"I'm quarreling with

Quinn rose and his gaze went flat, even taking on a hint of menace. "What is the nature of your present complaint, madam?"

"Stop it," Jane retorted. "Don't give me that Yorkshire growl, as if you'd tear me to pieces when I know you feed wild birds, marry stray widows, and work yourself half to death for your family. It won't wash, Quinn. You can intimidate every rolled-up title in Mayfair with that performance, but I know better."

A swift knock sounded on the door and Quinn startled.

"Food," Jane said. "Lest you snack on the bones of your contrary wife." She brushed past him, intent on going to the door.

He caught her by the wrist, his grip firm without hurting. "The performance is the civilized banker, the considerate husband. The real man isn't somebody you'd care to meet."

"How would you know? You keep him hidden from even yourself."

HIGH ACCLAIM
FOR GRACE BURROWES

"Sexy heroes, strong heroines, intelligent plots, enchanting love stories...Grace Burrowes's romances have them all."
—Mary Balogh, *New York Times* best-selling author

"Grace Burrowes writes from the heart—with warmth, humor, and a generous dash of sensuality, her stories are unputdownable! If you're not reading Grace Burrowes you're missing the very best in today's Regency romance!"
—Elizabeth Hoyt, *New York Times* best-selling author

A ROGUE OF HER OWN

"With flawless prose, delicious wit, and an unerring ability to bring complex characters to life, Burrowes revisits the engaging Windhams and delivers another winner; pure reading gold."
—*Library Journal* (starred review)

"Plenty of humor, sensuality and poignancy....A swiftly moving plot with engaging characters is sure to charm anyone seeking an enjoyable, emotionally satisfying read."
—*RT Book Reviews*

NO OTHER DUKE WILL DO

"Compelling, sympathetic characters and a rare blend of passion and humor result in another exquisite gem from a master of the genre. Gorgeously done."
—*Library Journal* (starred review)

"Those who prefer their historical romances to sound and feel historical will savor *No Other Duke Will Do*."
—NPR

TOO SCOT TO HANDLE

"A well-plotted, beautifully written story made all the more satisfying by its delightful secondary characters."
—*Library Journal* (starred review)

"Top Pick! Burrowes's delightful plotlines, heartfelt emotions, humor, and realistic, honest characters have turned her Windham series spinoffs into a fan favorite...a gem of a read. 4 ½ Stars."
—*RT Book Reviews*

THE TROUBLE WITH DUKES

"The hero of *The Trouble with Dukes* reminds me of Mary Balogh's charming men, and the heroine brings to mind Sarah MacLean's intelligent, fiery women.... This is a wonderfully funny, moving romance, not to be missed!"
—Eloisa James, *New York Times* best-selling author

"*The Trouble with Dukes* has everything Grace Burrowes's many fans have come to adore: a swoonworthy hero, a strong heroine, humor, and passion. Her characters not only know their own hearts, but share them with fearless joy. Grace Burrowes is a romance treasure."
—Tessa Dare, *New York Times* best-selling author

Also by Grace Burrowes

The Windham Brides Series
The Trouble with Dukes
Too Scot to Handle
No Other Duke Will Do
A Rogue of Her Own

MY ONE AND ONLY
DUKE

A Rogues to Riches Novel

GRACE BURROWES

FOREVER

NEW YORK   BOSTON

Forever

Hachette Book Group

1290 Avenue of the Americas, New York, NY 10104

forever-romance.com

twitter.com/foreverromance

First Edition: November 2018

Forever is an imprint of Grand Central Publishing. The Forever name and logo are trademarks of Hachette Book Group, Inc.

The publisher is not responsible for websites (or their content) that are not owned by the publisher.

The Hachette Speakers Bureau provides a wide range of authors for speaking events. To find out more, go to www.hachettespeakersbureau.com or call (866) 376-6591.

ISBNs: 978-1-5387-2895-6 (mass market), 978-1-5387-2893-2 (ebook)

Printed in the United States of America

OPM

10 9 8 7 6 5 4 3 2 1

To The Innocence Project

Acknowledgments

And we're off! To a new series with a new family in all its fascinating complexity. While the adventure of embarking on the *Rogues to Riches* stories fills me with enthusiasm, it has taken the proverbial village to transform my vision of a happily ever after into the tale you're holding in your hands. To Leah Hultenschmidt, my editor, and to the whole lovely team at Grand Central Forever, big thanks. To my readers, who inspire me every day, even bigger thanks and endless hugs. Happy reading!

MY ONE AND ONLY
DUKE

Chapter One

"You isn't to be hanged on Monday!" Ned declared. "Old Fletcher's got the bloody flux. Can't stir but two feet from the chamber pot. Warden says no hangings on Monday!"

Joy was the first casualty in Newgate prison. When Ned skipped into Quinn Wentworth's cell, the boy's rare, angelic smile thus had a greater impact than his words. An uncomfortable emotion stirred, something Quinn might once have called hope but now considered a useless reflex.

"You mean I won't be hanged *this* Monday."

Consternation replaced ebullience on the grimy little face. "Old Fletcher might die, sir, and then who would they find to do the business? Your family will get you out, see if they don't."

Quinn had forbidden his siblings to "get him out." Abetting the escape of a convicted felon was itself a hanging felony, as were 219 other crimes, among them stealing anything valued at more than twelve pence.

"Thank you for bringing me the news," Quinn said. "Have you eaten today?"

Ned studied ten dirty little toes. "Not so's I'd notice."

All manner of strange protocols applied in Newgate. One of the most powerful and feared bankers in London could invite a pickpocket to dine, for example, simply because the banker had learned that company—any company at all— was a distraction from impending death.

Despite the signed warrant dictating Quinn's fate, his cell might have been a successful solicitor's quarters. The floor was carpeted, the bed covered with clean linen, the desk stocked with paper, quill pen, two pencils, ink, and even— such was the honor expected of a wealthy felon—a penknife. The window let in fresh air and a precious square of sunlight, which Quinn valued more than all of the room's other comforts combined.

Even in the relatively commodious state quarters, the foodstuffs had to be kept in a bag tied to the rafters, lest the rodents help themselves uninvited. The pitcher of ale on the windowsill was covered to prevent flies from drowning themselves along with their sorrows.

"Fetch the ale," Quinn said. "We'll share some bread and cheese."

Ned was stronger and faster than he looked, and more than capable of getting the ale without spilling a drop. Quinn, by contrast, usually tried to appear less muscular and fit than he was. The warden had taken one pitying look at him and muttered about the big ones dying quickest on the end of a rope.

That comment—a casual, not intentionally cruel observation—had made real the fact of execution by order of the Crown. Hanged by the neck until dead, as the judge had said. The proper fate in the eyes of the law for most who violated the Sixth Commandment.

Though to be accurate, Quinn's crime was manslaughter rather than murder, else even all of his coin might have been insufficient to earn him quarters outside the dungeons.

"Shall I get the bread?" Ned asked.

The child was being polite, which ought not to be possible, given his upbringing—or perhaps he was being cautious.

Incarceration had also revealed in Quinn a latent propensity for rumination. What would death by hanging be like? Was the point of the proceeding to end the felon's life, or to subject him to such awful, public indignity that he welcomed his own demise?

"The bread, sir?" Ned's gaze had grown wary.

"And the cheese," Quinn said, taking down the sack suspended from the rafter. Cutting the bread required patient use of the penknife. Davies, Quinn's self-appointed man-of-all-work, and Penny, the whore-turned-chambermaid, were privileged to carry knives, but Quinn shuddered to contemplate what improprieties those knives had got up to when their owners had been at liberty.

Quinn set the food on the table, cut two thick slices of bread for the boy, situated cheese between them, and poured the child some ale.

Pewter tankards, no less. That would be Althea's influence, as was the washstand with the porcelain pitcher and basin. Quinn had been born in the poorest of York's slums, but saw no need to die looking like a ruffian.

"Aren't you hungry, sir?" Ned had wolfed down half his sandwich and spoken with his mouth full.

Quinn took a sip of fine summer ale. "Not particularly."

"But you must keep up your strength. My brother Bob told me that before he was sent off. Said when the magistrate binds you over, the most important thing is to keep up your strength. You durst not go before the judge looking hangdog and defeated. You can't run very far on an empty belly neither."

The boy had lowered his voice on that last observation.

"I'll not be escaping, Ned," Quinn said gently. "I've been found guilty and I must pay the price." Though escape might be possible. Such an undertaking wanted vast sums of money—which Quinn had—and a willingness to live the life of a fugitive, which Quinn lacked.

"Why is the Quality all daft?" Ned muttered, around another mouthful of bread and cheese. "You find a bloke what looks half like you and has the consumption. You pay his family enough to get by, more than the poor sod would have earned in his lifetime, and you pike off on Sunday night leaving the bloke in your place. The poor sod ends his suffering Monday morning knowing the wife and brats is well set, you get to live. It's been done."

Everything unspeakable, ingenious, and bold had been done by those enjoying the king's hospitality. That was another lesson Quinn had gleaned from incarceration. He'd seen schemes and bribes and stupid wagers by the score among London's monied classes, but sheer effrontery and true derring-do were still the province of the desperate.

He'd also learned, too late, that he wanted to live. He wanted to be a better brother and a lazier banker. He wanted to learn the names of the harp tunes Althea so loved, and to read a book or two simply to have the excuse to sit quietly by a warm fire of a winter night.

He wanted . . .

What he wanted no longer mattered, if it ever had. The reprieve Ned spoke of was more burden than blessing, because Quinn was fated to die, awfully, publicly, and painfully, whether he'd committed murder, manslaughter, or neither.

"If you're not going to eat that, guv, it shouldn't go to waste."

Quinn passed over his sandwich. "My appetite seems to have deserted me."

Ned tore the sandwich in half and put half in his pocket. For later, for another boy less enterprising or fortunate than Ned. For the birds—the child loved birds—or a lucky mouse.

Quinn had lost not only his appetite for food, but also his interest in all yearnings. He did not long to see his siblings one last time—what was there to say? He certainly had no desire for a woman, though they were available in quantity even in prison. He had no wish to pen one of those sermonizing final letters he'd written for six other men in the previous weeks.

Those convicts had faced transportation, while Quinn faced the gallows. His affairs were scrupulously in order and had escaped forfeiture as a result of his forethought.

He wanted peace, perhaps.

And justice. That went without saying.

The door banged open—it was unlocked during daylight—and the under-warden appeared. "Wait in here, ma'am. You'll be safe enough, and I see that we're enjoying a feast. Perhaps the famous Mr. Wentworth will offer you a portion." The jailer flicked a bored glance over Ned, who'd ducked his head and crammed the last of the food into his mouth.

A woman—a lady—entered the cell. She was tall, dark-haired, and her attire was plain to a fault.

Not a criminal, then. A crusader.

"Bascomb," Quinn said, rising. "My quarters are not Newgate's family parlor. The lady can wait elsewhere." He bowed to the woman.

She surprised him by dropping into a graceful curtsy. "I must wait somewhere, Mr. Wentworth. Papa will be forever in the common wards, and I do not expect to be entertained. I am Jane Winston."

She was bold, as most crusaders were. Also pretty. Her features were Madonna-perfect, from a chin neither receding nor prominent, to exquisitely arched brows, a wide mouth, high forehead, and intelligent dark eyes. The cameo was marred by a nose a trifle on the confident side, which made her face more interesting.

She wore a voluminous cloak of charcoal gray, bits of straw clinging to the hem.

"As you can see," Quinn replied, "we are a company of gentlemen here, and an unchaperoned lady would not be comfortable in our midst."

The warden snickered. "Wait here or leave the premises, ma'am. Them's your choices, and you don't get a say, Wentworth. I don't care if you was banker to King George himself."

As long as Quinn drew breath he had a say. "I am convicted of taking an innocent life, Miss Winston. Perhaps you might see fit to excuse yourself now?"

He wanted her to leave, because she was an inconvenient reminder of life beyond a death sentence, where women were pretty, regrets were a luxury, and money meant more than pewter tankards and a useless writing desk.

And Quinn wanted her to stay. Jane Winston was pleasing to look at, had the courage of her convictions, and had probably never committed anything approaching a crime. She'd doubtless sinned in her own eyes—coveting a second rum bun, lingering beneath warm covers for an extra quarter hour on the Sabbath. Heinous transgressions in her world.

He also wanted her to stay because frightening the people

around him had stopped amusing him before he'd turned twelve. Even Ned didn't turn his back on Quinn for more than an instant, and Davies remained as close to the unlocked door as possible without giving outright offense. The wardens were careful not to be alone with Quinn, and the whores offered their services with an air of nervous bravado.

Miss Winston's self-possession wafted on the air like expensive perfume. Confident, subtle, unmistakable.

"If a mere boy can break bread with you, then I don't have much to fear," she said, "and my father will expect me to wait for him. Papa is easily vexed. Do you have a name, child?"

Ned remained silent, sending a questioning glance at Quinn.

"He is Edward, of indeterminate surname," Quinn said. "Make your bow, Ned."

Ned had asked Quinn to teach him this nicety and grinned at a chance to show off his manners. "Pleased to meet you, Miss Winston."

"I'll be leaving," the guard said. "You can chat about the weather over tea and crumpets until..." He grinned, showing brown, crooked teeth. "Until next Monday."

"Prison humor." Miss Winston stripped off her gloves. Kid, mended around the right index finger. The stitching was almost invisible, but a banker learned to notice details of dress. "I might be here for a good while. Shall you regale me with a tale about what brought you to this sorry pass, Mr. Wentworth?"

The lady took the seat Ned had vacated, and she looked entirely at ease, her cloak settling around her like an ermine cape.

"You don't read the papers?" Quinn asked.

"Papa would have apoplexies if he caught me reading that drivel. We have souls to save."

"I don't think I'd like your father. Might I have a seat?" Because—for reasons known only to the doomed—Quinn wanted to sit down with her.

"This is your abode. Of course you should have a seat. You need not feed me or offer me drink. I'm sure you can better use your provisions for bribes. I can read to you from the Bible or quote at tiresome length from Fordyce's Sermons if you like."

"I do not like," Quinn said, slicing off a portion of cheese. He was a convicted felon, but he was a convicted felon who'd taken pains to learn the manners of his betters. Then too, somebody had to set an example for the boy. Quinn managed to cut off a slice of bread with the penknife and passed the bread and cheese to Miss Winston.

She regarded his offering with a seriousness the moment did not warrant. "You can spare this? You can honestly spare this?"

"I will be grievously offended if you disdain my hospitality," Quinn said. "Had I known you were coming, I'd have ordered the kitchen to use the good silver."

Ned cast him a nervous glance, but Miss Winston caught the joke. Her smile was utterly unexpected. Instead of a prim, nipfarthing little pinch of the lips, she grinned at Quinn as if he'd inspired her to hilarity in the midst of a bishop's sermon. Her gaze warmed, her shoulders lifted, her lips curved with glee.

"The everyday will do splendidly," she said, accepting her portion of the humble fare. "So whom are you supposed to have killed?"

Chapter Two

That Papa would forget his only daughter was nothing new. Jane had learned to appreciate his forgetfulness—let others listen to his moralizing—though he was growing worse.

He always grew worse around the anniversary of Mama's death. Then his visits to the prisons and poorhouses became incessant. Jane accompanied him because he demanded it, also because she feared for his well-being.

She needn't have. Few places were safer than the inside of Newgate jail during daylight. Her present host—not the first condemned man she'd met—watched her guardedly, as if she were the unpredictable element in the room.

Courts erred all the time. The guilty went free and the innocent were convicted, but Mr. Wentworth had not one shred of innocence about his bearing. He struck Jane as dangerous rather than wicked. If he had taken a life, he'd faced his opponent head-on and waged a fair fight.

"Surely, Miss Winston, we can find a more cheerful topic

than my late victim? One mustn't speak ill of the dead, and in my present situation, speaking well of the deceased eludes me."

The delicacy of Mr. Wentworth's words was undermined by a Yorkshire accent that suggested generations of hard winters and harder work.

He would have made a fine picture behind a plough or at a forge. His height came with a pair of broad shoulders that some tailor had clad in an exquisite lawn shirt. The tucks where the sleeve gathered at the shoulder were so small and numerous, Jane would have gone blind stitching them. His waistcoat was burgundy with gold embroidery and perfectly balanced ostentation with good taste.

He wore no coat—a terrible breach of propriety elsewhere—but different rules applied in prison. He might be paying for these comforts with that coat, or the guards might have plucked it from him "for safekeeping." Hanging was a messy business, and few men went to their executions in Sunday attire.

Mr. Wentworth took down a pewter mug from the quarter shelves built into a corner and poured half a tankard of ale.

"We're fresh out of tea." He set the mug before her and resumed his seat. "I do apologize. Is the fare not to your liking?"

The question became...mythological, with shades of Persephone in the underworld. Hades in this case was dark-haired and blue-eyed. His hands were as clean as a gentleman's, his hair was neatly combed if longish. His minion was an anxious urchin watching the adults as if one of them might hurl something breakable against the whitewashed stone walls at any moment.

Hades would not yield to that impulse, not today. Mr. Wentworth regarded Jane so steadily his gaze was a force more powerful than time. Patience and inscrutability looked out at her in equal, infinite measures. If the eyes were windows to the soul, Mr. Wentworth's soul was a bleak, silent moor under a gray December sky.

Though, ye angels and saints, he was a stunning specimen. His features were both masculine and beautiful—a slightly full mouth, perfectly proportioned nose, brows with a bit of swoop to them, and a jaw that put Jane in mind of Roman sculptures. Add the wintry blue of his eyes, and he was breathtakingly attractive.

And by offering Jane sustenance, he was being gracious.

"I am a preacher's daughter," Jane said. "I know better than to be ungrateful, and I've dined in humbler surroundings than this. For what I am about to receive, I am sincerely thankful."

She took a bite of surprisingly fresh bread, a small bite. She had in fact dwelled in surroundings less luxurious than Mr. Wentworth's prison cell. He came from means as clearly as she came from righteous penury—now.

"Himself is not to be hanged." The boy's voice was high even for one of his tender years, and he'd spoken as if a lapse in the conversation might permit some foul miasma into the room.

"Your sentence has been commuted to transportation?" Jane asked, washing her bread down with a sip of cool ale. Commutations for capital offenses were regular occurrences, though far from certain.

"Ned misspoke. I am not to be hanged this Monday. The executioner is otherwise engaged, and this is not a suitable topic to discuss with a lady."

"Old Fletcher's got a terrible case of—"

"Neddy." Mr. Wentworth's expression was amused.

The child fell silent, his little chin showing a hint of sullenness.

"A reprieve, then," Jane said. "Is that welcome or a particularly cruel blow?" The bread and ale were sitting well—breakfast had not—so Jane tried a nibble of cheese.

"Both, I suppose, or neither," Mr. Wentworth replied. "It simply is. The end is the same; somebody else's downfall will be the object of gossip when I can no longer oblige. Ned, would you be so good as to determine where Miss Winston's father has got off to?"

The child bolted out the door with a speed that had likely frustrated many a constable.

"Cutpurse?" Jane asked.

"Jack-of-all-trades and as good a lad as he can be."

Mr. Wentworth's gaze remained on the half-open door, as if he harbored regrets where the boy was concerned. Condemned felons were people, Jane had learned, as were soiled doves, pickpockets, confidence tricksters, grave robbers, and other criminals. They loved, they laughed, they had their rules and regrets.

Mr. Wentworth might well have saved lives during his years on earth, but he had taken a life that mattered to somebody, and that was prohibited by the Commandments. On the field of battle, men forgot the Commandments, though they called upon the same God in their various mother tongues. On the field of so-called honor, the Commandments never earned a mention.

Would that Gordie had been more devout and less honorable.

"You're supposed to eat the bread," Mr. Wentworth said. "I make sure to have extra of all my provisions and to never finish my portion, so that Ned, Penny, and Davies have enough to share or use for bribes. From the warden right down to the charwomen and the petty swindlers, Newgate's population has a fine appreciation for goods and coin."

Nobody had as fine an appreciation for coin as a poor minister's widowed daughter. "You were a banker?"

"I am—I was."

Mr. Wentworth wasn't a cit in the usual sense. He'd not been born to wealth, and he'd not been lucky at the tables. From gossip in the prison's common, Jane had gleaned that nobody was sure where his fortune had come from.

"Are you sorry for your sins?" Jane asked. "My father would gladly hear your confession, if you're of that persuasion."

Papa was good at sitting with the guilty and the sick and listening to their regrets. Jane had regrets, and the last person she could confide in was her father.

"Sorry?" Mr. Wentworth sat back. "I am angry, Miss Winston. Angrier than I have ever been, which impresses even me. Of course I have regrets. Ned has already found regrets that will haunt him all his days, short though those days are likely to be. I am not *sorry*."

Jane was sorry. Sorry she'd trusted Gordie not to get himself killed. Sorry she had chosen a man of unsteady temperament to pry her loose from Papa's household. Sorry Papa had lost his congregation, sorry her mother had died. . . . The list was endless.

"I might be able to help Ned," Jane said. "If he's awaiting transportation, arrangements can sometimes be made—for coin, you understand."

Mr. Wentworth was a banker in Newgate, and he'd been the one to mention money. If Mama were alive, Jane would not be having this conversation with this man in this place. Mama had departed from the earthly realm three short years ago, but Jane could barely recall a time when genteel rules and polite conventions had defined her world.

She had resented those rules with the bitter fury of a minister's daughter, more fool her.

"What sort of *arrangements* will free Ned?" Mr. Wentworth asked.

"If you think I'd sell him to a brothel, you are sadly mistaken. Ask anybody in the common wards, Mr. Wentworth. Reverend Winston is the genuine article, pious to the much-mended soles of his boots, and I am his loyal offspring. This is good cheese."

"Made on my properties in the north. If Ned is released, I want him sent to my sisters. They will be in need of projects and they have the means to see to the boy."

Ned struck Jane as a child who wouldn't tolerate much *seeing to*. He had run wild too early and too long to be tamed at this stage. Mr. Wentworth had the same air, despite his fine tailoring and clean fingernails.

But Ned could be freed, while Mr. Wentworth's death warrant had been signed.

"I will need some time," Jane said, "and you will need a day or two to make arrangements. Ten pounds will be more than sufficient to see Ned released into your siblings' care."

"A boy's life is a matter of ten pounds?"

Ten pounds was two years' wages in some households. "A girl wouldn't have cost you half so much."

An emotion flared in the man across the table, gone before Jane could label it. "You've freed girls, Miss Winston?"

"They aren't safe here. The whores try to protect them, and if the girl has a parent or older sibling with her, she'll fare better, but your door is locked at night in part for your safety, Mr. Wentworth. In the dark, the guilty and the innocent are indistinguishable."

A convicted killer should know that.

"Excellent point. How long does your father usually tarry among his flock?"

Mr. Wentworth wanted his privacy. Jane would have resented being sent on her way, but he was facing death. How did anybody remain sane under that burden?

"Papa is much too enthusiastic about his calling. I'm to visit with the women, but this late in the week, we're down to some regular offenders, and they prefer to be left in peace." The women had been polite about it, but they'd shooed Jane off, warning her to mind where she stepped.

Mr. Wentworth took a sip of his ale. The tankard was appropriate for that large hand, though he likely knew his way around a tea service too.

"Tell me, Miss Winston: Do you honestly prefer to remain here among the lost souls when you could be enjoying London's fresh air, such as it is, and your liberty? I account myself impressed."

Jane finished the last of her bread and cheese. The meal had fortified her. One could be hungry and bilious at the same time—a recent revelation.

"Your window has bars," Jane said. "Some of us live behind bars invisible to the eye."

"Profound, but the only way I will be freed of these bars is on the end of a rope. Achieving your own liberty is likely a less fraught undertaking. What do you suppose has happened to Ned?"

His gaze held worry for the child, despite a casual tone.

"Young Edward is sitting in a corner, his eyes glazing over, every particle of his body longing to fidget, while Reverend Winston maunders on about sin, salvation, and scripture. Every time Papa pauses to take a breath—which occurs about twice an hour—Ned will attempt to say, 'Excuse me, sir,' and Papa will ignore him, talk over him, or shush him."

"Would you care for more bread and cheese?"

Jane consulted her belly, which was calm for the first time in days. "I'd best wait a bit. I can fetch Papa."

Mr. Wentworth put a hand over Jane's wrist when she would have risen. "A little preaching won't hurt the boy. Stay and tell me how I'm to get him out of this place."

His grip was light. Jane was being asked to help a child whom society had discarded as unworthy of notice. She'd aided four other children, three girls and a boy, all of whom had disappeared back into the stews as if snatched by the fairies.

"This scheme must go right the first time," Jane said, lowering her voice. "Ned must do his bit perfectly, and you can't tell a soul. Not your favorite guard, not the kindliest of the wardens, not the charwoman who sneaks you a cigar, and especially not the whores. Absolute discretion, Mr. Wentworth."

She'd almost said he must be as silent as the grave, and he seemed to realize her near-slip.

He patted her wrist and withdrew his hand. "I am a banker, a successful banker despite my present circumstances. My discretion eclipses even that available in the confessional. Not a soul will know."

Mr. Wentworth smiled, mostly with his eyes. His gaze conveyed the intimacy of conspirators intent on a delightful prank, and when he looked at Jane like that, she could not believe he'd taken a life.

Though he likely had. Killers did not announce their vile deeds on street corners and then go sniveling and slinking into the nearest alleys.

Jane explained which charwoman to approach, how the straw bedding in the common area was changed, what Ned needed to say to be identified as the child whose freedom had been purchased. Mr. Wentworth listened, he asked a few questions—how was the money handled, how soon could this be accomplished—and all the while, Jane was plagued by a question of her own.

What sort of condemned killer troubled over the fate of a boy he'd just met, was no relation to, and had no reason to help?

* * *

"We've found him! Sir, we've found him at last!"

Mr. Thaddeus Dodson set down his quizzing glass. "Must you find him so loudly, Timmons?"

The clerk was tall, graying, and thin as a coachman's whip. Dodson had never seen Timmons perturbed, much less aquiver with excitement. Quivering was frowned on at the College of Arms and dignity much respected.

"But after three years, sir, three years, of searching and searching…We have a legitimate heir to the Duke of Walden. A legitimate male heir *and* a younger brother *and* two sisters of childbearing years."

Beyond the door to the pursuivant's office, the other clerks bent over their documents, though their pens were still. An heir was a victory for them all, a spare gilded the victory, and sisters of childbearing age spoke to underlying titles being preserved through the heirs general.

Three feathers in the cap of the College. Of course the clerks were proud.

"Good work, Timmons. Good work indeed. The Crown will be most grateful. Let's have a look at what you've found, and please do close the door. Damned draft can give a man a lung fever."

Timmons closed the door and spread out his genealogical research on Dodson's desk. To rescue the Walden dukedom from escheat—and the Crown from an enormous pile of debt—Timmons had had to go back nine generations. He'd racketed all over the North of England, visited graveyards

without number, and studied parish rolls so dim with age as
to be mere whispers of records.

He'd interviewed grannies, taken tea with earls, and
called upon vicars no London gentleman had called upon in
years.

His diligence had been rewarded. "Thank God the heir is
not some shepherd living in a hut," Dodson said. "I do so
hate to see noble titles thrust into the hands of those unprepared for such responsibility."

"He's wealthy," Timmons said. "Rich as a nabob, beautiful London house, equally lovely estates in Yorkshire, gives
handsomely to charities and doesn't make a great fuss about
it. We have only one problem, sir."

There was always a problem and seldom only one. "The
king is in Brighton, where he's expected to bide for the next
fortnight at least. We have time to tidy up a few loose ends,
and it's to His Majesty that this good news must be conveyed."

Timmons's excitement dissipated, and a tired, aging clerk
stood where a dedicated royal herald had been a moment before.

"Waiting a fortnight makes sense, sir, because the present
candidate for the title is enjoying the king's hospitality, so to
speak, though he's not likely to do so for long."

"Have a seat, Timmons, and pray do keep your voice
down. You said the heir was wealthy, generous, propertied,
and in good health. In what sense is he enjoying the king's
hospitality?"

"The bad sense, sir. The criminal sense."

Damn and blast. Why couldn't a man blessed with every
possible advantage in life keep himself from the magistrate's
clutches?

"Tell me about the brother."

Timmons lit up like an ember finding a fresh breeze. "The brother's a right enough fellow of seventeen years, not yet married. He should inherit all that wealth in less than two weeks. His Majesty will like that part. Can't fault a man for having his affairs in order, even if he is convicted of taking a life."

Dodson took up his quizzing glass and pulled Timmons's painstakingly detailed family tree closer. "There's nobody else? We have the criminal's brother or nobody?"

"That's right, sir, but for a distant cousin. We can have the convict or his brother—who's young enough to need a guardian, of course—and I can guess which option His Majesty will choose."

"So can I."

Chapter Three

Nothing helped.

Not reading, though how many times had Quinn promised himself he'd read all the classics his lordly customers were always quoting? He'd been beguiled by numbers, while words were simply a means to an end: *Pass the salt. Can't you see I'm busy? The bank is not in a position to make a loan to you at this time.*

Showing Davies how to play chess did not help. He was a clever young man, but impatient, and chess wanted nothing so much as patience. To teach Quinn chess, Cousin Duncan had needed patience without limit and a Wentworth's full complement of strategy.

Teaching Ned to read did not help, because the boy would never be able to afford books, and in his own words, he couldn't eat books or use them to stay warm unless he burned them.

Which he would do without a qualm.

Training Plato, Ned's favorite mouser, to shake paws did not help. Only a bedlamite tried to train a cat—even a hungry cat—to do anything. Plato doubtless knew this and occasionally performed the desired waving of a front paw, likely out of pity. The beast was all black with yellow eyes that never seemed to close or blink in the presence of food.

When Plato appropriated a place on Quinn's lap and commenced rumbling, that truly did not help. Purring when death was less than a fortnight away made Quinn want to pitch the cat out the window, and that reminded Quinn that every window was stoutly barred.

A knock sounded on the door, which was open only a few inches.

"Come in." Even in Newgate, a man didn't have to be home to callers, one of the many odd dignities the prisoners granted one another.

Miss Winston—Quinn forgot her first name, something that began with a *J*—peeked around the door. "Do you have a moment, Mr. Wentworth?"

All he had were moments. "I can fit you in to my schedule."

She was attired in the same gray shroud of a cloak, the straw flecking her hems up to midcalf today.

"I won't take up much of your time," she said. "Ned should be warned to remain alert on Wednesday. These situations are always subject to change—routines shift, people fall ill—and Wednesday is the next opportunity."

Less than a week away, but before Quinn's scheduled departure, as it were. "Then you need the ten pounds. Could I interest you in some lemonade and gingerbread?"

He'd given Ned all the strawberries. The boy had lined them up on the windowsill in order of size and consumed them from smallest to largest, one at a time. He'd sniffed each berry before popping it into his mouth, and Quinn had added another regret to the list:

I wish I'd taken the time to enjoy all the sustenance I consumed so absentmindedly, a pencil in my left hand, a column of figures absorbing my attention.

Figures would wait, while strawberries rotted all too soon.

Miss Winston pulled off her gloves. "*Lemonade?* You have lemonade?"

"And butter. My sister sends me a daily basket of provisions and one for the guards, as well. Theirs includes a bottle of port, which they immediately consume, so mine finds its way to me."

"She sends a decoy," Miss Winston said, taking a seat at Quinn's table. The legs of the table were uneven, so that it rocked when anything was placed upon it. A month ago, Quinn would have had the table burned for firewood.

"I would...give a lot for gingerbread with fresh butter," Miss Winston said.

I would kill for gingerbread with fresh butter, she'd been about to say. The poor thing was blushing. In light of her familiarity with the criminal element, that blush charmed Quinn.

He set the pitcher of lemonade on the table along with two clean tankards. The gingerbread was wrapped in plain linen, as was the butter dish. Such ordinary fare, and yet Miss Winston was clearly pleased with it.

She used the penknife to cut thick slices of bread and slathered both with butter.

"No plates," Quinn said. "The chophouse uses pewter, because the ceramic kind can be broken and used as weapons. I send my plates back across the street with each meal."

Ned had explained that to him. No ceramic, no porcelain,

no glass. Wooden bowls or beakers, metal flasks, pewter mugs. Nothing sharp, heavy, or too valuable. Cravats were frowned on, because they had been used to strangle both guards and inmates.

The boy had stoutly ignored the pitcher and basin sitting on the washstand as he'd delivered his tutorial.

"Aren't you having any?" Miss Winston asked, licking her thumb. "The gingerbread is quite good."

She'd barely sipped the lemonade—sweet, as lemonades went—while the gingerbread was rapidly meeting its fate.

"Of course," Quinn said, taking a bite from his slice. "I woolgather now almost as consistently as I used to dwell on bank business." At Davies's urging, he'd purchased a quantity of opium, but the considered wisdom of the house was to save the opium for the day Quinn was...the day he died.

The effect would be greater that way when an effect was most needed.

"Have you contacted your sisters?" Miss Winston asked. "Getting Ned out of here is only half the battle."

"I have written a note to my business partner, Joshua Penrose, and having conferred with you, I'll have it sent. I'll tell Ned on Tuesday night."

Ned would spend a day hiding among a pile of straw so vile even the rats avoided it, and then by night he'd be carried off to freedom. A simple plan, though it required that the escapee fit into the charwoman's muck cart, which could accommodate only a child or a very small adult.

The warden knew better than to allow the women to use larger carts, and his books would doubtless reflect the sorry truth that children died behind Newgate's walls all the time.

"I take it Davies can't be freed." A true injustice in Quinn's opinion. Davies had been an innocent bystander when a pickpocket had done a toss and jostle. The victim had set up a hue and cry, and the thief had taken off through a crowd, depositing the stolen money not in his accomplice's pockets, but in Davies's. The accomplice had decamped hot-foot, after pointing at Davies and implicating him loudly.

Merry Olde London indeed.

"Mr. Wentworth, I have asked you twice who Davies is. For considerably more than ten pounds, he might be able to improve his circumstances."

"He's innocent. Stolen goods were essentially thrust into his hands, but the judge did not believe him."

Plato sauntered around the door, tail up, not a care in the world. He'd doubtless smelled the butter.

"You have another visitor," Miss Winston said. "What a fine specimen."

Plato squinted at her—approvingly, Quinn thought. "He has a reputation for favoring the company of the condemned. Davies and Ned won't touch him."

"Now that is ridiculous." Plato leapt onto the table, and Miss Winston aimed her nose at the cat. Plato treated her to an almost-nose-kiss, then rumbled like thunder when the lady used her left hand to scratch behind his ears.

A sense of sweetness stole over Quinn, of innocence in the midst of insanity. Miss Winston was fond of cats, apparently, and Plato was fond of the butter he'd soon try to lick from the fingers of Miss Winston's right hand. For a moment, everything—the stink and noise of Newgate, the reality of death a week from Monday, the vague worry about what Ned and Davies were up to—receded as woman and cat charmed each other.

"He'll get hair all over your skirts."

She sat back. "Do I strike you as a woman who has the luxury of taking exception to cat hair?"

Well, yes, she did, or she should have. Miss Winston

should have had a maid brushing out her hair every night, bringing her chocolate first thing in the day, and fretting over her wardrobe. Not her two gray dresses, her *wardrobe*.

Quinn went to the sideboard and extracted twenty shiny coins. He took them to the table, tied them up in his last monogrammed handkerchief, and slid it across.

"A bit extra," he said, "in case any of the parties involved require additional remuneration. Any excess you may keep for yourself."

She put the cat on the carpet and set about untying the bundle. "That is not necessary, Mr. Wentworth. I'd free every nonviolent offender on the premises, every child, every—" She fell silent until she'd worked the knot loose and spread the coins on the square of linen.

"This is *twenty pounds*." Miss Winston struck Quinn as a woman of great self-possession, and yet she was agog at the sum on the table. Once upon a time, twenty pounds would have been a fortune to him too.

"You said ten pounds would see Ned free. That means a great deal to me." Though Quinn wasn't about to examine why Ned's freedom meant anything at all. A last gesture of defiance, perhaps, or a sop to a conscience past redeeming.

"But that's *ten pounds* too much."

"Is it? Complicated sums have ever defeated me."

She looked up sharply. "Do not mock me."

"Never disdain money, Miss Winston. The coin is innocent of wrongdoing, and you can use a new pair of gloves."

Quinn brushed a few crumbs from the table and dusted them onto the windowsill. Birds would feast on them, and Ned would delight in the birds.

"What are you doing?" Miss Winston asked.

"Feeding pigeons. And you?"

As Quinn had swept the crumbs into his palm, she had

done likewise with the coins, then tied them up in the handkerchief.

"I should not take your money," she said. "Not more than the ten pounds agreed to. One behaves charitably and properly for the pleasure of doing the right thing."

She believed that twaddle, which was a sign of either great integrity or a weakness of the mind.

"So allow me this small, final pleasure." That was bad of him, bringing death into the conversation. Doubtless the Almighty had added another year on to the eternity Quinn would spend regretting a life largely wasted.

Miss Winston stuffed the coins into a pocket of her cloak. "Why are you doing this?"

"Because a week from Monday, I will hang from my neck until, gasping, choking, and soiling myself, I die. I would like to be recalled as something more than a fine show for the guards on a Monday morning."

She put a hand to her throat, the first indication that she wasn't impervious to the brutality of Newgate.

"You haven't eaten your gingerbread," she said.

He broke it in two and held out half the slice. Miss Winston looked at the treat, then at him, then at the treat. She must have had a fondness for gingerbread, because she took the proffered sweet.

They ate in silence, while Quinn studied his companion. Was she pale today? Tired? Resentful of her father? Or had arranging Ned's escape taxed her composure? Something about the lady was off. If he'd met her at the bank, he would have put her in the category of customers about to explain a late payment but not yet in default.

"I apologize for my remark about your gloves," Quinn said. "You have gloves. Mine were among the first casualties of the local economy."

She took a considering sip of her lemonade. "But you have coin."

"I do now. That took some time and ingenuity." How that had stung, to be a banker without coin, without anything of value. Then old skills had reasserted themselves, and Quinn had bartered his way into a private cell and regular meals. The rest had been common sense and the inertia of a population for whom ingenuity was the difference between life and death.

"This lemonade is quite sweet," Miss Winston said, wrinkling her nose. "Or perhaps I've grown unused to anything made with sugar."

"Are your father's circumstances that limited?" Preaching and penury did not necessarily go hand in hand.

"His tolerance for anything other than necessities is limited. We were comfortable once. We're on appallingly good terms with the pawnbroker now." She put her hand to her throat again. "The lemonade is disagreeing with me."

Sickness was rampant at Newgate. Jail fever, consumption, venereal diseases, bad food…Misery concentrated here, and it spread.

Quinn came around the table and put the back of his hand to Miss Winston's forehead. "You're not fevered. Does only your digestion trouble you?"

"I'm sure it will pass." She rose and braced herself against the table, but made no attempt to reach the door.

"If you're unwell, then you're better off staying here."

She wasn't coughing, wasn't hot to the touch, didn't appear chilled, though many illnesses began slowly and gathered momentum until suffering reached a crescendo that made death welcome.

"I'm not ill." She hunched her shoulders and leaned over, as if winded. Her weight was on one hand, while the other hand pressed to her belly.

No. Not her belly. Lower.

Her hand pressed against her womb, which bulged slightly, now that she'd smoothed the billowing folds of her cloak.

"Sit down." Quinn nudged the chair closer with his foot. "Sit down, and tell me who the father is."

She didn't sit; she swayed into him. Quinn wrapped his arms around her, and for the first time in years, embraced a woman of his own free will.

Chapter Four

"Sir, I've found another small problem." Timmons had ambushed Dodson outside the College offices, right on the London street, where more privacy was to be had than under the noses of a lot of scribbling clerks.

"Life is nothing but problems," Dodson replied as Timmons fell in step beside him. The week had been productive, though disappointing. A duke was facing the hangman, a doleful thought. Dodson consoled himself that Mr. Quinn Wentworth would go to his death with that much more regret if he knew he was also saying good-bye to a lofty title.

Though Dodson had stumbled upon one very significant problem where His Grace of Walden was concerned: Quinn Wentworth had technically become the duke three years ago and should have been tried in the House of Lords. They'd have sentenced him to death too, quite possibly, Wentworth being not of their ilk. Yet another reason to let the matter resolve itself quietly.

"About the Walden situation," Timmons said, keeping his voice down. "I fear I must report a development."

"You couldn't let it go." Tenacity in a subordinate was a wonderful quality, when preserving the interests of the Crown. Contrariness was hard to overlook. "I told you how we'll proceed, Timmons, and the sovereign is yet enjoying the restorative pleasures of the seaside. Unless this development is another legitimate adult son in great good health, I doubt it's relevant."

"The development is relevant, sir. Mr. Wentworth—His Grace of Walden, rather—is a banker."

"We do not hold that against him. He's also a condemned felon, which is rather more problematic."

They paused on a street corner to allow a hackney to rattle past.

"A banker," Timmons said, "would have his affairs in order. I bethought myself to have a look at those affairs."

"Bethinking yourself is not what the Crown pays you to do, Timmons. We had that discussion last March." Timmons had bethought himself to see about any afterborn Elizabethan heirs in a situation where the Crown had very much wanted an estate to revert. Timmons's *bethinking* had cost King George a lucrative viscountcy that had gone—God save the realm—to a Cheshire farmer.

"I do apologize for my wayward impulses, sir, but in this case—a wealthy banker, a dukedom nearing insolvency—I could not stop myself. Wentworth's younger brother will inherit little."

Dodson came to a halt in the middle of the street. "How is that possible?"

"Stephen Wentworth, the boy of seventeen, will inherit

an enviable competence to go with the ducal honors. He can live as a comfortable gentleman of means, assuming his guardian does not squander his funds."

Guardians were always trouble. "Who is the guardian?"

"Wentworth's business partner, Joshua Penrose, and a second cousin who serves as the young man's tutor."

A fishmonger's donkey cart went by, perfuming the air with haddock. "What does the cousin inherit?"

"Mr. Duncan Wentworth will have mementos, guardianship of the boy, and an old horse."

"Good God. The sisters?"

Timmons glanced up and down the street. "They have handsome portions, all tied up in the funds. Each has a dower property, which becomes hers in fee simple absolute upon Wentworth's death or her twenty-eighth birthday, whichever shall first occur. Wentworth has provided well for his family, left his partner a thriving business, and tied it all up with enough knots and bows that even Chancery won't be able to untie it."

This was what came of commoners amassing too much wealth. "Then where in perdition does the rest of the money go? Is the problem a mistress? An aging auntie?"

"I am sorry to be the bearer of bad news, sir, but the bulk of the Wentworth fortune, and a great fortune it is, will go to charitable interests in Yorkshire."

"Yorkshire is nothing but sheep farms. How can there be any—"

A beer wagon came around the corner, harness jingling, the hooves of the great draft team churning thunderously against the worn cobbles. Dodson marched for the opposite walkway, Timmons at his side.

"Charitable interests in Yorkshire," Dodson grumbled. "Of all the notions. That will not serve, Timmons."

"I thought not."

A disagreeable breeze wafted on the air, and a crossing sweeper darted out to collect dung from the middle of the street.

"That money cannot go to charity while our good king is left with a lot of useless debt."

"Certainly not, sir. Shall I pack for a jaunt down to Brighton?"

"No need. I'll handle this. What is that smell?"

Timmons's gaze fixed on the retreating beer wagon. "I believe you might have stepped in something, sir. Something left by a passing horse."

Dodson darted a glance at his boots, which he prided himself on maintaining at a high shine.

Most of the time. "Well, damn. You say the family dwells in Mayfair?"

Timmons recited a direction in a very pleasant neighborhood.

"I'll pay a call on Mr. Wentworth's siblings, and then I'm off to Brighton."

"Best hurry, sir. Mr. Wentworth has only a few days left."

* * *

Until conceiving a child, Jane had felt little more than passing sympathy for the unfortunates whom Papa harangued at such holy length. She'd been too preoccupied with her own tribulations. Besides, if the prisoners hadn't sinned to the point of breaking man's laws, they wouldn't have been a captive audience for any preacher with a nose strong enough to tolerate the Newgate common.

Impending motherhood had caused Jane to re-examine her conclusions. Had the prisoners sinned or had they been unlucky one too many times, such that sin was the price of survival? Were they victims of circumstance and bad luck, or of criminals yet running free?

She sank into the chair Mr. Wentworth considerately held for her. "You ask me who the father of this child is. The father is no longer relevant. He will never be relevant again."

Mr. Wentworth's glower would have sent a lesser woman fleeing from the room—the cell—but vertigo was another of the charming indications of Jane's condition. She no longer fainted outright, mostly because she took seriously the first glimmerings of unsteadiness or fading vision.

"The father," Mr. Wentworth said, "was relevant for the five minutes required to get you with child. He forfeits any claim to irrelevance for the duration of the child's minority, at least."

Mr. Wentworth's words were carried on a Yorkshire winter wind of conviction.

"He was relevant for the five minutes necessary to speak our vows as well," Jane said, "but he entangled himself in a matter of honor and did not emerge victorious."

"Dead?"

"Quite, and these matters are not discussed." Ironic, that in the eyes of the law, Gordie had been murdered. The killer had gone back to his club, sat down to a breakfast of beefsteak, and probably had a sound nap thereafter.

Mr. Wentworth, by contrast, had a date with the gallows.

"My condolences." He put a hand on Jane's wrist as she reached for her tankard. "No more lemonade for you. You should be eating as much red meat as you can."

He was right. The lemonade had not agreed with her. His touch should have felt presumptuous—he was a condemned killer—but he meant to protect Jane from further misery, and his fingers whispering over the back of her hand were gentle.

"We have beef on Sundays, usually. Or ham," she said. "Fish or game other days, in the most modest portions."

"Not enough. Why did you introduce yourself as Miss Jane Winston?"

Why had he remembered such a triviality? "Because for all but one of my twenty-five years, that's who I was. My spouse and I eloped. He was of Scottish extraction, and galloping up to Gretna Green was a great lark to him." Everything had been a great lark to Gordie MacGowan, and that had made Jane uneasy. The thought of spending the rest of her life as Papa's sole support and companion had driven her past reason.

Mama had known how to soften the worst of Papa's zealous excesses, and if Mama had lived, Papa would not have become so...difficult. Gordie had regarded the reverend as a harmless old sermonizer with good intentions, which had boded well for the role of son-in-law.

"By representing yourself as unmarried," Mr. Wentworth said, "you consign your child to unrelenting criticism from the moment of birth."

Jane's stomach was calming, though this discussion had her temper heating. "My father refuses to recognize my union, Mr. Wentworth, because I ran off without his blessing. He introduces me as Miss Jane Winston. I can either make him look daft, and carry my marriage lines with me everywhere, or focus on more significant issues, such as how I will provide for my offspring."

Nobody else would provide. Papa ministered to a flock without means, and almost all of the luxuries Mama had brought to the marriage had been sold or pawned. Mama's wedding ring hung on a ribbon around Jane's neck, lest Papa recall that even that specific bequest to Jane could be sold.

"So instead of calling your father the liar he is, you

let him shame you, shame your child, and deny yourself a widow's freedoms. Why?"

Jane rose and leaned across the table. "Because I need to eat, because I need a roof over my head. Because as long as Papa thinks I'm ashamed, he won't cast me out for being too proud. Because I am exhausted and soon to acquire the dimensions of a farm wagon. How long do you think I'd last on the street, Mr. Wentworth?"

Of all things, he smelled lovely up close. Pregnancy had given Jane a mercilessly acute sense of smell, and Mr. Wentworth's scent eased the last of her nausea. Most of the fragrance was spices—ginger, cinnamon, clove—finished with subtle floral notes.

An expensive, proprietary blend that had the power to do what nothing else had for the past four months: calm Jane's stomach.

"What of your widow's portion?" Mr. Wentworth asked. "Surely your husband left you something?"

Jane resumed her seat rather than be caught sniffing her host. "My husband signed an agreement leaving me a small competence to be paid by his uncle, who has both means and standing. I suspect marriage to me was supposed to curry Uncle Dermott's favor. I am a minister's daughter, and Dermott is a devout Presbyterian."

Devout when it came to clutching his coins. "Uncle Dermott's London man of business explained to me," Jane went on, "that the circumstances of Gordie's death required utmost discretion, lest the other participant in the duel be needlessly troubled. The story has been put about that Gordie went off to India, but he perished of a fever less than two weeks into the journey. Once I've served my year of mourning, I'll see a bit of coin." *Possibly.*

"Unless you've succumbed to a difficult birthing, jail

fever, or consumption. With such parsimonious in-laws to hurry you to your own demise, why not remarry?"

Mr. Wentworth's inquisition was a curious relief. He was applying logic to a situation that had long since reduced Jane to a progression of fears—would Mama's ring be worth enough to pay a midwife?—and unpleasant symptoms.

"Who would willingly take on responsibility for a fallen woman and her illegitimate offspring?" This was the real burden Papa's intransigence effected. He labeled Jane not a respectable widow, but a jade. His willingness to overlook her "lapse" made him appear all the holier.

Jane had realized only recently that self-interest and self-abnegation could dwell side by side in her father's mind.

"You are beautiful," Mr. Wentworth said, in the same tones he would have remarked pleasing architecture on a Christopher Wren chapel. "Why not use a few wiles and charm the willing?"

"I tried that. My wiles were unequal to the challenge."

The smile came again, the conspirator's fleeting admission of humanness. He patted Jane's hand, the gesture purely friendly.

"Faulty wiles are to your credit."

Silence descended, broken only by the rumbling of the cat, who had curled up on the bed, where he had a fine view of the windowsill.

Jane's situation hadn't changed. She was still carrying a child, still entirely dependent on her father, and still facing an ordeal that claimed the lives of too many women. But she'd confessed her situation to the most unlikely confidant imaginable—a convicted killer—and felt calmer as a result.

"Faulty wiles will not keep a baby warm and fed, Mr. Wentworth. I was an idiot to think a man willing to elope with a penniless spinster could behave responsibly, but my husband boasted endless Scottish charm, and I was starved for joy."

"Did he at least provide that?"

Jane had lacked the fortitude to put such a question to herself. "No. What should have been a great lark became a forced march, then a misery. We anticipated the wedding vows, though, and Gordie hadn't the courage to abandon me on the Great North Road. He was drunk for the entire return journey."

Likely he'd been drunk for most of the trip to Scotland as well. Jane hadn't kept company with enough inebriated men to know high spirits from bottle courage.

"I am not drunk. I am condemned," Mr. Wentworth said. "You might consider that a better bargain, because I will not leave you or the child to the backward charity of your lying father." He picked up the cat, who curled against his chest and regarded Jane with the same regal self-possession shown by the man. "We'll need a special license, and I have time—barely—to procure one, if you're interested in marrying me."

* * *

"I was hoping to speak with your man of business," Mr. Dodson said, "but he's apparently otherwise occupied, and his office directed me here. I apologize for intruding on your privacy at such a difficult moment."

Althea Wentworth took her time preparing Mr. Dodson's tea. In the wing chair opposite the low table, Constance also held her peace, while Mr. Dodson barely hid his gawking. The Wentworth town house was tastefully appointed.

Very tastefully. He'd expected something else, of course. They all did.

"A death warrant has been signed for my brother," Althea said. "Difficult is putting it mildly, when we know him to be innocent."

"Your loyalty does you credit," Mr. Dodson replied. "Without having met Mr. Wentworth, I sincerely hope that if he was convicted in error, then the timely intervention of the Almighty or a nearly comparable force will save his life."

Constance was tapping the arm of the chair with each finger in succession eight times—a piano exercise, played silently when she was troubled.

"Your tea," Althea said, passing over the French porcelain cup and saucer. She prepared Constance's tea next, though Constance had no use for tea.

"Do you ladies have any idea what the College of Arms does?"

"Also called the College of Heralds," Constance said, fingers moving at the same steady tempo. "The College has authority to grant new coats of arms, research matters of heredity, and oversee the recording of pedigrees. They also have authority over the flying of flags on land. Their charter dates from 1484 and was granted by King Richard. The Court of the Lord Lyon performs comparable duties for our neighbors to the north."

Constance had the same azure eyes as Quinn, and they gave her a feline ability to look imperious when she stared rather than simply rude. Althea's eyes were plain blue, though she saw clearly enough.

Mr. Dodson was a man quivering to deliver exciting news. Althea and Constance had had enough excitement of late, thank you not at all.

"Just so," Mr. Dodson said, bouncing a bit on his cushion. "Just exactly so. We at the College undertake our efforts on behalf of the sovereign, who relies utterly on our discretion.

As you might imagine, when it comes to pedigrees and in-heritances, that discretion can be sorely tried."

Althea stirred her tea. Quinn had insisted his sisters know how to preside over a tea tray. Even he hadn't the power to make them drink the wretched stuff.

"Mr. Dodson, Constance and I are coping with a signifi-cant strain. Our patience is *sorely tried* by any who seek to take advantage of us at this most challenging time. We are furious with the Crown on behalf of our brother and not in-clined to tolerate flummery."

"Enraged," Constance added. "One might say murder-ously so." She smiled, an apology for her honesty that made her all the more intimidating. Truly, she had learned from Quinn's example.

Dodson set his cup on its saucer and deposited both on the tray. "The College of Arms does not deal in flummery. Just the opposite. We unearth the truth, no matter how un-comfortable that truth might be. We've uncovered illegit-imacy in the best families of the realm, we've unearthed secret marriages that resulted in bigamous unions by titled men. We—"

"Why are you here?" Althea asked. "If there is a grief worse than mourning, we're enduring it. You offend decency itself by wasting our time over tea."

Dodson was a small, tidy man, though lack of height imbued some with a need to posture, witness Constance's histrionics. As he rose and started a slow tour of the room— admiring the bust of George III, peering at shelves of classic literature—Althea spared a thought for Quinn.

He'd asked them not to visit him again, asked them to cease pestering the barristers for appeals and pleas that would only waste money. Quinn had ever been too prag-matic for his own good, and now he was to die for it.

"I'll get straight to the point, ladies," Mr. Dodson said, grasping his lapels with pale, manicured hands.

Constance shot a glance at the clock on the mantel.

"Your brother," Mr. Dodson said. "Your brother Quinton Wentworth has inherited the Walden ducal title, along with various minor titles, properties, and financial appurtenances thereto. I'm off to Brighton, where I hope to convince a compassionate king that a man facing such responsibilities, even a man convicted of a serious crime, should be shown mercy by his sovereign."

"Get out," Constance said, rising and pointing at the door. "Get out, and take your greedy, rotten little scheme with you. Quinn is innocent, and you'll not get him to hand his fortune over to the Crown with this ramshackle farce."

Constance was ever one to surprise people—men especially—with her intelligence, though the logic she'd applied was all but obvious. Quinn had not left any of his siblings a great fortune, and he'd had reasons for that, good reasons.

Ergo, if the Crown was intent on producing a title to preserve Quinn's life, then the Crown was in truth interested in preserving Quinn's fortune, though not Quinn's possession of it.

"You are overset," Mr. Dodson said. "I do apologize for causing you to be discommoded, Miss Constance, but I tell you nothing less than the truth."

"The truth is what the Crown says it is," Constance retorted, "and the Crown has said my innocent brother, who never cheated or killed anybody, and who has shown generosity to more than a few, is to die next Monday."

By rights, Quinn should already have met his fate. Joshua had explained the reprieve, if a reprieve it was. Constance's description of Quinn's character was accurate, but very much a minority view.

"Tell the rest of your truth in the next five minutes," Althea said, "or Ivor and Kristoff will see you out."

The footmen standing on either side of the doorway, a pair of blond Vikings in livery who were not twins but as good as, didn't so much as blink. Quinn had found them in Stockholm, though like many of his finds, their story remained a mystery. They went everywhere together on their half day, shared a room, and bickered in their own language like an old couple.

More than that, Althea did not need to know.

Dodson resumed his seat and used four of his remaining minutes to sketch a genealogy that dug a rabbit warren of family history back through three centuries.

"So you see," Dodson concluded, "your brother truly is the Duke of Walden, and you would be Lady Althea Wentworth and Lady Constance Wentworth. I cannot imagine our gracious king allowing such a lofty and respected title to lapse when a legitimate heir is yet extant to claim it."

Oh, of course. Dear George was occasionally gracious, but he was invariably greedy and ran up debts with the enthusiasm of a debutante shopping for hair ribbons.

"This will destroy Stephen," Constance said. "The boy is wild with rage at Quinn's situation, and inheriting a title will drive him past reason. You may keep your dukedom, Mr. Dodson."

Stephen, at seventeen, did not enjoy a solid grasp of reason most days. He had all of Quinn's intelligence and none of Quinn's self-restraint. Stephen was ungovernable at present, and, as Cousin Duncan had observed, understandably so.

"No, madam," Dodson said, hands on hips. "At the risk of contradicting a lady, I may *not* keep the Walden dukedom. Titles don't work that way. I cannot expect you to understand the details of titular succession, but when legitimacy has been established, and letters patent provide that male heirs—"

"Your five minutes are up," Althea said, gently, because Dodson was only trying to do his job. When Quinn had done his job, many had criticized him for it, called him flint-hearted, greedy, and unprincipled.

"The difficulty," Althea went on, "is that you might well be right: Quinn has inherited this title, he's due all the honors and whatnot, and you may even manage to wrangle a pardon from King George."

"You'd best be about it, if you intend to try," Constance said, checking the watch pinned to her bodice. "Though it won't do George any good. He's not getting Quinn's money."

Any mention of wealth was vulgar. Bedamned to vulgar, Quinn had always said, when ignoring financial realities meant his family went hungry.

"If the king signs a pardon, then your brother will not die," Dodson retorted. "A duke might be plagued by scandal, but polite society is usually willing to overlook peccadillos when His Majesty's example does likewise."

Manslaughter was not a peccadillo. The last doubt about Dodson's scheme evaporated. The Crown wanted Quinn's fortune, but Quinn had made sure his fortune was safe from royal plundering.

"We wish you every success obtaining a pardon for an innocent man," Althea said, rising. "But Quinn will refuse his sovereign's mercy. Our brother is all but dead, and we have the Crown to thank for that. No piece of paper obtained at the last minute, the better to steal from a grieving family, will earn Quinn's notice. Good day, Mr. Dodson."

"Safe journey," Constance added, coming to her feet.

Ivor and Kristoff opened the double doors at the same moment. Althea had caught them practicing that move, like the acrobats at Astley's practiced their tumbling.

"Your brother shall not die," Dodson said. "I know my duty."

Althea said nothing. Constance linked arms with her.

And Dodson stalked out, Ivor on his heels.

Kristoff closed the door and passed Constance a handkerchief, then tidied up the tea tray and left both sisters their privacy.

"Why must Quinn be so stubborn?" Constance lamented, dabbing at her eyes. "And how shall we manage without him?"

"He's stubborn because that's all he knows how to be," Althea said. "Quinn's stubbornness saved his life and ours—and he's not dead yet."

Though, of course, he soon would be.

Chapter Five

Quinn had been offered marriage on a few occasions, and he'd been propositioned many times, but he'd never asked a woman to be his wife. Based on Miss Winston's worried gaze, he'd made a bad job of his first and only proposal.

"I can leave you enough to live comfortably," he said, returning the cat to the bed, "you and the child. My only condition is that you not squander the money on your father's unholy schemes. The child will be considered my legitimate offspring in name, because I'll leave a witnessed letter with my man of business attesting to same. I assume you've been in London for most of the past year?"

Miss Winston unfastened the frogs of her cloak and let the collar fall open. "I've spent my whole life in London. Are you sure of that part about the child being your legitimate offspring?"

No, Quinn was not, not with a prior marriage that had ended only months ago.

"I'm sure the law complicates the whole business, or barristers and solicitors would go hungry. If you are my widow at the time of the child's birth and you have the means to provide for your offspring, then who will even raise the issue?" Quinn moved his chair, so he sat at Miss Winston's elbow rather than across from her. "Your goal should be to gain security and independence, which marriage to me will accomplish easily."

Was she paler than she'd been five minutes ago?

"If you're feeling charitable, Mr. Wentworth, why not simply hand me a banknote?"

Her question was valid, in light of the fact that Quinn would be giving the child a convicted killer for a father.

"Banknotes can be stolen, and as long as your status is simply a disgraced daughter rather than a widow or a wife, your money all but belongs to your father. I have sisters. I know what machinations are necessary to guard their independence, and we haven't time to pursue those."

She arranged the folds of her cloak, which did nothing to shake the dirty straw free. "I came to dislike being married the first time, and I like being widowed even less."

"I won't relish making a widow of you again. Think, though: How will your child fare as an orphan without means? I can tell you from experience, such a fate isn't pleasant. I was lucky—York is tiny, compared to London, and people knew me to be a hard worker. What assets will your child have if you fall prey to jail fever?"

She gazed at him for a long moment, while birds flitted through the bars and stole the last crumbs from the windowsill. Beyond the door, two of the whores were in a shrieking altercation about a garter.

Where was Ned, and why wouldn't Jane Winston accept an offer of help?

"Why me?" she said. "This entire jail is full of misery. I'm better off than all of them, and yet, you choose to assist me."

Her greatest asset by far was her caution, earned, as most caution was, at high cost.

"You are a victim of misfortune. I know what that's like. I also know what it's like to be a child upon whom fate has turned an unrelenting frown. To my great surprise, my experiences now include the perspective of a man facing ignominious death. Perhaps I'm arguing with the Almighty in mitigation. A convicted killer I might be, but I'm capable of protecting innocent life as well."

Jane spread her hands on the table. They were clean and feminine, though where was her wedding ring?

"I am not innocent," she said. "I am willful, reckless, ungrateful, stupid, and pregnant."

Quinn tore off a corner of gingerbread and crumbled it over the windowsill, then remained by the window, gazing out at the bare courtyard where his life would end.

"My mother was no different from you," he said. "Marrying in haste, for reasons that seemed paltry in hindsight but mattered very much to a sixteen-year-old girl. We do the best we can."

The birds would not come back as long as Quinn remained by the window, so he took a seat on the bed, jostling the cat, whom he appeased with a scratch behind the ears. Plato was a mouser. He enjoyed frightening the birds, but mostly left them to their crumbs.

"Where is your mother now?" Miss Winston asked.

Her name was not Miss Winston. Like almost everybody else in this armpit of the king's justice, she was traveling under false colors.

"In a pauper's grave in Yorkshire. She was gone shortly after I turned five." Few people knew that.

"I had my mother until three years ago. She caught a fever, and even as her health waned, she insisted on accompanying Papa to visit the less fortunate here and at the Magdalen houses."

The birds came again: a crow, a sparrow, a little wren, always one at a time, never staying for more than a moment.

"What would your mother tell you to do, Jane?"

The whores fell silent, though somebody else was ranting, gibberish punctuated by profanity.

"I'm not saying yes," Miss Winston replied, "though how do we procure a special license?"

"That part's easy, but I'll not put my man of business through the aggravation unless you agree to marry me. Five thousand pounds ought to see you comfortably established without setting the fortune hunters on you."

She touched her forehead to the table, as if felled by an excess of spirits, then sat up. "Five...Five *thousand* pounds? Five thousand *pounds*? You can toss that at me as a casual gesture on your way to the gallows?"

He could toss her ten times that amount and have nobody the wiser.

"If you invest at five percent, that gives you 250 pounds a year to make a home for yourself and the child. Not a princely sum, but many clergy make do on less. My business partner, Mr. Joshua Penrose, will see to your finances if you have nobody else in mind for that role."

"Five thousand pounds," she muttered, looking about as if to make sure she hadn't been magically transported to a different realm. "I cannot fathom..."

Her expression had gone from cautious to anxious.

Quinn grasped her dilemma. Money always came with conditions, with complications. Instead of struggling against her father's incompetence, Miss Winston would have to deal with being a murderer's widow. She would figure prominently in the broadsheets and tattlers in the coming weeks, and ten years hence, somebody would considerately wave those horrors in the child's face.

Miss Winston would have to draw firm lines between her household and the prying public.

She'd have to sort out what to tell pious Uncle Dermott, if anything.

She'd have to explain to the child how a condemned felon had stepped into the legal role of father.

Quinn could help her with none of it. "Money changes everything. It changes how you're perceived and treated, how you approach others. The changes aren't always for the better, but not having money can be fatal."

In his case, *having* money had proved equally dangerous.

"A child must eat," Miss Winston said, linking her fingers on the table before her, as if somebody was about to bind her wrists. "I must eat, if my child is to be born healthy."

Quinn held his peace, because the lady had apparently come to a decision. She'd take his money, she'd let him make one gesture in defiance of the court's judgment of him. Althea and Constance would grasp his logic, and Joshua would see to the funds.

Stephen...Quinn could not bear to think about Stephen. Thank God that Duncan was on hand to think about Stephen.

Miss Winston scooted to the edge of her chair. "Get that special license, Mr. Wentworth, and prepare to become my lawfully wedded husband."

She pushed to her feet, then swayed. Quinn was off the bed and had his arms around her in the next instant.

* * *

"I'll go next week," Ned said, keeping his voice down.

Newgate was the epicenter of tragedy in London, as full of despair and hard luck as the sewers were full of waste. Of all the prison's horrors—the stink, the sickness, the violence, the graft—the plight of the children appalled Jane most.

Papa's response was the predictable mumbling about God's will, which only confirmed that Jane wanted no part of her father's God.

And yet, who but the Almighty could have inspired Ned to remain captive?

"We might not have a next week," Jane replied. "The charwoman might lose her job, the warden might decide that wheelbarrows will replace the muck carts, the wagon that picks up the straw might be delayed by a lame horse."

Ned hopped down from the common room's windowsill. "All of that might have happened this week, but it didn't, Miss Jane. I don't want him to die alone."

"We all die alone, Ned. That can't be helped."

He kicked at the straw, doubtless disturbing a legion of fleas. "I've seen other men hang. He'll go quick 'cause he's so big."

Mr. Wentworth was tall and strong. Jane had had occasion to appreciate that strength when she'd nearly fainted several days earlier. He'd gathered her in his arms, his warmth and scent enveloping her. He was a killer—Jane had never once heard him protest his innocence—and yet, his embrace had been a comfort.

He'd held her as if he had all the time in the world to humor her wayward biology, as if she weighed nothing. He knew how to shelter a woman against his body without awkwardness or impropriety intruding.

Gordie hadn't known that, and he'd legally taken on the role of protecting Jane. His embraces had been exclusively carnal from the first, and Jane hadn't realized a man might offer her any other sort of intimacy.

"Next week," Jane said, "I want you to go, Ned. I'll make you promise Mr. Wentworth if you won't promise me." Because Mr. Wentworth could make the boy do anything—except abandon him.

"Next week you'll be a missus. You won't have to come here ever again."

Jane didn't want to visit Newgate again. Mama's stubborn devotion to charitable work had resulted in her death. Jane wanted to get the wedding ceremony over with, leave, and never, ever come back. Mr. Wentworth's generosity made that dream possible, even as eternal damnation awaited him.

In a few minutes, Jane would become a wife for the second time. She was waiting for Davies, Mr. Wentworth's self-appointed footman, to let her know the preacher had arrived. The license had been obtained only that morning, and on Monday—the day after tomorrow—she'd become a widow once again.

She'd considered telling Papa about the wedding and decided against it. He'd never approve, and he'd meddle, and a great ruckus would ensue, and then Jane would be sick, poor, and unwed.

Davies emerged from Mr. Wentworth's quarters—they hardly qualified as a cell—and beckoned.

"The parson's in the warden's room. You look a right treat, Miss Winston."

Davies was at the awkward age when boyhood refused to entirely part with the emerging man. His voice hadn't settled, his muscles hadn't caught up with his bones, and he hadn't learned to hide his emotions.

Though he was trying. Pity lurked in his pale blue eyes, for all he smiled at Jane and offered his arm.

The polite gesture was ridiculous, as was Davies's compliment. Jane had sewn this dress in haste, hoping against all the evidence that she'd never need it.

"Come along, Ned," Jane said. "Mr. Wentworth will expect you to join us."

Papa was elsewhere in the prison this morning, thank goodness, likely hearing the confession of somebody bound for New South Wales. Penny, one of the whores, had told Jane that Mr. Wentworth would be the only convict sent to his reward on Monday.

The thought was horrid. In the abstract, capital punishment brought a violent symmetry to justice. A life for a life. All good Christians ought to consider that approach outdated, but on a human level, the formula was logical. When the execution involved a man who fed wild birds and arranged for a child to regain his liberty, the logic failed.

There was good in Mr. Wentworth. There might have been a murderous impulse, a bad moment, a misjudgment, but there was also good.

"Miss Winston," Mr. Wentworth said, bowing when Jane entered his quarters. "Any second thoughts?"

He was resplendent in morning attire, which must have cost him significantly. The fine tailoring turned blinding good looks into male perfection, and—most perfect of all—he seemed unaware of his own attractiveness.

"No second thoughts, Mr. Wentworth." Jane had misgivings, doubts, and regrets in quantity, but she and her child needed to eat.

He extended a hand to her. "May I introduce Mr. Perkins? He has the honor of joining us in holy matrimony. Davies and Penny have agreed to stand as witnesses. We've room for a few more, if you'd like any other guests to join us."

His tone skirted the edge between jocular and ironic, and his grip on Jane's hand was warm.

That grip was all that prevented her from fleeing. She'd married Gordie in haste, and within months, Gordie had died. At least in this case, Mr. Wentworth's fate was a foregone conclusion rather than a damnable surprise. Cold comfort, but comfort nonetheless.

"Sophie and Susie would enjoy the ceremony," Jane said. They were good women, doing what they could to keep the children safe and to look after the older inmates. What they did for the guards was none of Jane's business.

"Ned, if you'd usher the ladies here?"

Ned took off like one of the birds stealing crumbs from the windowsill.

The minister offered Jane an awkward greeting, then went back to paging through his prayer book. The cat sat upon the bed, looking the most dignified of anybody present, and a crow strutted back and forth on the windowsill.

"Not what you envisioned when your girlish fancies turned to marriage, is it?" Mr. Wentworth asked.

"Nor you," Jane replied, "when you thought about taking a bride."

When Susie and Sophie crowded in behind Ned, Penny, Davies, and the preacher, the ceremony got under way. The words were beautiful, or would have been had not Mr. Perkins been in such a great rush. Midway through Jane's vows, a commotion erupted behind the witnesses.

"Jane Hester Winston, what is the meaning of this?"

Papa had used his Wrath of God voice, of course, and genuine consternation shone in his eyes. Had he been merely raging, Jane might have stood firm, but that doubt, that glimmer of fear, had her slipping her hand from Mr. Wentworth's.

Jane was half-turned toward the door—whether to flee the premises or cast up her accounts in the common, she could not have said—when the groom spoke up.

"Reverend Winston, I am so glad you could join us. The circumstances are unusual, but a father's presence at a wedding is always welcome."

Mr. Wentworth's fingers closed around Jane's hand as Papa's outrage faltered.

"A wedding? To *you*?"

"In order that I might leave your daughter provided for, and minimally ease the conscience of a man soon to face his Maker."

Provided for—that mattered. That did matter a very great deal. Jane studied the carpet, which bore a worn pattern of peacocks and doves amid lotus blossoms.

"Shall we proceed?" Perkins asked.

"No you shall not!" Papa thundered. "This is beyond irregular, and I see plainly that my daughter is again failing to heed the guidance of a loving parent. The minds of women are easily disordered, and I have no doubt this scoundrel, this murderer, this, this—"

Jane's belly threatened rebellion, as if even the babe objected to Papa's dramatics. "Hush, Papa. You've no need to shout."

"I have every need to shout. This is a travesty, a mockery of the holy union God intended. Will you shame me once again, Jane Hester?"

Mr. Wentworth wrapped his free hand over Jane's knuckles. "I see no shame here, sir. We contemplate a union between consenting adults who have made sensible choices. My hope is that you will stay and give your blessing to your daughter's decision. She is marrying a wealthy man, at a time when both she and you have few resources.

Taking me as a husband, even for the few days I'll fulfill that office, cannot be easy for her. Your support would mean much to her."

Not support. Papa was incapable of supporting his only child. The best Jane could hope for from her father was fuming tolerance.

"Jane?" Papa no longer shouted. "Does this wretched man speak the truth? You do this of your own free will?"

Wealth had been mentioned. Very shrewd on Mr. Wentworth's part. Now Papa would turn up reasonable—wounded and bewildered but reasonable. Jane wished dear Papa were anywhere else; she wished *she* were anywhere else.

She also, sincerely and to her surprise, wished Mr. Wentworth were anywhere else. When this ceremony concluded, Jane could leave, taking Mr. Wentworth's name and a portion of his means with her.

Mr. Wentworth would leave Newgate in a shroud.

"Marriage to Mr. Wentworth is very much of my own free will, Papa. He does me a great courtesy when I am much in need of same."

"Mr. Perkins, please resume the service," Mr. Wentworth said.

"But this is…" Papa began, clutching his Book of Common Prayer to his heart. "I fail to see…"

A circle of tired, resentful faces turned on him, every expression impatient and annoyed. Ned's little hands were balled into fists. Penny, Susie, and Sophie looked ready to add to the list of murderers incarcerated at Newgate. Davies had a hand on Ned's bony shoulder.

Mr. Perkins cleared his throat.

"I, Jane…" Mr. Wentworth helpfully supplied.

Right. "I, Jane Hester Winston…Jane Hester Winston *MacGowan*, do take this man…."

With no interruption or hesitation whatsoever, Mr. Wentworth completed his part of the service. They were pronounced man and wife, and gingerbread was served to all present, including the birds.

The ceremony could not have been stranger, and yet, when everybody had partaken of their gingerbread and left the new couple some privacy, Jane's relief was enormous. She hadn't fled, hadn't run off, and thus she would have five thousand pounds.

"I might have capitulated to Papa." She'd nearly done just that. "I would have let him lecture me back into my corner because I pity him. He has no congregation to respect him anymore, no wife to raise his spirits, no bishop to debate theology with." Why was Jane explaining this to a man who'd soon be dead? "I'm glad you were able to make him see reason."

Mr. Wentworth loosened his neckcloth. "So am I. The old boy has prodigious volume, but I gather he's not altogether what you'd wish for in a parent."

He was all Jane *had*—as a parent, as family, as a provider. "He used to be stern but reasonable. Mama could jolly him out of his excesses of piety. When he lost her…."

Mr. Wentworth folded the cravat and set it on a shelf in the wardrobe across the room from the bed. He hung his coat inside the wardrobe and then took the sleeve buttons from his cuffs.

"I won't be needing any neckwear on Monday," he said. "Ned and Davies are to divide my effects, though you should have this ring." He wiggled a gold signet ring off his smallest finger and set it on the table. "You're pale, Mrs. Wentworth. Shall I cut you another slice of gingerbread?"

Mrs. Wentworth. *Mrs. Wentworth.* Jane had wanted out of the prison before, because it was a prison, because a place very like this had made Mama ill, because marrying Quinn Wentworth was even more out of character for her than eloping to Gretna Green with a handsome Scottish officer.

Now panic beat hard against her ribs. "We are alone, Mr. Wentworth, and you are disrobing. Might I inquire as to why?"

Chapter Six

Quinn had learned early and well how to inspire fear. His first weapon had been a murderously fast pair of fists—still quite in working order—and his second had been equally fast feet. Then he'd perfected his aim with knives and pistols. Nobody got away from Quinn Wentworth. Not debtors fleeing their creditors, not cutpurses, not those with information sought by the authorities.

In York's medieval warren of poverty and privilege, he'd learned how to turn speed and power into money. Then he'd learned how to turn money into yet still more power, until neither criminals nor countesses dared cross him.

None of which made the trepidation in Miss Winston's eyes easier to look upon.

Not Miss Winston, never again Miss Winston. "The accommodations are dusty," he said, turning back his cuffs. "These clothes will fetch more coin if they're clean, and both Ned and Davies are short of funds at the moment."

She picked up the cat and cuddled him to her chest—like a shield? "You could leave them money."

What an awful conversation to have following one's nuptials. "Ned and Davies have both refused a place in my will. They prefer to earn coin. They'll accept a casual bequest, but they will not become objects of charity. They have the luxury of pride. Your circumstances require you to be more practical."

Quinn sat on the bed next to his wife, and she scooted away. He reached over to scratch the cat behind the ears, and the new Mrs. Wentworth drew back.

Her reaction was understandable and should even have been a relief. "Jane?" He had the right to address her by name now.

"Mr. Wentworth?"

"I gather MacGowan's connubial devotions were more enthusiastic than considerate. You have nothing to fear from me." Of all men, she had the least to fear from Quinn Wentworth, who'd also learned early and well what folly indiscriminate lust led to.

The cat scrambled free of her grip, leaving a shower of dark hairs in his wake.

"Nothing to fear, Mr. Wentworth?"

Quinn took her hand, which was cool. "Contemplation of a grim death in less than forty-eight hours is a poor aphrodisiac."

Her fingers were limp in his.

He tried again. "I could not do justice to you or the occasion, Mrs. Wentworth. Ours will be a short, cordial union free of conjugal intimacies. I apologize for not making that clear earlier."

Jane had apparently assumed otherwise, doubtless a reflection of how badly she needed Quinn's help.

She let out a breath, and the hand she'd placed over her belly slid to the mattress. "Will the marriage still be legal?"

"Absolutely. Nonconsummation is not grounds for an annulment, and who is to say, given your condition, what we're getting up to behind that closed door?"

Her expression lightened considerably, which was mildly insulting. Also humorous, on a level Quinn had learned to appreciate only since becoming incarcerated.

"Then tell me about yourself," she said. "I'll have to explain you to the child, for he or she will bear your name. What shall I tell my child about the person who provided safety and comfort to him or her, and to me?"

An interrogation regarding Quinn's past was probably the next least enjoyable fate besides a grim death, though if he had to endure questioning, he would do so holding his wife's hand.

"You will tell this child as little about me as possible," he said. "The less your offspring is associated with a convicted killer, the better. If pressed, you can allow I was a self-made man, but in truth I was simply lucky. In a situation where many children are born sickly, I was born big, strong, fast, and good with numbers. My father doubted my legitimacy, which offense he recalled when in his cups. He was a cooper by trade, though as a young man, he aspired to the status of wine merchant. One branch of the Yorkshire Wentworth family is titled, others are well respected. My father's was not among them."

A ducal family not far from York shared the Wentworth name, though Quinn had never so much as knocked on His Grace of Walden's kitchen door. Wentworth was a common name, and Quinn had had no wish to be forcibly ejected from the premises.

"Your good luck outweighed the bad?" Jane asked.

A fair summary, but for recent events. "My father died, which was most fortunate for his offspring, and I prospered. I eventually took on a partner, whom you will meet next week. You can trust Joshua Penrose in all matters relating to money."

Jane might just as easily have removed to the chair at the table, or declared herself ready to leave, and Quinn would have politely accommodated her choices. That she remained beside him, holding hands on the bed, was the first real comfort he'd had since losing his freedom.

Her hand in his gave him relief for a moment from the rage that had been locked in this room with him. The fury would return when she walked out, so Quinn allowed himself the respite.

"What of you?" Quinn asked. "Tell me about my wife."

"She's nobody. A study in obscurity who hadn't the sense to appreciate even that station. I was a good girl, until I wasn't. When Mama died, I lost my papa, too, in a sense, and I could never be what he needed me to be, so I gave up. When Gordie introduced himself to Papa in the churchyard one Sunday morning, I was easily charmed."

A mortal sin in her lexicon, apparently. Did she know that good boys could be preyed upon by the shallow charmers every bit as easily as good girls?

"The Gordies in this life excel at locating virtuous young women on the brink of surrender. Don't castigate yourself overmuch about it. Have you brothers or sisters?"

"None. You?"

He briefly described his sisters, two of the brightest, most stubborn, resilient people he knew, though even thinking of them was painful.

"And then there's Stephen," he went on. "The boy was under my father's roof for the shortest amount of time, but in some ways suffered his influence the most. Don't underestimate Stephen, whatever you do."

"Were you speaking rhetorically, or am I to make the acquaintance of your family?"

Quinn had taken only Joshua into his confidence regarding this marriage, because Joshua's assistance had been needed to obtain the special license, and Joshua would manage the funds promised to Jane.

Quinn would write one more letter—each of the last six letters was to have been his final correspondence—and explain Jane to Althea, Constance, and Stephen. Joshua could pass along the missive at the appropriate time, for Quinn would have no opportunity to send it.

"You will meet my siblings. Your confinement will be most safely passed in my—in my siblings' household. Althea and Constance are difficult by nature, but they will be protective of you. Where you dwell after the baby arrives will be up to you. I suggest you distance yourself from any association with the Wentworths for the sake of the child."

Jane rested her forehead against Quinn's shoulder. "You are being very kind."

"I am being contrary, which has ever been my nature." Long ago, Quinn had been a boy much in need of kindness. Now he was a man in need of a miracle. Having never seen one, and having seen too many tragedies and precipitated more than a few himself, Quinn did not expect aid from the Almighty.

He wrapped an arm around Jane's shoulders, searching his sordid past and short future for some useful words to give her.

"Look forward, Jane. You can't change the past, and dwelling on it serves no purpose. The origins of your improved circumstances mean you'll be outcast by good society, but you'll eat well, you'll be warm in winter. Get away from London and you'll be safe. I like thinking of you and the child, safe and happy."

A fine little speech, and Jane seemed fortified by it.

"I want something with your scent on it," she said, sitting up. "The fragrance you wear settles my stomach, and it's pleasant. Unique."

A bloody miserable request for a bride to make on her wedding day.

Quinn rose and rummaged in the wardrobe, then passed her the bar of hard-milled soap from the wash basin. "My sisters know where to get more. The shop is owned by a Frenchman, and he makes these products only for the Wentworths. We have soap, sachets, and *eau de parfum* with this fragrance."

She sniffed the soap and rose. "I'm a Wentworth now. Thank you."

Quinn was a businessman. He did not expect thanks for lending money or making shrewd investments. He expected payment on time, honest dealing, and profit. He was thus not prepared for Jane to pitch herself against him and wrap him in a ferocious embrace.

"I wish you could walk out of here with me," she said. "I wish I could hide you in a muck cart and spirit you away. I wish you could live to see the child who will bear your name."

She clung to him fiercely and wasn't letting go. In deference to her condition, Quinn wrapped his arms around her.

"If I could afford wishes, I'd wish that yours might come true." He could afford a prison wedding and a private execution, but not a single wish.

A triple knock sounded on the door, Davies's signal that the guard would soon be coming to escort Jane and her father from the prison.

Jane rested her cheek against Quinn's chest. "I will tell the child that you were decent, kind, and generous, and I will be telling the truth."

Quinn was angry, bitter, and condemned. He could have insisted to his wife that she not mislead the child, but what would be the point? Jane, he suspected, could be as stubborn as Althea or Constance, and that was fortunate. Soon enough the new Mrs. Wentworth would see reason and establish a household far from any mention of the late, disgraced Quinn Wentworth.

"Time to go, Jane. Be well, have a fine, healthy baby, and if you can, be happy."

She kissed him on the mouth, surprising a man who'd thought life held no more surprises and certainly no more rejoicing.

But her kiss held joy, an affirmation of her vows, regardless of the circumstances, a loud cheer for having put to rights at least one injustice in a wicked world. She persisted, wrapping Quinn close and taking a taste of him, and then Quinn was kissing her back.

Jane Wentworth was formidable and brave, also pretty and pragmatic. With more time, she and Quinn might have made something together besides a hasty legal arrangement. He permitted himself three heartbeats' worth of regret, then eased back.

"Away with you, Mrs. Wentworth."

Still she held him. "I wish..."

He put a finger to her lips. "Time to go. You promised to obey me."

She kissed him again—*to blazes with obeying you, sir*— and then slipped out the door.

* * *

Despite Ned's every wish, hope, and prayer, Monday morning did not see a commutation order arriving for Mr. Wentworth. The shackles clinked and dragged as the prisoner was led from his cell, and now the damned guards stood about in the courtyard—four of them—as the same chains were removed.

"Bloody crime," Ned said, "making a man pay to have the shackles put on, then pay to have them struck not five minutes later."

"Bloody crime," Davies replied from beside him, "when no writ of transportation shows up for such as him. Every other cove who's committed the same offense gets transportation. He gets the noose."

Ned wanted to mash his face against Davies's skinny ribs and howl. Instead he mashed his fist against Davies's arm. "Stop crowding me."

Davies tousled his hair, and Ned was so enraged he didn't bother hitting him again.

"This is wrong," Ned muttered, turning back to the barred window. "He's not a killer, not like them other poor sods."

The condemned were usually kept segregated in miserable conditions in the prison's bowels. Had Mr. Wentworth been confined thus, Ned would be dead.

"Don't watch, Neddy. He'll be just as dead if you stand guard over his things. I'll stay here."

"Nobody will dare steal his clothes. He left them to us, and he made sure everybody including the wardens knew that." Which made no sense. "If he could bribe the wardens not to steal his clothes, why couldn't he leg it, Davies?"

The guards formed a circle around Mr. Wentworth as the right shackle came off. The courtyard was drenched with early morning sun, an obscenity given what the new day held for Quinn Wentworth. The Ordinary had been sent for first thing to say prayers for him, another obscenity, for the Thou Shalt Not Kill man to ease the king's conscience about taking a life.

"He's not stupid, Neddy."

"What's that supposed to mean?"

The left shackle was proving stubborn, which was bad and good. Mr. Wentworth couldn't bolt until it was off, but they wouldn't hang him in chains either.

"Think about it," Davies said, gaze on the scene in the courtyard. "Quinn Wentworth is as rich as Fat George, but he's not a lord, not Quality. Penny's solicitor friend was at the trial. He said the physician was lying through his teeth, the witnesses were all familiars. Somebody wanted Quinn Wentworth put in jail, and that same somebody saw to it that his sentence wasn't commuted to transportation."

Almost everybody condemned to die, even the typical manslaughterer, got a commutation. Execution was usually reserved for an outright murderer or a counterfeiter. Familiars—witnesses whom the court knew from frequent testimony—were on the take or had agreed to testify lest they be charged with a crime themselves.

"Half the nobs must owe him money," Ned said, as the damned shackle gave way.

"They'll still owe that money when he's dead. Somebody hates him, worse than the Quality hate the rest of us anyway."

An argument rose in the courtyard, between the guards and the executioner. Nobody had thought to bring out a white hood to place over the condemned man's head.

"They even muck up a damned killing," Ned said.

"They know he's innocent. Even that lot know they're doing the devil's work today."

"They know he's innocent," Ned muttered, "we know

he's innocent, and *he* knows he's innocent, so why didn't he just buy his way onto a ship?"

Davies was innocent. Ned could smell it on him, smell the stalwart bewilderment of one who'd been caught up in the crooked, stupid net of the king's justice. Bewilderment was all that stood between Davies and the despair that made a good man give up on goodness altogether. His own, and anybody else's too.

Mr. Wentworth wasn't innocent in the same way, but he hadn't killed anybody. Ned could smell that too.

"I have a theory," Davies said. "He's innocent, but somebody wanted him hanged—the worst death there is, much worse than a knife in an alley. If somebody is powerful enough to make that happen, despite Mr. Wentworth's fortune, they're powerful enough to go after his family. He has sisters and a little brother, a business partner. If Wentworth were to bolt, or get a commutation to transportation, what would happen to that lot?"

One of the guards trotted off to fetch the damned hood. Mr. Wentworth was smiling as his hands were bound.

Smiling.

"I used to want to be like him," Ned said. "I'll never be like him. What if your theory is wrong? What if whoever put him in here will go after his family next?"

"If they're his family, they'll be careful. He will have warned them and put protections in place. He's gambling with his life that they'll be careful enough, and that this is personal."

"You think he knows who did this to him?"

The guard who'd gone for the hood lumbered across the gravel, a scrap of white cloth in his hand. Mr. Wentworth's hands were secured with a yank to the rope, and the hood was placed over his head.

"He knows or suspects who's done this to him. Don't watch, Neddy."

Ned couldn't watch and he couldn't look away. "I was starving when he got here, Davies. I wasn't hungry anymore, hadn't been hungry for days. I was seeing things that wasn't there. He made me eat. Made me take a bite of meat, and when that stayed down, two bites. Nothing but meat and eggs at first, and plain, weak tea. Like he knew what it was to starve."

The gallows was a simple crossbeam with nooses dangling from it. Under the crossbeam was a plank floor that dropped when a lever was pulled. The whole contraption was drawn out into the street for public executions. In the bare expanse of the courtyard, the same apparatus loomed like an obscene altar.

Ned wiped at his cheeks. "I wish he'd let me starve."

The length of rope was such that the condemned dropped eighteen inches at most, not enough distance to develop the speed that would assure a quick end.

"I'd starve right along with you," Davies said, wrapping an arm around Ned's shoulders. "But first I'd kill a few guards, the warden, and if I ever learn who put Mr. Wentworth's neck into that noose, I'd make very sure to kill them too."

Thus did Newgate turn a decent man murderous. "And I'd help you."

Up to the gallows Mr. Wentworth went, despite the hood. He was in no hurry, but certainly not dawdling either, damn him.

Damn them all, and damn this stupid, starving life.

The rope was snugged about his neck. He wore only a shirt and breeches, not even a waistcoat, because the waistcoat hanging in the wardrobe would fetch a pretty penny.

The whores had come up behind Ned and Davies at the window. They stood in a semicircle, some of them sniffling. An ominous quiet settled over the group, in a prison that tormented with noise as much as with dirt and deprivation.

"This is wrong," Penny said. "This is bloody, damned wrong."

The guards lined up, as if standing straight and tall could contradict Penny's truth. Davies's arm tightened about Ned's shoulders, and still, Ned could not look away.

* * *

Quinn had started to drink the laudanum Joshua had purchased for him, then thought better of it. Laudanum was in precious short supply among the incarcerated, and others needed it more than Quinn did.

Besides, why make this killing any easier for those taking a life? Why provide them a dazed, distant victim, one beyond pain, beyond reality?

So Quinn had been marched out into the courtyard only a little the worse for medication. Ned and Davies would find the laudanum in the wardrobe along with clothes and coin. No soap, though. That bequest had gone to Mrs. Wentworth.

Quinn pushed thoughts of Jane aside as the shackles were struck and the guards began arguing about the hood. Whose job was it to bring it out? Where was the damned thing? Why was this damned show taking place in the courtyard rather than on the street like a proper doin'?

The gallows were in the courtyard because Quinn had spent a thousand pounds to make it so. The warden had quietly told him that fifty thousand would not be enough to buy a commutation.

"So save your coin for your family, my friend."

The jury had been kind as well, observing the courtesy of finding that Quinn was without resources, and thus preserving his wealth from forfeiture to the Crown. In the usual case, that had become a formality decades ago. Quinn's was not the usual case.

The sun on Quinn's face was kindest of all, a gentle warmth that hinted of a beautiful day.

Jane would see the end of this day. Quinn would not.

The ordeal ahead no longer troubled him, perhaps because of the laudanum, perhaps because of a fatigue of the heart. He'd suffered physically on many occasions. He'd wished to die, the pain had been so unrelenting. His dignity had been ripped away just as often, his pride left in tatters.

Quinn had spent years at the foot of the gallows; now he was to learn the view from the top of the steps. A minor shift in perspective.

And yet...Jane would mourn him, which was both a comfort and a torment. A child would have the Wentworth name and a bit of the Wentworth wealth. An innocent child, one who'd have a mother's love from the moment of birth.

A mother's love, and a killer's name.

The hood was twitched into place over Quinn's head. "Up ye go, lad. It's time. They don't count to three or say any more prayers. Just drop the rope, then drop you. You're almost done."

This was intended as encouragement. That the guard spoke with a heavy Yorkshire accent was fitting.

Somebody took Quinn's elbow and guided him gently toward the steps. He was given time to navigate the stairs on his own, one of the guards quietly instructing him as the top step approached. This ritual was surrounded with etiquette, of all the ironies. Couldn't have the condemned plunging down the steps and breaking his neck.

The rope was dropped over Quinn's head—new from the smell of it, and rough against his skin. New ropes were stiffer, and thus undesirable under the circumstances because they resulted in death by suffocation rather than a broken neck.

Quinn did not want to die. He'd known that since the farce that had been his questioning at the magistrate's office. Life was not sweet—life was a relentless challenge—but being brother to Althea, Constance, and Stephen had been sweet. Being a partner to that bufflehead Joshua had been sweet.

The rope was tightened, the knot pressing against Quinn's jaw and brushing his ear.

Being married to Jane had been odd and sweet. Quinn's siblings and Joshua would manage—they'd none of them ever forget the lessons learned in York—but Quinn worried about his bride.

The guards stepped back. A hush fell, the morning air fresh and still. Quinn wasn't ashamed to have been outsmarted—bad luck befell everybody sooner or later—but he was furious that the author of his misfortune would not be held accountable.

For the first time in decades something like a prayer formed in Quinn's mind. *See my enemy brought as low I've been brought. Take care of my family, and take care of Jane and the child.*

A thump sounded, and then the world fell away from Quinn's feet. He could not breathe, could not stop fighting to draw breath. His chest exploded in pain, and the white of his hood faded to an awful, airless black.

Chapter Seven

The clock ticked relentlessly in the quiet of the morning room. Althea stitched, Constance stared at a treatise on the symbolic use of light in oil portraits, and Stephen went mad.

"He's gone by now," Stephen said.

Over at the door, Ivor flinched.

"Joshua will bring us word," Althea said.

Joshua would bring them Quinn's body. Murderers were turned over to the doctors for anatomical studies. Stephen knew exactly what that meant, despite the general unwillingness of his siblings to tell him anything useful. A mere manslaughterer's remains were returned to the family for a proper burial.

"Thus endeth the short and merry tale of Quinton Wentworth," Stephen said. "From footman to felon, by way of Mayfair's finest neighborhoods."

Constance exchanged a look with Althea.

"That's enough, Stephen," Althea said, but without the usual whipcrack tone she used on him.

"Quinn is gone," Stephen retorted. "We're on our own now." Stephen hated the idea that he was supposed to meekly sit in his wheeled Bath chair and grieve for a brother who'd been arrogant to a fault, for all Quinn had also been ferociously conscientious regarding the bank's business.

"Quinn got above himself," Constance said. "He made sure we didn't commit the same error."

The Wentworths lived quietly, but they lived quietly and well in London, a far cry from the quagmire of misery that had spawned them in York.

Stephen was seventeen and should have gone up to university. He would never go to university, for two reasons. First, he already knew more than most of the professors teaching at either Oxford or Cambridge about the subjects that mattered to him.

Second, the damned Bath chair.

But his wheeled chair offered lessons of its own, such as how closely madness hovered near the unsuspecting. Stephen had frequently considered taking his own life, before Quinn had brought Duncan down from York. With the implacable assurance of a man equally expert in Socrates, biology, and scripture, Duncan had insisted that a laboratory and greenhouse be added to the town house. To Stephen's amazement, Quinn had listened, and life had changed.

Today, life was changing again.

"Quinn has himself to thank for this day's work," Stephen said.

Constance tossed her pamphlet onto the low table. "What would you have us do, Stephen? Post notices in shop windows that we'll meet our brother's killer in Green Park at dawn? Quinn told us not to interfere."

Althea pulled a thread taut. "Quinn was forever telling us what to do. When did we listen?"

"We did sometimes," Constance said. "When he was sensible, not simply blustering and being overprotective."

Stephen wheeled himself to the window, where a sunny London morning was bustling to life. He'd spent much of his life looking out of windows, until Duncan had said that the mind needed fresh air to invite fresh ideas.

"Quinn was always overprotective," Constance said, "and when it mattered, he had no one to protect him. I tried. I sent a hundred pounds to the warden, simply seeking an interview. He sent it back."

"Two hundred," Althea said, "and that was also returned."

In the complicated economy of a prison, a returned bribe meant one of two things: Somebody else had paid a much larger bribe, or had made a more effective threat.

Stephen's sisters didn't need him to spell that out for them. He'd been eight years old when Jack Wentworth had died, old enough to know, as Duncan said, which from that. His sisters were both older than he and knew all manner of subjects not taught in any finishing school.

Constance took up one of the fine porcelain teacups that sat unused on the tray Ivor had brought in. She loathed tea and had a secret fondness for gin. Perhaps grief had deranged even her formidable mind, for she set the cup down and reached for the teapot instead.

This she hurled against the fireplace, resulting in a satisfyingly loud crash. Althea stared at the shattered porcelain and the tea splattered all over the bricks, then did the same with three teacups in succession.

The sisters would manage. Stephen signaled to Ivor, who opened the door. Stephen wheeled himself from the room amid the loud, messy destruction of a fortune in porcelain, and pretended not to notice that Ivor was crying.

* * *

Quinn's first impression of the celestial realm was that it smelled a lot like prison. Dirty straw, dirty people, despair saturating the air. Somebody was in a taking worthy of Althea holding forth on the subject of women's rights.

Women had no rights. Perhaps in heaven, that oversight had been addressed.

"He's breathing," a man said. "He'll wake up in a moment."

Quinn's head was lifted and the white expanse of the great beyond—or of the executioner's white hood—was replaced with the warden's office at Newgate prison.

"I've been sent to hell after all." Quinn's throat ached, but he could speak intelligibly.

"Praise be," said a dapper little man with a full head of white hair. "Thank the everlasting powers. Somebody fetch His Grace a glass of water."

The company boasted a His Grace, more proof that Quinn had been weighed in the scales and found wanting, for this was surely not the afterlife. He struggled to a sitting position, his brain sluggish, his neck burning like the devil.

Perhaps not *the devil*.

"Here you go, Your Grace," the dapper fellow said, passing Quinn a mug. "Soon you'll be feeling just the thing."

The water tasted metallic, but was cool and soothing to Quinn's throat. In no version of hell he'd been threatened with were new arrivals offered water.

"Who are you?"

"Thaddeus E. Dodson. My card." The fellow passed over a card printed on linen stock. The College of Arms. Perhaps this truly was eternal damnation, or the lingering effects of laudanum in an odd version of the hereafter.

The warden's expression was carefully neutral. Two guards stood by the door impersonating well-trained footmen—erect posture, expressions blank.

Quinn took another sip of the holiest water he'd ever tasted. "Somebody had better start explaining."

The warden cleared his throat. "You've been pardoned, Your Grace."

"The king himself has seen fit to grant you clemency," Mr. College of Arms said. "He has forgiven your error as an unfortunate tragedy mishandled by the courts. You are free to go."

The warden was studying the truly awful portrait over the mantel, a well-fed beldame with a pug in her lap.

"What aren't you telling me?" Quinn asked. "Fat George never does favors without expecting something in return. I'm a convicted felon. What could he want from me?" A convicted felon who had cheated death. The shock of that truth spread over Quinn like a summer sunrise. He could not trust his good fortune to last, if good fortune it was, but he was undeniably *alive*.

"You are a *pardoned* felon," Dodson replied. "We need not speak of that when more good news is at hand. Did you know, sir, that you were heir to the Walden ducal title?"

The only people who called Quinn "sir" were people who wanted money from him or people who owed him money.

And the whores, Ned, and Davies. They had called him sir.

"I suppose you'll have to hang me again," Quinn said, pushing to his feet. "I'm not the duke of anything, and I hope to die in that fortunate state. Shall we get on with it?"

He was not bluffing. The only explanation he could concoct for this reprieve was that he'd now be expected to commit some fraud or deception for the Crown. His father had attempted any crime, any betrayal of decency for the sake of another bottle of gin. Quinn would not follow in those scapegrace footsteps, even to save his own neck.

"You'll not be hanged," the warden said. "The bugger has papers, royal seal and all. To hang you now would be both treason and murder."

Quinn experienced the same dread that had come over him when he'd returned home after a day of looking for work and he'd heard Papa ranting from half a street away. Drunk and mean, drunk and maudlin, drunk and murderous. Those had been the choices when Papa was loud. All of Quinn's options had stunk then, and they doubtless reeked now.

"Mr. Dodson, you will explain yourself."

"The situation is simple, Your Grace. You are heir to the Walden dukedom, the seat of which lies in the north, not far from the place of your birth. Given your exalted station, the king has spared your life so that you might carry out the duties of your office, in gratitude to a benevolent sovereign."

Gratitude, to the very Crown that tried to hang him? *Had* hanged him?

"Bloody bedamned to your pardon, Mr. College of *Alms*. If King George thinks I'll hand over my fortune for his rotten title, ye can tell him to shove his seal up the royal bunghole—if he can find it."

Quinn's speech had reverted to the dialect of the York slums, and Mr. Dodson had retreated to the door. One of the guards snickered, then began coughing when Quinn turned a glower on him.

"Think of it as a commutation," the warden said. "You were in a prison of one sort—ugly maids, bad food, poor company. With a title, you'll be in a prison of another sort.

Better food and comely maids, though I can't vouch for the company you'll find."

That perspective had merit. Then too, Quinn had siblings and a business partner, and they needed the money his will provided. Then there was Jane, waiting for her five thousand pounds. Quinn marched over to Dodson and treated him to what Stephen called his damnation-and-doom glower.

"Tell the truth, or I'll hunt you down and use a dull, dirty knife to relieve you of body parts your missus might once have been fond of. What happens to my money if I accept George's pardon?"

Dodson blinked twice. "You keep your money."

"And?"

"You inherit the debts that the Walden estate has amassed."

"To the penny, man, or I swear I'll find a way to have a fatal accident."

Dodson named a sum that would have felled any mortal who hadn't spent the last ten years assessing which lords were worth lending money to and which were hopelessly bankrupt.

"Income?" Quinn pressed.

"From five different estates. They have been more than self-sustaining in the past and include tenancies under lease."

If the task was clawing a path out of debt, Quinn was better suited to that challenge than any other subject of the Crown, and King George likely grasped as much. What His Majesty could not know was how determined Quinn was to bring his enemy to justice.

The laws of the slum were few and simple. One directive stood foremost among them in Quinn's mind: Show weakness to those who disrespect you, and you'll be devoured like the prey you are. An eye for an eye meant wrongdoing was punished, and honor upheld. Any other course was as good as begging to be victimized again.

"Mr. Dodson and I are in want of privacy," Quinn said, "and send my footman to me."

The warden smiled faintly. "He means the prisoner Davies."

Quinn ran a finger around the collar of his shirt. "I mean *my footman*, Davies. When I depart this cesspit of injustice, I'll need the services of my tiger, Edward, as well as my chambermaids, Penny, Susie, and Sophie."

Dodson looked pleased, the idiot parasite. "Anything else, Your Grace?"

Forgive me, Jane. "I have a duchess. I must inform her of my good fortune."

* * *

"He's alive!" Joshua Penrose never shouted, never displayed even the cold temper that characterized his business partner, but a damned roll of black crepe sat on the sideboard, and the footman already sported a black armband.

"The bloody sod's alive and pardoned. Althea! Constance! Stephen! Quinn is alive and he's coming home."

Joshua had posted eyes inside the prison, and what those eyes had related nearly restored his faith in a God with a sense of humor.

Althea, dressed head to toe in black, appeared on the landing. "Mr. Penrose, have you taken leave of your senses?" She descended one dignified step at a time, until she was on the bottom stair, which put her nearly eye level with Joshua.

She was beautiful in her grief, but then, she was beautiful

all the time. "I have indeed taken leave of my senses, and so has the Crown. Quinn Wentworth received a royal pardon. The news is all over the prison, and he'll be home this afternoon."

Althea's knuckles showed white as she gripped the newel post. "He accepted the pardon? I did not want to hope." She bit her lip and stared past Joshua's shoulder.

Overhead the clank of metal and the sound of ratcheting chains suggested Stephen was using the lift to descend from the upper floors.

"Get Miss Wentworth some damned brandy," Joshua said, taking Althea's hand. "She's had a shock."

"Yes, Mr. Penrose," the footman replied. "At once, sir."

The footman—Ivor or Kristoff, Joshua could never tell them apart—sprinted for the steps that led belowstairs, though the closest decanter was two doors away in the library.

"Not the morning room," Althea said, drawing her fingers from Joshua's grasp. "I'll be in Quinn's study. Fetch Constance and Stephen."

She swished away, then stopped ten yards down the corridor, her hand on the door latch. "He's truly alive?"

Joshua closed the distance between them, because an uncertain Althea was painful to behold. "Quinn's alive, giving orders to the warden and guards, taking half a dozen common prisoners out with him, and threatening riot."

Althea rested her forehead against the door, more weakness than Joshua had ever known her to show. "He likely beggared himself for his freedom. Money well spent, I say."

"There's more," Joshua said, "and it's not bad news."

Constance came up the corridor. "He who shouts in a house of mourning had better have a good explanation."

"Quinn's alive," Althea said. "He's coming home."

Constance studied the parquet floor, a complex mosaic of oak. "He outbribed somebody. Thank God and the greed of the average Englishman."

Stephen wheeled himself down the corridor, Duncan trailing behind. "Quinn's alive? He's cheated even the hangman?"

"Barely," Joshua said, "but one of the guards had a very sharp knife when a knife was much needed, and Quinn's only slightly the worse for his ordeal."

"Let's discuss this in the study," Althea said.

They filed in, a radiant footman bringing up the rear with a tray bearing a decanter and five glasses.

"Half holiday belowstairs, Ivor," Althea said. "A double round for everybody in honor of the glad tidings, senior staff outside the kitchen may have the evening free. A cold collation for lunch will do."

Ivor set the tray on the low table and bowed. "Very good, ma'am. Felicitations on the wonderful news."

His accent was so thick—*vonderful nuis*—as to make the words nigh unintelligible, but his smile needed no translation. The servants' hall would host a near-orgy, though somebody would remain sober enough to answer the bellpull.

"Burn the crepe," Constance added, "or donate it to the poor, but get it out of the house before Quinn comes home."

"And the armbands," Stephen added. "Go naked from the waist up if you must, but get rid of the armbands."

Duncan, ever a practical fellow, busied himself pouring the brandy. He was a cousin at some remove, recruited to manage Stephen, but he had the Wentworth dark hair, blue eyes, and height. He'd come when needed and Quinn considered him family, so family he was.

While Joshua remained a business partner.

"A toast," Althea said, "to Wentworth resilience."

To Wentworth money, which was a result of that resilience. Joshua had no doubt that Quinn's fortune had come between him and death—this time.

"To Wentworth resilience," Joshua murmured. "Or should I say, to the Duke of Walden's resilience?"

Stephen set his glass on the tray. "He got the title too? I told you lot it was real, and you wouldn't believe me. If Quinn's a duke, then I'm a courtesy lord, and you have to listen to me now."

"If you're a lord," Constance retorted, "I'm a lady, and so is Althea. You'll have to learn a whole new set of manners."

Stephen doubtless already knew all the protocol, all the forms of address. As fast as Duncan threw subjects at him, Stephen gobbled down the knowledge. The boy was what Quinn could have become, had Quinn been allowed to think about anything but survival.

"Speaking of ladies," Joshua said, "we'd all best have a seat."

Duncan brushed a glance at Stephen, who lived half his life seated. The women arranged themselves on the sofa, leaving the wing chairs for Joshua and Duncan. They might have been any well-to-do family enjoying a glass of cordial on somebody's birthday.

"You've said there's more," Althea prompted. "What could be more than a reprieve from death and a lofty title to go with it? Doubtless Quinn will have to take some neglected estate and put it to rights, probably a half dozen of them, but that's a stroll down the lane for him."

The extent of the Walden debts would be a challenge even for Quinn, though exactly the sort of challenge he was equipped to meet.

"The dukedom, as Stephen has noted, is real," Joshua

said. "In typical Quinn fashion, he's anticipated his obligations and already found himself a duchess." And a potential heir. Joshua would let Quinn explain that development, if any explanation were needed.

"Quinn is engaged?" Althea asked, drink halfway to her lips.

"Not engaged," Joshua said, with the same direct gaze he used when he foreclosed on a mortgage. "Married. Quinn has taken a bride, and she'll be coming to live with you here."

A historic beat of silence went by, for the three younger Wentworth siblings were all quiet in the same room at once.

Stephen stared at his cordial, his lips moving in a silent pattern of what appeared to be French profanities.

Constance muttered, "I believe I'll have another," and reached for the decanter.

Althea, dignified, self-assured, lady-of-all-she-surveys Althea, spluttered her drink all over her skirts, while Duncan patted her back and said absolutely nothing.

Chapter Eight

"But from whence cometh your late husband's wealth, Jane Hester?" Papa asked, for the dozenth time. "The god of Mammon is a jealous god, and you cannot think to prosper by worshipping at his altar."

"Not prosper, Papa," Jane said, folding her mother's last good shawl into the battered trunk. "Survive. An infant needs food, shelter, and safety, and I intend that my child have those blessings."

Before Jane had been old enough to put up her hair she'd realized that Papa used his voice as a weapon. Everything, from the piety of his King James syntax to the sheer volume of his declamations, was intended to bludgeon the conscience if not the nerves.

She had learned to wield the same weapon, to appropriate the vocabulary of holiness and faith, and to quote scripture or misquote it as the occasion demanded.

"You'll bless your child with the filthy lucre of a *felon*?"

Papa could not pace, for Jane's quarters were too small to afford him that bit of stage business. "You'll use Wentworth's ill-gotten gains to surround yourself with *luxuries*? Did your misadventure in Scotland teach you *nothing*?"

"My *marriage* to Gordie taught me that life is precarious, and I must provide for his offspring as best I can."

Papa put a hand on the bedpost as if she'd hurled a dagger at his heart. "Jane Hester, what would your mother say?"

Get out while you can, probably. Mama had been a dutiful wife and a pragmatic mother.

"Mama would rejoice that an innocent life will not be born into undeserved hardship. She'd be grateful that some good fortune has come my way, despite the great sorrow of Mr. Wentworth's passing."

Jane had lain on her side in bed that morning and watched the sun creep down the cracked, water-stained wall. Executions were held first thing in the day, the better to accommodate a crowd that could not miss work to take in its entertainments.

Davies had told her that Mr. Wentworth's execution would happen in the courtyard, by some miracle of bribery, meaning Jane's husband had died almost three hours ago.

She could not bear to dwell on that reality for more than a moment or two.

He's gone. That great, complicated, beautiful beast of a man is no more.

I'm widowed again.

Mr. Quinn Wentworth has been put to death.

This should have been a relief, that matters had for once proceeded in exactly the fashion promised. For the first time in her life, Jane was free, she was possessed of a small fortune, and she could order her affairs as she saw fit.

She was anything but relieved.

Mr. Joshua Penrose had arranged for a coach to fetch her and her "effects." When that coach arrived, she'd be ready. Perhaps then—once she was away from these cramped, miserable quarters—she could cry for her late husband.

"You disappoint me, Jane Hester," Papa said in his most funereal tones. "You break your father's heart. Sharper than the serpent's tooth—"

"My child would not thank me for giving birth in these surrounds when a cleaner and more wholesome alternative is available," Jane said. "My child would not thank me for being unable to afford a trained accoucheur. My child would not thank me for—"

Papa had taken out his handkerchief. The last, most potent weapon in his arsenal. He eschewed violence—Turn the other cheek, Jane Hester!—but his definition of violence was limited to the physical.

Much destruction of the spirit could be rendered with mere words, with inaction, with indifference. Jane's heart suffered a blow every time she noticed that another of Mama's mementos had been carted off to the pawnbroker's.

Papa touched the worn linen to the corners of his eyes. "Jane Hester, never did I think that a daughter of mine would seek worldly riches, much less worldly riches of such an unfortunate origin. I shall pray nightly for Mr. Wentworth's soul, but I shall pray without ceasing for yours."

Jane tried mentally counting to three and praying for patience, her mother's preferred prescription for life's aggravations. No patience was to be found where Papa's posturing was concerned, not today, not when Quinn Wentworth was likely being measured for a shroud.

She closed the trunk and fastened the straps, then dragged its dead weight from the bed.

"And for your grandchild, Papa? Will you pray for that innocent soul as well? Will you give thanks that even as Mr. Wentworth faced certain death, his concern was for a child he'd never have a chance to know? Will you be grateful that I was not forced to take up with another Gordie, or worse, simply to keep body and soul together?"

Papa folded his handkerchief, his gesture a well-rehearsed study in sorrow.

"I have made inquiries regarding Mr. Wentworth, Jane Hester. His antecedents are most irregular, and all agree the source of his initial fortune is unsavory. You leave this house without my blessing."

She was supposed to apologize and beg Papa's forgiveness, for leaving, for having been widowed, for a lack of faith in the very Deity who had taken both Mama and Gordie before Jane had been prepared to deal with either loss.

"Judge not, Papa, lest you be judged. I've left my direction with Mrs. Sandbridge downstairs. You will always be welcome to visit in my home."

Not to dwell there. Mr. Wentworth had made that clear.

Mr. Wentworth, who was dead.

Jane used the fury that thought inspired to wrench the trunk across the floor—she hadn't the strength to lift it—and to the top of the stairs. Papa sat on the bed looking forlorn and bewildered, which he did well.

What sort of father watches a pregnant daughter wrestle a heavy trunk and lifts not a finger to help her?

The question popped into Jane's head in Quinn Wentworth's voice. She hoped she'd be hearing that voice frequently in the coming years, because she had genuinely liked her late husband. She'd respected him, and she was endlessly, endlessly grateful to him.

Getting the trunk down the stairs was a noisy business—

thunk, scrape, thunk, scrape—and Jane was put in mind of the steps a convicted felon climbed to ascend the gallows.

Light-headedness assailed her. She knew better than to ignore it, so she sat on the trunk in the foyer until coach wheels and shod hooves clattered to a halt in the street. A large conveyance judging from the racket, not a mean little gig.

Jane rose—slowly, always slowly—waited a moment, then cracked the door.

A smart black town coach drawn by four matched grays sat at the foot of the steps. The coachman and grooms wore black livery trimmed in red, and the coach's appointments were also done in black with crimson piping.

Lucifer would arrive in such a conveyance, somber and dashing at the same time.

"I have grown fanciful," Jane muttered, grabbing her cloak and opening the door wider. In truth, she was famished, but had dared only half a slice of dry toast with a few sips of ale to break her fast.

She had not met Mr. Penrose. She'd communicated with him only in writing, and thus when a largish gentleman stepped down from the coach, she wasn't shocked. He was attired in sober perfection for the time of day, top hat brushed to a sleek shine that matched equally handsome boots.

His linen was immaculate, his clothing exquisitely tailored. His arrival on this street would be talked about for days, so uncommon a sight was he. The fellow knew how to make an impression, and his height helped in that regard. Put a high-crowned beaver hat on a man as tall as Mr. Wentworth had been…

A queer feeling came over Jane as the gentleman mounted the porch steps. The same mental dislocation that an impending faint caused, though she wasn't dizzy.

"Mr. Wentworth." And not a version of Mr. Wentworth

who had any concern regarding his liberty or his continued existence. A splendidly turned-out version of a splendidly self-possessed, handsome man.

"Mrs. Wentworth."

Same deep voice, same steady blue eyes that gave nothing away.

Jane pitched into her husband and wrapped him in a tight hug.

"You are alive. Thank heavens, you are alive." She wept tears of joy and relief, wrinkling his cravat, breathing in the lovely, lovely scent of him. "You did not die. I am so glad you did not die. You are alive."

He drew Jane aside, so two footmen could take her trunk down the steps, but Jane could not turn loose of him.

"I was pardoned," Mr. Wentworth said. "I take it you regard this as a cheering development?"

Jane squeezed him again, though hugging him was like hugging a stone cross. "I am *ecstatic* to see you hale and at liberty, sir. Nothing could please me more. A pardon—a royal pardon, I take it. You are so wonderfully alive."

She beamed up at him, while he regarded her coolly. "I rejoice to be alive. Have you only the one trunk?"

Five words? He gave his resurrection from the dead a mere *five words*? Jane used the sleeve of her cloak to dry her eyes, until a square of white linen, initials monogrammed in red silk on one corner, was dangled before her.

"My mother's cedar chest is at the pawnshop." An inane reply. Mama's hand mirror, her jewelry box, her earbobs, her writing desk—they all gathered dust at the pawnshop. "The one trunk suffices."

"Then let's be on our way. We have matters to discuss."

He offered his arm, Jane took it and descended to the waiting coach. Before she gathered her skirts to climb into the most elegant conveyance she'd ever beheld, she spared her former home a final inspection.

Papa stood in the doorway, his expression blank. Jane felt again the compulsion to apologize, to beg forgiveness, to protect Papa's dignity even at the cost of her own.

Mr. Wentworth waited in silence, Jane's hand on his arm. A footman stared straight ahead; not even the horses dared fidget.

Jane did not know her husband at all. Having her for a wife might be a great inconvenience to him now. Having him for a *husband* might be something of an inconvenience as well.

Oh, dear.

She climbed into the coach and settled onto the padded comfort of the front-facing seat. Her husband took the place beside her, rapped the roof once with a gloved fist, and the coachman gave the horses leave to walk on.

* * *

As Quinn's town coach pulled away from the curb, his wife—*his duchess*—let down the shade over the window.

"All of London will soon know we're married," he said. "Not much use trying to hide."

Jane sat back. "The sun causes everything to fade. I close curtains out of habit."

She looked tired, and Quinn was growing to hate her damned gray cloak. "I prefer curtains and windows open in all but the coldest weather."

They regarded one another, two strangers now legally one flesh.

Jane's joy at seeing Quinn had been unexpected and not entirely welcome. Not entirely unwelcome, either.

She no longer radiated exultation. "We hardly know each other, Mr. Wentworth."

Quinn knew she needed help, knew she'd been genuinely glad to see him. Those factors alone would not have sent him to her doorstep, but he also knew she was with child. The evidence of her pregnancy had been pressed to his very person, and yet, her father had watched her departure with complete indifference.

"We have time to become better acquainted," Quinn said, though they'd be at Joshua's town house in less than an hour. "What would you like to know?"

She rolled up the window shade. "Do you have children?"

Interesting place to start. "I do not—yet." This topic needed to be raised. With Quinn's family underfoot, the requisite privacy for such a discussion would be scarce. "We are married, Jane."

"I was present at the ceremony, Mr. Wentworth."

Quinn had been present in body. He still wasn't sure where his wits had got off to. "Do you intend to honor your vows?"

She fussed with her cloak, the dreariest excuse for an outer garment Quinn had beheld in years. The wool would keep her warm even when wet, and thus qualified as that most offensive of wardrobe items, the practical garment.

"What are you asking me, sir?"

"You did not anticipate becoming my wife in truth, did not anticipate sharing a household with me. The marriage can be annulled, for a sum." He would make this offer, though it rankled. Vows were vows.

"You are correct that I did not foresee myself married to you, and in the general case, I dislike surprises. What if I said yes, I'd like an annulment?"

Quinn would be disappointed, but *not* surprised. In the

course of this long and strange morning, he'd been plagued by regrets and memories, though among the flotsam in his mind had also been treasure: Jane had kissed him on their wedding day.

Kissed him like she'd meant it from the heart.

She had trusted him to safeguard her future, taken him at his word, and never once inquired into his guilt. Quinn knew better than to hope for some marital fairy tale, but her kiss had been stubbornly unforgettable.

"If you want an annulment," he said, "I'll notify the requisite bishop, and you'll have your freedom. The sum put in trust for you will remain yours to do with as you please."

For yet more sums, any word of their prison ceremony would be stricken from memory, and Quinn would go on with his life as before, getting and spending.

While he also hunted the varlet who'd sent him to an ignominious death.

"Would *you* like an annulment?" she asked, folding her hands over her belly. "If you're laboring under the notion that a gentleman doesn't cry off, you needn't be so delicate."

She thought him a *gentleman*? "I spoke vows, Jane. I keep my word. At times, my word has been the only possession I had of any value. Once broken, it will never mend as strong as it was before. I make an exception in the case of our vows because nobody could have foreseen that I'd walk out of that prison. If you decide to honor your promises, then we will be man and wife in every meaningful sense."

She wiggled around on the bench, like a hen on a nesting box. "Do you drink to excess?"

Gordie MacGowan deserved to roast in hell. "I drink strong spirits only sparingly. The last time I got drunk I was twelve years old."

"Would you raise your hand to me in anger?"

On second thought, hell was too good for MacGowan. "I will never raise my hand to you. I will probably raise my voice, and you are free to do likewise in response."

She considered Quinn frankly, and he resisted the urge to look away. "I might enjoy that," she said. "Shouting matches instead of sermonizing would be a novelty. I might enjoy that rather a lot."

In her shabby cloak and mended gloves, Jane was yet dignified. Quinn liked that about her. Liked that she could interrogate him despite the upheaval of the day—she'd had a shock, after all—and he liked that his finery hadn't intimidated her. He'd also like more of her kisses, provided those kisses were freely given.

"Shall we be married, Jane? I will never be a doting swain, never shower you with flattery or romantic nonsense. You and your children will know every material comfort, and I'll make every effort not to annoy you."

The coach swayed around a corner, while Quinn made himself wait for Jane's answer. He could go on, elaborating settlement terms—pin money, dower portions, morning gifts, life estates, and so forth. He could warn Jane in detail regarding the obstreperous trio he called siblings, or he could ask her if she had any more questions.

This was not, however, a negotiation at the bank.

"You mention children, plural," Jane said. "You expect to have a family with me."

A duke was expected to have heirs. Quinn had come to this realization while soaking in the first tub of truly hot water he'd enjoyed in weeks. For himself, he wanted nothing to do with a title, much less with paying off debts the king was too miserly to take on. Nonetheless, Quinn was damned if he'd set an ailing dukedom to rights just so the Crown could snatch his wealth away through escheat.

"I would like to have a family with you."

She treated him to a frowning perusal. "Why haven't you married? You're well to do, gorgeous, and temperate."

"Because I have been busy becoming well to do, and any woman who'd leap at a man simply because an accident of nature made him attractive is asking for trouble."

She laughed. "Touché, Mr. Wentworth, and Gordie was far from temperate. Still, you are a handsome devil, you can be charming, and you're of age."

Quinn had no problem discussing money, which was vulgar of him in the extreme. Discussing his appeal to women made him want to dive from the moving coach.

"My antecedents are lowly, my trade is finance, and my nature is difficult. I hold mortgages on nearly a quarter of the recently purchased homes in Mayfair, and can't ride in the park without running into some viscount or baron who has sought an unsecured loan from my bank. The only club to admit me hasn't a lord to its name. Finding a young lady who can overlook my shortcomings would require time I don't have."

Quinn was being honest, though soon enough, Jane would find out how very lowly his antecedents were—and how lofty his title. He refused to tempt her with a tiara, though, when he'd be the man sharing her bed.

"I like you," Jane said, which pronouncement left Quinn more uneasy than ever. "You were decent to Ned and Davies. You fed the birds."

He'd fed the birds for entertainment. "Ned and Davies will be employed in my household, as will Susie, Penny, and Sophie, if they so choose."

"I also respect you."

What in seven flaming hells was he to say to that?

"We spoke vows," Jane went on. "I did not anticipate becoming your wife, but I much prefer it to being your widow. I'll honor my vows if you'll honor yours."

"I keep my word, Jane." Quinn reserved for later the matter of Jane's firstborn, for sad to say, birth could be fatal for both mother and infant.

She let her weight sink against his side. "Then we shall be man and wife, Mr. Wentworth, until death do us part, shouting matches and all."

"Man and wife," he said. "For better or for worse, and all the rest of it. I have siblings. They come under the 'worse' heading. Let me tell you about them."

Chapter Nine

"You are dithering," Joshua said. "You've nothing to dither about. Your family is ecstatic that you've been pardoned. Even Duncan was offering toasts to your continued good health when I left your house, and he's the next thing to a Presbyterian. Now he can boast that his cousin is a duke."

Quinn tugged at the cravat that Joshua's valet had tied too snugly around a brutally sore and abraded neck.

"Are you ecstatic at my continued good health?" Quinn asked.

And how long did one woman need to soak in a bathtub before she'd completed her ablutions? More than an hour ago Joshua's housekeeper had whisked Jane abovestairs, muttering about daft men and a lady's nerves.

"What sort of question is that?" Joshua retorted, opening a desk drawer and extracting a deck of cards.

They waited in Joshua's library, which in bachelor quarters doubled as an office and game room. Joshua pulled out a chair opposite Quinn at an ingenious little table that could be used for chess, backgammon, cards, writing, and several other tasks, depending on which hidden lever Joshua manipulated.

Joshua Penrose liked his intrigues.

"Somebody put my neck in that noose," Quinn said. "The usual motives are greed, revenge, or passion. I haven't inspired anybody's passion for years, I am scrupulously fair in all my financial dealings, and you benefitted the most by my death."

Joshua dealt cards with the smooth practice of an expert—or an expert cheat. "In your shoes, I'd ask the same question, which is why I won't lay you out flat for your suspicions. If you're looking for who benefitted from your death, all of your family members did, but the charities stood to gain the most and I doubt they had any inkling of their impending good fortune. How long can one woman soak in a bathtub?"

"My wife may take as long as she pleases." Though even Quinn, desperate to wash off the stink of prison, hadn't been able to linger more than a half hour at his bath.

He'd detoured back to Joshua's town house with Jane because the Wentworth residence was yet mobbed with reporters. Even that menace would not prevent Quinn from spending the night in his own bed.

A desultory hand of piquet ensued, one of thousands Quinn and Joshua had played when no food was to be had and no fuel was to be burned. Soldiers did likewise, whiling away the evening before battle.

Quinn tossed down his cards twenty minutes later. Joshua was either distracted or he was letting Quinn win.

"What did you tell my family about Jane?" Quinn asked.

"That you had taken a bride and would be bringing her home to them. Shall I deal again?"

A soft tap on the door nearly startled Quinn out of his chair, though he moved not at all. Prison had brought forth the reflexes that had kept him alive as a boy.

The housekeeper, a prim article who likely regarded mud on the carpets as a sign of the end times, opened the door and stood aside so Jane could enter the room. The dress Joshua had found for her was aubergine velvet, suitable for a new widow newly remarried, also suitable for a woman in anticipation of an interesting event.

Quinn stood. "Madam."

Joshua rose and bowed. "Ma'am." His manners were a dig at Quinn. They did that for each other, kept one another alert and aware.

She curtsyed with unhurried grace. "Mr. Wentworth, Mr. Penrose."

"You may be excused," Quinn said to the housekeeper, "and please have my coach brought around." The inevitable had been put off as long as possible, and interrogating Joshua would get Quinn nowhere.

The housekeeper remained by the door. "Mrs. Wentworth?"

Jane's confusion was fleeting, showing mostly in her eyes. She was Mrs. Wentworth, until Quinn found a way to explain that she was Her Grace of Walden.

"You are excused, Mrs. Gaunt. My thanks for your assistance."

Some sort of alliance had formed between the women in the space of one bath. That was good, because Jane would need allies.

"Penrose," Quinn said, "my thanks for your assistance as well. I'll see you at the bank tomorrow."

Joshua was wearing his harmless, charming look, which meant he was up to no good. "You are newly married and newly risen from the almost-dead. Mightn't you want to spend some time with your family before resuming your duties at the bank?"

Jane watched this exchange with veiled curiosity.

"I will spend the balance of the afternoon at home," Quinn said, "and endure as much of my family's joy as one day can hold, but then I have business to attend to."

The business of finding and putting period to an enemy, first and foremost.

"I will wish you both good day," Joshua said, "and extend my sincere felicitations on your nuptials."

He accompanied them to the front door, and an awkward silence ensued while Quinn waited for his coach to arrive and Jane discreetly gawked at the stormy Dutch seascapes displayed on Joshua's walls.

Silence had always been a friend to Quinn, assuring him his father was away from home or sleeping off another drunk in his filthy bed. Silence had remained an ally in the banking business, because customers who'd mis-stepped prattled of their stupidity when Quinn allowed a silence to last too long.

Silence was uncomfortable now, because it was shared with Jane and Joshua and the butler hovering near the porter's nook.

"Will you undertake a wedding journey?" Joshua asked.

Trying to get rid of me? "Perhaps later," Quinn said. "My wife's health must come before any other consideration."

Her health and her safety, for somebody's scheme had been thwarted by that royal pardon, and that somebody had wanted Quinn dead. Such a person might think little of hurting Jane or her child in a second attempt at ruining Quinn.

The coach pulled up and Quinn once again took his place beside Jane inside. To have company in the carriage was different. Quinn's sisters had their own conveyance, while Stephen preferred traveling on horseback if he had to go any distance.

Jane remained quiet as the coach pulled into the street.

"Did you have anything to eat?" Quinn asked. The new Mrs. Wentworth had had a trying day, and her condition was delicate.

"The housekeeper brought me some ginger biscuits with the tea tray. I was in heaven."

While Quinn had spent the past month in hell's family parlor. "We didn't finish discussing my siblings." Though where to start?

"I don't expect them to like me," Jane said, smoothing a hand over her velvet skirts. "We don't have that sort of marriage. I'll be agreeable, Mr. Wentworth. I excel at being agreeable when needs must."

"You sound determined on your penance." Also surprisingly fierce. Alas, Quinn hadn't an agreeable bone in his body.

"You were kind to me when I was in desperate need of kindness. I'll endure much to repay that consideration."

She saw the marriage as a bargain, a transaction. Quinn understood business dealings, so a commercial frame of reference ought to suffice.

Except it didn't. "My family might be unruly when they greet me. Loud, undignified." Foul-mouthed, if they'd been at the brandy. Constance could swear like a sailor, though she usually exercised restraint out of deference to Duncan's delicate sensibilities.

Jane took Quinn's hand. "I was loud and undignified when I saw you, also overjoyed."

She had hugged him as if he'd been a prodigal son lost in a hostile land during a time of famine.

"I will not be undignified," Quinn said. "I am disinclined to displays of passionate sentiment." He *could not* engage in displays of passionate sentiment was the more accurate admission.

"No matter," Jane said, stifling a yawn. "In my present condition, I'm the next thing to a watering pot. I'm not half so interested in maintaining my figure as I am in maintaining my dignity, all to no avail. I'll doubtless be sentimental enough for the both of us."

"Are you interested in taking a nap?"

Jane looked unwell to him. The dark dress accentuated her pallor and her fatigue, and ginger biscuits weren't the steak and kidney pie she ought to be eating.

"I have become prodigiously talented at appearing awake," Jane said. "Before I retire yet again, you will introduce me to your family, please, for they will be my family now too."

She alluded to some bit of scripture, a laughable source of authority in the life of Quinn Wentworth. As the coach horses clip-clopped along, Quinn turned his mind to the list of suspects he'd pursue starting first thing tomorrow.

Joshua most likely did not belong on that list. He had an abiding respect for money, as would anybody raised in Yorkshire poverty, but more than money, Joshua Penrose had a taste for power. He liked the role of *éminence grise*, influencing parliamentary debates, bringing down enemies by stealth and indirection.

Having Quinn arrested for a hanging felony was indirect but hardly stealthy. Still, Joshua bore watching.

As did Quinn's family.

Quinn's younger half-siblings had withstood Jack Wentworth's dubious care for years before Quinn had been able to intervene. Stephen, Althea, and Constance lacked a motive to kill him, though, unless resentment qualified. Jack Wentworth was to blame for Stephen's ill health, and God alone knew what horrors Althea and Constance had borne.

"Are you worried?" Jane asked.

Determined. "Like you, I am plagued by fatigue. Perhaps the relief of a pardon has that effect." Or the weeks in Newgate, unable to sleep, unable to find quiet, unable to pursue true justice.

"Then I'll see that your siblings don't keep you overlong. They must reassure themselves that you're alive and well, but you shall be allowed your rest."

Jane subsided against him, not exactly a cuddle—Quinn wouldn't know a cuddle if it pounced on him in a dark alley—but something wifely and trusting.

How odd. Of all the people in Quinn's life—family, business associates, employees, enemies, neighbors, and old acquaintances—Jane alone was free from suspicion.

Perhaps that in itself ought to make Quinn cautious with her, but he could not sustain the burden of such zealous vigilance. She was expecting a child, without means, and all but a stranger to him.

He wrapped an arm around her shoulders and steeled himself to endure his family's welcome.

* * *

"Pardoned, can you believe it?" Beatrice, Countess of Tipton, crumpled up the handbill, intent on hurling it into the dustbin, then thought better of the impulse. She would read it again, read every word, when she had privacy.

These little announcements—a combination of obituary and lurid fiction passed out at executions—were popular with the lower orders. The printer would be sold out by sundown, and a woman of Beatrice's station wasn't likely to come by another copy.

"How can so much resilience and good fortune attach itself to such an unworthy object?" she asked, pacing before the fire. "How can a man who's earned the enmity of half the good families in the realm, a jumped-up gutter rat in fine tailoring, earn the clemency of the very king?"

A handsome, *shrewd* jumped-up gutter rat. Beatrice had noticed Quinn Wentworth's good looks too soon and seen the shrewdness too late.

"Perhaps Wentworth's wealth played a role?" The Hon. Ulysses Lloyd-Chapman had casually passed over the handbill, as any caller would share the gossip of the day. Ulysses was Beatrice's favorite sort of man—handsome, idle, venal—but what did he know about her connection to Quinn Wentworth and how had he learned of it?

"Money should have resulted in a verdict of innocence," Beatrice retorted, "if money had been effective. Might you add some coal to the fire? The afternoon grows chilly."

The afternoon was no colder than most April afternoons. Beatrice simply liked giving orders, especially to men.

Ulysses rose gracefully, prowled over to the hearth, and put half a scoop of coal on the flames. He was a blond lion of a male specimen, though in later years he might run soft about the middle. He set the scoop back on the hearth stand.

On Beatrice's next circuit of the room, he made an elaborate, mocking bow.

Subtlety was a lost art. Quinn had been subtle, damn and drat him. "What are they saying in the clubs?" Beatrice asked.

"About Wentworth?" Ulysses lounged against the piano, looking both elegant and indolent. "The usual: He has the devil's own good luck, he's the symbol of everything wrong with society today, where did he get his money?"

Beatrice had some suspicions regarding that last item. She wasn't about to share them with Ulysses.

She patted his cravat, adding a few creases to his valet's artistry. "If that's all you know of the matter, then you'd best be on your way. Give your sisters my love."

Ulysses caught her hand in his and kissed her bare knuckles. "The Fashionable Hour approaches. By the time you've donned your finery, I can have my phaeton on your doorstep. The park will be full of the latest news, and Wentworth is bound to figure in several conversations."

They would be quiet conversations, for nobody admitted to borrowing coin from Quinn Wentworth; nobody admitted to wishing him dead either.

Ulysses kept hold of Beatrice's hand, stroking his thumb gently over her knuckles.

The wretch was coming to know her too well. "Away with you. My finery is not donned in an instant."

He kissed her cheek, a small effrontery. "As my lady wishes."

Ulysses sauntered off, letting himself out of Beatrice's personal parlor. He wasn't Quinn Wentworth—the Creator had fashioned only one Quinn Wentworth—but then, Quinn had caused far too much trouble in the end.

And he was causing trouble still.

* * *

"This is where you live?" Jane asked as the coach slowed on a quiet Mayfair side street. The trees were leafing out, though most of the stoops and porches had yet to boast of flowers. A competitive display of housekeeping wasn't required here, in other words. This neighborhood was built on established wealth rather than the upstart variety.

"I live a short distance away," Mr. Wentworth said. "My front steps are aswarm with that variety of pestilence known as the London journalist. We'll make a private approach to the family abode."

The carriage stopped. The door opened. Mr. Wentworth emerged first, then turned to assist Jane, who felt more like sleeping for a week than trotting all over London. She had barely gained her balance when Mr. Wentworth escorted her across the street to a plain coach drawn by bays whose white socks didn't quite match.

Respectable rather than showy. The larger vehicle drove away, and one footman attached himself to the back of the humbler conveyance. The interior of the smaller coach was spotless and comfortable, though less roomy.

"You live a complicated life," Jane said as her husband took the place beside her.

Her belly was protesting the coach travel, or the lack of sustenance, or the shock of finding her husband hale and whole.

Or possibly the mixed blessing of leaving the home where she'd dwelled for most of the past five years. Leaving without Papa's blessing.

"My life is complicated, not by my choice." Mr. Wentworth lowered the shades on both sides of the vehicle. He'd leaned across Jane to pull down the shade on her side, giving her a whiff of his shaving soap.

Lovely, lovely stuff, that shaving soap. Jane spent the next three streets parsing the scent: clove, cinnamon, ginger, a dash of allspice, and possibly pepper, along with something more masculine. Sandalwood, cedar...a scent with enough sylvan substance to anchor the whole.

"Wake up, Jane. We're almost there."

She opened her eyes. "I'm not asleep." *Yet.*

The neighborhood had changed; the houses here were larger, the street wider. Not a grand neighborhood, but a fine neighborhood. She was again assisted to alight from the coach, and her husband escorted her to a mews that included a carriage house.

Like most structures of its kind, the building Mr. Wentworth led Jane to had an upper floor over the carriage bays. He took her to a harness room, then down a set of steps.

"I need a moment," Jane said, as the closer air below street level aggravated her digestion. She breathed through her mouth while Mr. Wentworth waited. His patience was absolute, giving away nothing of restlessness or annoyance.

Jane was annoyed. What manner of bride arrives to her new home through a tunnel?

Mr. Wentworth had taken a lamp from a sconce on the whitewashed brick wall and held it up to illuminate a cobbled passageway.

"That way. Only a short distance."

Jane set aside her hunger, nausea, and fatigue, and let Mr. Wentworth lead her through the passage. Entire London streets covered underground passageways, and Roman walls and drains were forever making new construction difficult.

She was soon ascending another set of steps and emerging into a well-stocked wine cellar. Mr. Wentworth hung the lamp on a hook, illuminating thousands of bottles all laid on their sides and stacked in open bins. Coaches and matched teams were for show. An enormous and abundantly stocked wine cellar was evidence of real wealth.

"We're home," Mr. Wentworth said. "Your trunk will take some time to arrive, but I'm sure my sisters will see you made comfortable."

What manner of man had a secret entrance to his Mayfair dwelling? What manner of man planned this much subterfuge about a simple trip across Town? What sort of husband…

A wave of unsteadiness cut short Jane's growing consternation. "If your sisters can see to providing me some bread and butter, I'll be most appreciative."

He paused with her at the top of yet another flight of stairs. "I don't want your gratitude, Jane, though I understand it. You've saved me the trouble of locating a woman willing to marry a convicted killer from the lowest orders of society. I'd rather you find some reason other than gratitude to remain married to me."

In the shadows of this subterranean space, Quinn Wentworth looked of a piece with the darkness. He'd come home this way often, had probably chosen this property for the secrecy it afforded. Jane stirred the sludge of exhaustion and bewilderment that was her mind, for his observation wanted a reply.

"You could give me some other reasons to be your wife." Friendship, affection, partnership. She'd settle for cordial strangers.

He reached toward her, and she flinched back.

"Sorry. I'm nervous."

Mr. Wentworth unfasted the frogs of her cloak so deftly his fingers never touched her. "I'm not about to start taking liberties with your person now, when a gantlet of family awaits us. The only sane one is Duncan, who endeavors to be boring on his good days, though I'm not fooled by his pretensions. My sisters and brother had an irregular upbringing and the effects yet linger."

"I have trouble with my balance lately," Jane said, as he folded her cloak over his arm. "I am exhausted, peckish, and adjusting to a marriage that requires secret passages and clandestine changes of coaches. If I'm less than the wife you bargained for, then I ask for your patience. I do not deal well with upheaval."

He smiled, his teeth a flash of white in the gloom. "That's better. We'll get some food into you soon."

"I like the 'soon' part." Jane was glad to be free of the heavy, unfragrant cloak. Better she meet her in-laws in this lovely, soft dress, one free of stains and strained seams. "Could you come near for a moment?"

The smile disappeared. "I am near."

"Nearer," Jane said, putting her arms around him.

He held the cloak, which meant he couldn't effectively shove her away. She leaned on him shamelessly and breathed through her nose.

"Your scent calms my belly, or my nerves. Something. I need to breathe you in for a moment."

He draped the cloak over the railing and cautiously wrapped his arms about her. "Take your time. We're in no rush, Jane."

No *roosh*. A hint of Yorkshire in the vowel, and in the high contours of the consonants. Perhaps he was tired as well.

Jane allowed herself five deep breaths, and the magic of his scent worked wonders for her internal upheaval. She liked that her husband could hold her without his hands wandering, without pushing unmentionable parts of himself against her.

"I'm ready now."

"You aren't, but you're as ready as you can be to meet the rest of the Wentworth family."

He left the cloak in the passage and led Jane by the hand through a warren of pantries. A startled scullery maid rose from her stool near a great hearth, her plump features wreathed in joy. Mr. Wentworth put a finger to his lips and winked, and the girl subsided back onto her stool.

"The servants are all in the hall," she said. "Miss Althea said half holiday, but it's a double holiday according to Mrs. Riley. Is that your duchess, sir?"

"I'm not a duchess," Jane said, "but I'm very interested in getting off my feet." Desperately interested.

"This is my wife," Mr. Wentworth said, "whom you will be formally introduced to at a later time."

The maid bobbed a curtsy. "Welcome to Wentworth House, Your Grace."

I'm not Your Grace. Jane had no time to offer that protest, for her husband was towing her toward yet another set of steps.

"Mr. Wentworth."

"Almost there."

"Mr. Wentworth."

"I can carry you," he said without stopping. "I believe there's some tradition to that effect."

Jane was about to faint, about to heave up two cups of tea and some ginger biscuits, and about to raise her voice. This was not a moment to silently count to three and pray for patience. She couldn't pit her strength against her husband's, so she knocked his hat off his head.

"I am not a load of coal to be hauled about at your whim," she said, as he slowly turned to face her. "Why did that girl address me as Your Grace? I have no title, and neither, as far as you've told me, have you."

He looked guilty. Chagrinned. *Bashful.*

Imprisoned and facing a death warrant, Quinn Wentworth had been self-possessed, even mocking. Now, in his London finery, in his own home, he looked like a small boy caught with his hand in the governess's personal tin of biscuits.

"I have inherited a title," he said, "which is the primary reason I was pardoned. We'll discuss it later." He made a production out of retrieving his hat from the carpet and brushing nonexistent dust from the brim.

He was leaving something significant unsaid—something *else* that was significant—or Jane's mind was going the way of her balance and her figure.

"You regard this title as the price of your freedom?"

He tugged on his collar with his right index finger. "The title is sunk deeply in debt. Old George wanted no part of such a liability, and I and my fortune were in a position to aid his interests. I also happen to be the legal heir, which is ironic given that my father assured me my paternity was irregular. I had planned to tell you, though a title honestly didn't signify compared to being able to walk out of that prison."

A *dukedom* did not signify?

As it happened, Jane agreed with him. "I cannot tell if you thought I'd leap at the title or away from it, when in truth I can't see that it makes any difference." She stepped closer and removed Mr. Wentworth's cravat pin, a plain gold sword in miniature. "I married you, not your title, not your fortune. We shall discuss our circumstances in greater detail when we are assured of privacy. Do your siblings know?"

"They do. Penrose told them, the rotter."

Jane retied the neckcloth in the same elegant Mathematical, but looser than it had been. "Mr. Wentworth, might I offer a suggestion?"

He brushed a glance at the small golden sword Jane held near his throat. "You're angry."

"I am hungry, queasy, tired, and"—Jane slid the pin through the lace and linen—"in need of a retiring room, if you must know, but I am not angry. We can rejoice in our good fortune, and still admit we face unusual circumstances. Might we face them as man and wife? As people who regard one another as allies if not friends?"

The looser cravat revealed the edge of a bright red weal on his neck. His expression was stoic, though the neckwear had to have been paining him.

"Mine is not a confiding nature," he said, "but you have no reason to regard me as an enemy. As for the rest of it... I will try to be the best husband I can be to you."

"Fair enough. I shall try as well." She kissed his cheek, mostly to take in a solid dose of his shaving soap, then ascended the steps with him, arm in arm.

Chapter Ten

Constance was tipsy and hiding it well, Althea was furious—she went through life in a perpetual state of annoyance—and Stephen had been fascinated with Jane on sight. Duncan, as always, was lending a veneer of sanity to the family interactions.

Quinn had endured thirty minutes of interrogation about everything from prison conditions, to the estates conveying with the title, to who benefitted from his death—dangerous ground, that—when Duncan sent him a look: *Constance will soon reach the end of her tether.*

As would Quinn, and yet, his family was owed this time with him.

"I must excuse myself," Jane said, shifting to the edge of her chair. "I am easily fatigued these days. Mr. Wentworth, if you'd see me to my quarters?"

Quinn shamelessly took his cue, drawing Jane to her feet. But where to take her? "The bedrooms are upstairs," he said when they'd left the family murmuring among themselves in the parlor. "Stephen uses a lift, if you can't manage the steps."

"Now, you ask me about steps. I shall contrive, Mr. Wentworth."

He'd spent years earning the right to be addressed as Mr. Wentworth rather than "boy," "ye little bastard," or "the Wentworth whelp." Jane's form of address was familiar, but not comfortable, and yet, the idea of becoming His Grace of Walden to her chafed like the abrasion on Quinn's neck.

Jane took the steps slowly, her hand wrapped around his arm. He'd had the kitchen send up beef sandwiches, which Jane had nibbled between sips of tea. He wasn't imagining her pallor, nor the lavender half circles beneath her eyes.

"You don't know where to put me," Jane said, as Quinn paused at the top of the steps. "I'm not particular. Clean sheets and some privacy will suffice."

He'd have to do something about her habit of guessing his thoughts. "I was giving you a moment to catch your breath. My quarters are this way." She was his wife. Where else could he stash her but in his own rooms?

His apartment had been kept clean, as if he'd simply been at the bank for the day, not rotting away in Newgate for a month. The window in the parlor was open, as he preferred if the temperature was above freezing, and the fire in the hearth had recently been built up.

"A bed," Jane said, marching straight through the doorway to Quinn's bedroom. "Ye gods, a bed. My kingdom for a bed, and such a magnificent bed it is too. If you'd unhook me, please." She swept her hair off her nape and gave him her back.

The gesture was disconcertingly married, but then, Quinn was not her first husband, and hooks were hooks. He undid the first half dozen, and still Jane stood before him, hand on the back of her head, holding her hair away.

He undid another half dozen. "That should do."

"If you could assist with my boots, I'd appreciate it."

Her boots. "Of course." He knelt before her when she sat on the hassock. "You have difficulty getting them on?"

"Some days, I manage quite well. Other days, bending to any degree upsets my digestion and leaves me light-headed."

He eased off one battered boot, then the other. "Your garters?"

"Please."

Quinn had not touched a woman beneath her skirts for years. What allowed him to exercise that familiarity now was Jane's utter indifference to the intimacy. She was exhausted, uncomfortable, and desperate for rest.

"If we have a daughter," she said, as Quinn untied the first garter, "I'll not tell her the fairy tales."

Quinn's mind tripped over the first part—*if we have a daughter*. As a father, he expected to write out bank drafts and pay bills, though Jane's ideas about parenting apparently involved something more.

"I thought children liked fairy tales." Quinn wouldn't know, having had no one to tell him pretty stories when he'd been a child.

"Some children do. I'm referring to the pernicious falsehoods told among women: When you hold that new baby, you'll forget the misery you endured for nine months, and the hours or even days of travail that brought the child into the world. That fairy tale. Our daughters will know that conceiving a child opens the door to indignities without number, and they go on forever."

Quinn draped two worn, mended stockings over the battered boots. "Let's get you into bed."

He hauled Jane to her feet, and watched while she wiggled, twisted, and muttered her way out of the aubergine dress. Something like panic rose inside him as she handed him the frock.

She wore neither stays nor jumps, but stood in only her shift, the slight protuberance of her belly obvious beneath the worn linen.

"We must have an awkward discussion, Mr. Wentworth," she said, climbing the step to the bed, "about conjugal intimacies."

They were up to three awkward discussions in less than a day, doubtless a record for newlyweds. "Must we have that conversation now? I was under the impression your sole objective at the moment was sleep."

She threw back the covers on Quinn's side of the bed—he always slept closest to the window—and scooted beneath the sheets, then snuggled down into his pillow with a great sigh.

"We are man and wife," she said. "I will accommodate you if you insist on consummating our vows now, though I will be fast asleep all the while. I don't require awkward professions or pretty words, which we both know you cannot sincerely offer. I love this bed."

She looked small amid the pillows and covers, like a hedgehog burrowing in for the winter.

"I will not trouble you now in the manner you refer to."

She regarded Quinn from amid a sea of pillows, snowy linen, and soft quilts. "You've had a trying day. Your neck has to be sore. Why not take a nap? This sumptuous abundance of a bed has room for half a regiment."

She was in love with his bed—or his shaving soap—while mention of Quinn's neck reminded him of a constant, burning ache.

"I typically sleep on the side of the bed you're occupying."

She thrashed to the other side of the mattress, a beached fish determined to reach the waterline.

"Now will you come to bed? Your siblings won't intrude or I'll swoon on them—or worse—and you probably haven't had a good night's sleep for weeks. We'll face your family again at dinner."

And at breakfast, and again tomorrow evening. Abruptly, Quinn was ready to drop. Mentally, physically, and in every other regard, he'd hit the limit of his reserves, the end of his tether.

"You won't mind if I grab a nap?"

"I'll be asleep. I promise you, Mr. Wentworth. I'm asleep now, in fact."

Jane might be comfortable with marital familiarity, but Quinn needed the modesty afforded by the privacy screen. Because Jane had said the scent of his soap soothed her digestion, he gave himself an extra wash in a few obvious locations, and got a wretchedly stinging neck for his troubles.

Better a stinging neck than a broken one.

Jane lay on her side, her breathing slow and regular, as if she'd settled in until the next change of season.

Quinn locked the parlor door and the bedroom door, opened the bedroom window, and climbed beneath the covers. He was aware of Jane, but she was so still that her company was more of an idea than a presence.

He hadn't shared a bed with a woman in years. Hadn't wanted to, hadn't seen the need. He was married, though, had spoken vows and taken a wife. They could sort out the details later. For now, Quinn gave himself up to the miracle of sleeping once again in his own bed.

His and Jane's.

* * *

"She's pretty," Stephen said. "Leave it to Quinn to find a wife in prison who's not only proper but pretty."

"I don't care how pretty or proper she is," Constance retorted, "Jane's on the nest. How does a preacher's daughter conceive a child then cadge an offer of marriage from one of the wealthiest men in England?"

Duncan Wentworth called these people family, but they were as much a tribulation as they were an entertainment. Most days, they were very entertaining.

"Jane is a widow," he said. "Conception likely occurred in the usual fashion, and this is not a fit topic for a lady."

"You've taken tea with many ladies to know their conversational habits?" Constance replied, reaching for the decanter.

Althea moved the brandy aside before Constance could serve herself more spirits. Ladies also did not take spirits, except for the occasional medicinal serving, but Althea and Constance had likely imbibed their first taste of gin while still at the breast.

"I do wonder how she gained Quinn's notice," Stephen said. "He's had plenty of options where the fair sex is concerned."

Althea rose to set the brandy on the sideboard. "We can't know what it was like for him to face such a death. He was supposed to die for somebody's convenience, despite his innocence, despite his wealth. That could change a man's heart."

Quinn had no heart, beyond a wild beast's devotion to its pack. Duncan reached that conclusion without judging his cousin. Quinn had been raised in hell and managed as best he could. The damage was lamentable but permanent, and the resulting lack of sentiment had made Quinn an enviably successful banker.

"You are certain of his innocence," Duncan pointed out. "Most of London is certain of his guilt."

"Fine thing," Constance said, rising and shaking out her skirts. "You put your feet under Quinn's table, take his coin, and call him cousin, but you don't defend him."

What need had Quinn of a defense when his siblings were on hand to pour boiling oil from the parapets? "I merely make an observation, and you have never once heard me condemn or criticize Quinn Wentworth."

"You're wrong about all of London thinking him guilty." Stephen's comment embodied an adolescent's oblivion to conversational subtleties. "The lords and MPs who owe Quinn money were doubtless happy to see him brought low. I don't think the real people—the people who work and worry and strive—feel that way about him. They know he's pulled himself up from nothing, and they respect him for it."

"I respect him too," Duncan said, lest Stephen's ferocious loyalty be stirred into a passion. "Apparently the king does as well."

Constance tipped her glass to her lips to shake a final drop into her mouth. "I was rather looking forward to having my own property, truth be told. I could get away from you lot and from Quinn's infernal hovering."

"Constance." Althea's tone was chiding rather than dismayed. The Wentworths raised blunt discourse to dizzying heights, a refreshing change from the hypocrisy of the academics and clerics with whom Duncan had come of age.

"Don't let us keep you," Stephen said cheerfully. "If you're determined to leave London, talk to Quinn. The brandy will last longer without you here."

Nasty boy, but then, Constance was a bitter young woman, and Stephen could not afford to be tenderhearted.

"I'd miss you," Duncan said. "You keep us honest." Such as the Wentworths could be honest.

Constance set her empty glass on the sideboard. "Quinn doesn't know what to do with her."

She refused to say Jane's name, which spoke volumes about this desire to leave the household.

"Quinn will get her sorted out," Stephen said, finishing his drink. "He's resourceful."

"We shall all adjust," Althea snapped. "Jane is family now and Quinn's wife. She married him thinking to be widowed again today, and she'll have some adjusting of her own to do."

"Truer words..." Duncan murmured, getting to his feet. "I have translations to work on, so I'll leave you three to dissect Jane's character in peace. You might consider that she faces the daunting prospect of childbirth among strangers, and the woman does not look well to me."

"She looks uncomfortable," Constance said. "Hard to hate somebody who barely nibbles her biscuits."

And hard to know how to go on in the absence of enmity. Duncan often wondered who lived with the greater pain: Stephen with his injured leg, Constance with her injured heart, or Althea, buffeted between love for, and exasperation with, her siblings. And then there was Quinn, who had doubtless lost the ability to admit any suffering before he'd been breeched.

"Perhaps Jane will be a good influence on us." Duncan left his cousins snickering at what had been a sincere hope, rather than a jest. He'd tried for years to exert a civilizing influence on his family, to no avail whatsoever.

So he'd given up trying, and they'd all been happier as a result.

* * *

Jane drifted amid the blissful comfort of a well-stuffed mattress, clean linen, soft blankets, and the soothing scent of her husband. In sleep she'd shifted closer to him, her belly to his back. The rhythm of his breathing suggested he slumbered on, a comforting presence, as opposed to Gordie's pawing and thrashing.

And snoring.

And worse. Jane's first transition to married life had consisted of that wild trip to Scotland—accomplished one rocking, jouncing mile after another—a few seedy inns, and Gordie rocking and jouncing on top of her at those seedy inns.

Eloping had been expedient rather than romantic. She saw that with the perfect hindsight of regret. No banns, no opportunity for the naïve bride to give in to second thoughts, crawl home, and beg her papa's forgiveness.

And then, just as she'd been reeling with the enormity of the mistake she'd made—Gordie drank, he consorted with other women, he squandered his half pay—he'd died.

Relief, sorrow, and guilt had had a moment to compete for the status of greatest source of misery, then had come a period of futile bargaining with the Almighty: *I'm simply upset, I'm grieving. I'm dealing with too much upheaval. This is a digestive ailment. I cannot possibly be with child.* Somewhere in the past several months, Jane had lost her bearings, such that life had become a matter of coping from moment to moment.

Mustn't be sick.

Must eat something.

Must find a chamber pot.

Why must Papa pawn Mama's cedar chest when she was very clear that chest was to be mine?

Must lie down.

In the last six hours Jane had acquired a new and far safer address, and with that development had come one conviction: The whirling in her life had to stop, and before the child arrived. Jane's best estimate was that she had another five months before she'd become a mother.

"You're awake," Mr. Wentworth rumbled. He remained on his side of the bed, lying on his back, his arms folded behind his head.

"For now. This is a lovely bed."

"So you've said. We needn't share it if you'd rather have this bedroom to yourself." He made his announcement without doing her the courtesy of looking her in the eye.

And here she'd been so comfortable. "Are you about to offer me another annulment, Mr. Wentworth?"

He darted a glance at her in the gloom created by the bed hangings. "And if I were?"

"I'm told you don't go back on your word, so why reopen this discussion?" Did she want him to renew this offer? On the one hand, he wasn't at all what she had planned, and Jane set very great store by her plans. On the other hand, he was warm and he smelled good. His hands didn't wander uninvited, and she liked him.

Mostly. She would very much like another beef sandwich. She did not like this conversation.

"You've met us," he said. "Duncan is the only Wentworth with pretensions to gentility. The uncle who raised him was a vicar, and Duncan was educated accordingly. He ended up as a teacher after a failed attempt at the church. Don't ask him why he changed course, for the tale is unhappy and even I am vague on the details. The rest of us..."

Mr. Wentworth was self-conscious about his family, which Jane understood all too well. "You met my father.

Your family might take a while to warm up to, but Papa is a trial to the nerves, for all he means well."

Mr. Wentworth sat up, resting his back against the headboard. His chest was bare, and a fine chest it was, all sculpted muscle with a dusting of dark hair. The occasional scar nicked at his anatomical perfection, making him human as well as handsome.

"We should resolve this before the child is born, Jane."

Resolve? Insight struck as if the child had kicked her. "You are a duke. You've realized your heir might be Gordie MacGowan's son." This was what Mr. Wentworth had meant when he'd referred to changed circumstances. He was a peer, and not just any peer. Dukes were rarities and their lineages ancient.

Mr. Wentworth—or rather, His Grace of... what was his title?—laughed, a single rusty guffaw.

"I don't give a stinking goddamn who gets stuck with the title after me so long as Fat George doesn't get his hands on my money. The easiest way to assure that outcome is to have sons, and you're apparently willing to be their mother. The issue for your firstborn, however, is that your current husband is a convicted killer."

Jane struggled to a sitting position and tucked the covers under her arms. "If you don't care about your succession and you aren't ashamed of marrying a preacher's disgraced daughter, then why not try to make something of this union?" The question was for herself as much as for her bedmate. "I ask myself, What are the options? Should I go home to Papa and resume being Miss Jane Winston of the inexplicably gravid shape and uncertain digestion?"

"Don't be daft."

That gruff rejoinder assured her that Mr. Wentworth would not abandon her. He might annul the marriage, but he'd honor the obligation to support her. Jane should have been relieved rather than resentful.

"So," she said, "that leaves either making a go of this situation, or annulling the marriage and doing what with me and the child? If you cast me off, I'll be doubly disgraced, and the child will be a MacGowan rather than a Wentworth. I suppose you'd put me in my own establishment, like a former mistress? Doubtless some MacGowan will appear claiming to be the child's guardian and getting his hands all over whatever pin money you grant me."

Mr. Wentworth likely had a mistress. He was wealthy, unmarried, and stunningly handsome. Of course he had a mistress. A slender blonde with limpid blue eyes and a tinkling laugh.

Jane didn't like that thought *at all*.

"You'll not be left for a MacGowan to prey upon."

Prey upon again, though that was unfair to Gordie's memory. Jane smacked a pillow and arranged it behind her back. "All manner of developments occur despite probability to the contrary, Mr. Wentworth. You never expected to end up in prison. I never expected to end up widowed and with child, but here we are."

Here they were, having a disagreement in the same bed on the first day as man and wife. Jane would find a credible explanation for that bizarre state of affairs after she'd had another serving of perfectly salted sliced beef.

And buttered bread. She was abruptly mad for buttered bread.

"Here we are. Where do you want to be, Jane?"

"In the kitchen eating fresh bread with butter."

He left the bed and crossed the room to use the bellpull, then he spoke into a cone-shaped copper tube protruding from the wall near the hearth. Black silk trousers moved over powerful muscles and rode low enough to reveal dimples at the base of a long, strong back.

Also another crop of scars, these more conspicuous than the ones on his chest. Old injuries, some casual, some nasty. Quinn Wentworth hadn't always been a well-dressed, well-to-do banker. Jane suspected he was making the point for her on purpose.

"Bread and butter," he said into the tube, "strawberries, ginger biscuits, and ginger tea."

"And roast beef," Jane said.

"And roast beef." He took a chair behind a large desk that managed to be both masculine and elegant. "You did not answer my question, Jane. Where would you like to be? If we make a go of this situation, as you term it, you'll be a duchess, regardless of my criminal past. Certain obligations accompany the title."

He lounged casually in exactly one article of clothing— even his feet were bare—and yet, Jane felt as if she were being interrogated by a banker: *And when was the appraisal done? By whom? Any fixtures or appurtenances? What about fungibles or livestock?*

"My first obligation," Jane said, "is to the child. I must situate myself however I can to give the child the best chance of a happy, healthy life. If that means being a duchess, then a duchess I shall be."

He studied the branches of the maple tree outside the window. The leaves were unfurling, from pink buds to softest green leaves. In a few weeks, the tree would provide shade. Now the gauzy foliage seemed to reflect the afternoon sunlight and spread illumination.

"Your commitment to the child does you credit," he said. "I assure you that you will have material security, regardless of how we arrange the legalities."

Jane wanted to close her eyes again and this time to sleep for a week. "I am a female. I cannot arrange any legalities, sir. My father refused to recognize my marriage to Captain MacGowan and if you declare this marriage void, by Papa's reasoning, I will remain under his authority. Despite my age, despite Scottish marriage lines, he will press his position upon the courts and I will have no practical means of thwarting him."

The last thing—the very, very last thing—Jane wanted to face was protracted litigation in courts famed for inquisitiveness rather than speed, not that she could afford a barrister and not that any respectable lawyer would take her case.

Mr. Wentworth retrieved an afghan from the foot of the bed, and draped the soft wool around Jane's shoulders.

"You have no idea what a burden a disgraced father is to a small child, Jane. You could establish your own household and keep your finances in a trust. Then the child would have my money and the guiding hand of an ordained grandfather."

For an instant, she was tempted. Perhaps such an arrangement could return to Jane the kind, if distracted, parent she'd known before Mama's death.

And perhaps not. "Trusts take time to set up," Jane said, sniffing the wool caressing her shoulders. "Where would that arrangement leave the baby if something happened to me?"

Mr. Wentworth hadn't an answer for that, which was just as well. Jane was trying not to stare at the red weal gouged into the side of his neck. She resented this conversation for the uncertainty it brought, but she also resented that injury.

Hadn't life put enough mementos to pain and suffering on her husband's body? The king's pardon had come at the very last possible instant. How was Mr. Wentworth dealing with that? How was he dealing with the torment of the whole last month? With the notion of having taken a life?

Though seeing him all but naked, Jane had reason to doubt the court's judgment. Only a fool would engage Quinn Wentworth in a physical altercation, and his nature would not allow him lethal intemperance.

"Wait here," Mr. Wentworth said.

He padded to the parlor and came back bearing a tray. The scent of ginger wafted across the room, a sweet, smooth ginger free of the bitterness found in the coarser varieties. Mr. Wentworth set the tray on the desk and carried a heavy chair to the side of the desk as if the chair weighed nothing.

"You'll catch a chill," Jane said, climbing from the bed and taking a dressing gown down from a hook on the bedpost. "Fresh air is lovely, but if you sit in a draft wearing less than nothing, you'll soon regret it."

Then too, she wanted to think about his scars later, after she'd done justice to the tray. She stretched up to drape the dressing gown around his shoulders, careful that the collar didn't touch his injury. Her movements put her close enough to her husband that her belly nudged against his side.

The child chose that moment to reposition itself, delivering a poke to Jane's innards.

"What the hell was that?" Mr. Wentworth stared at her belly as if he'd only now noticed her condition.

"The baby," she said, arranging the collar of the dressing gown and stepping back. "When I lie down, he or she wakes up. Shall we have some tea?"

"The tea is for you," he said. "We'll continue this discussion later."

A fine suggestion. Jane did justice to the food, while Mr. Wentworth—*what* was his title?—sat across the desk, nibbling a ginger biscuit and sending dubious glances in the direction of her belly.

Chapter Eleven

"Whom King George pardons," Joshua Penrose said, leafing through the open stack of morning correspondence, "society pardons. Your thirty-day rule saved us."

"Snobbery saved us," Quinn countered from across the polished mahogany table. "Let me see the list again."

Within a fortnight of Quinn's conviction, half the bank's customers had given notice of intent to close their accounts. Joshua had spared him news of that development until Quinn had been soaking in a bathtub the previous day and unable to do more than curse at length.

Fortunately, the depositor's agreement required that the bank be given thirty days' written notice of any intention to make a major withdrawal or close an account, and thus none of the money had yet been removed.

The list of the high and mighty who'd been prepared to flee Wentworth and Penrose's felonious clutches read like an excerpt from Debrett's. The same names, save for a few, had changed their minds overnight.

"I have more good news," Joshua said, passing over the bible.

The bible was the main ledger book, the one that kept a daily tally of the bank's available assets and outstanding liabilities. Either Joshua or Quinn signed the bible at the close of each week, then it was countersigned by the head teller and the auditor.

The auditor was a little drill sergeant named Mrs. Hatfield, though Quinn suspected she'd had other names at other times. She was passionate about her accounting and knew every possible avenue for embezzlement, fraud, deceit, and sharp practice. How she'd come by that knowledge was a secret between her and Joshua.

She'd greeted Quinn that morning with the first smile he'd ever seen from her, and a wink. "Well done, Mr. Wentworth." She was pretty when she smiled, in the manner of a buttoned-up librarian preparing to host a reading of the Bard.

Jane was prettier, in a blooming, ungainly, grouchy sort of way.

"Quinn"—Joshua spoke somewhat loudly—"if you need more time with your family, you have only to say so. Nobody would begrudge you a chance to recover from your ordeal."

"My ordeal," Quinn said, "is only beginning. Who put my neck in a noose, Joshua?"

He could ask that, because the partners' conference room was the holiest of holies at the bank, and no sound escaped when the doors were closed. Customer privacy mattered, but not half so much as the privacy of the partners.

"I thought you had convicted me of that folly?"

"Upon reflection, you haven't a credible motive. The

bank was in the process of collapsing until this morning, and you've worked as hard as I have to make this place what it is. You might well hate me, but you grasp my usefulness and bear no ill will toward my family."

Joshua tidied the stack of letters, which was already tidy. "When will you leave it behind, Quinn? When will you realize you are no longer scouring the sewers for a stray lump of coal, burying corpses by day, and guarding them by night? You've food in your belly, a roof over your head, and—"

"And somebody is trying to kill me, in the most ignominious, shameful way possible. They would have succeeded but for a twist of fate nobody could have foreseen. They have cunning, influence, and substantial resources."

Joshua came around the table and set the papers at Quinn's elbow. "I fit that description; so do many of these depositors and most of our investors."

As did Stephen, Duncan, and half the peerage who owed Quinn money, in addition to one northern countess who owed Quinn her silence.

Quinn rose, ignoring the papers. "You see the problem." Though something Joshua had said teased at Quinn's mind. A stray penny of a thought, about...

"The bank is prospering as a result of your situation," Joshua said. "Whoever wished you ill would be frustrated to know that for every viscount who sought to withdraw his funds, a butcher, a baker, and a jeweler came in to open an account. The damned flower girls and opera dancers now bank here, and they expect better service than a dowager duchess receives. Look at the bible tallies for the last three weeks."

Quinn always purchased a bouquet for his desk when there were fresh flowers to be had, and he'd directed Althea to purchase the house flowers from the street vendors rather than from a professional florist. The choice was pragmatic. Flower girls were out and about at all hours, every day. They knew the comings and goings of a neighborhood better than anybody.

Look after the flower girls, and they looked after you. The concept wasn't complicated, though few in Mayfair seemed to grasp its utility. The small accounts opened in the last fortnight went on for pages, the flower girls prominent among them.

"We'll need a new bible soon." The christening of a new volume of the bank's master account book always merited a toast after hours for the staff.

"I've hired two new tellers, one of them female. The milkmaids, flower girls, and opera dancers prefer dealing with a woman."

One of their own kind, somebody who'd realize that a task as simple as putting on boots could become a challenge when a woman carried a child. Althea had already set up appointments for Jane with dressmakers, milliners, and glovemakers, and had also made arrangements for her to meet with an accoucheur.

While Quinn had been trying to talk Jane into an annulment. He'd never go back on his word, but neither would he hold a woman to a marriage she resented. His father had made that mistake, and Mama had paid with her life.

"Quinn, was your hearing damaged in Newgate?"

"Perhaps. Wretched place is noisy. What were you saying?"

"That we might want to let some of these accounts"—Joshua waved the stack of papers—"move elsewhere. Detwiler was among the first to give notice, and he's teetering on the brink of ruin."

"He's been teetering on the brink of ruin for two years."

Ever since his oldest daughter had left the schoolroom. She or her ambitious mama had beggared Detwiler with millinery, dancing slippers—

Jane would need a cobbler's services. Her boots would disgrace a muck heap.

"So let's push his lordship over the edge," Joshua said, propping a hip on the edge of the table. "He's arrogant and stupid. All we need do is lose today's letter from him and prepare him a bank draft."

"We do not engage in sharp practice," Quinn retorted, closing the bible. "We have a fiduciary relationship with our customers, meaning their best interests must come before all else. I have an appointment. You will excuse me."

"We do occasionally cull the herd, Quinn. Detwiler is perilously close to overdrawn in all regards."

"Then we ask him for a meeting and call upon him at his convenience. Not his man of business, him. I'll threaten to close his account, you'll console him with a prepared budget, and he'll bumble into better finances over the next few years."

Quinn retrieved his hat and cane from their customary places by the door. Two private offices opened on to this room—his and Joshua's—and both also had entrances on to the mezzanine above the bank's main lobby.

The bank's public area might have been any fashionable set of assembly rooms, complete with potted palms in various corners, fine wool carpets over an oak parquet floor, and cloudy Low Country landscapes on the walls.

Quinn liked the lobby, liked to look down on the people coming and going, liked the feel of commerce in the air, but now was not the time to linger here. He had put in an appearance, greeted his tellers and a few customers by name, smiled at all and sundry despite the stares and whispers.

Business as usual, while I hunt a killer.

"Where are you off to?" Joshua asked, joining Quinn at the mezzanine's railing.

"To hire a grave robber."

"You didn't kill Robert Pike? Didn't knock him arse over appetite in that alley?" The questions could not have been more casual.

"Mr. Pike and I spoke for a few minutes. He wanted money—a fellow Yorkshireman, down on his luck—I obliged with a pair of sovereigns. When I left the alley he was still muttering about life's many injustices and them as gets above theirselves." Quinn had dropped into street patois to imitate his supposed victim. Pike was an acquaintance from the old days who'd learned that not all of Quinn's transactions were made through the bank.

"That's what you told the jury."

"They did not believe me. Now I'm off to find a body."

Joshua smiled down at a young couple in expectation of an interesting event. They smiled back up at him. Did they know that the lady's feet would swell? That she'd become exhausted from her burden in a few months?

"I should have thought of that," Joshua said. "No body, no crime. The court had a coroner's report."

"I'll talk to the coroner too. His demeanor on the witness stand was less than scientific."

An errand boy sidled up to one of the assistant tellers. Children were safer conduits of information on London's streets. They were more reliable than running footmen, less conspicuous, and cost less to feed and house. Pickpockets left them alone, though half of Quinn's messengers had been pickpockets themselves.

The Wentworth and Penrose errand boys also slept on the premises, adding to the bank's security—and their own.

The teller nodded, and the child wafted away. The assistant teller made a leisurely path to the head teller on duty, who occupied a windowed corner office. Another conversation ensued.

"Something's afoot," Quinn said.

"You cannot be twice put in jeopardy of losing your life for the same crime, Quinn. Even if Pike is dead, you cannot be again convicted of his murder."

"I know the law, Joshua. I also know my neck will bear a scar for the rest of my life."

That silenced Joshua—a feat for the history books—or possibly the head teller's ascent of the side stairs did.

"Mr. Penrose, Mr. Wentworth, good morning. I bring a message from home for Mr. Wentworth."

The message had been brought discreetly, per bank policy. Quinn's belly did an odd flip, nonetheless. Ever since Jane had bumped up against him and the child had nudged at Quinn's ribs, Quinn's concentration had been off, his mind prone to wandering.

A child nestled beneath Jane's heart. One who put demands on her even months before birth.

Joshua nodded to an old gent in a tailed wig below. "Say on, Peters. Mr. Wentworth is a busy man."

Peters was a tidy little fellow who put Quinn in mind of Mr. Dodson. Both were dapper, aging men whose prosperity manifested in a small, comfortable potbelly.

"Mr. Wentworth is wanted at home."

"Is my wife well?"

"The message was simply that you are wanted at home, sir."

Quinn managed a decorous pace down the steps, though only just.

* * *

"I'm staying," Susie said. "Man saves me from transportation or the damned Magdalen houses, and I'll stick around long enough to give him my thanks. Hold still, Penny. I'll do up your hooks."

Sophie had already piked off, taking pockets full of bread, butter, and cheese, which had been freely on offer in the servants' hall. She had family somewhere in the stews and two little girls to see to. Susie wasn't about to judge a woman for returning to her children.

"Never thought I'd be back in service," Penny said, twirling a lacy white cap on the end of her finger. "That Miss Althea don't mince words."

"'Don't steal,'" Susie mimicked. "'Don't drink to excess, don't lead any footmen astray and think to profit from their interest. You will be loyal to this house for the duration of your employment or leave now.' Poor thing could use a good rogering." Though Miss Althea had also said Penny, Susie, and Sophie were to be allowed to sleep late on their first morning, to recover from their "recent tribulations."

Susie finished with Penny's hooks, then turned around so Penny could return the favor.

"That Mr. Duncan isn't a bad-looking sort." Because Penny spoke with the slow cadence of the Caribbean Islands, her every observation carried a knowing weight. "Miss High-and-Haughty didn't say nothing about keeping our filthy paws off of him."

The housekeeper had burned Susie's only dress and consigned her and Penny to a lengthy soak in the laundry. Susie's hands were clean—truly, truly clean, even under her fingernails—for the first time in months.

"Mr. Duncan is right handsome," Susie agreed, "if you

like a man past the stupid years. He has that quiet-but-interesting look about him. Has a brain in his head."

"Them kind can be inventive. D'ye suppose Mr. Quinn Wentworth trifles with the help?"

Susie donned her own cap. The cotton was light as a virgin's wish, the lace spotless. "We're proper housemaids now, Pen. You mustn't be lusting after Mr. Wentworth."

Penny sat on her cot to don a pair of black wool stockings, not a rip or darn to be seen. "You were in service before. Housemaids are only as proper as the menfolk they work for. I understand why a man facing death might not fancy a poke, but he's been pardoned, ain't he? Cor, these stockings are lovely."

Quinn Wentworth was lovely to look at, also *off*, somehow. What sort of pardoned killer collects five other prisoners on his way to freedom?

Susie tied the ribbons of her cap beneath her chin, the bow off to left. "He never even looked at us, you know? Not like that. Didn't look at any of us like that."

"Maybe he prefers gents or boys. Maybe he only likes fancy pieces, the kind that don't land in Newgate. If he'll keep me in wool stockings, he can have anybody he pleases with my blessing."

Susie passed Penny a pair of boots. "I have big feet. These might fit you."

A whole collection of newish boots lined the bottom of the maids' wardrobe, which sat at one end of the long dormitory. Eight beds were neatly made, a spare quilt folded across the bottom of each mattress. Beside each bed was a washstand and small table, and two of the tables bore vases of fragrant irises.

The far end of the room had been fitted out as a sitting room, with a sofa and chairs grouped around a big parlor stove, and a flowered oval rug on the floor. The damned place even had paintings on the walls—more flowers—and an orange cat curled up on the mantel.

"This is respectable, Pen. I don't know if I can stand it."

Penny stuck her foot in the air, showing off her half boot. "This house is safe and warm. We'll be fed, and we won't have to spread our legs for any gent with the coin or a notion to steal what he should be purchasing."

"I was raised respectable. Poor, but respectable."

"Of course you were. Put your boots on, Susie. I smell bacon."

Susie grabbed the largest pair of boots in the wardrobe. "My name's Susan. I don't think Mr. Wentworth was raised respectable."

"He weren't. I heard a couple of the guards talking. Some say Mr. Wentworth were a highwayman, some say he stole jewels off rich women. Some say he did worse than steal. The guards didn't bother him, I know that. Why do I feel prettier in this ugly dress than I ever felt on the stroll?"

"'Cause you're daft. These boots fit. I haven't worn a pair of boots that fit, ever."

"You know who I really fancy?" Penny asked, putting on the second boot.

"The man with the most coin," Susie replied, though that was a whore's response, and she was done with whoring. Maybe.

"Him too, but I do think young Mr. Davies cleans up nice."

Davies was likely the same age as Penny, but he was also young in a way Penny could never be. "He's sweet. He'll make a fine footman. Don't scare him, Pen. Prison takes a toll on a fellow the first time he's locked up."

"D'ye think Mr. Wentworth has been locked up before?"

Locked up for sure, though maybe not in prison. "He's cold, Pen. Cold right down to his bones. He didn't get us out of Newgate because of his kind heart. He took us along like spoils of war, a hearty up-yer-arse to King George. That's a cold man what gives it back to the king who pardoned him."

Susie stood, the boots feeling odd on her feet. Real heels, that added more than an inch to her height and made noise when she crossed the room. Laces without knots, stockings without holes or darning to give a blister a place to start.

"So Quinn Wentworth is cold," Penny said, dropping her skirts around her ankles. "What about marrying Miss Jane? Was that a cold man, speaking his vows to a woman in her condition?"

Susie's belly rumbled, and for once she didn't have to ignore her own hunger. "We'll keep an eye on Miss Jane. She didn't bargain for none of this, least of all on being the wife of Quinn Wentworth. I'm tellin' you, Pen, something's not right with that man."

"We look a treat, don't we? Newgate yesterday, respectable today. Let's go find some bacon and flirt with the footmen."

"You flirt with the footmen. I'm for the bacon."

* * *

"Miss Jane might not be dying," Ned said, over the clatter of the wheels on the cobbles.

Quinn's personal gargoyle of doom was perched on the back of the phaeton. Ned had been offering helpful pronouncements through half a mile of snarled traffic and pedestrians with nothing better to do than inspire Quinn's rage.

"A tiger occupies his post silently," Quinn said, steering

around a costermonger's cart only to face a parked coal wagon.

"Why call me a tiger if all I do is lounge about up here on me rosy feak and watch you drive like a parson's granny?"

Quinn backed the phaeton up several yards—no mean feat—and pulled around the coal wagon. "You wait, silent as a tiger, until you are required to pounce to the cobbles and hold the horse. Goddamn it, take the reins—"

Ned was already off his seat, wading into a verbal conflagration between a portly dandy in a gig and a pair of beldames in a dogcart.

"His worship hasn't time to watch you lot heckle away the day," Ned bellowed, seizing the bridle of the dandy's prancing bay and dragging the horse from the intersection. "You should be ashamed, all o' ye, making a spectacle in a decent neighborhood when folk have pressing matters and the king's business to be about. Your mothers couldn't peg out the wash stone sober on a sunny day and neither of ye can steer worth a draft horse's Sunday fart."

Quinn drove through the opening Ned had created, and Ned jumped up behind as the gelding trotted past.

"Impressive, Ned."

"A tiger's got to roar sometimes. Maybe Miss Jane fainted. She used to do that, at Newgate. She always woke up. She tossed up her accounts a time or two as well. The whores said it weren't nothing to fret over."

Ned kicked his feet idly, while Quinn reviewed the litany of emergencies that could have pulled him away from the bank: Jane's baby was coming too soon—though what was Quinn supposed to do about that besides curse fit to scour a London sewer?

Perhaps Stephen had taken a fall. The boy had no sense of his own limits, not when it came to aggravating his sisters, not when it came to his physical problems, and certainly not regarding his temper.

Maybe Constance had secreted a bad bottle of gin in her rooms, which had last happened when she'd been fifteen and as wretched as a girl that age could be.

Althea....If a summons had gone forth from the house, then Althea hadn't been in any condition to prevent it.

Or some evil had befallen Duncan. He was the only family member not given to drama, and if he'd taken sick, had a mishap, got the worst of one of Stephen's rages...Duncan had never once hinted that managing Stephen was a thankless or difficult task, though Stephen on a bad day was a human tempest. If Duncan was planning to leave the household, panic was warranted.

"You didn't look this thunderous when they was striking off your shackles," Ned said. "If tragedy's afoot among your family, then somebody woulda said."

Quinn took a corner as fast as gravity allowed. "You saw the guards taking off the chains?"

"We all did. Had box seats. You made the whores cry." Ned's voice was casual—and vaguely accusing—suggesting the boy had also lost his composure. When a child had nothing else to his name save a few ragged clothes, composure was precious.

Quinn had neither the time nor the focus to spare for a lad's scolds, however deserved they might be. "I can never again swing for the crime of killing Robert Pike, Ned. And you should not have seen me hanged."

"You should not have been hanged. You didn't swing, you dropped like a horse turd hits the street. Bloody bad business, and you'd best get to the bottom of it."

A tiger also dispensed advice, apparently, and took an inordinate interest in equine digestion.

"I do intend to get to the bottom of it, but as far as you're concerned, I was the victim of a simple judicial error. These things happen."

Ned snorted as Quinn turned the vehicle into the alley behind the house.

"Ju-di-ci-al error," Ned said, as if tasting a new batch of ale. "I like that. Sounds big. You should take Davies with you to and from the bank, you know."

Quinn pulled up as a groom ran out of the carriage house to take the horse. Ned leapt down—nimble as a tiger— before Quinn had brought the gelding to a halt.

"You don't take on my battles, Edward."

Somebody had washed the boy's hair and dragged a comb through it, put him in clean clothes, and even managed to get a matching pair of boots on his feet. By a street urchin's standards, Ned had come into a dukedom, and all the dignity of his office glowered up at Quinn.

"When it comes to me mates, nobody tells me what to do, guv. I'll hold your horses, I'll trot around fetching your shirts from the tailor, I'll eavesdrop on the maids for you, but I'm me own man."

I bloody don't have time for your juvenile dramas. Quinn managed to keep the words behind his teeth, barely, as raised voices cut across the morning air.

"You got trouble with your womenfolk," Ned said, not a trace of gloating in the words. "Best make haste."

Quinn made haste—at a decorous pace—Ned trotting at his heels. "You will be relieved to know that as I travel to and from the bank, a running footman always accompanies me. I've let it be known that I never carry cash when I'm on the bank's business, and I don't wear enough glint to attract notice."

"I didn't see no footman and I kept a sharp eye."

Quinn let himself into the back stairway. "You won't see them. They aren't in livery, and they know how to blend in. They carry knives as well as pistols and a pocketful of sand."

Ned snatched an orange from a bowl on the sideboard. "Knives is good and quiet. Sand has blinded many a man at a handy moment. Your womenfolk are loud."

Never had Quinn thought the sound of domestic discord would reassure him, but if Althea—that was Althea, plain as day—was bellowing like a robbed fishwife, then nobody had died.

"Eat that in the kitchen," Quinn said, "and don't let the maids catch you eavesdropping."

Ned tossed the orange into the air and caught it behind his back. "I never do. Good luck with the warring parties, your worship."

Quinn wanted to take the stairs two at time, for the altercation was happening in the family parlor. He instead proceeded at a reasonable pace, nearly knocking over the Jamaican maid—Penny?—on the landing.

"She's not come to any harm," Penny called.

The words allowed Quinn to slow, marginally, but they also underscored the problem he'd wrestled with across half of London: He was responsible for his wife. The law and his own conscience agreed in that regard, and Quinn was prepared to write bank drafts, see to the succession, and put a roof over Jane's head accordingly.

Nothing on his list of husbandly duties required him to *worry* about her, though, to fret over her worn boots, watch her while she slept, or wonder what she'd name the baby. And—God save him—what if she took to worrying about him?

The voices rose, and Quinn broke into a run.

Chapter Twelve

"I will not have this discussion before an audience, Althea."
In truth, Jane didn't want to have this discussion at all.

She remained sitting, rather than go toe-to-toe with
Althea, much less take on Quinn's sister while Stephen,
Constance, a matched set of oversized footmen, and Susie
gawked at the spectacle.

Quinn sauntered into the room, not a care in the world,
while Jane was ready to do somebody—anybody—a grievous injury.

"Greetings, all," Quinn drawled. "Althea, if you'll join
Jane and me in the—"

"Mr. Wentworth," Jane snapped, "I'd like a word with
you in private." Man-fashion, he had no idea what the substance of the altercation was, no inkling of the stakes, but he
was ready to arbitrate and expect his judgment to be final.

Jane would never disrespect her husband publicly, though

neither would she allow him to lose this battle for her. He needed her to win. He simply didn't grasp that yet.

"You are in a delicate condition," Althea said. "Shall you give birth on Bond Street? Shall you have the Wentworth heir in the middle of Piccadilly? This family works too hard—"

Jane held out a hand to her husband. "Your assistance, please." Jane was now a part of *this family*, and while Althea was well intended, she was also wrong.

Mr. Wentworth's inherent good manners had him helping Jane to her feet. She kept hold of his arm—it was one of those days, when her vision dimmed and her balance wavered whenever she stood.

"We'll talk later," Mr. Wentworth said to his sister.

"Indeed we shall," Jane added, because in this case, having the last word—as rude and undignified as that might be—mattered.

Constance smacked Stephen on the shoulder, though for once, the boy wasn't smirking.

"Where's Duncan?" Mr. Wentworth asked as he and Jane gained the corridor.

"Being prudent, leaving the battlefield to those invested in the conflict. I am not a turtle, Mr. Wentworth."

"I beg your pardon?"

"You were happy to haul me all over creation yesterday, up hill and down dale. I am in sufficient good health that you may trust me to reach our sitting room before sundown."

"Perhaps it's my nerves that are overset, Jane."

"Doubtless, you are a quivering mass of near-hysteria, contained by only a gossamer thread of self-control. Why else would you have scampered off to the bank the day after your own scheduled execution?"

He opened the door to their sitting room. "I own half of

that bank, and I'd been absent from my duties for weeks. Showing up and pretending I'd been on holiday was of utmost importance." He closed the door rather firmly.

Having reached a private location, Jane could study her husband. His hair was windblown, the knot of his cravat a quarter inch off-center. For him, that was doubtless serious disarray, though the result of very slight dishevelment was to make him look more dashing.

"How was your morning at the bank?" She could not read his expression, which probably meant that he was upset, to the extent Quinn Wentworth became upset.

Would that Jane had his ability to weather all vicissitudes with calm.

"Do you know how often I've been summoned home from the bank?"

"Of course not."

He paced over to the sideboard, took a glass stopper from a decanter, and held it to his nose. "I have *never* been summoned home from the bank, Jane. My family knows better. At that bank, I'm an actor on a stage, and if I miss my cues, if I'm anything other than the personification of equanimity and decorum, then the play fails. In recent weeks, I have missed cue after cue, spectacularly, and half of London—half of *titled* London—was watching to see what I'd do today."

He breathed in through his nose, as if he were taking smelling salts.

"I didn't send for you, didn't foresee the discussion with Althea becoming a pitched battle, and didn't take any satisfaction from the dramatics. I'm sorry your performance was disrupted. Are you alone of all the bankers in London forbidden to pop home for a midday meal?"

He took another whiff of his glass stopper. "Yes, Jane. I

alone of all the bankers in London am not to leave my post for anything less than urgent business."

Jane crossed the room, wrapped her hand around his, and brought the stopper to her nose. "This is lavender water?"

Mr. Wentworth put the stopper in the decanter. "The scent is pleasant. What were you and Althea arguing about?"

A clumsy change of subject, but useful when Jane disliked even discussing an altercation.

"On one level, we were arguing about whether I'd make an outing to Oxford Street. On another level, we were arguing about who shall be the lady of your house."

The master of the household scrubbed a hand over his face and settled behind the desk. Why did he need a handsome desk in both his bedroom and his sitting room?

"Explain."

"Would you like some luncheon?" Jane asked. "I'm a bit peckish." She'd glossed over breakfast with tea, toast, and two ginger biscuits. Perhaps that accounted for the light-headedness.

"Order whatever you like," Mr. Wentworth said. "Use the bellpull in the bedroom once, wait for the count of five, then speak into the tube."

Jane asked the kitchen to bring up trays, though where should those trays be put? Mr. Wentworth's quarters held two desks and one enormous bed, but nowhere to take sustenance.

She sank onto the sofa, which was devilishly well padded. "Shall we eat on the balcony?"

"Jane, what in all God's creation was so important that somebody called me home from the bank?"

He hadn't raised his voice. Jane suspected Quinn Wentworth never had to raise his voice.

"I have no idea. I did not call you home from the bank. I do know that Lady Althea, doubtless thinking to be helpful, decided to jail me on the premises. Without a word to me, she arranged a procession of modistes, milliners, mercers, and other tradesmen to invade this house, destroy my peace, and generally keep me from making a single adult decision regarding even my own attire without both her and Constance to supervise me."

Mr. Wentworth was back to studying the maple. "You're upset because my sister tried to be helpful?"

Jane preferred diplomacy and tact for resolving delicate matters—"Turn the other cheek, Jane Hester!"—or she had before marrying Quinn Wentworth. Turning the other cheek, in this one instance, would not do. She pushed off the sofa, wobbled a bit, and crossed the room to slap both palms on the desk blotter.

"Lady Althea," she began, "is not being helpful when she decides how my time is spent, with whom, or where. I can understand that she has been the lady of this house, and I would never attempt to divide your loyalties. Neither will I permit her to treat me as some dimwitted child who can't be trusted to cross the street without a nanny. My own father seldom sank that low."

Mr. Wentworth picked up an engraved gold snuff box and rotated it, dropping each edge in succession onto the leather blotter. *Thunk, thunk, thunk, thunk . . .*

"Althea wasn't treating you like a dimwitted child. She was trying to keep you safe."

"From what? The baby isn't due for months."

He set aside the snuff box, rose, and took down a sachet bag that hung on the balcony curtains. The bag held a key, which unlocked the balcony door.

"Remember where the key is," he said, replacing it in the bag, "in case there's a fire and the balcony becomes your only route to safety."

The day wasn't quite warm, but the balcony was on the lee side of the house, the air was still, and sun was strong. Jane took a seat on a wrought-iron chair while her husband faced her, leaning against the railing. He made a handsome picture backdropped by the maple—a handsome, annoyed picture.

"The Wentworths aren't like any other family on this street," he said.

They weren't like any other family in all of England. "One gathers as much."

"We started off in the gutter, Jane. We're as lowborn and disreputable as a family can be this side of Newgate, and now the distinction of a prison record has befallen us as well."

A man unused to explaining himself was trying to make something clear. Jane ignored her rumbling belly and set aside the argument with Althea.

"And yet, you are a duke."

He folded his arms and gazed upward, which made the edge of the injury to his neck visible above the linen of his cravat.

"Dodson agreed that no announcement would be made regarding the title. I'll be invested as quietly as possible, and the dukedom will be a matter of gossip and speculation unless and until I take my seat in the Lords."

This apparently was a relief to him, the poor man. "You'd be better off using the title and having done with the gossip. A dukedom is impossible to keep quiet for any length of time. Just get it over with, and let people draw their own conclusions. Refuse to discuss your personal situation and you can't be drawn into gossip."

He took the chair beside her, then took her hand. "The matter isn't that simple. I am legally the son of a destitute drunk and a desperate woman. What I did to escape that upbringing is grounds for one scandal after another. I dug graves, Jane. I emptied privies for the night soil men. I collected debts. I drove a knacker's cart. If there was a low, contemptible job available for coin, I did it. I made enemies, very powerful enemies."

Those enemies haunted him, whoever they were. "Your foes have had years to bring you low and they haven't succeeded."

He kissed her knuckles, an odd gesture. "Yes, Jane, they did. They brought me all the way to the gallows."

The angry red weal hadn't faded from his neck. A mere half inch was visible above the white of his neckcloth, and his clothing had to be a constant irritation. Still he hadn't told her the whole of it, and he might never.

What he was saying became obvious between one beat of Jane's heart and the next.

"You didn't kill Robert Pike," she said. "You never laid a hand on him."

* * *

Quinn watched as Jane went on rearranging puzzle pieces. She sat very still, her hand cool in his.

She had married him thinking him capable of taking a human life. Perhaps that meant she was foolish—or brave—but it also signified the lengths she'd go to for the sake of her children.

"If you didn't kill that man, then why . . . ?"

Quinn was reluctant to explain, but he dared not leave her in ignorance. "Because somebody wanted me not only dead, but disgraced. A previously thriving bank was approaching ruin until this morning, and our fortunes are still far from secure."

"The crumbs," Jane said, making no sense whatsoever. "Ned, the women, Davies...marrying me. They were simple decency rather than gestures of atonement. I should have known."

Quinn had no idea what mental flights drove those words. "Anybody associated with me is in danger, Jane, and I can't keep you safe if you're flitting all over Oxford Street." The arrival of a child would only complicate the whole challenge, for babies were so very vulnerable.

Jane's grip on Quinn's hand became firmer. "I haven't flitted anywhere for months. This is why you mentioned setting me aside. You think I should distance myself from you not because of the scandal, but because you have enemies."

He did not want to set her aside. He'd reached that conclusion somewhere between the third and fourth hours after midnight, the previous five hours having been spent watching Jane thrash about in her sleep, get up almost hourly to make her way behind the privacy screen, then flop back to the bed and resume thrashing about.

She could not find rest, she could barely keep a meal down, she never complained, and she hadn't asked to become a member of the Wentworth family. She could not possibly foresee the sort of evil that put a noose around an innocent man's neck.

Quinn would never be much of a husband to her, but neither would he leave her to fend for herself. He'd worry about the child's situation later, assuming the infant made a safe arrival into the world.

"You are innocent," Jane said, her voice low and hard, "and I am furious."

"Furious at me?"

"Of course not at you. You've done nothing wrong. What sort of vile, crawling, contemptible maggot accuses an innocent man of taking another's life? The witnesses abetted this disgrace, as did the journalists, the—"

She winced, putting her free hand to her side.

"Jane, you must not become upset. Think of the child."

"The child will never be safer. What about your poor family? They are reeling with how close they came to burying you. They'd be lost without you, and I daresay they are a bit lost *with* you. The authorities cannot turn a blind eye to such a perversion of justice."

"The authorities were in on it, love. The judge was bought and paid for, the coroner, the witnesses, all of them. The warden told me not to even try to bribe my way to an escape and that appeals would be pointless. Whoever did this was determined and powerful."

"And that means," Jane said, "you are more in need of Althea's concern than I am. I have a suggestion." She rose, balancing with a hand on Quinn's shoulder. She lowered herself to his lap, an awkward perch that required him to steady her with his arms about her.

"This is friendly, Mrs. Wentworth." Awkward, but friendly.

She scooted, which was like a load shifting in a wheelbarrow. "You usually call me Jane. I have a suggestion."

"While you never call me Quinn."

"Quinn, you will please consider my suggestion before you roar and stomp about and splutter."

Despite her awkward shape, she made a nice armful. "I haven't roared or stomped for years, and I never splutter."

"You will," she said, patting his chest. "The child will make you splutter and curse—and laugh, I hope. My suggestion is that you consider allowing me to protect you."

Allowing *her*...Quinn could get his arms around the lady, but his mind refused to wrap around her words.

"But that's... You can't... I don't see..." He was spluttering. "Explain yourself."

"Think about it. Whoever laid you low could do so because at some point, you were alone with Mr. Pike, or you could not account for your whereabouts when witnesses placed you at his side. Your wife—a minister's daughter, a military widow, no less—can vouch for your whereabouts at all hours, day or night, because you only leave her side to attend to business or escort your sisters socially."

Jane smelled of flowers and soap, and holding her appeased some purely protective need Quinn tried to ignore.

"Wentworths don't socialize."

"You're newly wed and newly titled. We shall socialize to the extent that I can."

"The family isn't invited anywhere, and we prefer it that way."

Jane's fingers began to work at his neckcloth. "Quinn—I do like that name—your way didn't work. Your way, being socially aloof, recluses in plain sight, left you vulnerable to a sneak attack. I daresay it also tries the nerves of your family and inclines them to sour moods."

She left the ends of Quinn's cravat trailing, unbuttoned the first two buttons of his shirt, then ran a gentle finger around the inside of his collar.

Irritation he'd been ignoring eased. "My siblings were born in sour moods. Stephen in particular cannot be blamed for being easily provoked, for his leg pains him without mercy. If we receive no invitations, how do you propose we commence socializing, assuming I'm even considering this notion?"

Which he was. Jane's suggestion had that whiff of strategy about it, the difference between brawling and pugilism, the difference between walking away from a fight and ending up facedown, bleeding onto the filthy cobbles.

"We start off humbly," Jane said. "You invite the vicar for dinner—he'll come. Vicars always appreciate a free meal. You take your sisters driving in the park. You ride out first thing in the day. You tip your hat to those whom you recognize, and you escort me to my outings on Oxford Street. At all times, you exert yourself to be agreeable, and society will see you for the gentleman you are. We must embark on this campaign immediately, for as my condition advances, I won't be able to protect you as easily."

Jane's plan—be gracious and society will be gracious to you—was the doomed hope of a minister's daughter. Quinn couldn't bring himself to deride her naïveté, foolish though it was.

He was too busy grappling with the other manifestation of her wrong-headed notions.

I won't be able to protect you. The words might as well have been in some heathen tongue Quinn had never heard before. His family was loyal, which wasn't the same as protective.

Jane—expecting a child, in a marriage she hadn't planned on, poor as a proud beggar—was determined to protect him. While she snuggled in Quinn's arms—*snuggle* being another foreign word—he sorted through vocabulary. In the privacy of his thoughts he was determined to put a name on the emotion his wife had inspired.

He'd make the effort to identify what he felt, the better to defend against it, lest ambush come from within.

"We should also visit the lending library," Jane murmured. "Put you on display before the spinsters and companions. Their good opinion matters."

I could barely read until I was older than Davies. "Fine idea."

She rubbed her cheek against the lace of his untied cravat. "I love your scent."

I stank worse than offal for most of my youth. "A gentleman's hygiene matters. Shall I carry you to the bed, Jane?"

She raised her head and peered at him. "If you think I'll miss my sliced beef for the sake of a nap, you have wandered far from the path of sense, Mr. Wentworth."

"Quinn." When he held Jane, he was three counties away from sense, which was a serious, serious problem. "Where did you think to start your shopping?"

She rattled off the names of a few mercantile establishments, while her hair tickled Quinn's chin, and he contemplated offensive maneuvers: Duncan could take Althea and Constance shopping, Quinn and Stephen could hack out in the park on fine mornings. Quinn, Stephen, and a groom, rather, there being safety in numbers.

The family would squawk at the change in tactics, they'd protest, they'd grumble—and enjoy every minute of their own noise—but they'd see the wisdom of Jane's idea. Joshua could be recruited to dine with Quinn occasionally at the club, and Quinn could carry on his own investigations all the more effectively for appearing to settle into married life.

A voice in his head that sounded like Ned warned against deceiving Jane in this regard—appearing to ingratiate himself with polite society while laying what traps and snares he could—but if there was protecting to be done, he'd do it.

Protect his family, Jane's innocence, and his own life.

"We don't have to accomplish all of this in a week," Jane went on. "My stamina is not what it used to be. I'd also like to interview some midwives and an accoucheur or two."

A tap sounded on the door. Quinn rose with Jane in his arms and settled her on the sofa.

Ivor and Kristoff came in, bearing silver trays and wearing smirks, for Quinn's wife had ordered him away from the donnybrook in the family parlor not twenty minutes past.

By now, a word-for-word re-enactment of that encounter had made its way to the kitchen.

"Please put the trays on the balcony," Jane said. "His Grace and I will be going out after we dine. You'll want to see to your own sustenance, for you'll both accompany us."

Ivor bowed, Kristoff did as well, an instant later. "Yes, milady."

"My wife is a duchess," Quinn said. "Might as well get in the habit now of addressing her as Your Grace."

The pair of them withdrew, no longer smirking.

Quinn got Jane situated on the balcony and took some pleasure in her appetite. She finished two beef sandwiches and a pair of ginger biscuits before pronouncing herself satisfied. Quinn saved her half of his sandwich, because she apparently didn't stay satisfied for long.

"We didn't say grace." Jane folded her table napkin and laid it beside her empty plate. "I am very grateful. Not only was I hungry, but my digestion appears to be settled for once."

That was it. "Thank you, Jane."

She took a third ginger biscuit and held it out to him. "For what?"

Quinn detested ginger biscuits. They were never sweet enough. "For sharing your ideas with me." *For trying to protect your husband.* He broke the biscuit in half and passed her the larger portion. "For being honest."

"Let's agree that our union will be characterized by honesty. The truth is serving us well, so far."

Oh, Jane. If Quinn were honest about the details of his past, they'd have no union at all. If he were honest about his plans for his enemy, they'd have no future.

"I will look forward to many more of your frank opinions, Duchess. Shall you rest before our outing?"

She nibbled her biscuit. "I believe I shall. Give me an hour, and we'll storm Oxford Street."

Quinn stood and kissed her cheek—she'd said she liked the scent of him near. "I'll send one of the maids to fetch you in an hour."

He needed to get away from her, needed time to think, to explain the situation to his family. He needed time to consider what it meant that he was *grateful* to his wife, purely, simply grateful.

And that he was determined to thoroughly deceive her.

Chapter Thirteen

"The news is all over the clubs," Cuthbert, Earl of Tipton, said. "Nobody's quite sure what to make of it."

Beatrice took a slow, stalling sip of her chocolate. She ought to have ordered a tray in her room, because her husband always broke his fast in the morning parlor and always read the paper from front page to back. A former diplomat's habits died hard.

"I beg your pardon?" she said. "Might I have the jam?"

The footman at the sideboard brought the jam pot to Beatrice's end of the table. She sat where no impertinent beam of sunlight could strike her face and otherwise blight the beginning of her day.

Her husband's relentless good cheer accomplished that feat most mornings. She didn't hate Cuthbert, but managing him was wearisome.

"That damned Wentworth," he muttered, turning a page. "You may be excused, Thomas."

The footman, whose name was Harold, withdrew.

"Wentworth?" Beatrice made a production out of choosing a slice of toast from the rack on the table. The toast was warm, and Cook had flavored half the batch with cinnamon.

"Quinton Wentworth, the banker. He was to be hanged for murder, and now he's larking about at liberty again, free as you please. One of King George's many queer starts. Butter, pet?"

"Please."

Cuthbert brought her the butter, for he was ever considerate. Beatrice wished he'd curse, rant, and accuse, but he never did. Not ever. Another relic of his days as a diplomat.

"Murder is distasteful so early in the day." Beatrice tore her toast in half. The crime had been manslaughter, though the difference mattered not at all to the victim. The distinction was one of intent. A murderer sought to end the victim's life. A manslaughterer might have shoved the victim to the ground or come at him with violence in mind, but without intent to take a life.

Ulysses had explained the nuances to her in tedious detail, as if the legalities should fascinate her when Quinn Wentworth had once again survived despite all odds to the contrary.

"His bank has to be reeling," Cuthbert said, in the same tones he'd report that a cricket team was doomed without its best pitcher. "Though with a royal pardon in his pocket, Wentworth will likely come right soon enough. Please do have more toast. I can't abide the cinnamon myself."

Was he baiting her?

Cuthbert was an odd combination of shrewd and oblivious. He'd come into a second cousin's title years ago, but the wealth had taken some time to free up from trusts and bequests. His solution had been to spend time in the diplomatic corps, living more cheaply overseas, drawing a salary, and periodically abandoning his younger wife for months at a time.

He made a credible earl, a touch of gray about his temples, his frame lean, and his wardrobe dapper.

Cuthbert wasn't ugly, wasn't stupid, wasn't anything in particular that a wife was entitled to complain of. He was a considerate and undemanding lover, when he bothered to recall he had a wife.

Beatrice wasn't sure which she resented more: his neglect or his attentions.

"I like variety in my treats," she said. "Plain toast grows boring even with butter and jam." She'd spoken without thinking, a simple truth about breakfast fare, but Cuthbert gazed at her consideringly over the top of his newspaper.

"If you're bored, we might take a trip to Lisbon before the weather grows too warm."

Any excuse to drag her off to his favorite haunts. "The social season has only started, my lord. What can you be thinking?"

He smiled, the diplomat's self-conscious, gracious smile. "I'm avoiding my parliamentary committees, if you must know. What difference does it make how many hackneys trot around London, or how loudly George begs for more money? Will I see you at Almack's tonight?"

"Possibly."

He folded the paper and rose. "I'll live in hope until this evening. Should I send Thomas back in?"

Harold-Thomas was handsome—footmen were required to be handsome—but he needed a better acquaintance with soap.

"No, thank you. I'll enjoy the rest of my meal in solitude."

Cuthbert kissed her cheek, the newspaper tucked under his arm. "Maybe we'll go to Lisbon this autumn or sail off to Rome. You'd like Rome."

All those ancient statues with their chipped noses and eternally staring eyes? Having a doting husband fifteen years Beatrice's senior was bad enough.

"Let's think about it. Autumn is months away."

Cuthbert patted her hand. "You ladies do so enjoy your waltzing. I'll take lunch at the club, see what the fellows have to say about this Wentworth debacle. A few of them bank with him, despite the availability of many more venerable institutions. Some say he stole his first fortune, the rest remain strangely reticent, even in their cups. All very interesting."

"Money," Beatrice said, putting a world of disdain into two syllables. "Was there ever a more boring topic?" Or a more interesting topic than Quinn Wentworth?

"A club man is easily amused," Cuthbert replied. "Enjoy your day, pet."

"Save me a waltz."

"I'll be happy to." He left the morning parlor at his usual brisk pace, though why—why in the name of every gentlemen's club in St. James—must Cuthbert focus on Quinn Wentworth now?

Beatrice closed the door after her husband, drew every curtain in the room, and resumed her seat. She rested her forehead on her crossed arms and hated her whole dreadful life.

And Quinn Wentworth. For good measure, she hated Quinn Wentworth too.

* * *

"You'd best tell me," Stephen said, patting his gelding. "Whatever has you half deaf at table, and off to the bank at all hours, is worrying the sisters. You've been out of prison for nearly two weeks, and yet you might as well still be locked away somewhere for all we see of you."

"The sisters always worry." They'd also taken to shopping like coachmen sampling free summer ale. Instead of bickering incessantly, Constance and Althea planned mercantile raids, compared prices between establishments, and tried on bonnets without number. Jane abetted these excesses, and when Quinn had arrived home last evening— half an hour earlier than usual—he'd heard feminine laughter coming from the family parlor.

Who would have guessed?

"The servants tell me everything," Stephen said, turning his horse down a quiet bridle path. "Everything, Quinn. If you want eyes and ears at home, I'm your man."

On horseback, Stephen looked older than when in his Bath chair. He was growing into Quinn's height, and he'd chosen a mount that stood more than seventeen hands. To compensate for the weakness in his leg, his upper body strength was significant, and his chest and shoulders were well developed as a result.

By the laws of the street, Stephen was a man.

"You're my baby brother. Asking you to spy for me only puts you in harm's way."

Quinn had forgotten that Hyde Park early on a spring day was a slice of heaven. Birds flitted overhead in the luminous canopy of new leaves, the Serpentine reflected brilliant morning sunshine. Here was peace and beauty, right in the midst of London's endless vice.

Stephen's horse shied at a rabbit darting across the path, dislocating Stephen from the saddle not one bit.

"I do believe those two words—baby brother—are my least favorite pairing in any language," Stephen said. "I wouldn't be spying. I'm simply summarizing the endless stream of gossip, news, and hearsay that is heaped upon me daily by our loyal staff. Kristoff and Ivor are having a row over the new maids, for example."

Kristoff and Ivor barely spoke when in livery. "What sort of row?"

"Don't be an idiot. You might be married to your bank, but the rest of us are human."

"I am married to Jane." Which made Quinn increasingly uneasy. He slept beside Jane every night, to the extent he ever slept, and to the extent he *could* sleep when she was in and out of the bed so frequently.

Quinn almost enjoyed squiring her about to the glove-maker's or the milliner's—almost—but did Jane enjoy her post as his self-appointed bodyguard?

"I like Jane," Stephen said. "She can't play chess worth a tinker's prayer, but she's a good sport and she puts up with Althea and Constance. I think you'd like Jane too if you'd give her a chance, *Your Grace*."

I do believe those two words... "I'm glad you and Jane are getting along. I'd take it as a favor to me if you'd teach her to shoot."

Stephen halted his horse. "You should teach her. She's *your wife*. Joshua says you're frequently gone from the bank, off doing God knows what. Jane is determined that we all help keep your ungrateful self safe, which is difficult when we don't know where to find you. Althea says the baby won't settle for months yet, but leaving word with me of your whereabouts would be a husbandly courtesy. Mind, I'm not suggesting you tell your duchess what you're about, be-cause I would never meddle between man and wife."

"What does that mean, the baby won't settle?"

"Ask Jane."

She and Quinn didn't talk about the child. Jane had chosen a midwife and an accoucheur, and made second choices for each in case the first was unavailable. Always sensible, that was Jane.

"I don't want to worry her. Please teach her to shoot."

"You teach her to shoot. You're her husband."

Wentworths were stubborn, and Stephen was enjoying himself.

"You're a dead shot," Quinn said. "By comparison, I barely know which end of a gun does what." Pistols were loud, they cost money, and they could fire at most four bullets, with little accuracy over any distance. Quinn was very good with a pistol, Stephen was brilliant. "A sharp knife is a poor man's best friend."

"You are not a poor man—or has that changed too? Is the bank in trouble?"

Stephen's question was reasonable, but he had waited for one of few opportunities to raise it in private. Jane had asked Quinn to make this dawn jaunt with Stephen for three mornings in a row, and Quinn had relented mostly to appease her.

"The bank is in good health for the moment," he said. "Any renewed scandal and we're done."

"Joshua says you're thriving."

Damn Joshua. "We've brought in some accounts from the working classes, I'm happy to report, though they have little in the way of funds. The major depositors are nervous. I've also been busy trying to learn the business of the dukedom."

"Such a pity nobody else in your family has a grasp of basic math or simple mercantile concepts. All alone you must struggle on, the uncomplaining hero of some tragedy you're determined to write in your own blood."

"You sound like Jane."

"I'm nearly quoting her on the subject of Ned and regular bathing, though I came up with the part about the tragedy myself. Jane said to ask you if I could help with the estate properties, because I have a fine head for numbers. Duncan seconded the motion, then Constance said if you hand me an estate to put to rights, she wants one too. Althea was at the glovemaker's at the time, or she would have demanded a property as well."

This was Jane being helpful. Also meddlesome as hell.

Another horseman rode toward them. A largish fellow on a largish bay, no white on the horse anywhere.

"I'll review the stewards' reports on the properties when I return from the bank this evening, but it's not bank business that has occupied me so much over the past two weeks."

Quinn's groom—who did carry a gun, a knife, and a pocketful of sand—closed the distance between his horse and Quinn's.

"That's Elsmore," Stephen said.

The Duke of Elsmore sat on the board of directors for the Dorset and Becker Savings and Trust. The bank was ancient, and Elsmore's family had been involved at a genteel distance since its inception. From what Quinn had seen, the Dorset and Becker was an honest organization, though it catered to wealthy gentry and titles from the northern shires, and its investments were uniformly unimaginative.

Elsmore met Quinn's gaze when the horses were a good twenty yards apart.

"Look bored," Quinn muttered, motioning the groom to hang back. "Say nothing."

Stephen snorted. "As *Your Grace* wishes."

Elsmore brought his horse to a halt a few feet up the path. "Wentworth, good day. Perhaps you'd introduce me to your companion?"

Elsmore was several years younger than Quinn, had dark hair, and preferred severe attire to the gold buttons and lacy finery some of his class favored. At the rare gatherings where their paths had crossed, Quinn had sensed only polite curiosity from Elsmore rather than the lurid interest most hid so poorly.

"Your Grace, good morning. May I make known to you my brother, Lord Stephen Wentworth. Stephen, I present to you Wrexham, Duke of Elsmore."

Lord Stephen Wentworth. That merited an upward twitch of Elsmore's eyebrow.

Dodson had informed Quinn that the royal hand had been put to the appropriate warrants. Three days ago, Quinn had observed the bare minimum of ritual with the Lord Chancellor, and the Wentworth siblings now sported courtesy titles.

With this introduction to Elsmore, all of polite society would soon hear that news.

"Congratulations are in order," Elsmore said, his smile surprisingly fierce. "One hears rumors. A ducal title?"

"Yes."

Silence fell. Quinn's horse snatched at the reins. Ruddy beast had no manners, but he was fast and fearless.

"Damned George probably saddled you with a load of debt," Elsmore said, simply an observation from a commercially astute peer. "My condolences must accompany my congratulations, but you'll sort it out. One hears rumors of a different sort, however."

You'll sort it out. From a duke, much less a director at a rival establishment, that was tantamount to sponsoring Quinn for vouchers at Almack's. Doubtless, Elsmore expected something in return.

"Lord Stephen is in my confidence in every regard," Quinn replied, and Stephen, who apparently aspired to reach his eighteenth birthday, did not fall off his horse overcome with mirth.

"One hears a certain viscount is considering moving his funds," Elsmore said, gaze upon the greenery overhead.

Was this a warning, a confidence, an inchoate request for a favor, or...? Ah. *Detwiler*. A request for help making a decision, then, though a banker never, ever violated client confidentiality.

"Some viscounts can move their assets about in a thimble," Quinn said, "while their debts would require a wheelbarrow."

Elsmore appeared fascinated by the surrounding maples. "A wheelbarrow?"

He'd never struck Quinn as slow before. "A bloody big muck cart."

"With a cloud of flies buzzing over it," Stephen added, "that you can hear from halfway up the street."

Accurate, given that Detwiler's finances were under discussion, though Stephen couldn't know that.

"I see." Elsmore gathered up his reins. "Such a pity when that's the case. Lovely morning, isn't it?"

"The best London has to offer," Quinn replied.

Elsmore touched his hat brim. "Your Grace, Lord Stephen, always a pleasure to pass the time in beautiful surrounds. I'll wish you good day."

He sent his horse at a walk between Quinn's and Stephen's mounts, his air of self-possession as subtle and bright as the sunbeams lancing down through the trees.

The bay's hoofbeats faded, while Quinn tried to make sense of the encounter.

"What the hell was that about?" Stephen asked.

"The Duke of Walden has made his come-out." Which Jane had doubtless known would happen on such an excursion.

"But that business with the muck carts and viscounts?"

"A test, and I passed, no thanks to your thespian capabilities." Elsmore would have a quiet word with his bankers, and they'd advise Detwiler to keep his funds with Quinn for the sake of investment continuity or some such fiction. Detwiler's financial muck cart would remain parked in its present location amid Quinn's accounts.

A courtesy done between banking establishments, one that coincided with Detwiler's best interests, or Quinn would not have even hinted to Elsmore of the viscount's true situation.

"When will you let me start at the bank in earnest?" Stephen asked, nudging his horse forward on the path. "I'm good with numbers, and I'm *entirely in Your Grace's confidence*. I can also keep an eye on you for Jane's sake."

Quinn's gelding kept pace with Stephen's mount. "You're entirely a pest." A loyal pest with quick wits, also Quinn's only brother. "Robert Pike's body was not in the grave where it was purportedly buried."

Stephen stared at his horse's mane while a squirrel started a racket overhead. "That's good."

"And it's bad. The poor sod in that coffin had his hair dyed dark to match Pike's, and he might have resembled Pike somewhat in life, but he wasn't Pike."

"You can tell his hair was dyed?"

"He was doubtless seriously ill, and chosen for his resemblance to Pike. His hair was dyed some time before he died. For however much longer he lived, his hair grew and nobody thought to touch him up in death."

"I wish you didn't know so much about dead people."

"I know about staying alive, I hope. His skull bore no sign of injury, though the physician's report said Pike's death was precipitated by a mortal blow to the head."

Abetted by exposure to a cold March night, lack of medical treatment, and six pages of nearly illegible lies, deceptions, and obfuscations by the physician, who was not regularly employed in the capacity of coroner. The author of the report hadn't testified at the trial, but rather, a coroner who'd read that report had mumbled and muttered under oath in his place.

Quinn had brought a retired physician with him to examine the deceased, though anybody could see the poor blighter's head hadn't been bashed in.

"You planning to have a chat with the coroner who wrote that affidavit?" Stephen asked.

"He's on indefinite holiday in a location his former housekeeper could not recall—somewhere far, far away."

"That's bad."

"Pike hailed from York, and his family still bides there. I'll be traveling north at the end of the week—*on business*, as far as Jane is concerned."

The Countess of Tipton hailed from York, as did her in-laws. Quinn had pushed that fact to the very edge of his awareness, where it refused to stay.

Stephen brushed a glance in Quinn's direction, presaging one of the lad's rare attempts at delicacy. "Jane won't like you disappearing onto the Great North Road even *on business*. She'll expect you to take an army of nannies, all of whom will tattle on you without a qualm."

"I know." And that was bad too.

Chapter Fourteen

Wellington must have felt this frustrated taking years to advance across Spain. Jane's only ally in her efforts to create a peer's household under the Wentworth roof was Susie—Susan, rather—who had been in service long enough to know a lax housekeeper when she saw one, and a lax butler, and a pair of footmen whose discretion belowstairs was sadly wanting.

The maids made a rioting mob look decorous by comparison, to the point that Penny had pronounced them less civilized than streetwalkers.

"They want to do better," Susan said, "but they haven't anyone to show them how to go on."

"The house is reasonably clean," Jane replied, toeing around on the carpet beneath the desk in search of her house mules. "The meals arrive to the table hot, the fires are kept lit and the hearths swept." But oiling the gears for Stephen's lift took precedence over blacking andirons, because Stephen hated when his use of the device made noise.

Dusting Althea's harps—she had four—was more important than cleaning the windows, and God forbid that Constance's cats should be occasionally groomed, the better to minimize the hair they left on every upholstered surface.

Worse, both felines roamed the house freely, and had graced one corner of the formal parlor with a decided odor of courting tomcat. Jane could detect that smell from the corridor, though Susan assured her the stink wasn't "that bad."

As if any stink was acceptable in a ducal domicile. The house was a monument to minimal efforts applied with minimal supervision, and Jane's entire day had been spent listing the work to be done in each room. Her usual habit of counting to three when in need of patience had become a slow count to ten.

Down in the foyer, the front door clicked open.

"The hearths are swept," Susan said, "but half the time, nobody's at the front door. The menus never vary, the staff bickers, and in the servants' hall they tipple gin like vicars swilling China black."

Masculine voices drifted up from below. Quinn and Duncan, and at an earlier hour than usual. Quinn had missed dinner—he usually missed dinner—and Stephen and Constance had started a row at the table over the Irish question. Duncan had tried to intervene—Duncan was nothing if not brave—and they'd both turned their cannon on him. Jane had pitched her table napkin at Stephen's head and prompted a ceasefire on the strength of the combatants' sheer surprise.

They'd stopped bickering, though Jane had vowed to herself not to resort to such an undignified tactic again, not that any strategy would work twice in succession with the Wentworth siblings.

"If you'd have the kitchen send up trays, please," Jane said. "Beef sandwiches and apple tarts."

"And ginger biscuits," Susan said, pouring a scoop of coal onto the hearth. "Aye, Your Grace. Your slippers are under the bedroom desk."

The bedroom desk, which was kept locked, just like the desk in the parlor was kept locked. Jane hadn't purposely gone looking for the keys, but she'd found them when she'd replaced the stale sachets hanging from the bedposts.

She'd not used those keys—yet. Susan took her leave, while Jane retrieved her slippers. It wouldn't do to meet her husband in bare feet.

Or would it?

Quinn let himself into the sitting room and stopped near the door. "You should be in bed, Jane."

"I took a nap this afternoon." Already, she was tempted by the Wentworth habit of dissembling, and that was unacceptable. She had promised Quinn honesty and expected the same in return.

He speared her with a glower. "You lay down. You never rest for long."

That Quinn saw through her half-truths was comforting, in a Wentworth sort of way. "I do the best I can. If you'd unhook me, I'll make another attempt at sleep once I've seen you fed."

He remained by the door, looking tired and beautiful. Jane did not go to him, because she'd tried that. Tried being his valet, tried being his companion at a late-night dinner, tried waiting for him to make any husbandly overture at all. When pressed into her company as an escort, he was polite but clearly bored.

Their marriage was much too young for boredom.

He shrugged out of his jacket and hung it over the chair behind the desk. "I passed Susan on the stair. She should have assisted you into your nightclothes. You must be firm with the staff, Jane. They won't know their duties unless you make your needs clear."

One...two...three. "Be firm with the staff," Jane said, taking Quinn's jacket into the bedroom and hanging it in the wardrobe. "Which staff would that be, for they adhere to no schedule I can fathom, except the bully boys you call running footmen. That lot is always ready to attend you, God be thanked."

Quinn squatted to examine the mechanism of the bedroom door latch. "Have you quarreled with my sisters?"

Jane closed the door to the wardrobe with a loud *snick.* "I'm quarreling with you, Quinn Wentworth. My husband. The man with whom I spoke vows. The person who will parent my firstborn with me."

He rose and his gaze went flat, even taking on a hint of menace. "We can refine on that impossibility later. What is the nature of your present complaint, madam?"

"Stop it," Jane retorted. "Don't give me that Yorkshire growl, as if you'd tear me to pieces when I know you feed wild birds, marry stray widows, and work yourself half to death for your family. It won't wash, Quinn. You can intimidate every rolled-up title in Mayfair with that performance, but I know better."

A swift knock sounded on the door and Quinn startled.

"Food," Jane said. "Lest you snack on the bones of your contrary wife." She brushed past him, intent on going to the door.

He caught her by the wrist, his grip firm without hurting. "The performance is the civilized banker, the considerate husband. The real man isn't somebody you'd care to meet."

"How would you know? You keep him hidden from even yourself." She tugged free and opened the parlor door.

Ivor and Kristoff brought in trays, set them down on the

low table, and withdrew on wordless bows. They were learning. Quinn would learn too.

He took a seat on the sofa. "I see two trays. Will you join me, or have you slacked your hunger by taking several bites from my backside?"

"I like your backside," Jane said, settling beside him. Sitting these days was an act of faith, a matter of descending to the last point where balance and strength controlled, and then casting off onto the cushions, perhaps never to rise.

Quinn paused with a sandwich halfway to his mouth. "You like my backside." The menace in his gaze was revealed for what it truly was: caution.

"You're quite muscular. One appreciates a well-made husband. The kitchen forgot the perishing mustard."

He took a bite. "This is a mortal sin?"

"The sin is venal, but compound it by a hundred, and it becomes another day in the Duke of Walden's town abode. Twice I have told the kitchen that you prefer mustard on your beef sandwiches. Three times, they have neglected to heed my guidance. In any proper household, somebody would be severely reprimanded for repeatedly ignoring an employer's preferences."

He opened his sandwich, which bore not a dash of mustard, then put the slices of bread together again. "I'll have a word with Althea."

The ginger biscuit Jane had been holding crumpled to bits before she could count to three.

"You will not *have a word with Althea*. Althea has ceded the domestic field to me, and properly so. She has discovered, ten years later than most females do, that attiring herself in flattering styles is enjoyable. She has closeted herself with her harps by the hour, she has read an entire Radcliffe novel and pronounced it ridiculous."

Finally, Jane had his attention. "*Althea* read a novel? Next you'll tell me Constance and Duncan have taken up pall-mall."

"We all played a round the day before yesterday, which is simply a normal family activity on a fine afternoon. In a duke's household, for the staff to forget the mustard is not normal. For the housekeeper to carry a flask of gin is not normal. For your brother to offer to teach me to shoot a pistol is *not normal at all*."

Jane swept the crumbs off her front—she would soon lose a lap altogether—and tried to rise, but the sofa was low and the baby was growing, and nothing, nothing, was going right about the whole dratted day.

The whole dratted marriage.

Quinn's reply to her diatribe was to pluck her up in his arms and carry her into the bedroom.

"Stephen needs to feel competent and safe," Quinn said, settling with Jane into the reading chair. "He taught himself to shoot and he's quite good at it. You'd be doing me a kindness if you'd let him show you around a lady's pistol. Constance and Althea are proficient with knives."

Jane was too tired to take umbrage at Quinn's high-handedness and too happy to be in his arms. He seldom touched her unless she made the first overture.

"Stephen beat us all at pall-mall. He stood to take his shots, which clearly pained him, but his accuracy was deadly. I don't want to learn to use a gun, Quinn. Guns kill people. Better to have a firm knowledge of reason and civility than a passing acquaintance with weapons."

His embrace grew more snug. "Guns can kill bad people. I need for you to be safe, Jane."

Not exactly a stirring declaration, but Quinn meant well. "If you arm me—and I'm not saying I'll allow that—my first victims will be your domestics. That they forget mustard means they forget to whom they owe their loyalty."

"You're upset about mustard?"

"Yes." Though now that Quinn was sharing a chair with her, Jane could be more honest. "And no. Are you trying to forget you're married? The midwife was very clear that normal marital activity will present no risk to the baby and is even good for me. When will we consummate our vows, Quinn, or are all your long hours at the bank about some problem you are trying to keep from my notice?"

He remained silent, his lips pressed to Jane's temple.

* * *

Every sin Quinn had ever committed, and there were many, every mistake he'd made, and those were even more numerous, haunted him in the person of his wife. Jane was bustling, scolding, and quarreling her way into his heart, the last place she should hope to be.

The town house had always oppressed Quinn, with its relentless geometry of portraits hung perfectly straight, carpets running down the exact center of the corridors, wallpaper patterned to precisely match, panel by panel. Who could thrive amid such endless, purposeless order?

And yet, the house had a musty smell in the corners, reminiscent of pets, dirty laundry, and winter damp, even in spring. The windows were seldom clean, which Althea attributed to London's coal smoke, and if somebody recalled to put flowers in the front foyer, just as often, the bouquet was left to disintegrate before it was replaced.

As if the squalor of the Yorkshire slums had followed Quinn hundreds of miles south, and would follow him all the way to the grave.

In the past week, the house had been thoroughly aired.

The windows sparkled, the flowers were fresh. The carpet in the formal parlor had been taken up, and the oak parquet floor polished to a high shine. Jane had done this—Jane had known how to do it—and she'd softened the pointless order of Quinn's home.

He'd first noticed her efforts in his apartment. The afghan folded over the back of the sofa was now laid at an angle, the pillows piled at one end rather than arranged symmetrically. The windows weren't open to the same degree, and the decanters no longer stood in order of height.

Jane was making his house a home, and he was helpless to stop her, for she apparently needed to domesticate and organize to be happy, and he needed for her to be happy. His penance for all transgressions past, present, and future was that one day—if he survived the next attempt on his life—she'd realize what manner of man she'd married, and look at Quinn with either pity or disgust.

Or turn her gaze from him entirely.

"Do you know how long it has been since Althea read a novel?" Quinn asked the wife so agreeably occupying his lap.

"I can't possibly know."

"Althea has never read a novel, to my knowledge. She learned her letters kicking and screaming. I had to bribe her with music lessons."

"Another stubborn Wentworth," Jane replied, removing the pin from his cravat. "Why am I not surprised."

"Stephen hates for anybody to watch him stand," Quinn went on. "Hates that his left leg can barely hold his weight."

Jane unknotted Quinn's neckcloth. "I hadn't realized that your brother is nearly as tall as you are. Has an impressive set of shoulders on him too. He seemed surprised when I remarked as much."

When had anybody, any female, given Stephen a compliment for any reason? At his age, Quinn had been starved for female attention to the point of utter witlessness.

"Let him teach you how to use a gun, Jane, or let my sisters start you out with knives. Both take time to learn well."

She drew his cravat away, making sure the linen didn't abrade his neck. "You're almost healed. Is your neck still sore?"

"I sleep more easily on my right side." Facing Jane's half of the bed rather than the window.

He was doomed.

"May I put a theory to you?" Jane asked.

"Could I stop you?"

"The household reflects its master." She moved against him, or her belly did. Not a kick, something else. "You adhere to no schedule, so the domestics have no schedule. You barely notice what you eat, so Cook sends up the same menus week after week. Your version of loyalty involves violence more than discretion, hence your staff will defend your citadel, but gossip like dairymaids churning butter."

As a boy, Quinn had loved the sound of dairymaids gabbling over their work. They'd often let him have a scraping from the churns, and nothing soothed hunger like a dab of butter.

"My household functions adequately for my needs."

Jane cuddled closer on a sigh, a weary woman yet determined on her objective. "The household does not function adequately for the needs of a duke, Quinn. Cook should know your favorite desserts. I should know your favorite flowers. Althea might inquire as to which composers I prefer so she can learn a few airs to play for us after dinner. There's no...I don't know the word for it. We're ready to repel boarders or send out pickets for the night watch, but that manner of being a duke ceased to be useful three hundred years ago."

She traced her finger over Quinn's lips. "You smile so seldom. I love your smile." She kissed him on the mouth.

Desire mocked Quinn. Of all women to be drawn to...Jane was approaching her confinement, worried about his taste for mustard, and determined to reform a family sprung from the lowest gutters, all without so much as raising her voice.

"I'm off to York tomorrow, Jane. The press of business requires me in the north." The lie stung as the rope had burned his neck. Quinn had survived the rope, and he'd survive to someday be the sort of husband Jane deserved.

She kissed him again. "Coward. Tear about all you like. If you miss the birth of this child I will name him something dreadful."

Her kisses were ginger flavored. On her, the spice was luscious. "I won't be gone long. Less than a fortnight." And yes, when it came to his marriage, Quinn was a coward, though the child wasn't due for months.

She drew away. "You needn't run off, Quinn. If you can't see your way to consummating the vows, then just tell me. I'm not at my best, and my charms are humble on a good day. A white marriage isn't unheard of, even for a peer, but you had said..."

She tried to stand and succeeded only in pressing against Quinn's half-aroused cock. He rose with her in his arms and set her on the bed.

"You should be thinking of the baby now," Quinn said, kneeling to remove her slippers. "If I'm not putting demands on you, it's because the time hasn't been right. You didn't marry me for that, and we have no reason to hurry."

"I lack the nerve to ask your sisters if you keep a mistress, but perhaps your feelings are engaged elsewhere. I apologize for complicating your life, if so, though heirs do require the participation of both husband and wife."

She ducked her head, and Quinn wanted to pitch himself out the window.

"No mistress, Jane. No time for that nonsense."

"You're lying," she said, skewering him with a gimlet scowl. "Gordie could rise to the occasion in three minutes and be done in five. The problem isn't time."

"I'm glad he's dead if that's all the consideration he thought you were owed." Quinn had any number of reasons to be glad Gordon MacGowan had gone to his reward.

"What consideration am I due from you?" Jane asked.

She would not give this up. Another stubborn Wentworth indeed. "You are due every consideration."

"Then take me to bed, Quinn. Make me your wife in truth."

Quinn didn't understand his own reluctance, though caution was part of it, as was a backward lingering shame. He desired women in the abstract, and after he'd parted company with Beatrice, Countess of Tipton, he'd spent a good year desiring them in the flesh, proving something to himself.

Then Papa had broken Stephen's leg, and Quinn had focused entirely on making money. Life had become simpler, and Quinn hadn't looked back.

He held out his wrists for Jane to remove his sleeve buttons. "I'm leaving for York in the morning on bank business. The man I supposedly killed hails from York, and I thought while I was in the area I'd make a few inquiries."

He hadn't meant to tell her that. Hadn't wanted her involved, and her glower confirmed she didn't want to be involved.

She took his sleeve buttons, hopped off the bed, and dumped them into the vanity tray.

"Leave it alone, Quinn. Don't borrow trouble. Let sleeping dogs lie, and let bygones be bygones. Whoever put you in prison failed, and you're a duke now. Act like one. Go on about your life in a dignified fashion, and all will be well."

She leaned into him, her arms about his middle.

She was very confident of her platitudes, though her naïve sermon confirmed that Quinn was right to spare her the details of his investigations.

So he'd offer her a platitude in return. "I've cheated the hangman, Jane. Nothing will happen to me."

Her gaze promised argument, even now, even about this.

In exasperation—and desperation—Quinn kissed his wife.

Chapter Fifteen

Jane usually spent half of her day spinning theories about her husband.

Maybe his ordeal in Newgate had disturbed his manly humors so badly he could not consummate his vows. This theory wanted supporting evidence, for in every way, Quinn had returned to his former responsibilities with impressive vigor.

Perhaps he'd suffered an injury that rendered him sexually incapable. Gordie, veteran of many a gruesome battle, had assured her such was possible.

Again, no helpful evidence was on hand to support Jane's theory, for she'd seen Quinn nearly naked. He bore many scars, none of them in a location that would affect his breeding organs.

The obvious reason for Quinn's conjugal indifference had ample supporting evidence: He was sexually capable, and simply not attracted to Jane. As considerate as he was, his touch bore no hint of desire, his gaze was never lustful. The obvious explanation was the most likely, and Jane was ridiculous for being upset over that.

And yet, one more theory had presented itself: Quinn did not know how to make love with a lady. He'd managed a luscious kiss on their wedding day, and that might have been luck or chivalry. Maybe when it came to greater intimacies a minister's daughter baffled him.

The first week following Jane's elopement, Gordie had offered a few amatory flourishes. Kisses, caresses, love words that had rung false but sounded well intended. Jane's eyes did not outshine the glory of the stars, her breasts were not more abundant than heaven's blessings, for pity's sake.

Her blushes had been profuse, however.

Maybe Quinn thought she needed those ridiculous metaphors. Maybe once upon a time, she had. Now she wanted only him, though her longings weren't merely sexual in nature. She wanted to be a wife Quinn could trust and esteem, a true wife, not one more family member expecting him to provide for her every comfort.

Though Quinn apparently did not care to be a true husband.

She formed the intention to step back from him, to give up and spend another night trying to ignore her husband's warmth in the bed beside her, but her body refused to obey the sensible decision of her mind.

Quinn pressed his mouth to hers, gently, gently. "You're tenacious as a badger."

A compliment. She smiled into his kiss. "Thank you. More, please."

He slid a hand to cradle the back of her head and held her still, while he explored her features. Nose, eyebrows, jaw, chin...He wandered by kisses and delicate brushes of his fingers to every aspect of her face, making her aware of herself in a new way.

Tension Jane had been holding forever slid away, until she was clinging to Quinn to remain upright, and for the sheer joy of embracing him.

He knew how to kiss. Holy winged cupids, did he *ever* know how to kiss.

"Do ye turn up shy on me now, Jane?"

She kissed him back, such as she could when he was so much taller. Her belly prevented her from pressing as close as she longed to, but she was near enough to know that her husband was growing aroused.

"The bed, Quinn. Please…the bed."

His laugh was low and knowing. "I'm still wearing boots, woman. My wife will ring a peal over m' head if I get the sheets dirty."

Jane pulled away and gave him her back. "My hooks."

An abbreviated version of their bedtime routine unfolded, with Quinn locking doors and opening windows while Jane used the privacy screen. She climbed onto the bed, heard the rag sopping in the basin behind the screen, heard the distinctive sound of a toothbrush tapped against porcelain.

Then silence.

* * *

Two devils haunted Quinn as he made a particularly thorough job of his ablutions.

The first devil was so familiar as to nearly qualify as a friend. An upbringing saturated in shame had driven Quinn to work harder and longer than other boys, to dream more ambitiously than other youths, to drink less than other men, and he was awash in money as a result. He used only the best tailors, the finest bootmakers, the most respected haberdashers, but beneath all of that finery, the boy Jack Wentworth had loathed still lived.

You're a disgrace to the family name.

I'd kill you but why should I have to pay for your burial?

Get over here and take your punishment like a man.

And the line Quinn would never, ever say to his children: *I'll give you something to cry about.*

In hindsight, all of Quinn's accomplishments were a protracted study in not becoming what his father had been: cruel, violent, weak, impulsive, contemptible. Though of course Jack Wentworth had hurled those labels at his son so often, the accusations had occasionally stuck.

I'm not a boy. I'm not that boy.

Jane rustled about in the bedroom, making Jane-noises as she smacked pillows, arranged them to her liking, and pulled the bed curtains closed. She was an orderly woman who thrived on a peaceful, orderly routine, and Quinn treasured that about her.

In the first hours after regaining his freedom, Quinn had promised her a true marriage, and he'd only gradually realized how unsuited he was to be her mate.

Let sleeping dogs lie, she'd said, as if a sleeping dog didn't stink, drool, and bring fleas wherever it went.

Don't borrow trouble, she'd said, as if Quinn hadn't been born with a lifetime supply of trouble.

Let bygones be bygones, she'd said, as if attempting to end Quinn's life in humiliation and pain was a spilled glass of punch.

And thus the second devil joined Quinn behind the privacy screen: He desired his wife mightily. She was good, lovely, and dear, and by every law known to humankind, he owed her his intimate attentions and was entitled to enjoy her company in the same fashion.

But not only was Quinn a slum rat in banker's clothing, he was also a man determined to exact an eye for an eye, *at least*, when he found the enemy who'd put him in prison. Jane could turn the other cheek, forgive and forget, and do good to those who persecuted her—her father came to mind—but Quinn lacked those virtues.

He would deceive Jane as long as possible—for the rest of their lives, if fate let him arrange his retribution discreetly—but how could he make love with a woman to whom he was lying and would continue to lie?

Jane sighed in the bed, a sweet sound that scraped across the arousal Quinn fought against every time he was near her. His cock knew nothing of deception or honor, and knew everything of impending pleasure.

You're a disgrace to the family name.

Take your punishment like a man.

I'll give you something to cry about.

Quinn wrapped his hand around his rigid shaft and closed his eyes.

* * *

Was Quinn gathering his resolve? Hoping Jane would fall asleep? She waited and eventually his weight dipped his side of the bed.

"Are you still awake, wife?"

Had he hoped she'd drifted off? "I am awake, and I am your wife. Do you want me to beg, Quinn?" A half-formed suspicion suggested some men might like that, might like hearing women plead for masculine attention.

Gordie's lovemaking had settled into an expeditious undertaking, but Jane had liked the cuddling afterward, the sense that for a few minutes, she and her spouse were in charity with each other and with the world. Gordie could be charming, and, in that brief postlude, affectionate.

An odd sympathy for her first husband plagued her: Had Gordie, who'd always been the initiator of marital intimacies, felt uncertain of Jane's affection? Had he hoped for overtures from her, as Jane had waited for overtures from her current husband?

Quinn shifted to the middle of the bed. "Ye'd never beg."

Jane scooted over against him and used his thigh to pillow her knee. "I might put demands to you."

Quinn shifted to his side and resumed kissing her. For once, he was unhurried. Even his mind seemed to have slowed to focus solely on Jane and the present moment.

"You must promise me," Quinn said, gliding his palm over Jane's thigh, "that you'll not overdo while I'm gone, Jane. Rome wasn't toppled in a day."

His hand was warm, his touch lovely.

"I wish you didn't have to go." *To leave me.*

"I'll be back before Althea has finished her current novel."

The next kisses trailed lower, over Jane's shoulders and neck. Quinn Wentworth could conjure magic with his mouth, leaving a path of heat and languor.

Jane's breasts were sensitive, and Quinn was careful, caressing rather than grabbing. Jane reciprocated by exploring his chest, tracing scars, finding a ticklish spot on his ribs. He caught her hand when she would have dared investigate lower.

"On your side, Jane."

Lovemaking spoon-fashion had been an early addition to Jane's wifely vocabulary. Several times she hadn't even been fully awakened to accommodate a husband intent on an early morning tup. She complied with Quinn's suggestion, though disgruntlement threaded through the moment.

She wanted to see Quinn's face when they made love.

"Here." Quinn passed her a pillow. "For your knee."

How could he know she was more comfortable with something under her knee? The midwife had suggested a creative use of pillows, and the improvement in Jane's rest had been significant.

"Thank you."

Quinn draped himself around her from behind, a large, warm, solid presence. Jane could lean against him and truly relax as his hand drifted from her neck to her shoulders to her back to her derriere.

"I want to touch you too, Quinn."

"Time for that later."

He was tall enough to be able to both kiss Jane and insinuate a hand between her legs. She wasn't on her back—Quinn was everywhere supporting her, and yet, she was frustrated too.

She could not touch him, other than to run a hand over his muscular flank or wrap her fingers around his wrist.

He took that frustration and used it to enflame her longing for him. He teased, he explored, he kissed, and caressed, until Jane was panting and writhing against his hand. She'd never been this bothered previously, this desperate.

She expected Quinn to slip himself inside her at any moment—*now* would do nicely—and ease the ache he'd built, to *make love* with her. His fingers were slick between her legs, almost penetrating, then dancing away.

He did something—the merest whisper of a touch—and lightning struck Jane from within.

"That's it, then," he murmured against her neck. "I have ye now."

Lightning could strike twice, and three times, and as often as Quinn Wentworth chose to make it happen. He set up a rhythm that counterpointed Jane's breathing and the undulations of her hips, until all of her focus centered on where Quinn touched her.

Pleasure ambushed Jane, a breathtaking gift cascading through her, a shock and a wonder.

Also a revelation. She lay panting against Quinn, his hand a comfort over her sex. Her heartbeat throbbed beneath that hand, while her mind was flung to the farthest, brightest corners of creation.

Quinn kissed her temple. "Will ye survive?" He was pleased with himself, the great beast.

Jane heaved over to lie against him. She was pleased too, but he was leaving in the morning, and the moment presented opportunities that might not return for weeks.

"I have questions, Quinn."

The self-satisfaction sighed out of him. "Will they keep, those questions? After such pleasures, you've earned a respite."

Ah, a respite. He wasn't through, then. "Yes, they'll keep. Suffice it to say..."

He kissed her, and Jane kissed him back, even as whatever thought she'd been about to express—pity for her first husband, gratitude to her second—flew out of her head. She fell asleep cradled in Quinn's arms, warm, wonderstruck, and determined to have some answers.

* * *

Quinn's early morning escape was thwarted by nothing less than the hand of God, or so it felt when Reverend Winston was ushered into the breakfast parlor by a bleary-eyed Kristoff.

"Good morning," Quinn said, as Kristoff laid another setting to the left of the head of the table, Jane's customary place being to Quinn's right. "I hope you'll join me for a meal."

Winston wore his usual rumpled, righteous mien. The breakfast parlor was redolent of warm toast and bacon, though, and the reverend took the proffered chair at his host's left hand.

"A cup of tea wouldn't go amiss," Winston said. "A visit from my prodigal daughter wouldn't go amiss either."

False paternal martyrdom was a sure way to drive Quinn onto the Great North Road, but Winston was family now, and he had answers to questions Quinn hadn't been able to put to Jane.

"Newlyweds," Quinn said. "We're an inconsiderate lot. Then too, Jane needs her rest."

Kristoff put a plate of steaming eggs and bacon before the reverend. Quinn passed over the butter, full pot of tea, and the rack of toast, then flicked a glance at his footman. Kristoff withdrew and closed the door.

"How is my Jane Hester?" Mr. Winston asked. "A father worries."

This father had been waiting in his musty garret for more than two weeks for Jane to crawl home. Quinn had taken a solitary tour of Jane's former abode when Winston had been off dispensing bibles and blame and the landlady had been at market. The upper apartment was the last, painfully tidy stop before the coach to penury reached its destination. The landlady's quarters on the ground floor had been more commodious.

Quinn's subsequent interview with the neighborhood pawnbroker had been illuminating.

"Jane is coping with much change," he said. "My family

has not had a genteel guiding hand, ever, and neither have I.
If you'd tell me about Jane's mother, I'd be grateful."

Jane had mentioned her mother only in passing, and those
mentions had been shadowed with grief.

Winston put down his fork. "I have a miniature." He withdrew a small likeness from his coat pocket, the typical oval
in a cheap gilt frame. "That's my Hester. Sweetest woman
God ever made, taken much, much too soon."

The face smiling up at Quinn was indeed sweet. Kindness
shone from her eyes, as did a glimmer of humor. She resembled Jane about the mouth and chin, though her gaze lacked
the snapping alertness Jane turned on the world.

Quinn passed the miniature back. "Would you allow me
to have a copy made of this painting?"

The portrait disappeared into Winston's right pocket.
"That is my only likeness of my Hester. I don't typically let
it out of my sight."

"You would be welcome to watch the artist at work. He
wouldn't even need to remove the painting from the frame."

Still, Winston's gaze was guarded. "I'll think about it.
When will you bring Jane around to visit her old papa?"

The urge to coerce was instinctive: *When will you allow
her to have an image of her mother?* In the alternative,
Quinn could nick that portrait from Winston's pocket without the pastor even realizing the painting had been removed
from his person.

Would serve the old hypocrite right too, though Winston's devotion to his wife's memory seemed genuine.

"I'll ask you again at a more opportune time," Quinn said.
"I suspect a copy of that little painting would be the finest
wedding gift you might offer Jane."

Another fine gift would be one genuine smile, aimed at
Jane with sincere approval. Her words came back to Quinn:

I love your smile. That Jane should be starved for smiles was wrong.

That Quinn was eyeing the clock, hoping to leave for York before Jane rose, was more wrong still. He wanted a few days to enjoy the memories Jane had given him before he submitted to her interrogation.

"I hear you've assumed a title," Winston said around a mouthful of bacon. "A lofty title. News is all over the prison, and the guards say it's true. My Jane is a duchess."

She's not your Jane. "The fellows at the College of Arms tell me I'm stuck with the title, and with the debts amassed by the entailed estate." Which were, indeed, substantial.

Under Duncan's supervision, two clerks were reviewing the ducal ledgers for fraudulent charges, double entries, overcharges, and bookkeeping "errors." In Quinn's estimation, the estate had been pilfered by disloyal subordinates more than it had been mismanaged by the aging titleholder. When the old fellow had died, the pilfering had expanded into outright pillaging.

Constance and Althea would *delight* in cleaning house at the family's newly acquired seat in Yorkshire, though that would leave Quinn more privacy with Jane in London, which would not do.

"I could use a spot of marmalade." Winston applied butter to his toast as if caulking a ship of the line for a voyage to China. "A duchess should have pin money."

Quinn's eggs curdled in his belly. "I'm well aware of what I owe my wife."

He owed her the truth regarding his past and his plans, likely the only debt he'd never repay. He rose to retrieve more bacon from the sideboard for his guest.

Winston aimed the butter knife at Quinn. "I am here as Jane's father, to ensure those responsibilities are generously met. You, by contrast, took advantage of a grieving young woman's disordered thinking, the better to enjoy her favors when your circumstances were dire. You all but made a harlot of my daughter, man's capacity for selfish pleasures being undaunted even by the prospect—"

"Shut yer filthy mouth, old man."

Winston set down the knife. "You reveal your true colors, Mr. Wentworth."

"When you sit at my table, you will refer to me and to your daughter as Your Grace. If you ever again use the word 'harlot' in the same house where my duchess dwells, I will do you the courtesy of teaching you to fly out of windows, like the winged angels whom you will never meet. You come here pretending to ask after Jane, but it's her coin that interests you. How much do you need?"

"How dare you?" Winston retorted. "Accusing me, Jane's father and only living relative, of having no more—"

Quinn snatched the carving knife from the ham platter and hurled the blade such that it embedded itself into the table two inches from Winston's elbow.

"How much?"

Winston's gaze went from Quinn's face to the hilt vibrating subtly amid the lace runners, crystal, and silver. The bombast went out of the reverend, replaced with fear and what might have been bewilderment. He'd scurry off to his holy callings, then gather his courage and his favorite self-deceptions, and be back spouting his pious venom.

"I wanted to redeem a cedar chest from the pawnshop," Winston said. "Belonged to my wife. I thought one day, Jane might...that is..."

The chest was in the housekeeper's parlor, awaiting a thorough cleaning. Quinn hoped to locate a hand mirror, two shawls, a jewelry box, and pearl earbobs as well.

"Last chance," Quinn said. "How much?"

"Five pounds."

"You need that five pounds because you are in arrears on your rent," Quinn said, setting the plate of bacon before his father-in-law. "You haven't paid the coal man since the first of the year, and your credit at the chophouse is gone. Instead of honest work carrying hod or tutoring the sons of merchants, you make a pestilence of yourself among the most unfortunate creatures ever to be incarcerated. You cling to your respectability like a terrier with a rat. Be glad I value that respectability for Jane's sake."

A soft click warned Quinn to leave unspoken the remaining half dozen dire admonitions he had for the reverend.

"Good morning." Jane stood in the doorway, looking pale and severe. "Papa, good of you to call. Your Grace, I trust I'm not interrupting."

Quinn had hoped to slip away before Jane rose, or, failing that, hoped to take a pleasant leave of her. Ah, well. So much for hoping, as usual.

"I'll be on my way soon."

She didn't so much as look at him, but she'd troubled over her appearance this morning. For Jane, this meant a slightly more intricate braid in her coiffure, and a lace shawl rather than the wool she normally favored.

And about her eyes, a surprising touch of self-consciousness.

Quinn held her chair and bent to brush a kiss to her cheek. "You're looking well this morning."

"Thank you."

Across the table, Winston ploughed through the remainder of his eggs. He might have made a grab for the rest of the toast but Quinn set the rack before Jane's plate, along with the butter and the honeypot. From the sideboard he retrieved a cellar of ground cinnamon mixed with sugar, for this was how Jane liked her toast.

"Tea, madam?"

"Please."

She typically took the first cup plain. If that sat well, she would add a dash of sugar to her subsequent two cups. Quinn liked knowing these details about her, though he wondered what details she was hoarding up about him.

Threatens old men simply for being lazy and selfish.

Leaves a new wife to fend for herself among the Visigoths barely a fortnight after the wedding.

Avoids intimacies with said wife, though that nearly costs him his sanity.

Hurls carving knives across the breakfast table.

"How are you, Papa?" Jane asked.

"Quite busy," Winston replied. "I've been asked to substitute for Mr. Carruthers on the last Sunday of the month. The sermon topic is turning the other cheek."

"One of your favorites," Jane said, sprinkling cinnamon over her toast. She murmured appropriately as her father sailed forth on a wind of scripture and self-importance, and Quinn stayed long enough to know that Jane's toast agreed with her this morning.

And then, lest he put off leaving for another day, he rose. "I must be on my way. I'll bid you both farewell."

Jane stood as well, too fast for Quinn to hold her chair. "I'll see you out. Papa, I'll be right back."

The coachman had been walking the team up and down the street for the past twenty minutes. Tarrying with Jane wasn't on Quinn's schedule.

"You needn't see me off," he said. "You and your father doubtless have catching up to do."

Jane turned on him that patient, determined expression

that wasn't so much a glower as it was a portent of doom. She was mentally counting to three. He was coming to know the look.

"Don't be silly, Your Grace. A wife wishes her husband farewell."

Well, damn. Quinn bowed her through the door, pausing only to offer his hand to his father-in-law and give the reverend a pat on the shoulder in passing.

"Good to see you, sir," Quinn said, "and you will please forgive my earlier harsh words. I am protective of my wife's peace."

"As well you should be," Winston replied around a mouthful of bacon. "Good day."

Jane would have walked Quinn to the front door, but he stopped with her at the foot of the stairs.

"Duncan will take the coach to the bank," Quinn said. "I'm leaving through the wine cellar. A precaution, only."

Jane leaned close, as if inspecting the folds of Quinn's cravat. "Papa asked for money, didn't he? That was doubtless difficult for him."

"He was working up to it. You are not to pass him a single farthing, Jane. He's in good health, he's literate, and I won't let him starve or jeopardize his respectability. Somebody in your family needs to at least look the genteel part."

Jane braced her forehead against Quinn's chest. "I'm sorry. He wasn't always like this."

Time to go, before she could change the sub—

"I'll miss you," she added, kissing Quinn's cheek. "And I'll dream of you. Very bad of me to drift off like that last night."

She was asking Quinn a question, and he needed to leave.

"Your father might have dropped this," Quinn said, withdrawing an oval miniature from his pocket. "That is your mother, isn't it?"

"Mama?" Jane took the portrait carefully, as if it might break when it had doubtless traveled safely in Winston's pocket for years. "I haven't seen this in ages. I thought he pawned it." She traced a finger over the glass as a tear trickled down her cheek. "The likeness is good. Very good."

"You should have a copy made before you return it. Your father would thank you. Little treasures have a way of going missing." Little treasures like Jane's entire inheritance from her mother, according to the pawnbroker.

Jane clasped the miniature to her heart. "Excellent suggestion."

"Duncan knows some artists. Consult with him, and now I really must be on my way." Quinn allowed himself one taste of Jane's lips—cinnamon and sweetness—and then he descended the steps two at a time.

Chapter Sixteen

"I give Quinn a head start," Duncan said, shrugging into his greatcoat. "Then I go to the bank in his place. Most will assume Quinn is the fellow climbing into the town coach and trotting up the steps to the bank's side entrance. He's an exceptionally wealthy man and exceptionally attached to his privacy. This is simply how he leaves London if he must travel on business."

Jane needed to get back to the breakfast parlor before Papa took to admiring the silver and forgetting that he'd slipped a place setting into his pocket. She also needed to take advantage of Duncan's willingness to talk.

"Does Quinn travel often?"

"Yes, and then he bides here in London for months at a time. I expect the dukedom will mean considerably more racketing about."

Duncan was nearly as tall as Quinn and equally broad-shouldered, but more civilized. Whereas Quinn's hair was sable, Duncan's was russet brown. Quinn's gaze was fierce, Duncan's watchful and intelligent. He tended more to leanness than muscle, but Jane suspected he'd be just as quick as Quinn with wits or fists.

She ought to like Duncan, for despite all the scrapping and bickering Quinn's siblings did, she liked them. He was certainly attractive, though where Quinn and Stephen unapologetically attired themselves in Bond Street splendor, Duncan's clothing was noteworthy for its plainness. No trio of gold watch chains, no elegant silver cravat pin or nacre buttons—nothing that called attention to him.

And yet, in his sober demeanor, in his understated dress, in his dedication to developing Stephen's prodigious intellect, Duncan had a dignity all his own. The siblings teased each other, and they even occasionally twitted Quinn, but they did not make jests at Duncan's expense—ever.

Someday, when Jane was feeling very brave, she'd ask him why his career with the church had been cut short, and if tutoring Stephen was a penance or a reward.

"Does Quinn take along any of his trusty running footmen when he travels?" She kept her voice down lest Papa eavesdrop while he pilfered the silver.

"Two, and they are both armed, as are his outriders and grooms. They know you expect His Grace to be guarded at all times. The traveling coach is a rolling arsenal and he changes teams frequently. He'll come home, Jane, safe and whole. He always does."

Jane refrained from pointing out the obvious: Quinn had nearly gone to his celestial reward a fortnight past.

"Shall I bid the reverend good day?" Duncan asked. "One doesn't want to give offense, and he has become family of a sort."

Was there no privacy in this house? "You'd best not. Papa

exerts gravity in the form of other people's good manners, and then you've spent half your morning listening to his well-rehearsed thoughts on woman's responsibility for original sin. Can you have a copy made of this painting for me?"

She showed Duncan the miniature, though she resented that another's gaze should fall on Mama's countenance when Jane had been deprived of that pleasure for so long.

"How soon do you need it?" No comment on the resemblance to Jane, though Duncan flicked a speculative gaze over her features.

"The sooner the better, and let's have two copies while we're about it." Because Papa lost what mattered to Jane most and took her treasures and memories 'round to the pawn shop when she was napping.

Jane told herself that Mama's personal effects evoked painful memories for Papa, and that Mama would have wanted him to be happy. Those excuses had worn thin before Mama's second-best shawl had disappeared.

Duncan pulled on his gloves, the briskness of the gesture reminiscent of Quinn departing for a day at the bank.

"Quinn has brought the reverend's accounts up to date," he said, "including his rent and his arrears at the chophouse. Your father is also to be paid a quarterly stipend. You must promise me you'll act surprised if Quinn ever tells you that himself."

Duncan's tone was severe, though in his blue eyes Jane detected a hint of devilment. He was *teasing her*, as none of the other Wentworths had, taking her into his confidence and treating her as family. The tears that had started when she'd seen her mother's portrait threatened again.

"I'm not surprised at Quinn's generosity, though I'm very, very pleased."

"Quinn's generosity required a bit of prompting," Duncan

said, taking up a gold-tipped walking stick. "Though only a bit. You would never have asked Quinn to look after your father, which point was made to Quinn at a moment when he was receptive to suggestions."

He tapped his hat onto his head, and that gesture too put Jane in mind of Quinn.

"You are a new recruit to the Wentworth ranks," Duncan said. "They are my cousins and I love them dearly, but five years after joining this household, I still often feel as if we must be from different species, much less from different families."

He surveyed himself in the mirror above the sideboard, and in the angle of his hat, in his posture, and in his grip on the walking stick, he was every inch a Wentworth male.

"I feel it only fair to warn you," he went on, "Quinn cannot abide a sneak. The first time you pawned a bracelet, he'd notice, and there wouldn't be a second time."

Jane owned no bracelets, and Duncan's gaze held no mischief now. He was warning Jane not to violate Quinn's trust—and perhaps not to violate his own—though the warnings were unnecessary.

"Hold still," she said, freeing a fold of Duncan's cravat from the lapel of his coat. "You don't want to arrive to the bank wrinkled...." She gave his chest a pat. "Better." For an instant Jane wondered if she'd given offense, so pure was the consternation in Duncan's gaze.

"Thank you." He tucked the miniature into his pocket. "Stephen is looking forward to your first lesson in the effective use of firearms later today."

"Then Stephen is bound to be disappointed. I'll see you at supper." For Duncan always attended family meals, usually in the capacity of referee or scorekeeper. One wondered what Duncan truly thought and felt. With the younger Wentworths, one *never* wondered.

"I'd best protect the cutlery from Papa's admiration," Jane said. "Until this evening."

Duncan bowed and strode for the front door, and even in his walk he had something of Quinn's air. Perhaps that was appropriate. If anything happened to Quinn and Stephen—angels forefend!—Duncan would become the Duke of Walden.

* * *

"Will it stink like this all the way to York?" Ned asked.

"You're smelling Smithfield Market," Quinn replied, as the coach turned onto St. John Street. "In the course of a year, a million sheep and tens of thousands of cattle are penned on less than five acres."

"Bloody lot of sheep shit," Ned said, wrinkling his nose. "Whose idea was it to put a livestock market in the middle of London?"

Long ago, Quinn's view of life had been equally circumscribed by inexperience. He'd known his neighborhood, then his town. The transition to working at the Tipton estate in the Yorkshire countryside had left him feeling very much a man of the world.

And then, very much a fool.

"The market was established when London was still contained within the City walls," Quinn said, "hundreds of years ago. I expect it will move eventually." Somebody would make a lot of money when that happened.

Ned's nose remained pressed to the glass. "Tell 'em to move it downwind."

That commonsense suggestion bore the inklings of profit. The livestock market would be moved someday not because of the stink—Londoners were far from delicate when it came to the city's myriad stenches—but because slaughtering that many animals created the sort of waste that threatened water supplies and public health.

Had Quinn not left Jane less than a quarter hour earlier, he'd have turned his mind to where—downwind of London—a livestock market might ideally be located, and how he could quietly buy that land now. Such a purchase might not yield a profit for decades, but profit and patience often went hand in hand.

Instead of land development schemes, Quinn's head was full of regrets. He wished he'd lingered with Jane in bed. He wished he'd not left her to deal with her father alone. He wished he'd lectured Duncan at length—at greater length—about the need to ease Jane's transition into a family that knew nothing of gentility.

"You miss her?" Ned asked, breathing on the window, then drawing his finger through the condensation.

"Would you like to ride on the roof, Ned?" Quinn used his most quelling tones, which would have had any bank employee trembling in his boots. "Two hundred miles of stink, wind, and rain might teach you to keep impertinent questions to yourself."

Ned wiped his palm over the window, erasing the lopsided *W* he'd drawn. "I miss her. Miss Jane is that sort of female. I hear her in me head, reminding me to wash behind me ears. I feel her hand brushing the hair outta me eyes."

Oh, yes. Jane was *that sort of female*. "Stop smudging up my windows and pay attention."

Ned grinned and breathed on the window again, but before he made another streak, Quinn snatched him onto the opposite bench.

"You will comport yourself according to my rules, Ned, or I'll toss you out of the coach now. You can go back to

sleeping in church doorways and hoping you don't wake up
in a brothel."

Quinn had had that experience when he'd been about
Ned's age. His abductors had neglected to tie his feet, leaving him free to break a window and hare off.

I hate that I must return to the north. The Walden ducal
seat was not far from York, and even closer to the Tipton estate.

"The abbesses won't get me," Ned said, kicking his boots
against the bench. "I'm too fast." His gaze had gone flat,
suggesting he too had had a near miss.

"They can make another attempt, so test my patience at
your peril. While we're traveling, you don't refer to me as
Mr. Wentworth or Your Grace. You don't gossip with the
stable boys. You keep your gob shut or I'll leave you in
Yorkshire, where winter starts in September and doesn't let
up until May."

A child living on the streets knew to fear the cold.

Ned popped off the bench and resumed peering out the
window. "Miss Jane would fetch me home, and she'd ring a
peal over your head if you left me behind."

True, and a comforting thought. "I've faced the hangman,
young Edward. A nattering female holds no terror for me."
Not that Jane nattered. She chided, she teased, she sighed,
she counted to three, and she yawned.

She nestled against her husband in the night, as trusting
as a kitten and a hundred times more dear.

"What's York like?"

Like an ancient slice of hell, for a hungry boy with no
safe place to lay his head. The enormous edifice known as
the York Minster cast its shadow over the entire city, a loom-
ing presence that marked a site even the Romans had used as
a gathering place.

Quinn hated the damned thing, hated its sheer size and durability.

"York is a cathedral town, with Roman fortifications, much like London and St. Paul's, though York Minster is older than the present version of St. Paul's by centuries. Why the Vikings didn't knock the damned walls down and use the lot to build a mead hall, I've no idea."

Ned continued to gawk as they crossed the New Road. Stretches of open fields ran between groups of houses, and the great bustling institution of the Angel Inn held pride of place on the corner.

The empty feeling in Quinn's belly grew worse. Perhaps he could send Jane a letter or two, though what could he say? *Don't forget your ginger biscuits in the morning. Trust no one except family.*

"You'd have the barbarians tear down God's house?" Ned asked.

"You see the Minster as God's house. I see it as a place I wasn't allowed to set foot on even the coldest winter nights, when I was no older than you. I see it as a fantastic monument to man's conceit, upon which many a coin has been spent while children starved in its shadow."

In every regard, the thought of York during daylight left Quinn feeling hemmed in, cramped, and uncomfortable. At night, the town expanded. All the winding streets, narrow alleys, and crumbling walls became so much darkness, where possibilities multiplied, most of them lucrative and dangerous, and some of them even legal.

"Stick close to me on this journey, Ned." Quinn pushed the hair away from the boy's eyes. "Don't wander off, don't explore, don't investigate."

"Right," Ned said, wiggling out of fussing range. "Not my town, not my turf. Best watch meself."

"Watch me," Quinn said, as the coach picked up speed. "Don't let me out of your sight if we go abroad. If John Coachman summons you to the livery, you stick to him like a cocklebur."

"Ned Cocklebur. I like it."

The boy would likely vanish a dozen times in the course of the journey. Jane would kill Quinn if anything happened to Ned, assuming Quinn lived long enough to return to her side.

* * *

When Jane rejoined her father, Kristoff was at attention by the sideboard, and no carving knife protruded from the breakfast table. Very little of the bacon had survived Papa's appetite, which suggested a significant portion was secreted in a table napkin somewhere on his person.

"What has you out and about so early today, Papa?" Jane asked, as Kristoff held her chair. Why did Papa never observe that courtesy?

"The Lord's work, of course. We can't all slumber the morning away, Jane Hester. Your husband lacks couth."

"If Quinn's manner was less than genteel, he was doubtless sorely provoked."

Papa chewed with the focus of a squirrel, gesturing with his toast to hold the floor. Mama had scolded him for that very mannerism many times. Jane sent up a prayer for patience.

"A man who will hurl knives at family members is no fit influence on my grandchild, Jane Hester." The same knife now lay innocently beside the ham, and Kristoff's expression was professionally blank. "I cannot dissuade you from giving credence to this farce of a marriage, but I intend to be a conscientious guardian of your offspring's morals. Make no mistake about that."

Papa had also appointed himself guardian of the butter. Jane took what remained in the butter dish and dabbed it on her toast.

"You will always be welcome to visit, Papa." She forced herself to recite that invitation, though the habit of deference was growing harder to maintain. *He means well, and he has suffered much. One... two...*

"To visit? Jane, do you forget the terms of your late husband's will?"

"You claimed I was too overset by grief to make sense of it, so of course I'm not familiar with every detail. I inherited what few possessions Gordie had, and those promptly disappeared to the pawnshop." Without her permission, not that Gordie had had much. Still, his regimental sword might have meant something to his only child.

Or to his grieving, overset widow.

"One doesn't provide a soldier a proper Christian burial without paying for the service. Will you leave me any butter?"

Kristoff set a fresh pat by Papa's elbow.

"Thank you, Kristoff," Jane said. "If Gordie intended to direct the details of this child's upbringing, he should have had the decency to remain alive and be a father."

Papa set down his toast and bowed his head. Jane took a sip of her tea rather than ask what troubled him. A frustrated thespian inclination troubled him, certainly, and, considering how much food he'd consumed, his belly might also be protesting.

"Jane, I will overlook your disrespectful tone because your condition is delicate and you are newly widowed. Trust me when I assure you that Gordie MacGowan expected me to serve as guardian of his child, should the Almighty grant the infant life. Reconcile yourself to respecting your late husband's wishes in at least this regard, and know that you too will always be welcome under my roof."

He aimed a gentle smile at her, and Jane nearly pitched the honeypot at him.

"Very generous of you, Papa, though I'm sure my current husband will be happy to provide for the child whom my previous husband left half orphaned."

"Your current husband is a barbarian. No grandchild of mine—"

The first cup of tea was sitting well enough, but the conversation was stirring in Jane a long-simmering rage. Papa could no more provide for a grandchild than he'd been able to provide for a daughter, and that was not Quinn Wentworth's fault.

"My husband might lack couth in your opinion," Jane said, arranging her toast on her plate, "but he has every bit of my loyalty. Because you are apparently out of sorts today, I'll leave you to finish your meal in peace. Feel free to call again anytime, Papa, but don't expect me to listen to you insult my husband."

Jane gathered up her tea and toast, sent Kristoff a visual warning not to leave the room until Papa was done gorging himself, and took her breakfast up to her apartment.

She had wanted to start the day with her husband, possibly even making love with her husband. She had wanted to apologize for falling asleep. She had wanted to tell Quinn that her rest had been sound for the first time in weeks, and that she would miss him.

Her toast was half gone before she admitted that under ideal circumstances, she would have asked Quinn to write to her—even demanded a note or two from him. York was hundreds of miles away, and the king's highway was dangerous.

A wife worried.

Jane ate the rest of her toast, mentally composing a letter to Quinn and getting nowhere. *Why didn't you finish what we started? Why not waken me with kisses? When will you come home?* Provoking a disagreement with her husband would be foolish and pointless, so she didn't even try to put that sentiment in writing. *Let bygones be bygones.*

The maids had yet to tidy up the bedroom, so Jane took her plate to the sideboard to be collected later. She washed her hands behind the privacy screen and reached for the cloth bunched beside the basin.

Somebody had already used it, though not recently. The cloth was half damp, half stiff. Jane shook it out, and a peculiar odor assailed her. Nothing else had the same smell, one she'd come across only after taking a husband.

She dropped the cloth in the basin and wiped her hands with her handkerchief.

At some point last night, Quinn had spent his seed behind this privacy screen rather than make love with his wife. Was that consideration, cowardice, or something else? Jane didn't like it, whatever the reason.

She rinsed the rag, wrung it nearly dry, and hung it on the towel rack. The day, which had begun with the lovely discovery of Mama's miniature, turned sour.

Jane got halfway through devising a schedule for the maids. Her progress had been slow, frequently interrupted by the necessity to pace and resent Quinn's odd behavior, when Stephen wheeled himself through the door, leaving it open behind him.

"Good morning, Jane. Are you ready to learn how to blow out a man's brains?" His question bloomed with eager good cheer.

An hour ago, her answer would have been different. Now

she was more aware of how little she understood about her husband, and how dependent she was on his honor and generosity.

And she was furious with her meddling, posturing father. "I am prepared to learn how to handle a gun. The knowledge is doomed to remain theoretical, though one should not neglect any educational opportunity."

"Spoken like a Wentworth," Stephen said, "and Althea and Constance can't wait to get you started with the knives."

"I have always appreciated a good, sharp blade. Let's be about it, shall we?"

Chapter Seventeen

"How can it take years to find the heir to a dukedom?" Joshua asked, tossing a pencil onto the ledger before him. "Dukes die, and old dukes die fairly predictably. The College of Arms can't say they were taken by surprise."

"They can," Duncan replied, "in this case. The old duke had heirs, a trio of second cousins, all between the ages of forty and fifty. One was married without issue, the other two bachelors in good health."

"What happened to the heirs?"

Duncan rose despite a protest from his right knee, a legacy from too many winter afternoons spent kneeling on the stone floor of Uncle's church.

"Bad luck happened, or so we are to believe. One bachelor was run down by a runaway team on his way home from Sunday services. The other bachelor had an ingrown toenail that turned putrid, but he refused surgery. The married fellow succumbed to a heart seizure soon after losing both of his younger brothers."

Joshua pinched the bridge of his nose. "When a dukedom is going begging, bachelorhood is a singularly stupid indulgence, and that is a prodigious streak of *bad luck* for one family."

Duncan refrained from pointing out that Joshua, wealthier than many dukes, was himself unmarried, and that Quinn Wentworth had enjoyed an even more prodigious streak of *good luck*, barring recent events.

"My numbers tally thus far," Duncan said, "but they are curious numbers."

He and Joshua had closeted themselves in the partners' conference room and each taken a year's worth of the ducal estate ledgers. The family seat was not far from York, though the dukedom held properties in several different counties. Each property had kept its own set of books, and the steward at the family seat—Mr. Harcourt Arbuthnot—had kept a general ledger.

Until he'd absconded for the Antipodes several months ago, likely taking the last of the Walden fortune with him.

"My numbers tally as well," Joshua said, "but who pays a Yorkshire housemaid twenty pounds a year?"

"Nobody, unless she's doing considerably more than polishing the silver."

Joshua picked up the pencil and threaded it over, under, and through his fingers. "The former duke was ancient, and he dwelled mostly at the Berkshire property. That well-paid army of maids in Yorkshire wasn't dusting and polishing him."

"Arbuthnot lived at the Yorkshire estate. The maid is probably on his arm as we speak, enjoying a life of ease in New South Wales. She might well be wearing some of the Walden family jewels too."

Joshua's pencil stilled, the point end protruding between his third and fourth fingers. "Leaving Quinn to put the whole mess to rights. I want Mrs. Hatfield to look over these books."

Mrs. Hatfield hadn't said more than six words to Duncan at any one time. She prowled the bank like a cat that had caught a whiff of a mouse in the environs of the larder, her fingers ink-stained, her spectacles spotless.

"The figures tally," Duncan said. "I thought auditors looked for figures that don't add up."

"Mrs. Hatfield has an instinct for what's going on behind the numbers. She'll spot when the maid's salary was increased, put that together with the duke's health failing as indicated by increased physician's bills, and establish cause and effect in a manner that boggles the mind."

Stephen had the same unnerving propensity, which made maintaining any sort of privacy around him—any sort of secrecy—nearly impossible.

"You admire this about her."

"I am in awe of that woman, and not a little intimidated."

Comforting, to know that something or someone could intimidate Joshua Penrose.

"You would not take her away from bank business simply to indulge idle curiosity about embezzlements of yesteryear." And the year before that, for several years before the previous duke's demise.

When Duncan and Stephen had discussed the ducal succession months ago, the fate of the real assets had been of particular interest to Stephen, while for Duncan, the peregrinations of the title itself had been fascinating.

Quinn's good luck truly *was* astonishing.

"Timing is everything," Joshua said, tossing the pencil in the air and catching it. "The estates were plundered, systematically and thoroughly, until three months ago, at which time Arbuthnot decamped in the dead of night. I suspect we'll find the stewards at the other estates all similarly slunk into the hedgerows about the same time. How did Arbuthnot know that the College was on the trail of an heir? He might have instead assumed the estate was languishing for the mandatory seven years prior to reverting to the Crown."

The conference room abruptly felt too close, too cut off from natural light and fresh air. "Perhaps he didn't know, perhaps he'd reached the limit of his greed, but what matters now is that he's gone and the debts remain—and that Quinn is alive."

Joshua tossed the pencil again. "Greed has no limit, no expiration date, much like Quinn's need for justice."

"For revenge, you mean."

The pencil rose in the air a third time, but Joshua let it fall to the ledger book, where it landed squarely in the crease of last year's journal.

"He was hanged, Duncan, for a crime he didn't commit. The College of Arms found him in the very nick. Five minutes later, two minutes later, and Stephen would be the duke."

Duncan closed the volume he'd been studying and began a slow circuit of the room. Sometimes his knee eased up with moderate activity. If bad luck were to befall Stephen, the title devolved to Duncan, another observation left unspoken.

"What's your point?"

"I have several. First, the College should not have taken years to find Quinn Wentworth. Jack Wentworth has been dead for nearly a decade, and you can still find people in York who spit at the mention of his name. He was notorious in a relatively small town. Why did it take so long to find Quinn?"

"Quinn no longer dwells in Yorkshire, and few would connect Jack Wentworth's grubby boy with your business partner." Quinn didn't hide his antecedents, but he assuredly did not advertise them.

"Somebody connected them in time for Arbuthnot and his merry band of felons to abscond before Quinn assumed the title."

Duncan's knee had gone from twinging to throbbing. "You think somebody threw the College of Arms off the scent, and then warned Arbuthnot when the herald doubled back and picked up Quinn's trail. Who would be in a position to do that?"

Who indeed.

"The aristocracy is inbred," Joshua said, "especially in the north, where titles are few and ancient. A countess with blunt to spare could easily keep track of who had called on the vicar, who had nosed about the parish records of births, deaths, and marriages. I can guarantee you she's kept track of Quinn. Arbuthnot might have piked off in an abundance of caution. More likely he was warned by a friendly neighbor."

Duncan resumed his seat and resigned himself to suffering until his knee was done lecturing him.

"Let's fetch Mrs. Hatfield, shall we? Your theory is fanciful at best, but it explains much, particularly if that neighbor was also benefitting from Arbuthnot's thievery."

"In other words, I'm right. Something stinks, all roads lead to York, and we've sent Quinn north with little more than a few grooms and a boy to guard his back."

"My money's on the boy," Duncan said. "He puts me in mind of Quinn at a younger age. Ferocious, principled in his way, and nobody's fool. Just like Quinn."

Though Quinn, for a time, had been the Countess of Tipton's very devoted fool.

* * *

"I see improvement," Stephen said. "We've been at this little more than a week, and already you have a good eye and a steady hand."

Althea had said something similar about Jane's use of knives. In both endeavors, aim was critical, because, as her tutors had explained, using the weapon meant giving away her location, and that meant greater risk of retaliation.

The weapon had thus best be employed effectively the first time. Jane had no objection to the theory, but having rejected the *lex talionis*, she wouldn't be carrying a knife or a gun on her person. An eye for eye left everybody blind, as Mama had often pointed out.

"I don't care for the noise of firearms," Jane said, "though hitting a target is gratifying."

She'd graduated to moving targets, and for that exercise, Stephen had taken her to some rural property on the edge of London. The footmen had set up jars suspended on ropes, which Stephen had them swing from overhanging branches.

As a way to pass the time, target practice distracted Jane from Quinn's absence, but each night she went home to a vast, empty bed, and equally vast worries. Where was Quinn—where was he really? What would he make of Papa's daft maunderings about assuming guardianship of Jane's child? What business required Quinn's remove from Town barely a fortnight after he'd been pardoned?

Were the grooms, Ned, and the footmen keeping Quinn in sight at all times?

Quinn's siblings worried as well, and thus Jane obliged

their need to instruct, arm, and protect her. All very different from how she'd envisioned married life, but not dull.

"Quinn would be proud of you," Stephen said, as the grooms gathered up the ropes, firearms, powder, and shot. "Give me that last pistol, Ivor."

The footman passed over the gun, a small, double-barreled weapon that would fit easily into a lady's reticule, then stepped back.

Safety mattered to Stephen, and thus Jane's first lessons had been simple: Always stand behind the shooter, always handle a gun as if it's loaded. Always. She moved behind Stephen, who surveyed the trees and hedges around them.

She hadn't seen him shoot previously, but she had seen him walk. With the aid of two canes, Stephen could navigate slowly, step by painful step. For these shooting expeditions, he chose that option while Ivor carried the chair behind him.

Stephen had settled into his chair, lips nearly white, and remained seated for the duration of today's lesson. He loaded the lady's pistol, took aim at some distant twig or branch, then, without warning, swung the pistol and fired such that a blooming sprig of honeysuckle dropped from over Jane's head to land at her feet.

He'd aimed *a loaded gun* in her direction and fired a bullet within inches of her head.

"Never relax around firearms, Jane." He fired the second bullet at a fencepost five yards away. "Never. They can misfire, land in the wrong hands, and as long as somebody—"

"How dare you?" Jane snapped, snatching up the murdered honeysuckle and pitching it at him. "You did that for the puerile pleasure of frightening me, you vile wretch. The risk you took with my life is inexcusable, and this is the last lesson I take from you."

She shook with a primal reaction that compelled her to get away, collapse, or strike back.

Ivor appeared at Jane's side. "Lord Stephen will apologize." His diction was perfect, right down to the *w*. His tone was arctic, worthy of Quinn.

"She needs to realize when she's not safe," Stephen shot back. "She needs to realize she's a Wentworth."

Jane marched up to him, Ivor hovering at her elbow. "You need to realize that a gentleman does not discuss a lady in the third person when she's participating in the conversation." She plucked the gun away and hoped Stephen's fingers were bruised in the process. "You further need to realize that I will not abandon your brother on a whim. I spoke vows, Stephen, and I keep my word. Quinn is honorable, he has been kind and decent to me, and he will always have my loyalty."

No sulky boy glared up at Jane, but rather a young man exercising a frightening degree of calculation.

"Quinn is not who or what you think he is," Stephen said. "He's my brother, but I owe you at least that much warning. Ivor, please escort the lady to the—"

Jane passed Ivor the gun and crossed her arms.

"I'll meet you at the coach," Stephen said, pushing to his feet and balancing on his canes.

Jane stood before him, unwilling to budge until she'd fired her own artillery. "Wentworths are stubborn because they've had to be, but you had no cause to upset me like that. You owe me an apology."

Ivor took the chair and left Stephen leaning on the canes. No pain showed in Stephen's gaze, only a long-cherished anger.

"I am sorry, dearest Jane. You were in no danger, and I meant well, but—"

"Must I teach you how a gentleman apologizes?" For she would if need be. She'd stand toe to toe with him until he toppled to the grass in a raging heap, and leave him there until winter before she'd relent one inch.

She who believed in turning the other cheek, in forgiving and forgetting, was angry enough to throw fragile blossoms and shout, which only made her doubly furious with Stephen.

And that, she divined between one breath and the next, was what he wanted. To test not her devotion to Quinn, but her respect for Quinn's maimed younger brother. Did she respect Stephen enough to hold him accountable for his actions?

"I'm trying to figure out what my sin was," he said, "so I can be at least somewhat sincere in my remorse."

The afternoon was waning, Jane was hungry, and the child was moving about, likely unhappy with the noisy target practice. Too blasted bad.

"Your sin was adding needlessly to my fears," Jane said. "I'm facing childbirth. Do you think the prospect of that excruciating and often fatal exercise fills me with good cheer? It's a miserable, lingering death, and would leave my child all but orphaned."

She paced away from him, battling the temptation to shout. "I'm afraid that my father, a bumptious, obnoxious bumbler who frequents jails and prisons, will fall prey to an illness as my mother did. He's a miserable excuse for a father, but the only blood relative I have. Then there's my husband, whom somebody has tried to kill, and who is even now attempting to reestablish normalcy by tending to business as usual. I have no time for your adolescent pride or its attendant histrionics, and I am in no way responsible for your ailments."

Stephen smiled at the golden eagles that formed the grips of his canes. "I'm sorry. I should not have aimed the gun anywhere near you, and it won't happen again."

"Better." Jane turned to stalk off toward the coach, but Stephen had put both canes in one hand, and caught Jane by the arm.

"I am sorry, and I should not have done what I did, but Jane, you should be a little bit afraid for yourself. Whoever brought Quinn low missed the mark, but only by merest chance. My brother is a duke now, and that might protect him or it might make him a more tempting target."

Jane took one of the canes. "Quinn's lofty station should make him even more intimidating than he already was, though what fool would challenge Quinn Wentworth even once, much less twice? Please take me home. I need to eat, and I've had enough drama for one day."

They made a slow progress to the coach, arm in arm, and were soon bumping and jostling back toward Town.

"How did you break your leg?" Jane asked.

"My own dear father broke my leg," Stephen said, "but let's save that charming recitation for another time. Enough drama for one day, right?"

She let him retreat into silence, because she grasped the important lesson of the day: A broken leg had likely been the least of Stephen's injuries.

Chapter Eighteen

"I saw the Minster in York," Ned announced. "It's ever so beautiful, with heaven-windows and echoes and no poor people. Himself said the Minster were there even when the Vikings ran the town."

Quinn let the child prattle on, because Ned's chattering provided a moment to study Jane. She was still at the Wentworth town house, which Quinn had not assumed would be the case.

She wore a claret-colored dress high enough at the waist to hide her condition, and her color was good. She'd kissed Quinn's cheek upon greeting him, but her mood had yet to make itself apparent.

Which suggested something other than jubilation at his return.

Quinn was furious, with himself, with anybody named Pike, with the Great North Road, and with God Almighty.

For the Countess of Tipton he reserved a special brand of ire that nearly equaled the hatred he'd felt toward his father.

"You were very kind to take Ned to see the Minster," Jane said. "Someday I'd like to see it."

"He didn't take me," Ned said, scuffing the toe of one boot with the other. "Mrs. Dougherty took me, and told me all about when himself were in service. He were a footman and a jolly good one. She were the housekeeper, and Miss Camellia were a maid."

"Ned, take yourself to the kitchen," Quinn said, as Jane peeled the greatcoat from his shoulders. "Regale the staff with your adventures, but for the love of God leave me in peace."

"Mrs. D said you were a footman to an earl's house, and nobody ever looked so fine in his livery as you did before you got old."

Where were the Vikings when a small boy needed carrying off? "The kitchen, Ned, and you will take a bath tonight."

"Tim takes baths, claims a young gent shouldn't smell like a shoat," Ned said, plucking an orange from the bowl on the sideboard. "Knows his letters, Tim does, and he's younger than me. Mrs. Dougherty is Tim's granny and she said nobody ever learned his letters faster than Quinn Wentworth, and it's a pity and a shame that—"

Quinn hauled the child up by the elbows and held him at eye level, the boy's feet dangling. "I desire privacy with my wife. Get ye gone."

"I'm gone," Ned said, tossing the orange in the air and catching it. "Ned Gone, that's me."

Jane stood holding Quinn's greatcoat, her expression puzzled. "The housekeeper taught you to read?"

"And write." *Thank God.* "Shall we go upstairs?" Where Quinn would not take a bath until he'd found a way to do so in solitude.

Jane hung the coat on a hook and joined him on the stairs. "Duncan had the miniature of my mother copied. The likeness is lovely."

"Has the reverend realized it's missing?"

"I had the original returned to him, and he's not paid another call." They reached the top of the steps, and Jane sent Quinn a measuring glance. She was doubtless gauging whether to inform him of some domestic disaster. Kristoff serving breakfast with gin on his breath, Constance wearing her nightgown to the supper table...

"I missed you," Jane said, kissing Quinn—on the mouth. "The bed is much larger without you in it."

Bloody hell, he'd missed her too. In one coaching inn after another, in the narrow bed under Mrs. Dougherty's eaves, along hundreds of miles of rutted roads, Quinn had missed his wife.

He let her wrap him in an embrace that felt all too right. "If you want to see the Minster, I'll take you there someday. It's impressive." That much, he could honestly say.

"Any edifice that has stood against vandals, neglect, Norse raiders, marching armies, more neglect, more marching armies, fire, reform, pillaging, and time itself has to be impressive—rather like you."

"My wife has grown fanciful in my absence."

"Your bath awaits," Jane said, twining her arm through his. "Come along and tell me if your business was successful."

Let the lying begin—again. "All went smoothly. My initial financial ventures were undertaken in York, and I keep some investments in the first bank to do business with me." Quinn had stopped to visit that bank for all of twenty minutes as an afterthought intended to give Ned an honest itinerary to boast of.

In other regards, the trip had been frustrating. Robert Pike was apparently in France, where Quinn could not easily follow him. Determining that much had taken tampering with the confidence of the posting inn's proprietor, dropping a few threatening hints, and listening to gossip at the pub frequented by Pike's brother—nothing illegal, fortunately.

"I'll likely need to travel again soon, Jane. A month-long stay at Newgate has left much to do, and a journey to France isn't out of the question."

In the middle of the corridor, Jane wrapped Quinn in a fierce hug. "I wish I could travel with you. Women do, you know, despite the approach of motherhood. I've always wanted to see Paris."

A knot gathered in Quinn's belly to go with the ache in his heart. "I can't speak French, Jane. Can't read or write it, and would not regard time on French soil as a holiday. I'll go if I must. I'd rather not." His siblings had all learned French, because Quinn had insisted they be educated properly, but he couldn't put them at risk of harm.

Jane opened the sitting room door. The tub sat by the hearth in the bedroom, with towels, soaps, and shaving kit, all arranged in anticipation of Quinn's ablutions.

"I'm fluent in French," she said. "My maternal grandmother was French and spent her last five years with us. She and Mama and I frequently resorted to French when we wanted to spare Papa our opinions. We can travel..."

Jane dropped Quinn's arm as four footmen, Susan, and Penny all trooped by carrying steaming buckets of water. They filed right back out again, leaving Quinn alone with his wife.

There was lying, and then there was deceiving. "Until this other situation is settled, Jane, you'll be safer here among my family."

"What other situation is there to settle?" she asked.

"You've been pardoned, we're married, I'm expecting a child, and life goes on."

She jerked the bow free on his shaving kit and unrolled the length of flannel. His razor gleamed silver in the firelight, as Jane tossed a handful of bath salts into hot water.

"Somebody tried to see me dead and disgraced, Jane. How can you expect me to ignore such a crime?"

The signature Wentworth scent rose from the bathwater, while Jane's aura of cheerful welcome faltered.

"I don't expect you to forget your ordeal, but vengeance solves nothing. You are a duke now, and anybody seeking to harm you should know that the peerage protects its own."

The peerage would rejoice to see Quinn Wentworth fail. "I'd rather not quarrel with you, Jane. We simply view the matter from different perspectives."

More to the point, Quinn didn't want to lose her. Didn't want to see that light of welcome permanently extinguished, didn't want to weather Jane's disappointment. She'd been disappointed by Gordie and the reverend, when both men ought to have been devoted to her happiness.

"Let's get you soaking while the water's hot," she said, "and you can tell me about your career in service. Here I've been thinking your household wants a guiding hand, while you know exactly how a staff ought to function, because you've seen the whole business from belowstairs."

She wouldn't leave him to bathe in peace. Weariness that had little to do with hundreds of miles of travel pressed on Quinn, weighting his limbs and his thoughts.

"My stint as a footman was years ago and is best forgotten. I've held many, many other jobs."

Jane tested the blade of his razor against her thumb. "Wearing livery is no disgrace, Quinn. Domestic service is honest work."

Someday, he'd tell her about the months working at Tipton Hall—the prettied-up version of his youth that Mrs. Dougherty was determined to recall.

Now, the simple sight of Jane, hair swept back in a tidy bun, hands graceful and competent, made him long to toss her on the bed and curl up next to her until her warmth, her scent, and her sweetness obliterated the memories even a few days in York had brought back.

"Domestic service is hard work," Quinn said, shrugging out of his coat. "I didn't last long."

He pretended to focus on unfastening his watch, sleeve buttons, and cravat pin, but he watched Jane in the cheval mirror. She dunked a ball of hard soap in the hot water, then closed her eyes and sniffed at the soap. Despite Quinn's guilt, frustration, and fatigue, the sight of Jane merely *sniffing soap* stirred erotic longings.

"When you were a footman, who was your employer?" she asked, unfastening her cuffs and rolling up her sleeves.

Her wrists—*her wrists*—made him hungry.

I am a man in trouble. "My employer was a mostly absentee lord who liked to roam around on the Continent and call himself a diplomat when he wasn't in London waltzing until all hours." Not a lie. "Might you have the kitchen send up a tray? Sandwiches and ale will do."

Jane used the speaking tube to order Quinn food he didn't want.

"I've eaten more beef in the past two weeks than in the previous year," she said. "The midwife told me to consume as much red meat as I can tolerate. I've become quite the carnivore."

"You do seem more vigorous." More at home handling Quinn's things, more the lady of his house. More married to him, God help her.

Having no alternative, Quinn went about removing his clothes and handing them to Jane, who hung up his shirt and folded his cravat as if husband and wife had spent the last twenty years chatting while the bath water cooled.

Quinn was down to his underlinen, hoping for a miracle, when Jane went to the door to get the tray. He used her absence to shed the last of his clothing and slip into the water. She returned bearing the food, which she set on the counterpane.

"I'm happy to wash your hair."

"I'll scrub off first. Tell me how you occupied yourself in my absence."

She held a sandwich out for him to take a bite. "This and that. The staff has a schedule, the carpets have all been taken up and beaten, Constance's cats are separated by two floors until Persephone is no longer feeling amorous."

Quinn was feeling amorous. He'd traveled to York and back, endured Mrs. Dougherty's gushing and Ned's endless questions—"Ned Nosy, that's me!"—and pondered possibilities and plots, but neither time nor distance had dampened his interest in his wife one iota.

Jane's fingers massaging his scalp and neck didn't help his cause, and when she leaned down to scrub Quinn's chest and her breasts pressed against his shoulders, his interest became an ache.

The water cooled, Jane fed him sandwiches, and Quinn accepted that the time had come to make love with his wife. He rose from the tub, water sluicing away, as Jane held out a bath sheet. Her gaze wandered over him in frank, marital assessment, then caught, held, and ignited a smile he hadn't seen from her before.

"Why Mr. Wentworth, you did miss me after all." She passed him the bath sheet, and locked the parlor door while Quinn stood before the fire and dried off.

"I missed you too," Jane said, taking the towel from him and tossing it over a chair. "Rather a lot."

Quinn made one last attempt to dodge the intimacy Jane was owed, one last try for honesty. "Jane, we have matters to discuss."

He could not tell her he was on Pike's trail, could not tell her he'd made a youthful fool of himself over a lonely countess, but perhaps if he told Jane more about life growing up in York, she might grasp why her husband was determined to have justice.

Not vengeance, justice.

"We'll talk later all you like, Quinn. For now, please take me to bed."

She kissed him, and he was lost.

* * *

Quinn's absence had given Jane two weeks to gain her footing with his family and his staff, and to rest. She'd needed the rest desperately and would need more in the months to come. The past year had gone from grueling to disappointing to heartbreaking, the burden of anxiety alone wearing down her energy and her composure.

While Quinn had traveled, she'd slept late, napped, and eaten regularly and well. She had pondered her situation, and made progress with her in-laws, though she was still angry with Stephen. Mostly, she'd missed her husband.

To see Quinn clearly aroused was reassuring and... stirring. To kiss him was invigorating in a way even sleep and good food could not be. Quinn was hale and whole, wonderfully male, and *hers*.

"Are we in a hurry?" he asked, drawing back half an inch.

Oh, *that smile*. "Yes. We are in a tearing hurry to get into the bed and... and..."

"Dance the mattress hornpipe?" he said, shrugging into a dressing gown. "Swive, fornicate, make the beastie with two backs?"

He was teasing her with his naughty talk, and Jane liked it. "Become as one flesh," she countered, turning and sweeping her hair off her nape. "Enjoy the pleasures of married life. Consummate our vows."

His fingers whispered across her neck, brushing stray locks of hair free of her hooks. "If you're sure, Jane, then I'm happy to climb into bed with you, but you're allowed to miss him, you know—your dashing soldier." Quinn's arms came around her from behind. "He was your first love. You needn't pretend otherwise."

She turned in Quinn's embrace, plunged into a depth of emotion she'd been ignoring. "It wasn't like that." She'd wanted her marriage to Gordie to be a romantic tale, more fool her.

Quinn put his lips near her ear. "He turned your head, filled your heart with foolish fancies. I envy him that."

Now was not the time to marvel at Quinn's perceptivity, or to explain to him that mostly, Gordie had filled Jane's head with nonsense. For he had, and only his death had allowed her to admit as much.

Lovely nonsense, and all the worse for being lovely. Then he'd been offended by some dandy's drunken insult, and his manly honor had cost him his life.

"Don't envy him," Jane said. "Don't even speak of him, please. Unlike you, he couldn't move past a bad moment and get on with life. You are my husband now, and it's you I've been missing."

Quinn regarded her, not the cold, analytical scrutiny she'd seen from him on other occasions, but an inspection tinged with concern. Then he enfolded her against the warm plane of his naked chest.

"I tried not to miss you," he said, fingers working at her hooks. "We've been married barely a month. I shouldn't know you well enough to miss you, and yet, I did. I missed the sound of you humming behind the privacy screen. Missed the way you keep the mattress bouncing all night. Missed the pretty, lacy, lady-clothes you leave draped about the bedroom."

Jane burrowed closer. "I slept in one of your shirts. I wanted your scent on me, and I think it helped settle my stomach."

"I'm a tisane for a dyspeptic expectant mother," Quinn said, giving her bum a pat. "My most interesting job yet. Let's get you out of this dress."

He was an aggravatingly competent lady's maid, and Jane could only imagine the coin in which he'd been paid for exercising those skills. He hung her dress in the wardrobe rather than draping it over a chair, her stays presented no challenge to him, and his touch with a hairbrush was gentle and soothing.

She was soon tucked under the covers while Quinn moved around the room blowing out candles.

"You are not to pleasure yourself behind the privacy screen," she said. "Not on my behalf." The heat of her blush should have ignited the bed curtains.

Quinn came to stand beside the bed. He hadn't banked the fire in the hearth, and thus he was illuminated in flickering shadows.

"Pleasure myself?" He opened his dressing gown and grasped himself in his right hand. "Like this, ye mean?" He stroked his arousal in slow, upward caresses, and Jane forgot all about blushes.

"You look wicked when you do that—wicked and luscious."

He laughed and climbed into the bed so he was crouching over Jane beneath the covers. "I am wicked, and you are wonderfully honest. Shall you be wicked with me, Mrs. Wentworth?"

He took her hand and wrapped it around his cock, which was new territory for Jane. Her knowledge of marital intimacy had been formed with a man who'd had more enthusiasm than self-restraint—or more selfishness than consideration.

"Do you like this?" she asked, sleeving Quinn's shaft, "or are you humoring me?"

"I'm not humoring you."

His voice had dropped to a growl, and when Jane would have asked another question—what did it feel like, to be caressed this way?—Quinn kissed her. He took her hands, lacing his fingers with hers and pressing her knuckles to the pillow on either side of her head.

"I want to touch you too," Jane said. "I need to touch you."

He trailed his open mouth along her shoulder and freed her hands.

Jane went exploring, down the smooth contours of Quinn's back, over lean hips and taut buttocks, up the stair-step of his ribs. He was everywhere masculine power, though with her fingertips she also traced the scars he'd collected.

A long, thin ridge across one shoulder blade, a puckered star on his biceps, a dent at the base of his spine. The wounds were many and varied, and she wished he'd trust her with each one's story.

Quinn bore her investigations, bracing himself over her on all fours, his forehead against the crook of her neck. His hair was damp and cool, his breath warm.

She had the sense her curiosity pleased him more than any erotic cleverness might have. "I am your wife," she said, kissing his temple. "Make me your lover."

He hitched nearer, and his cock brushed her belly. His kisses were soft and meandering—a failed attempt at distraction—and by lazy little nudges he eased inside of her.

Jane was sorting through ways to urge him *on*—she wasn't a blushing virgin—when she realized there was more of him than she'd anticipated. Much more.

"Breathe, Jane. We'll get there if we go easy."

She let out a breath, and Quinn sank deeper. He was diabolically patient, pausing to brush her hair from her brow with gentle fingers, to tug at her earlobe with his teeth. She was ready to pull his hair when it occurred to her she needn't remain passive.

She met his next languid thrust with a roll of her hips and Quinn gathered her close.

He liked when she moved with him. The tension in his body told her that; the slight rasp of his breathing confirmed it. His loving consumed her, narrowing her awareness to movement, pleasure, sensation, and *him*.

With the sliver of her mind that could still reason, she realized Quinn was waiting for her, monitoring her reactions even as he pushed her more and more deeply into yearning. He was being intimately considerate, and Jane was infinitely frustrated.

"You too, Quinn. *Together.*" Four words was the limit of her coherence. She locked her ankles at the small of his back and went after his monumental self-control with every physical argument she could command. Hips, hands, mouth, breath—everything.

The joining became fierce, and *mutual*, as pleasure cascaded through Jane in a roaring torrent. Quinn never sped up, never gave quarter, and thus Jane could not relent either. He groaned softly against her shoulder, then shuddered and shook as he hilted himself inside her. When Jane was convinced the storm had passed, Quinn ambushed her with another series of powerful thrusts, and she soared again, high and hard.

He was making a point, for which she'd thank him once she could form sentences again. In the absence of words, Jane settled for letting her legs fall open as she stroked his backside.

Quinn stayed with her for long, sweet moments, breathing in counterpoint, keeping her warm.

"I'll fetch you a flannel," he said, easing away.

Jane rolled to her side, the better to watch her husband prowling across the bedroom in the altogether. He was a magnificent specimen of manhood, though she suspected he didn't see himself that way. While he wasn't self-conscious about his nakedness, he also had none of the swagger Jane had seen in her first husband.

As if Gordie had invented the marital act himself, clever fellow, and bestowed its blessings on all of creation.

A cloth sopped in water, then Quinn was frowning by the bed, a damp flannel in his hand. "I was trying to be considerate."

He was unhappy—after *that*?

Jane took the cloth and used it beneath the covers—awkward business—but she wasn't about to flip the covers back so a brooding, scowling Quinn could watch her wash.

"You were very considerate," Jane said. "If you'd been any more considerate, I'd be witless and panting into next week." She tossed the cloth in the direction of the privacy screen. "Get under the covers, Quinn, and explain what has you in a swither."

He remained silent by the bed, likely his version of a protest at being told what to do, then he obliged by walking around to his side of the mattress.

"You are with child," he groused. "I'm not a rutting bull."

Oh, for the love of...Jane bounced across the bed and insinuated herself against his side, which was like cuddling up to a block of granite.

"Maybe I am a rutting heifer," she said. "I hadn't realized one can move. Two can move. Gordie hadn't your...he couldn't last, and I wasn't to move lest I cause him to spend too soon, and it was all very awkward when it went awry, which it usually did, and now you've made me blush."

This marriage would doubtless involve a deal of blushing. "You've demanded honesty of me," she went on, "and by heaven you shall have it. I *liked* being passionate with you, I liked being free to touch and talk and let go. I liked that we pleased each other. I liked it a lot, Quinn."

He wrestled her over him, so Jane was straddling her naked husband. His sex was cool and damp against her tender flesh, which seemed to bother him not at all.

"A rutting heifer? I married a rutting heifer?"

"Apparently so."

Quinn snorted, then rumbled, until he was laughing outright. Jane smacked him on the shoulder, then tucked herself against his chest and smiled herself to sleep.

Chapter Nineteen

Holding Jane while she dozed was exactly the ambush Quinn had feared it would be. The daft woman liked swiving him, liked touching him, liked talking with him. The touching was bad enough—Quinn well knew the danger of sweet touches—but the talking would be his doom.

For Jane not only expressed herself well, she *listened*.

"I'll be back," she said, pushing up off his chest and scampering to the privacy screen.

Quinn had not even bothered to get that damned shift off of her, hadn't done a moment's homage to her breasts. Maybe next time...if there was a next time.

Jane came back to the bed by way of the hearth, where she banked the fire for the night. "You never did tell me exactly what business awaited you in York."

She resumed her place straddling him, cuddled to his chest, a fiendishly distracting interrogation posture.

"I'll be ready to go again with no provocation whatsoever, Jane. Mind yourself accordingly."

She drew her fingernail in a circle around his right nipple. "Go? To York?"

He flexed his hips. "No, love. Not to York."

"Ah, well then." She kissed him and drew the covers up over them both. "I'll be ready to go again too. Tell me about York. You are very dear to pay a call on an old friend."

"I stay with Mrs. D when I have to visit York. She doesn't let on that I'm in town, and between her and her daughter, they hear most of the market gossip." Quinn also paid for the roof over Mrs. Dougherty's head and the food in her larder, as much out of loyalty to a former fellow combatant as to twit Lord and Lady Tipton.

"Gordie was a great one for gossip and it led to his death."

Quinn had brought up Jane's late husband before they'd climbed into bed, thinking to make an awkward situation easier. Clearly her mourning for Captain MacGowan included some anger.

"Gossip doesn't fire real bullets, Jane. I understand that you loved him, but any soldier would know dueling is dangerous."

Jane nuzzled Quinn's neck, her nose cool against his skin. "The danger in Gordie's case was stubborn arrogance. The older brother of a fellow officer made some comment about me, or about a new husband who chose to drink rather than enjoy his wife's company—nobody told me the details. All I know is, Gordie brooded and paced and drank, and then he hunted through half the pubs in London, until he found the man who'd made the comment."

The moment should have been marital—a confidence shared between a wife and her husband amid warm blankets, while the pleasure of lovemaking yet lingered. Quinn stroked Jane's hair and silently cursed Gordie MacGowan.

"You tried to talk him out of this foolishness, I take it?"

"Quinn, I wept, I bellowed, I threatened, I *begged*, and all he'd say was that a slight to my honor must be avenged. He would not let it go, and now he's dead."

Let sleeping dogs lie. Forgive and forget. "I don't intend to stand in front of any loaded guns on account of a few stupid words, Jane. You may rest easy on that score." Nothing less than public disgrace would do for Quinn's enemy. "I didn't work myself to a shadow, ignore gossip without limit, and pinch pennies until they screamed just so some drunken lordling could put period to my existence."

Not when married life included pleasures such as falling asleep with Jane draped over him like a contented cat.

"I married a brilliant man."

"You married a determined man." Also one who couldn't think when his naked wife wiggled about like that. "Jane, have mercy."

She peered at him, even her expression catlike in its impatience. "We are *husband and wife*. I have missed you. I am awash in the glow of newfound delights, and you turn up missish. I know I'm not the stuff of naughty fantasies, but the midwife said that a certain abundance of appetite in regard to—"

He put a gentle hand over her mouth. "For the love of God, Jane, hush. These delights are newfound for me as well."

And more precious than she could possibly know.

She slowly pushed his hand away, then winnowed her fingers through his hair. "You'll look a fright in the morning, going to bed with wet hair. What do you mean, these delights are newfound for you too? You are so far beyond handsome that words fail, and you have scandalously abundant means, according to your siblings. I am benefitting from your amatory experience, of course, but my comprehension in certain areas...What do you mean?"

Quinn cradled the back of her head, urging her to snuggle so he'd at least not have to look her in the eye. She thought him handsome. Not hulking, coarse, or common. Not pretty either.

"When a man has a certain vitality," Quinn said, "the attention that comes his way is the same as that aimed at a prancing colt. All and sundry assume the ride will be spirited in a purely athletic sense, and that the colt is eager for the outing. If the stud is afraid of rabbits, backsore, or missing his pasture mates, that's of no moment. He's to charge and leap on command, while his rider shows off her new habit and her fancy mount. I learned that I did not care to be that stud colt."

Please let her understand. Let that be explanation enough forever.

"I'm told the life of a debutante is not to be envied," Jane said, fussing with the quilt. "Always on display, never putting a foot wrong, flattering everything in breeches without once offending propriety. I'd never have thought the same misery would befall an attractive young man, but then, my upbringing wasn't worldly. I'm easily shocked."

Quinn was shocked. For all the lures that had been cast at him, all the desperate innuendo tossed his way at the bank, nobody had ever called him *attractive*. His damp hair had resulted in a chill about his shoulders. Jane's maneuvering with the quilt had restored warmth, while her words . . .

"I've kept to myself," he said. "Left the ladies alone. For years. Life is simpler that way."

"Your perspective is understandable, and on behalf of my gender, I apologize for all the times you were importuned without invitation. Nonetheless, you and I are married. Leave every other lady alone but neglect me at your peril."

Her apology washed over Quinn like an extra blanket on

a chilly night, comfort he hadn't known he'd been missing, also a surprise. While the warmth was lovely, a part of him had to clutch that blanket by a corner, lest it be stolen from him should his vigilance lapse.

"Close your eyes," Jane said, kissing Quinn's cheek. "You've earned your rest, and God knows I'll waken you with my nocturnal travels soon enough."

"Yes, Jane."

She drifted off, a sweet weight on his heart, though Quinn could not fall asleep for a long, long time.

* * *

"He were a ghost," Ned said, taking the towel from Davies. "I was to wait up for him, so I sat by the back door, like he told me, and I watched him turn into darkness."

"You fell asleep," Davies replied, snatching the towel back and scrubbing it over Ned's wet hair.

"I did not fall asleep, you donkey's bunghole. Mrs. D gave me coffee, because it keeps a fellow awake better than tea. That's how a proper footman stays on the job all day. Bitter stuff and made me have to piss something awful, so I was awake. One moment himself were on the garden path behind Mrs. D's cottage, plain as moonlight, the next he were gone. Came back the same way. Didn't wake up the sow at the foot of the garden or the cat sleeping on the wall."

"So you didn't follow him," Davies said, scooping a bucket of dirty water from the tub and sluicing it down the scullery drain. "That was smart."

"Not my town, not my turf." Besides, His Grace had promised Ned he'd be shipped off to France for disobeying orders. Of course, the duke had also threatened to sell Ned to the Vikings, toss him into the sea, and leave him behind.

Had a colorful imagination, did His Grace. Miss Jane might like to know the terrors a small boy endured while racketing about with her man.

Ned wrapped himself in the toweling—an acre of soft, dry, lavender-scented fabric—and sat by the fire. Bathing wasn't all bad, not when the kitchen was warm, the water was warmer, and dinner had been tended to first.

Davies scooped more water from the tub. "You're to sleep late tomorrow. Miss Jane's orders."

"She'll want a report."

Davies dumped the bucket and watched the water drain away. "You have to decide, Ned, whether you're his man or hers. She has Susan and Penny, but you're the duke's tiger. Bear tales carefully."

Good advice. "Are you Penny's man yet?"

"For fifteen minutes last Tuesday, she was nearly my woman. What else happened in York?"

"The Minster was huge," Ned said, getting comfortable on the warm stones of the kitchen hearth. "Bigger than St. Paul's, bigger than—"

"You told us all about the bloody Minster. What *happened*?"

Davies had done what he could for Ned in Newgate, which meant they were mates. Then too, Davies had never seen the Minster, never seen a hill with more sheep on it than Covent Garden had people on a sunny market day, never traveled the Great North Road. He'd hidden his disappointment, but being left behind clearly hadn't sat well with him.

"We went out to some big house in the country, maybe ten miles from York. A palace, like if you took a whole square from Mayfair and made one house out of it. Himself drove right by the gates, but he noticed that house, not in a good way. Noticed it by ignoring it to death. Went to the village, had a pint, and we come back a different way, past another great house, which he also ignored. I stayed with the horses in the village, because I'm his tiger."

"You stayed with the horses because you're a nosy bugger, and himself didn't want you eavesdropping."

As if that mattered? "I might 'ave heard a word here and there."

Davies dumped yet another bucket. "And?"

"He were right turbulent about something. Didn't raise his voice, but he were fuming."

Davies rummaged through a basket of clean laundry and pitched clothes at Ned. "Get dressed, or the maids will be consoling you on the size of yer wee pizzle."

Ned pulled the shirt over his head—a clean shirt, of all the miracles. The kitchen was also cleaner, now that Ned noticed the details. The windows were clear, the copper pots shiny, the floor swept and scrubbed.

The kitchen hadn't been dirty before, not by Ned's standards, but now the place was worthy of a duke.

"Don't be insulting my pizzle," Ned said. "Isn't like your pizzle is the size of the York Minster."

"Ask Penny if she'd rather spend time with my pizzle or your perishing Minster. What were his dukeship fuming about?"

When had Davies become such a nosy cove? "Couldn't understand him. He was talking thee and thou and summat and t' this and t' that. Never heard such talk afore in my life."

"That's Yorkshire, then. Don't forget your inexpressibles, young Neddy. Shall I give your hair a trim?"

Ned looked at his feet, clean right down to a set of wrinkled toes. "Not too much, just a trim. The choirboys at the Minster—"

"I'll trim you bald if you don't cease bletherin' about the damned Minster."

"I'm trembling with fear, I am. Ned Tremblin', they call me. The dread Viking Davies Dog-Pizzle has threatened to snatch me bald."

Davies laughed and found a pair of scissors, then trimmed the back of Ned's hair so it wouldn't touch his collar. All the while, Davies continued to question and speculate and pass the time, and Ned dodged, distracted, and pretended to yawn.

Davies had never been this curious about the duke in Newgate, which left Ned with questions: For whom was Davies asking questions, and why? Until Ned had those answers, he'd not be letting on that the duke had been in a right taking over some countess who hadn't been anywhere near where His Grace had expected her to be.

* * *

"So Pike's in France?" Joshua asked.

"He was as of two weeks ago," Duncan murmured, his penknife shaving a fine point on a goose quill. "Fat lot of good that does us."

In the privacy of the partners' conference room, Quinn let them bicker, because that's how Joshua and Duncan went on. They never came to blows or insults, though they scrapped over the last word like dogs sniffing about a knacker's yard.

"Knowing Pike's alive does me plenty of good," Quinn said. "Whoever sent him to Calais likely did so without giving him the proper travel documents. Pike can kick his heels indefinitely in the port itself, but without papers, the French will keep him buttoned up there. I can send a man to watch him, so I'll know if he sails for home."

"Papers cost money," Joshua said, propping his boots on

the corner of the reading table. "Papers for a man who's doubtless traveling under an assumed name will cost more money, and take time. Then too, Pike likely has about four words of French."

Quinn hadn't even that many.

Duncan leapt back into the discussion, debating how long forged papers would take to prepare, how much they'd cost, whether they'd be more easily procured in London or Calais, whether they'd been acquired weeks ago, before Quinn's arrest.

Quinn listened with half an ear, because the papers wouldn't be procured anytime soon. Whoever had sent Pike to France wanted to know where he was in case Pike needed killing. Talkative conspirators tended to meet with accidents.

"A diplomat's wife would know how to quietly get hold of any papers she needed," Quinn said.

Joshua's boots hit the carpet with a thump.

"Her again." Duncan packed a load of contempt into two words, a veritable fit of temper for him.

"Makes sense," Joshua said. "Lady Tipton has means, she's carrying a grudge, she's well connected."

"You're planning to go to bloody France, aren't you, Quinn?" Duncan's tone implied a trip to France was a felony in itself. "So you bring Pike back, get his sworn confession. He'll say he simply asked you for a bit of blunt in an alley and then left the country. He'll declare ignorance of your trial and conviction, because whoever set this up isn't stupid. If somebody took the trouble to send you to Newgate, they'd take the time to coach Pike on what to say if he's flushed from his covert."

Quinn had reached the same conclusion before he'd left York.

"Pike isn't the key," he said, getting to his feet. "Pike

would be a fine bargaining chip if I spoke French or had a French translator I could trust. I don't, and I'm uncomfortable leaving Jane again while my enemy can maneuver freely."

"Jane," Joshua said, as if referring to a particularly thorny banking law. "She's...well?"

Since Quinn's return from York, his household had never known such calm and order, and his thoughts had never known such chaos. Althea played only sweet, languid airs on her harps, while Constance painted portraits of her cats. Stephen was researching the history of the dukedom with the single-mindedness that characterized his happiest pursuits.

"Jane thrives." She also desired her husband passionately and often. The frequent lovemaking was as disconcerting to Quinn as it was delightful, but worse—far worse—was Jane's affection, her laughter, her *wifeliness*. She assumed Quinn would be interested in hearing about the petty battles and victories of her day, and that he'd enjoy sharing his own frustrations and triumphs with her.

Which...he did.

"Any more visits from the reverend?" Joshua asked.

Duncan swept the trimmings from the quill pen into his palm and tossed them into the dustbin in the corner.

Perhaps he hadn't been the one to mention Winston's visit to Joshua. Quinn wasn't sure how much actual spying Joshua did on the Wentworth household, how much casual gossip found its way to his ear, and how much Joshua's possible interest in Althea accounted for his knowledge.

"No sign of the reverend since my departure for York," Quinn said, "thank the divine powers. If you gentlemen have nothing more to discuss, I'll be off."

"You announce that Pike's presence has been verified in Calais," Duncan said, folding his penknife closed. "You confirm that he's written to his family in York. You knew him when he was a gardener on the Tipton estate, and you are all but certain that the Countess of Tipton has authored your demise. What aren't you telling us?"

"I've told you everything I know, except that the countess is no longer biding in the north. The earl is in Town on parliamentary matters, and her ladyship is buying out half the shops in Mayfair."

Joshua muttered something having to do with the back end of a sheep. "How could we not know she's here in London?"

"Because," Duncan said, his knife disappearing into a pocket, "the Wentworths are not received, and thus all of Mayfair could be on fire and it would be of no moment to them."

"You are a Wentworth," Quinn replied, though in all likelihood he and Duncan shared no blood.

"One of five who refuses to read the society pages. What else do we know about the earl and his lady, and why they're in Town this year of all years?"

"Six Wentworths," Quinn said, "unless Jane has taken to reading the papers. I know precious damned little about Lady Tipton's habits in Town, but I have an appointment with somebody who should be better informed than I am."

"Would you like some company when you pay this call?" Duncan asked.

"I have nothing pressing this afternoon," Joshua added.

If Quinn took one of them, he'd have to take both. "Thank you, gentlemen, I'll pay this visit on my own. Perhaps we should ascertain where Lord Tipton keeps his London accounts."

By making it a competition, Quinn was sure to have the information that much sooner.

"Good question," Joshua said, heading for the door. "Shouldn't be too hard to come up with an answer. I bid you both good day." He departed on a soft click of the door latch, leaving a not entirely comfortable silence.

"Tipton banks at Dorset and Becker," Duncan said, "the same as most of the northern aristocracy does. Penrose and I spent the last two weeks poring over the estate books from the Walden seat. Even I, who don't care for ledger books, can read a tale of fraud and embezzlement there. When will you take an interest in your dukedom?"

The publican in the Walden village coaching inn had cheerfully confirmed in twenty minutes of gossip what Duncan and Joshua had taken two weeks to deduce: The previous duke's steward had been a bold, greedy, *shrewd* thief, and the entire district had known it.

"I took a look at the ducal seat while I was in the north," Quinn said, "but I wasn't inclined to linger in the neighborhood. If you knew where Tipton banked, why not speak up?"

"Because finding a moment alone with you has become impossible. You're either closeted with Jane, riding out with Stephen, haring off to York, or impersonating a doting brother where Althea and Constance are concerned."

Duncan, who never raised his voice, never lost his composure, was...complaining. Possibly even pouting, because of Jane's scheme to keep Quinn safe.

"If I attempted to dote on my sisters, they would fillet me, and Jane is my wife and in a delicate condition. Stephen is my brother and at a dangerous age."

Duncan took inordinate care pulling on his gloves. "Speaking of Stephen..."

"If he's got a maid with child, I'll deal with it." Though how was Quinn to beat the stuffing out of a brother confined to a Bath chair?

"Did Jane tell you he nearly blew her head off?"

Cold washed through Quinn, the sort of bone-deep cold he'd felt as a boy when his father's voice acquired a whimsical sneer.

"I beg your pardon?"

"Ask Ivor. Jane wasn't in any danger, but Stephen showed very poor judgment. She was upset."

"I am upset."

"Glad to hear it," Duncan said, tapping his hat onto his head. "You should be. I'm away to Berkshire tomorrow."

"You're jaunting off to the shires *now*?"

Duncan turned a look on Quinn reminiscent of Jane marshalling her self-restraint. "I'm off to inspect the most neglected of the estates you've inherited. I shouldn't be gone outside of a fortnight, and from our discussion before you *jaunted off* to see the Minster, I thought you expected this of me."

Quinn wrestled with a sense of being abandoned, of events spiraling out of control, but Duncan was only seeing to a task Quinn himself had delegated.

"Safe journey," Quinn said, and... *Let me know what you find?* Of course Duncan would prepare a report. What else needed to be said? Duncan waited, a look of patient forbearance in his eyes.

"Thank you," Quinn said. "Don't leave without saying good-bye—I might have some specific tasks for you to tend to on your travels—and for all that you do, thank you."

Duncan's brows rose, a gratifying reaction, however slight. "You're welcome."

Chapter Twenty

"I never thanked you for summoning Quinn from the bank when Althea and I had our disagreement," Jane said.

Constance turned a page of her book, though first she had to gently draw it out from under Hades's paw. The cat reclined on the reading table, the front third of him sprawling over a volume on French portraiture.

"How do you know I summoned him?"

"Althea was too busy arguing with me, Stephen was too fascinated with the altercation, and Duncan clings to the misguided belief that most domestic difficulties will sort themselves out. You acted, and I'm glad you did."

Constance scratched Hades's ears, which inspired feline rumblings of contentment. "You are in a delicate condition. Althea ought not to have provoked you."

Jane was beginning to know her husband, though she'd be decades learning his history. Althea held nothing back, announcing her opinions and intentions to all and sundry.

Duncan wished to be left alone, and Jane's curiosity about Stephen was dampened by caution.

Constance remained an enigma, but by summoning Quinn, she'd sided with Jane against her own sister. Or had she sided with the child?

"Althea was trying to look after me," Jane said. "I appreciate the motive, if not the method. I also appreciate that you brought Quinn from the bank to resolve the situation."

"Can't have a lot of yelling and strife when a woman's carrying." Constance slid the book out from under the cat, which put an end to his purring and earned her an annoyed squint. She returned the book to the library shelf and regarded Jane from across the room. "What did you want to talk about?"

So much for pleasantries. "I found a packet of letters addressed to Quinn. Old letters, from a woman. If I stumbled upon them, any chambermaid could chance across them, and yet if I don't replace them in the same spot, Quinn is bound to realize they've been moved."

Jane put the packet on the table, complete with the green satin garter securing them.

Constance took down another book. "Those are not your letters, but if Quinn were concerned about keeping them private, he should have chosen a different place to store them."

Constance did not appear the least bit dismayed that her brother was secreting correspondence in his own home, in his own sitting room, when he doubtless had safes, vaults, and strongboxes that would better serve to conceal them.

A man kept letters near because they meant something to him.

"Quinn chose a fine hiding place," Jane said, "but when I discovered the letters, they tumbled free and I have no idea what order they should be in. If I knew something of the context, or how long they've been stashed away..." *Something about the enraptured woman who'd sent them...* The greetings alone confirmed that Jane had stumbled upon love letters.

"Constance, you will excuse us."

Quinn stood in the library doorway. Jane hadn't heard him come in; apparently even the cat hadn't heard him, because Hades scrambled from the table and shot out the door ahead of Constance. She followed her familiar, book in hand, pausing before her brother.

"If I hear a raised voice, Quinn Wentworth, I will be right back in here, and no lock will deter me. Jane is *with child.*"

"I am well aware of my wife's condition."

Quinn closed the door behind his sister, then turned an icy stare in Jane's direction. "I'll take those letters." He held out a hand, not an olive branch.

She could pass the letters over, apologize for having found them, and pretend she'd never seen them. She did not, because nowhere in the definition of letting bygones be bygones or allowing sleeping dogs to lie did Jane see a requirement to engage in self-deception.

She undid the garter and picked up the first letter. "'My darling, most dear, desirable, Wentworth...'" She flipped to the next one. "'My delightful, exasperating, inventive fellow...'" Then the third: "'To the most well-endowed specimen ever to bring delight to his lady's bed...'"

She never made it to the fourth. Quinn had crossed the library and snatched the packet from her hand.

"This is personal correspondence, Jane. Shall I start reading your letters?"

She could not discern his mood, but her own was very clear to her—she was angry, and beneath that, unsure of her husband.

"You told me you haven't kept mistresses. You told me we shared newfound pleasures. You told me you were too busy to bother with affairs of the heart, and I believed you."

"I spoke the truth."

His calm mendacity only enflamed Jane's temper. "My *darling, dear, desirable* Wentworth? Does your solicitor exercise his alliterative talents thus? Perhaps the fine fellows at the College of Arms open their correspondence to you with such effusions." She marched up to him and jabbed his chest with a finger. "New. Found. Pleasures."

He stared down at her, a single furrow appearing between his brows. "Are you *jealous*?"

That hypothesis clearly pleased him. Jane whirled away lest she start shouting.

"I am not jealous, you mutton-headed gudgeon. I am angry. You *lied* to me, and about an intimate matter. Perhaps you sought to spare my feelings, but we agreed that we'd have honesty between us, Quinn, and then I come across passionate letters. How am I to trust you?"

He set the packet on the mantel. "You married me, I spoke vows. You either trust me or you don't. I've fed you, clothed you, housed you, made love with you—"

"And lied to me."

Quinn stared off across the library, as if doing sums in his head. "I take it the late, lamented Captain McGowan had an unreliable grasp of the truth."

"We are not discussing him." And yet, they were. Quinn's instincts were, as usual, deadly accurate. "We are discussing a man who assures me his affections have not been elsewhere engaged, the same man who keeps these letters affixed to the topmost drawer of his desk."

"Have you read them?" Such a casual question.

"One can't help but glance at what's in plain view, which

was sufficient to establish the nature of the correspondence. I did not read them." Hadn't been able to read them.

"You sound like you're giving a sermon, Jane. If you take to task every man who has a few old letters in his possession, then I daresay—"

"Quinn, *you lied to me*. We don't tiptoe around one another's feelings like the shepherd boy and the goose girl. Why not simply admit that once, long ago, you lost your heart and never entirely regained it? Why not sigh and smile, and allude to a lady you loved dearly in your youth? My expectations of this marriage were honesty, civility, and a certain mutual accommodation. Of the three, you seemed to value the honesty most highly."

Though those expectations had become augmented by hope on Jane's part, and where hope flew, fears followed.

"How did you find the letters?"

"The drawer jammed—the lace of the garter was caught in the mechanism. They spilled onto the floor at my feet."

"Why were you rummaging in my desk?"

Jane took a seat at the end of the sofa and tapped her fingers on the armrest in a slow triple meter.

"In point of fact, Your Grace, that is *our* desk, I being your wife and having no desk of my own. I was neither rummaging nor pillaging. I must sit somewhere when I draw up the menus and schedules for the maids and footmen. Am I now to ask you where I might sit?"

He scrubbed a hand over his face, his granite inscrutability slipping to reveal wariness.

Why was he home several hours early, today of all days?

Jane's ire ebbed, as if somebody had turned down the wick on a lantern. "What's wrong, Quinn? Something is amiss or you'd be at the bank."

He took the place beside her, and more of Jane's indignation slipped away. She could not cling to her anger when Quinn was troubled, though neither could she allow the situation with the letters to remain unresolved.

"I paid a call on the College of Arms."

"Mr. Dodson was doubtless pleased to receive you. Constance and Althea mentioned him."

"I wanted to discuss a banking matter with him, the dukedom being in some disarray, but he attempted pleasantries with me."

Poor Mr. Dodson. "You have exquisite manners, though your patience wants work."

Quinn took her hand, and the last of Jane's anger skittered back to where she stored other vexations—Papa's pigheadedness, Hades's mating urges. What remained was worry— why had Quinn lied?—and determination.

"My patience wants major repairs," Quinn said, "particularly since I've acquired a wife."

They weren't to discuss the letters, though Jane's immediate problem—what to do with them—had been solved. They were Quinn's letters, and he'd find a new place to store them.

"Odd, acquiring a husband has similarly tried my own usually placid nature. What did Dodson have to say?"

"Little of any moment, though he did mention that one of his heralds had a lively correspondence with Stephen going back several months. Not the same fellow who researched the Walden dukedom, else Dodson would have known of Stephen's inquiries sooner."

Jane was glad for the warm grip of Quinn's hand in hers. "Stephen *knew* you were heir to a title?"

"He certainly had inklings, and his intellect is in better working order than most people's. If anything happens to me, the title becomes his. When were you planning to tell me that he nearly blasted you to kingdom come, Jane? I thought we'd agreed to be honest with each other."

Jane withdrew her hand. "Did you really? How disappointed you must be. Try counting to three when you're vexed. I used to find that habit helpful when my patience was tried."

Quinn had the grace to wince. "The letters are more than ten years old, and I keep them to prove that my attentions were not forced on the woman who wrote them."

Ye gods, marriage to Quinn was complicated, and that explanation only replaced one worry with another.

"After *ten years*, you still fret that this woman could cause you trouble?"

"The statute of limitations on rape is considerably more than ten years." He offered that observation with such a bleak, remote expression that his earlier claims about having refrained from romantic entanglements in recent years gained credibility.

"Whoever she is," Jane said, scooting to the edge of the sofa, "she needs to forget her youthful indiscretions and leave you in peace." *This is what happens when a woman clings to her hurts and disappointments.*

"Verily." Quinn's hand on Jane's arm stayed her from trying to rise. "But rather than discuss my misspent youth, I'd like to hear about Stephen's asinine behavior with a gun."

"Ivor tattled."

"We agreed to have honesty between us, *Your Grace*."

"That we did." Jane sat back. "Stephen exercised poor judgment, and he apologized. He felt it imperative to warn me that Wentworths aren't safe, and must never let down their guard. I gather this woman is among those who taught you that same lesson."

Quinn remained silent, staring at the peacocks and doves

patterned into the library carpet. He was an articulate man, but the conversation had apparently taken a turn even he hadn't anticipated.

Instinct leapt ahead of reason, and dread closed around Jane's heart. "You think the lady who sent those letters had you arrested, tried, and sentenced to death. Who is she, and what happened that, years later, she'd still hate you enough to see you hanged?"

* * *

Nobody save Quinn and her ladyship knew the entirety of his involvement with Beatrice, Countess of Tipton. He'd kept his gob shut, and prayed to whatever god took pity on stupid young footmen that her ladyship had done likewise. Having lent money to many a titled family, Quinn could now see—at a distance of more than a decade—that he'd been embroiled in a silly affair with a neglected aristocratic wife. He'd been an idiot of sixteen, too randy for his own good, and much taken by an older woman's overtures.

Jane was making no overtures whatsoever. She rose from the sofa and paced across the library, a worried lioness whose claws were sheathed—for now.

"I have no proof that her ladyship is behind my arrest, Jane."

"Not your arrest, Quinn, your attempted murder and ruin, years after you've given any grounds for offense. Tell me the rest of it."

"There isn't much to tell. I was sixteen when I became a footman for the Earl of Tipton. I was big, fit, and sufficiently good-looking that a lack of polish could be covered up by handsome livery. Footmen aren't required to speak, only to step and fetch and endure endless boredom."

Jane tidied up a pile of books that Stephen had doubtless left on the reading table. "Was her ladyship bored?"

"Bored, lonely, neglected, and angry at her husband. At the time, all I could see was that she..."

Jane organized the books on the table by color—red leather bindings in one stack, brown in another. "She was attracted to you?"

The countess had sought to possess Quinn, to *own* him like a dog on a leash. "I hate discussing this."

"I hate casting up my accounts, but sometimes that's the only way I'll find relief."

"Hardly a genteel analogy, Jane." But apt. Good God, was that analogy apt.

"I am a Wentworth," she said, coming close enough to pat Quinn's cravat. "We're sometimes a little rough around the edges. If you feel like an idiot for becoming entangled with a predatory older female at sixteen, imagine how stupid I must feel for having succumbed to Captain MacGowan's dubious charms at twenty-three."

She wafted away when Quinn had wanted to catch her by the hand. "You? Stupid?"

"And desperate. I'd lost my mother to influenza, or to stubbornness, to be more accurate. My father wasn't getting over his grief and had quarreled with his bishop, and Papa hasn't been assigned a living since. Month by month, he's pawned the little treasures Mama brought to the marriage or accumulated over the years. Even the cedar chest Mama left me was sent to the pawnbroker's.

"Ahead of me," she went on, "I could see nothing but impoverished spinsterhood, while Papa's mind grew more vague and our situation more precarious. Then one day, he 'accidentally' brought one of Mrs. Sandridge's teaspoons upstairs. I slipped it back into her apartment, but what if she'd accused Papa of stealing? I was frightened, lonely, and tired of being the only adult in a situation where I was constantly belittled, and yet, I was supposed to honor my father."

Jane had stroked a hand over her belly, probably a reflex when she was upset.

"You're human, Jane. To be constantly criticized and mocked by the parent who is supposed to stand up for us makes running away from home a sane choice." Quinn had debated with himself whether killing a parent was ever justified, though the hand of fate and some bad gin had allowed the question to remain theoretical.

Jane's smile was commiserating. "Running away from home is a sane choice unless we run into the arms of a jealous countess?"

Quinn's world shifted with that smile and became a brighter, lighter place. He traveled the distance from a youth hauling a wagonload of self-recrimination to a man with a few regrets. His childhood home had been a hell of hopelessness. Of course he'd been bedazzled by a sophisticated woman who'd pretended to see something special in him.

Of course he had.

Jane came around the table and into Quinn's arms, though he hadn't made a decision to reach for her. He held her—held on to her—unable to say what exactly the conversation had accomplished, though Jane was no longer jabbing him in the chest and hurling thunderbolts.

"I thought she liked me." Quinn's admission was foolish, pathetic even, but Jane's honesty—or her courage—was apparently contagious.

She nuzzled the lace of his neckcloth. "Imagine Stephen embroiled with some lordling's castoff wife. Would you expect him to know liking from manipulation?"

"That's…"

"Different? I suppose so. Stephen has had years to observe polite society at close range, to tip his hat to the ladies in the park, to smile at them in church. He comes from wealth, he's exquisitely turned out, and can likely keep up in French, Latin, Greek, and German. You were the veriest lamb, by comparison."

On his most innocent day, Quinn had not been a lamb, but when it came to women—to ladies—he'd been staggeringly ignorant.

"One doesn't like to admit to having been seduced."

Jane peered up at him. "One doesn't like to admit to having married a handsome buffoon simply because he looked dashing in his uniform and had such a charming accent. I like your accent too, by the way."

Quinn had spent years with elocution tutors trying to eradicate that accent. "I hope my speech is that of a gentleman."

"Of course it is, but when we're in bed, it's the speech of a gentleman from Yorkshire. Tell me about this daft countess."

Jane led Quinn by the hand to the sofa, and he allowed it—not because he was a lamb, but because she liked his accent. Or something. Why had the notion that a *gentleman* could sound as if he'd been raised in Yorkshire never occurred to him?

"Beatrice was kicking her heels at the earl's estate, which was to say she was going mad while he played at diplomacy on the Continent. I'd worked my way into a position in the stables, and she noticed me and promoted me to footman."

"Get comfortable," Jane said. "This tale will take some telling."

How was one—?

Jane shoved at his shoulders, and Quinn realized he was to stretch out on the sofa with his head in her lap. He accommodated that suggestion, because she was right. This tale—which he'd never shared with another—would take some telling.

"She smiled at me, she took me with her everywhere. She casually brushed against me, had me carry her parcels up to her private parlor. She took my arm in public and asked my opinion when I escorted her from shop to shop. Then one day, when I had delivered some purchase or other to her sitting room, she kissed my cheek."

In hindsight, Quinn could see the progression, could see how calculated the dance steps had been. Too late, he'd learned that he hadn't been her ladyship's first little project, though he might well have been her last.

"What a disgraceful woman," Jane said. "She couldn't be bothered to frolic with one of her own class; she had to prey on a boy."

Jane's fingers stroking Quinn's hair were gentle, her tone disgusted.

"I wasn't a boy, Jane. At sixteen, I was a strutting, snorting acolyte of the god Priapus, and convinced of my own manliness. She looked at me, and I was in torments. She ignored me, and I was in worse torments still. I was seventeen before we became intimate." Not lovers. Whatever role Quinn had played in the woman's life, he hadn't been a lover.

"I hate her," Jane said, kissing Quinn's brow. "Even if she didn't send you to prison, I hate her."

And I love you. For surely, this affection and liking, this desire and willingness to trust, had to be love?

"I don't hate her," Quinn said. "She taught me many valuable lessons. I learned to read and write because of her."

Jane's fingers paused. "To read her letters? Oh, Quinn."

"At first to read her letters, but then I realized that if I ever wanted to be more than her plaything, I needed to better my circumstances, not simply work harder, but work smarter. My father's rages had grown constant, the girls were getting older, the children never had any food, and something had to be done."

"Then your father broke Stephen's leg."

The words still hurt, still hit Quinn with an inner blow. "Stephen told you about that?"

"No details."

"He's never shared the details. He was only four at the time. I assume Papa fell on him or dropped him, that the injury was accidental. In any case, Papa could not afford a doctor. By the time word got to me at the Tipton estate, setting the leg would have been difficult if not impossible, but I vowed then and there to disentangle myself from the countess."

"Did she let you go?"

No, she had not. She'd raged, pouted, threatened, and promised, until Quinn had been as desperate to escape her as he'd once been to secure her approval. Would that Beatrice was more like Jane, determined to forgive and forget.

"I left, eventually. Took a job with a banker for whom I'd once been an errand boy. With better manners, better speech, some literacy, and clean clothes, I made a passable clerk."

Jane smoothed his hair back. "You were a brilliant clerk, and your employer noticed."

"I wasn't brilliant. I was honest. The old man left a five-pound note on the floor one night. I found it and returned it to him the next morning. He'd been testing me, and of all the clerks he'd tested in that manner, I was the first in twenty years to return his funds to him."

She traced a fingertip over Quinn's eyebrows, then down the length of his nose. "Five pounds must have been a fortune to you then. Why didn't you keep it?"

"Because I am not my father. I do not willingly break the law. I accepted any work, no matter how wretched, because Jack Wentworth had had a trade and refused to ply it. I had no trade, but was determined to be the better man. The banker bequeathed me a modest sum along with advice regarding its use. I made discreet, sound investments, worked hard, had some wildly good luck in the spice trade, and became a wealthy man."

Jane hugged him. "You're the best man. I still hate the countess. The very last thing you should do, though, is gratify her need to meddle by giving her any further attention. Ignore her. Her machinations failed, if indeed they were her machinations."

The baby moved where Jane's belly pressed against the back of Quinn's head. A kick, perhaps?

"I cannot ignore a woman who uses her influence to threaten my life and my good name. I'll at least make a few discreet inquiries." More discreet inquiries, in France, in Yorkshire, all over the stews and alleys of London.

Jane wrapped her hand around his nape and gently shook him. "If you kick over a hornet's nest, you'll be stung— badly. Do you know how my mother died?"

He *should* know. Should have asked the reverend, if nothing else. "Tell me."

"She was devoted to the Magdalen houses, or to the women in them. She'd accompany Papa to the prison and sing the praises of those establishments to the fallen women. Papa admired her for this, while I attempted to dissuade her."

The Magdalen houses were little better than forced labor for the women admitted to them. The task assigned was typically laundry—heavy, uncomfortable labor for females in poor health, though the house made a profit off of their work, despite the stated agenda being the saving of souls. Wages were nominal, the food poor, and the sermons never ending.

"You objected to women being judged and overworked?" Quinn asked.

"If I took up that fight...No, Quinn. I objected to my mother consorting in close quarters with a population carrying every possible illness. When influenza struck Mama's favorite charitable home, nothing would do but she must tend the sick herself, though she'd already contracted a fever of some sort visiting the jails."

The lady's husband had doubtless applauded her kindness, while Jane had gone mad. "Your mother fell ill?"

"Of course, and Mama refused to rest, because she cared so very much about the soiled doves who would not have spared a farthing for her medical expenses."

Jane twitched the afghan over Quinn's shoulders, though he hadn't realized he'd grown chilled.

"I'm sorry you lost your mother thus, Jane. She was clearly a good woman and dear to you."

A good, foolish woman. What sort of mother leaves a daughter half orphaned for the sake of strangers? But then, what sort of woman abandoned her five-year-old son to be with a paramour, when that son was left in the care of Jack Wentworth?

"Mama would be alive now, Quinn, if she'd not been determined to take on the evils of the world. Papa said she died a saint's death. I say she died of misguided stubbornness. My compassion for women in need is genuine—there but for your proposal I might have gone—but Mama wouldn't listen, she wouldn't give up, she wouldn't take the prudent course even long enough to see to her own health."

And thus, Jane's personal commandments included avoidance of anything resembling a dangerous quest.

Or a dangerous countess. Good God, what a coil, and what a motivation for seeing Lady Tipton held accountable sooner rather than later.

Quinn meant to ask Jane why her father didn't simply apologize to the affronted bishop and exchange the charms of Newgate for ministering to some rural flock, but Jane stroked his brow, and her silence suggested further interrogation would pain her.

Instead, he mentally drafted pronouncements about family safety, women in a delicate condition, and husbandly authority, but Jane's caresses beguiled him, and then he was asleep.

Chapter Twenty-one

Jane needed to cry. To rage, weep, and curse for the young man who'd been served so many ill turns so early in life, but she instead remained sitting on the sofa while her husband dozed. Quinn's recounting of his past had only made her respect him more and worry for him more.

Why would a scorned lover come after Quinn now, when he was infinitely more powerful than he'd been as a footman?

Why wait more than ten years to seek revenge, if that's what this was? Why go to the excessive effort of bribing judges, prison officials, guards, witnesses—

Jane's thoughts were interrupted by a soft knock on the door. She eased herself around her sleeping husband, tucked a pillow under his head, and draped the afghan over him. If vengeance was the province of the Almighty, Jane hoped the countess soon stepped into the path of a celestial crossbow.

She kissed Quinn's cheek, smoothed his hair, and went to the door.

"Beg pardon, Your Grace," Ivor said. "Reverend Winston has come to call." The footman scrupulously avoided peering into the library, though Quinn was fully clothed and merely napping—for a change.

"His Grace fell asleep while reading," Jane said. "Let him rest. I'll wake him after I've dealt with my father."

Which ordeal Jane did not anticipate with proper daughterly joy.

"Mr. Winston is in the family parlor. Would you like a tea tray, ma'am?"

Jane would like Ivor to stand at the door of the family parlor, looking formidable and fierce, but if Papa thought he had an audience, he'd likely stay even longer.

"Please bring a tray, and then return here to ensure nobody disturbs the duke."

"Yes, ma'am. Shall I send Kristoff to attend you in the family parlor?"

Stephen's words came back to Jane: *You need to realize when you're not safe. You need to realize you're a Wentworth....* But what havoc could Papa wreak, besides pilfering knickknacks or overstaying his welcome?

"Thank you, no."

Ivor's shoulders tensed, suggesting that Jane had given offense to a loyal retainer. She hadn't time to smooth ruffled feathers when Papa was unattended on the premises.

When she reached the family parlor, Papa was peering at the underside of a French porcelain bowl that held dried rose petals scented with a dash of nutmeg. Because the bowl was full, he'd had to lift it over his head to read the maker's mark.

"Papa, good day."

He set the bowl on the piano. "Jane Hester."

Filial affection dictated that she go to him and embrace him—Papa had a half dozen sermons on the requirement to honor one's progenitors—and yet she didn't. "The tea tray is on the way. Shall we be seated?"

He took the middle of the sofa, leaving Jane an armchair. "You're looking well, daughter."

"I'm feeling somewhat better. I've been able to catch up on my rest." Also to stuff herself with red meat, fresh fruits and vegetables, and the occasional sweet.

Papa picked up a gold snuff box that held lemon drops. The lid was embossed with an ornate *W*, and the formal parlor held others like it.

"He treats you well, then?"

Put it down, Papa. "If you refer to His Grace, my husband, I am abundantly happy under his roof. Help yourself to a lemon drop."

The reverend helped himself to three. "I have worried for you, Jane Hester. Prayed for you."

"Prayers are always appreciated. How did your service for Mr. Carruthers go?"

"Carruthers? What has he—? Oh, right. Turn the other cheek. Very well received, as always. A central tenet of faith for the true believer. In that same spirit, I find myself on your doorstep, despite the lack of manners with which you last received me."

He had been received with a full breakfast buffet. "If my manners were wanting, perhaps your own needed improvement. You taught me not to malign a man behind his back."

Two more lemon drops were crunched into oblivion. "I don't malign, Jane Hester. I speak the God's honest truth. Your husband is a man of dubious antecedents, and you might be blinded by his filthy lucre or the pleasures of the flesh, but you are still my daughter, however wayward your path."

What answer could Jane give that was both respectful and honest? "I took vows in the eyes of God and man, Papa.

My path is not wayward, and I esteem my husband greatly."
Please, in the name of all that's holy, let the tea tray arrive,
so that food and drink might distract Papa from the sermon
he was determined to deliver.

"I beg the Almighty nightly to forgive me for ever allowing you to come with me to minister to the less fortunate,
Jane Hester. I get on my knees and fervently importune Him
to expunge that guilt from my soul. Had I not permitted you
to aid me, then you would never have—"

"You did not *permit* me to come with you, Papa. You insisted. You berated me for wanting to stay home and rest,
for not measuring up to Mama's standards. You harangued
me about God's distaste for the slothful. What you thought I
could accomplish in such an environment still eludes me."

Jane knew better than to react to his provocation, but the
past weeks of rest, good nutrition, and *being a Wentworth*
had put some of the fight back in her. Papa was not honest,
not with himself, not with her, not with the world.

Papa turned loose of the snuff box and bowed his head.
"Jane Hester, you wound me."

Before Papa could elaborate on the mortal nature of his
injury, Ivor brought in the tea tray, and Papa revived mirac-
ulously. For a few minutes, tea, shortbread, cakes, and or-
anges delayed further sermonizing.

Ivor hovered by the door and pretended to ignore the look
Jane sent him.

You are a Wentworth. You aren't safe.

Stephen had been so serious with that warning, so sure of
his point. Had Jane been a tea cake, she might have agreed,
for Papa had consumed them all, and yet, she wanted her father out of the house. Talk of scheming countesses with long
memories had made her uneasy, particularly when Quinn's
nature was to confront rather than to ignore a slight.

"How is Mrs. Sandridge?" Jane asked.

"A bit more tea, if you please," Papa replied around a mouthful of shortbread. "Mrs. Sandridge is well, though you might call upon her yourself, if you're truly concerned. I've asked her to look about for a wet nurse when the time comes."

Jane did not expect her father to make a great deal of sense, but that pronouncement baffled her. Mrs. Sandridge was well past childbearing age.

"I beg your pardon?"

"For the child," Papa said, gesturing with his shortbread. "Though of course there's time to sort all of that out." He held up his teacup. "The tea, Jane Hester. A guest should not have to ask twice."

Jane poured out as foreboding filled her belly. Either Papa had lost his last claim to sanity, or he'd found a new way to plague his only child.

"What do you mean, 'for the child'?"

"Thank you, Jane Hester. I want to be entirely prepared to receive MacGowan's offspring into my household, of course. His will was very clear: I'm to be guardian of any afterborn heirs and see to their welfare. I can't very well see to the welfare of a child being reared by a convicted felon, can I?"

On his best day, Papa was not a fit guardian for a well-trained lap dog.

"You have taken leave of your senses if you think I'll surrender any child of mine into the keeping of a man who can't pay for his own coal."

"Temper, Jane Hester. The female mind is so easily overset. Thank heavens that men of sound faculties can make arrangements for innocent children, lest a mother's frailties condemn the child to a wayward path. Might we have more tea cakes? They're quite small."

Jane rose to tug the bellpull, mind whirling. Gordie had left a will—officers were required to—and she had no idea what the will said.

"Do you suppose Uncle Dermott will allow you to raise a MacGowan, Papa?" Though as to that, Jane would rather the child be raised in London than on some godforsaken Scottish moor.

"Dermott MacGowan refused to make any provision for you or the child. I'm not about to consult him on so significant a matter as my grandchild's well-being."

Ivor brought more tea cakes, Papa maundered on about the expenses of raising a child, and the baby kicked at Jane's insides. Quinn would never allow Papa to have custody of the child, and Papa would never let this issue drop. He'd go to the courts—a certain path to scandal. He'd drag all of Quinn's past into public view, tarnish Gordie's memory, and hold Jane up to public scrutiny as an example of an ungrateful, stubborn, selfish woman.

How on earth was any daughter to honor such a father? To forgive and forget this degree of hypocrisy?

"Papa, I am ashamed"—bile rose in Jane's throat— "of…" *You. You and your pious cowardice, your righteous arrogance. Your failure to live up to Mama's image of you.*

"Well you should be ashamed, Jane Hester. Your mother, God rest her, encouraged a certain independence in you that I have come to regret, meaning no disrespect to the dead."

Jane pushed to her feet when she longed to defend her mother's memory. "You will excuse me, Papa. I'm about to be unwell. Ivor will show you out." She snatched the bowl of dried rose petals and managed a dignified exit—only just. Then she was on her knees in the linen closet, retching into the antique French porcelain.

* * *

Stephen had learned years ago how to take apart and re-assemble his Bath chair. He regularly oiled the metal surfaces, because any fellow with three older siblings needed to move quietly about his own home.

He was thus proceeding silently down the corridor when an odd noise from the linen closet caught his ear. Either one of Constance's cats had eaten a mouse that disagreed with it or somebody was in distress.

He opened the door and the scent that assailed him ruled out the mouse theory. "Jane? Are you well?" Inane question. Quinn's wife was on her knees, a porcelain bowl before her.

"Go away."

Not dying, then. "Shall I fetch Quinn?"

"I will kill you if you don't close that door immediate—" She fell silent and put a hand over her mouth.

Stephen rose from his Bath chair and knelt by her side. "The sachets and soaps probably aren't helping. Ruddy stench permeates everything. Let's get you to bed and find you some ginger tea, and—" And what? Quinn would know what to do—Quinn knew what to do with aggravating reliability—but where was Quinn when Jane needed him?

"Stephen, every moment you remain in this linen closet you risk your continued existence."

He got a hand under her arm and lifted her to her feet. "I'm a doomed man, then, but hold off annihilating me until we get you down the corridor, hmm?"

She leaned on him, which felt awkward and good. Good because he had the height and strength to support her. Awkward because Jane was soft, feminine, and not at her best. If Stephen had it to do over again, he'd probably not have shot the honeysuckle from above her head, but he didn't have it to do over again, and he and Jane hadn't spoken much since.

"Are you able to walk, Jane?"

"Of course."

He waited, and she remained for a moment right where she was, against his side. Of all people, Stephen did not associate "of course" with the ability to walk.

"I hate this," Jane muttered.

Tarrying in an odoriferous linen closet with a dyspeptic sister-in-law wasn't high on Stephen's list of ways to spend a day.

"I got drunk once," he said. "Felt like the devil the whole next day. If it's anything like that..."

She left the linen closet, still leaning on him, and shuffled with him past Satan's chariot.

"It's exactly like that, while you have no energy and your figure comes to resemble that of a...a heifer on summer grass. I'm whining."

"You're also making progress toward your bed, so don't stop on my account. I really ought to fetch Quinn."

"He's napping in the library. I'll nap in my bed."

Quinn never napped. He didn't laugh, he didn't chase women, he didn't waste a day reading the paper or playing cards. He was a bloody paragon, as long as lack of imagination was a virtue and loneliness a high calling.

He also avoided the library. "You left him asleep in the library?"

They paused outside the door to Quinn's suite of rooms. Jane shook herself free and peered up at Stephen. Lovely that, to have a woman looking *up* at him.

"You don't have your canes."

Shite. Shite, bollocks, and bother. "I have good days and bad days. Damsels in distress inspire me to heroic feats." He was blushing, damn it all to hell, and Jane wasn't buying his load of goods. Quinn never blushed, may he be condemned to a purgatory full of other humorless paragons.

"If you have too many good days, Duncan will be out of a job, is that it?"

Stephen peeled away from her to rest his back against the wall. "Do you do that to Quinn? Fire off insights without warning?"

"Yes, and he returns the favor. Shall I fetch your chair?"

Stephen's stamina was improving, slowly, but he paid for his excesses, and he needed a moment to gather his wits.

"Please."

Jane returned with the Phaeton of the Doomed and held it steady as Stephen settled onto the cushion.

"You're feeling better?" he asked.

"One often does, physically. My dignity is another matter."

Stephen had considered his regard for Jane, and decided that he liked her but he wasn't at risk of falling in love with her. She was too much Quinn's, too clearly devoted to her husband. Then too, she was expecting a child. A daunting prospect.

"Was that your father I saw coming up the walk?"

She straightened a painting hanging above the deal table—drooping roses and green apples. "Yes. He's probably still in the family parlor appraising the portable goods."

"Quinn will march him off to the magistrate if he steals."

Rather than upset the lady, this seemed to interest her. "Quinn would be that unforgiving?"

"That scrupulous. Quinn does not bend rules. He has a little speech that he gives all the courtesy lords and dowagers who seek to borrow money from him. He warns them not to go in debt to him unless they understand that he will see them jailed and bankrupt should they default. They smirk at him, but he's sent the sponging houses a lot of custom."

"No exceptions? That seems harsh."

Stephen agreed, but then, the Quality squandered fortunes on gaming and vice. "Quinn says he gives his word, they give theirs. Exceptions and special cases only muddy the waters. It's all in writing, so they know exactly the terms of the loan."

Jane left off fussing with the furnishings. "Quinn is nothing if not logical. If you'd see my father out, I'd appreciate it. If Duncan were here, I'd ask him."

"Are you well, Jane?" Stephen was no judge of the fairer sex, but Jane's indomitable air was like Althea's temper and Constance's discontent: always there, just below the surface. Jane was trying to get rid of him—all the siblings did—and yet, she seemed off to him, daunted.

"I'm well, considering."

The corridor was empty, and another opportunity to converse with Jane privately was unlikely. "I've learned something you should know."

"I should know many things." Her smile was wan. "Such as why you hide your strength from your family."

"I'm honestly not that strong. I do my exercises, and...maybe someday. You mentioned Duncan."

"He's away to Berkshire to look in on one of the ducal estates, or so Quinn told me."

Meaning Duncan had lied to Quinn—had gone out of his way to lie to Quinn. "He's not off to Berkshire, Jane. He'd have taken the coach for a journey of that length. He's on horseback, and he took only a pair of full saddlebags."

"Perhaps he'll stay with friends along the way."

Jane was only half listening, one hand on the door latch,

the other on her belly. How many more months did this go on, and where the hell was Quinn?

"Duncan doesn't have friends, Jane. He has books. He has ideas." Stephen doubted Duncan even had a mistress.

Jane pushed the door open and leaned on the jamb. "You must excuse me, Stephen. I'm truly not feeling well. You'll tell Quinn what you've told me?"

Stephen had been hoping Jane would pass this development on to Quinn. Tidier that way. "I'll tell him."

"My thanks, and do look in on the reverend. I left him rather abruptly." She withdrew and softly closed the door.

Stephen wheeled himself down the corridor, nearly running into Quinn outside the family parlor.

"Have you seen Jane?"

"She's in your sitting room, not feeling quite the thing. She asked me to keep her father company."

Quinn scowled at the door to the family parlor. "He's back?"

"His daughter lives here. Some fathers do this, I'm told. Look in on their offspring, not that we'd know."

Quinn aimed his scowl at Stephen. "Don't turn your back on him. He's every inch the respectable parson, but he cites scripture for his own purpose and hasn't done an honest day's work in years."

No greater transgression existed in the gospel according to Saint Quinn, which left a brother in a wheeled chair feeling ever so decorative.

"If you have a moment, I've a few things to talk over with you, Quinn. The reverend can stuff himself with tea cakes in solitude."

"No, he cannot. We'll talk when next we hack out in the park. I need to see to Jane." He stomped off down the corridor more purposefully than Moses had crossed the Red Sea.

Perhaps he'd noticed the traveling coach sitting in its bay, perhaps Jane would mention Duncan's odd behavior.

And perhaps she wouldn't. "Quinn!"

He turned outside his door, expression impatient. "Not now, Stephen."

"Let's ride out tomorrow."

"If the weather's fair." Then he slipped through the doorway and left Stephen to the thankless task of entertaining company.

"I want them to treat me as if I'm normal," he said to nobody in particular. Not exactly the truth. Stephen wanted to *be* normal. A slight, manly limp would be acceptable, but not the ungainly lurching that meant he'd never turn a lady down the room. "Dealing with inconvenient callers is normal."

On that cheering thought, he let himself into the family parlor. The reverend set down the little gold snuff box, a guilty expression suggesting that the Eighth Commandment had been in jeopardy, or perhaps the Tenth.

Quinn hadn't the patience for the old twattle-basket. If life in a Bath chair taught a fellow one thing, it was patience. Tomorrow, Stephen would share his observations regarding Duncan with Quinn. Now, he'd defend the family's monogrammed snuff boxes, and wonder where the hell Duncan had got off to, and why he'd lied to Quinn.

Chapter Twenty-two

Jane had apparently sent forth a decree, and Quinn had acquired a battalion of nannies where previously only a devoted duchess and a few watchful siblings had been. Going to and from the bank, the running footmen kept pace with the phaeton, and Ned clung to his post as tiger.

If Quinn stepped outside the bank to pass the time with the flower girls, Ned appeared four yards away. If Quinn took a notion to stop by his one and only club to eavesdrop on gossip at midday, Joshua took the same notion. At the pawnshops, Ned waited outside, nose pressed to the window like a neglected puppy.

A week went by, while Quinn's patience ebbed like the funds in the royal exchequer. Lady Tipton was biding not four streets away from where Quinn's family dwelled, and something had to be done. Tracking Pike down in France might prove impossible. Then too, Quinn was being followed, and not by one of his own footmen.

"This is not the way to the park," Stephen said as Quinn turned his horse out of the alley. "I wait days for you to find the time to ride out with me, comport myself like the soul of fraternal patience, and you forget where the park is."

"And yet," Quinn replied, "if anybody inquires, you will tell them we enjoyed a lovely hack on a pretty morning." The streets were already busy despite the early hour, and today wasn't Monday. Nonetheless, Quinn grew queasy as he guided his horse toward the City.

"You put me off for a week," Stephen said, "then drag me across London when I'm looking forward to the bucolic splendor of Hyde Park? I can't exactly confide my woes to you in the middle of the street, Quinn."

"The rain put you off for a week." Quinn's need to ensure Jane's day started pleasantly had also played a role. If he brought her plain toast and ginger tea before she got out of bed, her belly was less rebellious.

Following the toast and tea, on two memorable occasions, Quinn had climbed back under the covers and Jane had started his day very pleasantly indeed.

"The rain put me off for two days," Stephen said. "Are we going to bloody bedamned *Newgate*?"

"Yes."

"Does it ever occur to you to ask other people what they want, Quinn?"

He'd asked Jane. She liked to be on top. "You're free to gallop off to the park, but because nobody has asked *me* if I'd like a little privacy, I suspect you'll stick to my side like a rash."

"A devoted rash. Why are we visiting the scene of your execution?"

"Please, Stephen. I had a brush with death, a misfortune, an unpleasant ordeal. You're a lord now—try to find some damned delicacy."

Stephen fell silent, which was delicacy enough. All too soon, the horror that was Newgate came into view.

"You'll stay with the horses," Quinn said.

"Because I can't hop down and chase you. Sometimes, I hate you." Said without heat.

"Sometimes," Quinn replied, "I hate myself." As when he sneaked away from Jane's side, because he didn't want her to worry needlessly. "I'm here to question a guard."

Stephen crossed his hands on the pommel and regarded the bleak façade. "Imagine that. You've come back to the scene of your misfortunate brush with death by the ordeal of hanging to question a guard. This has to be the ugliest piece of architecture ever to house mortal man."

And women and children. "That's the intention, to intimidate and frighten." Quinn did not want to be here, but the person he needed to speak with dwelled on the premises.

He dismounted at the entrance and passed his reins to Stephen. "Don't go far."

"Don't stay long. Duncan is up to something."

"About damned time he got his head out of the learned tomes. I've asked him to look into a few delicate matters for me." Among them, a ducal estate in Berkshire that stewards and solicitors had picked cleaner than bleached bones. The family seat in Yorkshire was in no better condition if the new steward's reports were to be believed.

Stephen peered down at him, which was disconcerting when Quinn was accustomed to looking down on his baby brother.

"*You* sent Duncan on his present errand? But then, why should I be told what my tutor has got up to. I'm merely his only pupil, his cousin, and the closest thing he has to a friend. No need to keep *me* informed." Having concluded his lamentation, Stephen led Quinn's horse away, hoofbeats ringing against the dew-slick cobbles.

At the street corner, the shadow Quinn had acquired shortly after returning from York pretended to read the bill of fare set outside a pub. A slow reader, apparently, or a footman new to the business of spying.

Getting inside Newgate was simple—a hard stare, a name—and then Quinn was again enveloped in the stench and filth that had been his temporary home. He'd been lucky to get into a state room, because the alternative was eventual death for most who dwelled too long in the common wards.

He was led up a set of steps to a dormitory portion of the prison. The smell wasn't as bad, and the noise was muted. Sounds from the street hinted at normalcy while iron rings anchored in the stone wall confirmed that nothing in this place was normal.

Quinn was left outside a partly open wooden door. He knocked and pushed the door open.

"If it isn't our Mr. Wentworth." The guard had yet to shave and was without his coat. His beard was a mix of gray and flax, his eyes the blue of northern summer skies. He rose from a battered table and smiled, revealing good teeth. "You're looking well, sir."

"I'd like to stay well."

"Wouldn't we all. Easier said than done. You wanted to talk."

Quinn closed the door, though it made him uneasy to do so. The chamber was small: one window, one door, a tiny hearth. The furnishings consisted of a bed, a table, a chair. Six pegs had been jammed into the wall opposite the hearth, and a worn Bible sat on the mantel.

Once upon a time, Quinn would have regarded these snug, dry, secure quarters as palatial.

"I want to live," he said. "To do that, I need to know who put me in jail."

The guard unrolled a shaving kit on the table and wrapped a tattered towel across his throat. He brought a basin of water from the hearth and resumed his seat, propping a speckled mirror against the side of the basin.

"You put yourself in here, guv. Took a man's life. Happen it might have been by accident, but the cove's just as dead."

"In point of fact, he is not dead. Mr. Robert Pike is kicking his heels in Calais, and has written at least twice to his brother in York. He's no more dead than you are."

A steel blade was held up to the meagre morning light. "Good for Mr. Pike. You're a free man, a wealthy free man with a royal pardon. Why can't you let well enough alone?"

Exactly what Jane had advised.

This rough, aging man had once been kind to Quinn, and he'd had a brutally sharp knife and quick reflexes when those had been the difference between life and death. He was trying to be kind now.

"I haven't the luxury of leaving well enough alone," Quinn said. "My wife is in a delicate condition, my sisters are unmarried, my brother spends most of his time in a Bath chair. If whoever had me arrested should attempt any more mischief, my family will not survive, my bank will fail, and then everybody from shop girls to courtesy lords will suffer. I would take the law into my own hands only as a last resort, but I cannot allow an enemy to threaten my family."

The guard opened a tin of shaving soap, swished a brush in the tepid water, and worked up a lather. The scent of bay rum wafted across the small chamber.

"They say you're from up north."

"York, born and bred. I don't make a secret of it." Quinn waited while his host scraped away whiskers and made the undignified, peculiar faces men made when shaving.

The guard tapped his razor against the side of the basin. "Mind, I didn't see anything."

"Understood."

"Didn't hear anything, don't know anything. Hand me that towel."

Quinn passed over a less-tattered square of linen.

"I've been here at Newgate for more than twenty years. Other than the warden and some of the state prisoners, I have the best room in the house."

Which spoke volumes for the accommodations at Newgate. "Go on."

"I can sit by this window and see who comes and goes. Who's got people waiting outside, whose children are coming around with a loaf of bread or a coin. We don't get many swells calling here."

"I'm surprised you get any."

The guard patted away the stray flecks of lather on his cheeks and chin. "You work here long enough, nothing surprises you, *Your Grace*."

"Point taken."

"So a while back, maybe three months ago, one of them fancy coaches pulls up after dark. The nights were cold enough that the window was closed, but I rarely hear a coach and four stop out front."

The main entrance was directly beneath the window. Late at night, iron-shod hooves on cobbles would make a racket.

"But one did."

"Twice. The crests were turned, nobody got out. Warden got in. The coach pulls away. Fifteen minutes later, he's back. I says to myself, 'Jock,' I says. 'Somebody's in for some trouble.' Warden's a good man, but he don't always have a choice."

"The warden nearly killed an innocent man."

"It happens, and the guilty go free. Not my job or the warden's to sort 'em out. It were a fine and fancy coach, guv."

With crests on the doors, confirming that wealth was, indeed, involved. "What color was the team?"

"Grays, both times. If you're trying to sneak about after dark, that's an odd choice."

Not if you were the Countess of Tipton, who'd always favored grays and was too arrogant to consider that they might be an indiscreet choice.

"Did you notice anything else about the coach?"

"The shades were pulled down, the lamps unlit. Just a fine coach and four matched horses."

Which proved exactly nothing. "Then I thank you for your time."

"They say you weren't born rich."

Quinn laughed. "I was born dirt poor in a room smaller than this one. All of my life, I told myself that poverty didn't entitle me to lie, cheat, steal, or break the rules. I worked to exhaustion, got lucky, and then got luckier still, and worked even harder."

"Until you got very unlucky." The guard set about cleaning his razor and rolling up his kit. The interview was over, in other words, and had been a waste of time.

"I don't consider it bad luck when somebody tries to kill me. Murder is evil and wrong, and I won't stand for it."

The guard tied his shaving kit with a tidy bow and set it on the mantel. "We're stubborn, we Yorkshireman. Wish I could be of more help."

Quinn extended a hand and shook. "If you think of anything, send word, Jock." He passed over a card with the bank's direction, because nobody needed to know the specific location where his family dwelled.

Jock studied the card. "You're not about to bribe me, are you?"

"If your word can be bought, then it's not trustworthy."

"Precious. Don't find many who see it like that." He folded the battered mirror and set it beside the shaving kit. "Up home, a man's word is still his bond, not here."

Homesickness colored that observation, while Quinn never wanted to see Yorkshire again. "You were raised in York?"

"Out on the dales. Had a wife, a baby girl. Lung fever got 'em the same winter. Tried to find work at one of the fancy estates, but a shepherd boy who took the king's shilling isn't much use in a household like that." No rancor colored these words, merely the soldier/shepherd's stoic acceptance.

"I wore livery once myself. Longest two years of my life." And the most confounding and regrettable.

The guard smiled. "Bet you looked a treat, all done up in lace."

Quinn was happy to leave on that note—he had looked a treat, damn it all to hell—but instead he asked one last question.

"I don't suppose you noticed the livery on the coachman or grooms?"

The guard folded his arms and leaned against the wall. "Happen I did. More foolishness if somebody's trying to keep their business quiet. Grooms wore pale blue and silver with black stockings. You'd think we were holding a fancy dress ball here. I recognized that livery because the earls of Tipton have fancied it for as long as I can recall, and their domestics have been strutting about York in that finery just as long."

"So they have." Finery Quinn himself had once been proud to wear, right down to the black stockings and silver shoe buckles.

* * *

The baby was growing, almost as if the good food and rest Jane enjoyed in the Wentworth household were going straight to the child, and that was lovely.

Her regard for her husband was growing as well. Quinn Wentworth was an affectionate man, though Jane suspected only Constance's cats had been privy to that secret. Behind a closed bedroom door, Quinn became a warm blanket of husband by night, and an inventive lover at all hours.

When Jane couldn't find sleep, she found Quinn, and he loved her into dreams and peaceful slumbers. If she asked it of him, he escorted her and his sisters about the shops, though she knew he'd rather be at the bank. Because she did ask it of him, he tolerated the company of footmen, siblings, Ned, grooms, or Joshua rather than let Jane fret that he was without the safety of numbers.

He explained complicated financial instruments to her—trusts, deeds, mortgages, promissory notes—though Jane found his recitations baffling. To Quinn, these documents were so many forms of sport, challenges to craft and enforce, works of art to admire. She came to understand that banking had provided a sense of order and predictability to a young man who'd grown up amid chaos and violence.

Jane's worries were growing as well. Papa had come by again, and Jane hadn't the heart to refuse him entry to the house. Stephen had stayed by her side while Papa had discoursed at length on the quality of mercy, confusing Shakespeare and holy scripture while swilling tea and gobbling cakes.

To Stephen, that recitation had likely been a mind-numbing bore. To Jane it had been laced with alarming innuendo. Papa clearly intended to have the raising of her child, proof positive that her surviving parent had become a candidate for Bedlam. By the time the courts found in Papa's favor—a theoretical possibility—Jane would be approaching old age.

But how to explain that to Papa, or how to put the situation to Quinn without Papa ending up *in* Bedlam?

The library door opened and Quinn entered. Jane rose to kiss his cheek, because such was a wife's privilege.

"You're home in the middle of day," she said. "Is something amiss at the bank?"

Quinn kissed her back—on the mouth. "Something is terribly wrong. I missed my wife and couldn't concentrate worth a damn. Joshua is in a temper over the clerks squabbling, the auditor is in a temper over Joshua's bad mood, and I bethought myself: I have a perfectly lovely wife at home and it's a beautiful spring day. Why am I subjecting myself to this drudgery, when I might instead be enjoying Jane's company?"

The house was quiet, it being half day and the sisters having retired to Constance's studio. Stephen was closeted with a new translation of Dante, and Jane had been contemplating composing a letter to Papa's bishop, begging for word of a congregation Papa might serve.

How much more agreeable to spend time with her husband.

Quinn came down beside her on the sofa. "What are you reading?"

"Dr. Smellie's treatise on childbirth." Constance had given it to her, a strange offering, but then, everything about Constance bordered on the eccentric.

Quinn propped his boots on the hassock and put an arm around Jane's shoulders. "I anticipate your travail with something approaching panic."

"Women give birth every day, Quinn. I'm healthy, I'll

have good medical care. Please don't worry." Jane was worrying enough for them both. She slid down against him, pillowing her head on his shoulder.

She worried about giving birth as all women did, and she worried about her father's increasingly odd notions. In the wrong mood, Papa might try to physically appropriate an infant—the accurate term was *kidnap*—and Quinn would be unable to overlook such behavior.

Should *anybody* overlook such behavior?

"Joshua says we ought to move to a larger house," Quinn said.

"Why?"

"I'm a duke. I'm supposed to involve myself in the House of Lords now, and ensure banking laws remain sane, because the present crop of titled buffoons will just pillage the exchequer in the usual fashion if left to their own devices."

Quinn's fingers started a slow massage on Jane's nape. Tension she'd held all day eased away, and she considered telling Quinn of her father's scheme.

"Does Joshua want you to take your seat, or is that your conscience talking?" Even after a morning at the bank, Quinn still smelled of his lovely shaving soap.

He toed off one polished boot with the other. "I was absent from the bank for weeks, Jane. Joshua had no warning I'd be unavailable, and he not only managed without me, he managed well. We've increased the number of depositors by twenty percent since I was arrested, and now that my title is becoming common knowledge, our customers include peers as well as shopkeepers."

Jane took Quinn's free hand. "And?"

"Joshua is delighted. He's hired more tellers, another amanuensis, two clerks... while I'm wondering if I cheated the hangman merely to keep a larger ledger book."

For Quinn, that was an expression of fundamental doubt. "You have doubtless worked just as hard as Joshua for just as long to make the bank succeed. You have been through hell, taken a wife, been saddled with a title, and will soon have an infant underfoot. You're due a little time to sort out your thoughts."

He nuzzled her temple. "So sensible. When you're all prim and proper I get bothered."

Quinn had a naughty streak, much to Jane's delight— a lusty, naughty streak. She sensed in his more exuberant overtures a newfound glee, a relief at being spontaneous and physical that was new for Jane as well.

"I like it when you're bothered, Quinn."

He rose and held out a hand. "Come upstairs with me, Jane. Help me sort out my thoughts."

When he smiled like that, his thoughts needed no translation. Jane took his hand, struggled to her feet, and let him escort her to their rooms.

She'd bring up the situation with Papa only if circumstances made that discussion imperative. By the time the child arrived, Papa might have a congregation again, preferably on a remote island to the west of Scotland.

* * *

"Where could he be?" Althea tossed herself into the reading chair by the hearth. All the comfortable furniture seemed to end up in Constance's studio, though how and when it migrated here only Ivor and Kristoff knew.

"Davies says Duncan is in Berkshire," Constance replied around the paintbrush sticking out of her mouth. "When Davies passes along gossip, it's usually trustworthy. He knows we rely on his reports. Perhaps our cousin came across a librarian flaunting a first folio of the Bard and became passionately distracted. Hand me that rag."

Constance was not an artist so much as she was a caricaturist. Her paintings were emotionally accurate—revealing character, motive, sentiments—while her physical representations were interpretive. She'd shown a respectable talent with watercolors by age fifteen, and then...

Then she'd taken up oils, which ladies were not supposed to do. Althea handed her a rag that was stiff with myriad blotches of paint and redolent of linseed oil.

"Duncan should be back by now," Althea said. "Berkshire's not that far."

Constance took the brush from her mouth and the brush in her hand and tucked one behind each ear, paint end out.

"Duncan deserves a break from us, Althea. He never chastises or criticizes, but in his very silence, I hear volumes of long-suffering. If he were a better man, he'd pray for us, but he's a Wentworth, so he simply endures. Stephen would have been lost without him."

Stephen would have been dead without Duncan. Five years ago, Ivor had found one of Quinn's cravats fashioned into a noose in Stephen's dressing closet. A further search had revealed a note—"The pain defeats me."—and enough arsenic to kill an elephant-sized rat. Quinn had left the evidence undisturbed. He reasoned that a twelve-year-old's melancholia need not be complicated by humiliation, and he'd sent a pigeon to Duncan in York the same hour.

Duncan had resigned his post as a schoolteacher and boarded the next stage for London.

"Of all of us," Althea said, "Duncan strikes me as the loneliest. He's a Wentworth who doesn't fit in among Wentworths."

"I like him for that. He's also brilliant, and doesn't lord it about, unlike certain younger brothers."

"You've never liked anybody."

The two paintbrushes jutting from Constance's hair made her look like a fanciful bull with one red-tipped horn and one black.

"I like my cats." Constance poured another inch of ale into both mugs, passed one to Althea, and perched on her stool. "Are you hiding in my studio?"

Yes. "Quinn's home in the middle of the day."

Constance took a sip of ale and drew her sleeve across her lips to wipe the foam away. "They are newly married. Allowances must be made."

Perhaps that explained why the portrait on the easel was Persephone and Hades, cuddled up on a hearth rug. The tomcat looked pleased with himself, while the she-cat licked the top of his head. Hades was half a lick away from having his ear gnawed off, did he but know it. Persephone, like her owner, did not suffer fools.

"They are newly married," Althea said, "but it's peculiar to see Quinn smiling with his mouth. He smiles with his eyes on occasion, such as when Stephen bests Duncan on some philosophical point, but Quinn smiles *at* Jane. At the dinner table, in front of everybody."

"Jane smiles too," Constance said, studying her ale, "at Quinn."

Worse, they smiled *with* each other, like, like a besotted couple sharing sweet secrets and private jokes.

Most peculiar. "Jane won't be smiling at him when she finds out he's hiding invitations from her, among other things."

The invitations had started as a trickle, after Jane had crossed paths with some other duchess at a glovemaker's. Althea had never seen more gracious curtsying, while the proprietress had hovered and cooed like a matchmaker eavesdropping on a proposal.

Several days later, a pair of calling cards had appeared in the perpetually empty crystal bowl in the foyer—a marchioness and a countess, whom Debrett's revealed to be related to the other duchess. Every day a few more cards and invitations showed up, only to be snatched away before Jane caught sight of them.

"Quinn means well," Constance said, withdrawing the paintbrushes from her hair. "He's being an idiot. A stint in Newgate will be a minor scandal compared to snubbing half the peerage."

"Better to be an idiot than have all of polite society looking on as you introduce your wife to the woman who tried to see you hanged. Do you trust Duncan, Con?"

Constance should have scoffed at Althea's question, should have snorted with laughter as only Constance could on the semi-annual occasions when she was amused.

Instead she set her brushes on the easel tray and took a considering sip of ale. "I trust Duncan. Do you trust Stephen?"

Uncomfortable question, but one Althea had pondered. "The Stephen who fired a gun in Jane's direction?"

"That Stephen, the same one who knew the Walden title was in search of an heir."

Althea had the damnedest urge to ring for a tea tray. Ale made one burp, and the taste was pedestrian. Unrefined.

"I do trust Stephen," she said, "but mostly because anybody trying to get away with Quinn's murder wouldn't announce their violent intentions by threatening Quinn's wife. Stephen is a pestilence of a brother, but he's far from stupid."

Constance put her feet up on a hassock, revealing slender ankles and bare feet. "I hate this, doubting family. Family is all we've had for so long. Jane is not to blame for Quinn's troubles, but I resent her nonetheless."

That was a considerable admission for Constance. "Do you resent Jane, or the fact that Jane arrived with a child on the way?"

"Both, of course, but there's something I haven't found a way to pass along to Jane, and catching Quinn alone has become nearly impossible."

By design, of course, because Jane wasn't stupid either. "Spill it, Con."

"Do you recall the day Jane met Her Grace of Moreland at the glovemaker's?"

"The occasion has doubtless been memorialized in dozens of genteel drawing rooms."

"Did you notice who was coming up the walkway, footman and maid trailing, as we were leaving?"

On second thought, ale was a fine drink. In sufficient quantities, it dulled the day's sharp edges and fortified against the sudden arrival of bad news.

"I was too busy pretending I knew what I was supposed to do," Althea said. "I must have curtsied six times."

"Five," Constance said, "but I wasn't too busy to notice the Countess of Tipton making her way to the very establishment we'd just vacated."

"Coincidence?" Althea asked, finishing her ale.

"We're Wentworths. What's the likelihood that Quinn's nemesis would cross paths with Jane on one of her few excursions without him?"

"No likelihood at all."

"Shall I ring for more ale?"

"Of course."

Chapter Twenty-three

Making love with Jane was the reward for every effort, the antidote to every ill, and—with her—simply another part of being married.

Quinn pondered that conundrum in odd moments at the bank, while staring at the estate ledgers, and in the quiet interludes after lovemaking. He'd spent the first eighteen years of his life scrabbling for survival, spent his entire adulthood amassing wealth from nothing, dodged the noose, been handed a failing dukedom, and left parts of himself scattered from York to London.

Jane was putting him back together. With her smiles and scolds, her shopping expeditions, her affection, her presence at his side, she was bringing a sense of normalcy to a family that had never been normal.

"Would you rather I'd stayed at the bank?" Quinn asked, as he closed their sitting room door. "I am a creature of routine. Perhaps you are too."

Jane led him into the bedroom. "I'd rather you do as you please, and I cannot imagine a circumstance where climbing into bed with my husband would not please me too."

She avoided addressing him as Your Grace or Duke, and used his name, or "husband." Occasionally, she referred to him teasingly as Mr. Wentworth. Even that small domesticity soothed Quinn, and reinforced the notion that with Jane, he could be himself.

Almost.

He tended to her hooks, she took his sleeve buttons. He opened the window, she folded back the covers. They had a rhythm about even this, though when it came to lovemaking, Jane was anything but predictable.

Quinn finished undressing, giving Jane the use of the privacy screen. She emerged in her shift, her hair a single braid draped over one shoulder.

"I'm getting fat." She regarded her belly as if the fairies had bestowed it upon her the previous night. "I'll soon lose sight of my feet."

She wasn't getting fat, but the swell of her middle was noticeable when she was unclothed. "You're growing luscious. If you lose sight of your feet, I'll find them for you."

Jane leaned against him, all soft, sweet woman. "How did you learn to be so attentive? You describe your father as a parental horror and barely recall your mother. Where did your considerate nature come from, Quinn?"

Considerate? "In all of creation, you are the only person who regards me as considerate, though I suspect my father's bad example played a role in forming my character. He treated my mother and my stepmother abominably, and when Step-Mama was too exhausted to deal with the children, I did what I could. I cannot ignore a crying baby."

Jane shifted closer, looping her arms around him. "I

treasure this about you. You notice what's amiss and do something about it, but what if that baby isn't yours to comfort?"

What an odd question, though technically, the baby Jane carried wasn't Quinn's to comfort. He'd consulted with solicitors and barristers, and their opinions were mixed. Gordie had sired the child but hadn't known Jane had conceived. He thus hadn't had an opportunity to acknowledge the baby as his. In the normal course, Gordie would have had little choice, because marriage obligated a man to support all children born to his wife during the period of coverture.

Which obligation, Quinn's father had chafed against at every turn.

"I'm not concerned about the babies who belong to others, Jane. At this very moment, I'm not exactly focused on the baby you'll have either."

He kissed her, lest she launch into a conversational flight about which room to convert into a nursery. He could taste the pre-occupation in her, the retreat into that place from which only an expectant mother regarded the world. She had secrets there—fears, physical sensations, hopes—and Quinn allowed her that privacy.

He had secrets too, and his reason for ambushing Jane in the middle of the day was one of them.

"Come to bed," she said, after a lovely, lazy spate of kissing. "Come to bed and love me."

He did love her. Loved her courage and her intriguingly complicated female body, her pragmatism and her generous heart. The words remained lodged in his heart, so he tried to show her his feelings with touches and tickles.

When Jane swung her leg over him and straddled him on the bed, Quinn was already having to do sums in his head to restrain his desire.

"You look so serious," Jane said, drawing a finger between his brows. "And yet, you make me laugh in bed."

"You're the one who referred to yourself as a rutting heifer."

Jane mooed against the side of his neck bearing the scar, then bit his earlobe. She had a curiosity about his body that went beyond the sexual, and suggested to Quinn that to her, he wasn't simply attractive, he was *interesting*.

"Shall we name the child Bossy?" Jane asked, straightening to lift her shift over her head. "Or perhaps I'll deserve that appellation." She studied her breasts quizzically. "I have never considered myself well endowed, but my proportions are changing."

"Will you use a wet nurse?" Quinn hoped not. This was ungenteel of him, a relic of his upbringing, but the notion that a stranger would nourish the baby sat ill with him. Some women nursed a child for a few months, then hired that stranger. Others never put the child to their own breast—others who could afford that choice.

"I haven't thought that far ahead," Jane said, touching her nose to his. "We haven't even decided where to put the nursery yet."

If he let her wander off on that topic she'd still be chattering away at sunset, and Quinn's schedule did not permit him that much patience.

"We haven't chosen a name," he said, lifting his hips to scoot closer. "Perhaps we can discuss that later."

He eased into the joining, and though he and Jane had made love a dozen times, he still marveled at the pleasure and intimacy. Lovemaking with Jane was more than physical union, it was…

The quest for words slipped away as Jane folded down onto Quinn's chest. Her caresses and sighs confirmed that she wanted a sweet, relaxed loving, and so he sent her over the edge only twice before permitting himself to spend.

His hands drifted over her back, tracing sturdy bones and elegant curves while Jane's breathing slowed. What did it say about him, that these moments of absolute contentment and closeness were as enjoyable as the erotic satisfaction?

"I'll fall asleep," she murmured.

She always fell asleep after lovemaking. Quinn was counting on her remaining true to form.

"You rest," he said, easing her to her side. "I'll be right back."

He kissed her shoulder, left the bed, and brought her a damp flannel. Before she passed it back to him, she was already yawning.

"You'll think me lazy," she said, cuddling down into the covers.

"I think you lovely." And worth protecting at any cost.

Quinn climbed in beside her and held her until he was certain she was lost to dreams. With one more kiss to her cheek, he slipped from the bed, dressed, and prepared to confront a murderess.

* * *

"Himself never comes home in the middle of the day," Ned said.

Davies was peeling apples, the long, thin spiral of skin hanging over the slop bucket. "Himself is married and a duke. He needn't get your permission to do anything."

Ned took an apple from the basket. This time of year, they were less than crisp but still fine for cooking—or juggling. He started with two, because he was out of practice.

"But we're not to leave him to his own devices. Miss Jane said."

"He's not alone, Ned Dunderpate. Where'd you learn to do that?"

"Taught meself. Juggling's good for a copper every now and then, a legal copper." He caught the two apples, selected a third, and started over. "Being a pickpocket is like doing a magic trick. What was in a bloke's pocket disappears and he's none the wiser."

"Being a pickpocket is how you ended up in Newgate."

Three apples required attention—five was the best Ned had ever done—and arguing with Davies required attention.

"I'm done picking pockets." Ned hoped this was true, though the duties he'd been given consisted merely of taking the air twice a day when himself went to the bank, and delivering the occasional message for the bank.

That and regular trips to the pawnshops.

Which was a worrisome state of affairs. In Ned's opinion, giving a boy a cot in the laundry, three meals a day, and new boots entitled His Grace to slavish devotion, not simply stepping and fetching around the neighborhood.

"If you're smart, you're done with all the games," Davies said, starting on a second apple. "Not another boy in all of London has gone from Newgate to a duke's household. Play your cards right, you could be a footman."

The back door closed. In the window above the sink, Ned saw a boot-level view of the duke crossing the garden.

Ned caught all three apples and tossed one of them to Davies. "A tiger's work is never done." He bolted up the steps and caught up with his employer. "So where are we off to, guv?"

The duke kept walking. "I am off to the bank, on foot. You will remain at your post in the kitchen in case the ladies need your services this afternoon."

Like hell. "It's half day. Where are the running footmen?"

"Probably getting drunk and flirting with the tavern maids, as is their right when they are not at work." Himself passed through the gate at the foot of the garden and pulled it shut behind him.

Ned clambered over. "You can't be running around London by yourself. Miss Jane said. Somebody put your neck in a bloody noose, and we have to keep you safe."

His Grace of Doom stopped in the middle of the cobbled alley. Ned had never seen such a cold expression on a man's face, and he counted many a hardened criminal among his acquaintances.

"Ned, I applaud your loyalty, but your insubordination will cost you your post if you don't desist."

"You'd *sack* me?" Ned's voice had cracked, so great was his consternation.

The duke slapped his gloves against his thigh, looked up and down the alley, then turned his glower back on Ned.

"I will turn you off without a character if you don't remain here as directed."

Which only confirmed that Miss Jane had been right: Himself wasn't used to having people look after him. Neither was Ned. Miss Jane had explained that Ned would have to adjust. Adjusting was hard, so Ned didn't haul off and smack his employer in the stones despite the temptation.

"We were in jail together, and you'd give me the boot?"

That cold gaze grew frigid. "Without a character. Tossed out on your ear, finished, sacked."

Ned had never had a character and wasn't exactly sure what one was. He did know that for the duke to march off across Town on foot, without grooms, without Miss Jane, was bloody stupid.

"Then I'll be Ned Sacked."

Had Ned not been returning glower for glower, he would have missed the gleam of humor that crossed the duke's features. Miss Jane had said His Grace was full of bluster. Ned hadn't wanted to test the theory.

In the next instant, he was scooped up and deposited on the ladies' mounting block.

"You," the duke said, jabbing a finger at Ned, "are Ned Wentworth. If you'd like a middle name, I can suggest Pestilential, Pigheaded, or Plaguey. Ponder your choice while I return to the bank, by myself, along a route I have traveled in safety for years. Any word to the rest of the staff of this altercation will earn you a severe dressing down, Ned. I mean it."

Whatever an altercation was. "You're giving me *your name*? The name of your own family?"

The duke pulled on black leather gloves. "See that you never dishonor it. Now get back in the house."

He stalked off down the alley, while Ned's throat went tight, and his breathing hitched.

"Ned Wentworth. I like it." He took another breath. "Edward Wentworth. Mister Edward Wentworth."

He wiped his eyes on his sleeve—the coal dust in London was awful—and began sorting through middle names. Himself was named Quinton.

"Edward Quinton Wentworth." That didn't feel quite right.

Something else wasn't quite right. If the duke was walking back to the bank using the route he'd followed safely "for years," he should have turned at the intersection of the next alley. He kept going straight, away from the bank. For half a minute, Ned debated what a loyal, insubordinate, pestilential Wentworth should do.

Then he hopped off the wall and started after the duke.

* * *

Jane dreamed of Quinn as she'd first known him, confined to a gentleman's cage in Newgate, coatless, serving her gingerbread, and offering her a miracle. She reached across the bed thinking that now, finally, was a moment when she could raise the topic of Papa's ridiculous notions regarding Gordie's will, but her hand encountered only cool sheets.

She opened her eyes and found herself alone.

"That dratted bank." She'd wanted to dance a jig at the idea of Quinn cutting ties with the day-to-day operation of the bank. At least five ducal estates needed his attention, and he'd enjoy putting them to rights.

He might also enjoy setting the buffoons in the Lords on their ears, though Jane hoped to make some progress socializing with those buffoons before her confinement began.

She rang for Susan to assist her with her hooks, pinned up her braid, and opened the copy of Debrett's she'd been studying for the past several days. Polite society was closely interconnected, and surely a ducal family could claim a few distant relatives among those assembling for the season?

"Will you need anything else, ma'am?" Susan asked.

"If Lady Althea is home, please let her know that I'd like a word with her."

"She and Lady Constance are having tea in the studio."

They weren't having tea. They had chocolate, cordial, good old English ale, and the occasional medicinal tot, but never tea.

"My request is not urgent. Lady Constance is welcome to join us. If Lord Stephen isn't otherwise occupied, he's welcome as well."

Quinn was a duke, and the time had come for polite society to acknowledge him as such.

Susan withdrew, and Jane opened the desk drawer to retrieve paper and pencil. A duchess was expected to entertain and to be entertained. She had the next eight weeks—the remainder of the season—to begin the arduous task of establishing her husband among his peers and neighbors.

The paper and pencils were in their usual places, but the letters Quinn had been personally safeguarding were missing.

"Cash, coins, and his letters patent can sit in a safe, but the letters from That Woman..."

Jane gave the rest of the desk a hurried inspection, then looked over the desk in the bedroom. No letters. Quinn had kept those letters for years. Why would he...?

Althea called to Jane from the sitting room. "You asked to see us?"

"I did." Jane joined them in the sitting room and closed the bedroom door behind her. "I wanted to discuss our social calendar."

Constance took the seat at the desk. "I don't socialize. There, we've discussed my calendar."

Althea remained standing. "Should a woman in your condition be socializing?"

"My condition is barely evident," Jane said, "at least when I'm wearing higher-waisted dresses. The baby isn't due for another several months, and I do not intend to spend that entire time as a recluse sitting on a velvet pillow sewing baby clothes. The Wentworths are now a ducal family, and the title brings certain obligations."

Constance drummed her fingers on the blotter. "You could do charitable work."

Charitable work had killed Mama, though for a duchess, charitable work was probably a version of sitting on a velvet pillow.

"Your brother is more than generous to the charities of his choice."

"You're a clergyman's daughter," Althea said. "You should have causes of your own."

This family was Jane's cause. "What aren't you two telling me? I expect grousing from you at every turn, but not dissembling."

Althea shot a glance at the door, confirming Jane's sense of something amiss.

"We should let her know," Constance said. "She'll find out soon enough, and not responding to invitations is rude. Even I know that."

Althea crossed her arms. "You tell her."

"Somebody tell me," Jane said, settling into a wing chair. "And do not think to mention my condition in your own defense."

"The invitations have started," Constance said. "The Duke of Elsmore was the first. We thought it was a fluke, a jest in poor taste, but the cards kept coming. Then the Duchess of Moreland sent a footman around with her card. That means we can call on her."

"The Duchess of *Moreland*?" Jane did not consider herself a duchess. She was a woman married to a man who'd happened into a title through a series of unfortunate events. Her Grace of Moreland was a duchess from her tiara to her embroidered satin slippers, and the power she wielded was legendary.

"We met her at the glovemaker's," Jane said, upset rising in her belly that had nothing to do with the baby. "She was so kind, and we've failed to acknowledge her card?"

"Stephen says there's honor among dukes," Althea replied, inching toward the door. "They take an interest in one another because there are so few of them."

"Devonshire sent a card," Constance said. "We're welcome to call on him too." She sounded bewildered rather than pugnacious. "There are others, any number of courtesy titles."

This was good news masquerading as a disaster, proof that polite society could forgive and forget, and Quinn would be so pleased....

"Does Quinn know about this?"

Althea became fascinated with a bouquet of pink and yellow tulips on the sideboard. "He asked us to set the invitations aside and said he'd deal with them later."

Oh, Quinn. "And the pair of you said not a word to me. When did Elsmore's invitation arrive?"

They exchanged a guilty glance.

"Two weeks ago," Constance said. "Give or take."

Jane rose, because for some situations counting to three was a complete waste of breath.

"My mother was a lady. She married down, as many ladies do, but she made sure I knew how to comport myself in all company. Do you know how inconsiderate it is to ignore an invitation? These matters are bounded by protocol, etiquette, an agreed-upon—" Why weren't they arguing with her? Why weren't they dismissing her concerns? "You have reminded Quinn about these invitations, haven't you?"

"We nag him," Constance said. "He puts us off, says we'll have time for all of that later. That marchionesses and countesses can wait to be acknowledged by a duchess."

Marchionesses and countesses? *Countesses?*

"*That man*," Jane muttered. "That stubborn, misguided, foolish...Quinn is trying to keep me from crossing paths with one countess in particular, a lady who will doubtless be in attendance at some of the functions I'll be invited to. This is why we don't go to the theater, why we don't drive out at the Fashionable Hour."

Constance looked confused. "What countess?"

"*Her*," Althea said. "The Countess of Tipton."

Constance, for once, had no terse retort.

"I've started reading the society pages," Jane said. "She's here in London with her husband." And Quinn's letters from her were missing. No thief could breach the Wentworth citadel, and the staff would not dare move letters without permission, which meant Quinn himself had those letters.

"You should sit down," Althea said. "You look pale."

Jane's mind was leaping from fact to conjecture to fear. "Quinn came home at midday for no reason. He didn't take his nooning here, didn't come home to retrieve a forgotten document. It's half day, so we have little staff about, and I would bet your oldest harp, Althea, that Quinn gave his running footmen the afternoon off too."

Constance sat up very straight. "What are you saying?"

The intimacies, the tender confidences, the oh-so-considerate lover leaving his wife to nap away her afternoon…

"He has gone to her," Jane said. "He's either attempting to placate her with offers of money or favors, or he's planning to do her an injury, which she well deserves."

In either case, Quinn hadn't confided in his wife. Worse than that, he'd *pretended* to confide in Jane, pretended he was considering leaving the bank, pretended he'd missed her so badly, he'd been truant from his ledgers….

Not you too, Quinn. Please don't let my husband be among those to ignore the sensible course and march off to certain doom in the name of his blasted principles.

The fear of that certain doom nearly paralyzed her, for a woman scorned who had a title, money, and a long, bitter memory wouldn't hesitate to take advantage of Quinn's honorable nature. Though Jane was furious with Quinn too. Gordie's true colors had always been evident; Jane had simply been too inexperienced and desperate to spot a handsome rascal wearing the king's colors.

Quinn, though, had deliberately set out to deceive her.

"What will you do?" Althea asked.

"What I should do is leave," Jane said. "I should do as many fashionable wives do and establish my own household, free from meddling papas, dissembling husbands, quarrelsome family, and unreturned calling cards. Quinn has gone daft if he thinks gratifying that woman with a pitched battle will work to his advantage."

Constance was on her feet. "You aren't making sense. Quinn hates the countess, as do I. You don't know what he was like before. He never rode in the park, never took us shopping, never read the paper at the breakfast table because we might see his lips moving when he came to long words. He's doing the best he can, and you can't leave."

Yes, I can. "How many times am I expected to forgive and forget willful dishonesty? What Quinn is doing—deliberately provoking a woman whose schemes have failed—is wrong, stupid, and dangerous. I've told him as much over and over, and rather than cede to my wishes or offer me any sound rebuttal, he lies to me, over and over."

Gordie had lied, saying he was off to the Horse Guards when in fact he'd been swilling gin at the pub and ogling tavern maids.

Papa had lied, whisking Mama's treasures off to the pawnshop, and then pretending they'd been misplaced.

Mama had lied, claiming she was on the mend, only to make her illness worse through overexertion.

That Quinn would lie as well...

"You're a *duchess*," Althea said. "You can't fly into the

bows over a misunderstanding. Quinn might well be back by supper with some perfectly reasonable explanation for why you can't find a batch of old letters."

A wave of weariness hit Jane, which was ridiculous when she'd just spent the better part of an hour napping.

"You don't believe that, Althea. Now you're attempting to deceive me as well, deceive me again."

Going home to Papa would never be an option, but Jane had pin money more than sufficient to establish a household, and she had her pride. She did not want to leave the man she loved, but condoning another betrayal was impossible.

"Beg pardon, Your Grace, your ladyships." Ivor appeared at the door. "Reverend Winston is in the sitting room and asking to see Her Grace. Shall I have a tea tray sent up?"

The day needed only this. Jane nearly told Ivor to send up an entire meal, but Constance was drumming her fingers against her skirts, tapping each finger eight times, her expression carefully blank.

That was a Wentworth in distress.

Althea had glanced at the clock three times and checked the watch pinned to her bodice twice. Jane would not have been surprised to see Quinn's sister drop to her knees and crawl out the door—or the window.

Another Wentworth in distress.

"No tea tray, Ivor. And you and Kristoff will attend me. Althea and Constance, we are not finished."

Though perhaps Jane and Quinn were, assuming he survived his altercation with the Countess of Tipton.

Chapter Twenty-four

The letters in Quinn's pocket felt as if they weighed twelve stone, something Jane would have understood. These epistles had likely put him in Newgate and put his neck in a noose. Better, as Jane advised, to forgive and forget. To move on and appreciate the joy of marriage to a woman who didn't live life in anticipation of the next ambush.

Jane Wentworth was the bravest woman Quinn knew, and she was his.

As Quinn strode down the Mayfair walkways, other gentlemen nodded to him. Two ladies he might have recognized from the bank smiled, and, without thinking, he tipped his hat to them. The flower girls all waved to him, and if he weren't on his way to put a certain countess out of his life once for all, he'd have bought a bouquet from each one.

Ned's absence also carried a weight, so accustomed had Quinn grown to the lad's chattering and swearing.

The tow-headed young man following Quinn was yet

another weight. He'd appeared intermittently after Quinn's return from York, his attempts at subtlety only making his presence more obvious.

A country lad, would be Quinn's guess, agog at London's size and busyness, but willing to do anything to keep the approval of his mistress. Quinn turned down an alley from which there was no exit. Afternoon sunshine didn't reach into this corner of Mayfair, though the stench of rotting food did. As a boy, Quinn had considered that odor an omen of good fortune, because where some discarded food rotted, other discarded food might yet be edible.

He didn't even have to crouch down. He merely took up a lean against a wall beside steps that led to a basement. In somebody's kitchen, an argument had broken out about missing muffins.

The quarry knew enough to pause at the mouth of the alley, but Quinn had chosen this place carefully. The alley angled around a turn before it came to a dead end, and the unwitting youth took the blind turn at a casual stroll. Quinn stepped out of the shadows and boxed the younger man in.

"Looking for your blue and silver livery?" Quinn asked. "I don't think you'll find it here. Perhaps ye might look under her ladyship's bed."

The man turned slowly. "I have no idea what you're talking about, sir. Let me pass." His accent proclaimed him to be a Yorkshireman, as plain as the sheep on the dales.

"I can't do that, lad," Quinn said. "You've been content to ride my coattails from a polite distance until this week, and now you're making a pest of yourself. Sooner or later my duchess or my family will notice, and they'll raise worrying about me to an art form. We can't have that, now, can we?"

The young man's gaze darted left and right. If he were clever, he'd also look up. Wash lines, trellises, drainpipes, and balconies all created options when flight was imperative. Instead he held up his fists, protecting his face and angling his stance with scientific precision.

A pugilist, then. God help the lad.

"I'm not afraid of you," he spat. "Living like a swell, when everybody knows you're a baseborn gutter whelp who deserved to be hanged."

Turn the other cheek, Jane said. Such sound advice, though Jane had never told Quinn what to do with his feet.

The old reflexes would never leave him, and that made Quinn almost as happy as the notion of handing the countess's letters back to their author. He casually—joyfully—snaked out a foot and tripped the budding prizefighter onto his skinny backside.

"Thanks, my boy. I might never get to use that maneuver again, being a swell and all."

The youth stared up at him, gaze surprised. Then the pain of banging his head on the cobbles set in, and his eyes closed.

A sudden acquaintance with London cobblestones was the very devil on a man's skull.

"Now here's what I need you to do," Quinn said, crouching over the fallen swain. "You'll take this coin, which I did earn most honestly, and toddle off to the nearest pub. You'll want to put ice on the back of your head, for it will be troubling you severely by nightfall. When the countess asks you how I slipped through your clutches, you'll tell her that a baseborn gutter whelp has ways that a decent young man can't fathom."

Quinn held up a sovereign, a fortune to a young fellow in service, and let the lad have a good long look.

"We shall let bygones be bygones, agreed?" Quinn said, allowing the fellow to sit up.

The footman took the coin with one hand while he rubbed the back of his head with the other. "Agreed, but I don't work for the countess."

He had the wheat-blond locks of a northern boy far from home. Quinn tousled his hair gently.

"Of course you don't work for her. Have an ale or two while you're cooling down that manly temper, though don't overindulge. You'll only make the headache worse."

The fellow remained sitting on the cobbles, rubbing his head and clutching his sovereign, while Quinn went in search of a countess whom he was determined to forgive and—ye gods, what a lovely notion—*forget*.

* * *

Papa was examining a white porcelain knight that usually graced the mantel in the family parlor. He didn't even bother to put the figurine down when Jane entered the room, Ivor and Kristoff on her heels.

"Jane Hester, good day."

The day had been good, then it had turned awful. "Put that back where you found it, Papa."

He turned the statue upside down, peering at the horse's belly. "Meissen. You have quite an eclectic collection, Jane Hester, or your husband does. Will he be joining us?"

That is none of your business. "His Grace is not at home. Was there something you wanted?"

Papa set the horseman on the windowsill. "Send one of those handsome fellows for a tea tray, why don't you. You there." Papa waved a hand at Kristoff. "Fetch some comestibles. To keep a guest waiting is inconsiderate, to deny him the hospitality of the kitchen rude. Your mother did not raise you to be rude, Jane Hester."

Papa smiled, a patiently chiding elder tolerating an oversight.

Ivor and Kristoff both remained by the door, staring straight ahead. Jane would ask Quinn to raise their wages, if she ever spoke to Quinn again.

"I am on my way out," Jane said. "Now is not a good time to entertain you."

"You don't have time for your old papa? My, how haughty you've become. Pride goeth before a fall, Jane Hester."

"No, it doesn't," Jane said. "If you're quoting Proverbs, then the passage says that pride goeth before destruction, and an haughty spirit before a fall."

Papa ran a finger down the length of the mantel, scowling at the lack of dust on his fingertip. "You presume to instruct me regarding scripture, young lady, when I'll have the rearing and education of your firstborn child?"

Jane was half tempted to placate her father, to cajole and appease, to stuff him with sweets as if he were a spoiled toddler.

But no. She'd done exactly that on too many occasions, which was why Papa could make such a nuisance of himself now, when she had pressing matters to see to.

"Stop talking nonsense, Reverend. You haven't the independent means to support yourself, much less a child. You can wave all the documents and sermons at me you please, but the truth is, you'd rather extort money from my husband than minister to a legitimate congregation. You should have apologized to your bishop months ago, but you're too stubborn, proud, and—"

One of the footmen had growled, but they were standing immediately behind Jane, so she didn't know which one.

Papa had *raised his hand*. Raised his hand as if he'd deliver a slap to Jane's face, a form of discipline he hadn't attempted since Jane had put up her hair.

He reached behind himself, smoothing a hand over the back of his head, as if violence hadn't been his intention a moment before.

"You are overset," he said, retreating to the window. "Your condition has made you prone to fits of temper, and you are doubtless regretting the hasty union that has separated you from your only family."

"Get out," Jane snarled, and that felt good. "Get out of my house, and don't come back until you can support yourself in the profession to which you claim the Almighty Himself has called you."

Papa drew in a long breath, clearly filling his sails for some discourse on Jane's many shortcomings. "Jane Hester, surely—"

"Tutor the sons of squires," Jane said. "Manage a Magdalen house such that its inmates aren't worked to death. Take up the chaplaincy at a hospital or herd a lot of stinking sheep, for all I care. You will no longer come around here spouting scripture while you appraise the porcelain and empty the larders."

"Come now, daughter. You don't mean these unkind words. I admit the past months have been difficult for you, and that grief can derange the best of us."

For an instant, a bewildered widower stood in the boots of a bombastic conniver, but the moment was so fleeting as to be nearly imaginary. Papa drew himself up like an aspiring actor preparing to deliver his few insignificant lines of dialogue.

"Sorrow notwithstanding," he said, holding up one finger, "Christian decency counsels us to magnanimity of spirit, Jane Hester, and I am willing to overlook your ungracious attitude and judgmental words. We are family, and turning the other—"

"Out!" Jane bellowed. "I have turned the last other cheek I intend to turn in your case. Get out of this house now or you will be shown the door."

One of the footmen cracked his knuckles, a rude, nasty sound that Jane heard like the pealing of cathedral bells.

"Her Grace said now."

Papa sniffed, he glowered, he tried to draw out a dramatic silence, but Jane stepped aside, giving the footmen a clear path to him, and thus did Papa march past her to the door.

Ivor and Kristoff followed him out of the room, and when the front door closed, Jane felt as if she'd been given a royal pardon. Slow applause came from the direction of the corridor, and Jane whirled to see Althea, Constance, and Stephen crowding in the doorway.

"I was right," Jane said. "Shouting at an opponent can be salubrious. Enjoyable even."

She nonetheless sank onto the sofa, because ejecting one's father from the premises apparently left one weak in the knees. Weak with relief, perhaps.

Stephen wheeled into the room ahead of his sisters. "Next, we'll teach you to curse. Constance and I can both curse in French, and I have enough German to get you started. Do you suppose the old windbag will stay gone?"

Althea and Constance chided him for disrespecting an elder. Stephen sensibly argued that no respect was due a man who insulted his hostess, much less his own daughter. Ivor and Kristoff returned, smiling shamelessly, and somebody ordered a bottle of cordial.

Jane was returning the white knight to the mantel when a

movement outside the window caught her eye.

"Why is Ned pelting across the garden as if the press gangs are after him?" she asked. "And where is Quinn?"

"Shall I fetch Ned from the kitchen?" Ivor asked, as Kristoff brought the bottle of cordial in on a tray with several glasses.

The moment recalled for Jane the day she'd met the Wentworth siblings. They'd been drinking cordial then too, tossing quips back and forth, subtly teasing each other as they welcomed Jane into their midst. She'd been exhausted, bewildered, famished, *and so glad that Quinn was alive*.

"No need to summon Ned upstairs," Jane said. "I can interrogate him just as easily in the servants' hall, and don't anybody try to tell me that I'm not permitted to breach that fortress. I'm a Wentworth and a duchess. I go where I please."

As Quinn had apparently done, *alone*, blast him to perdition.

"We're coming with you," Althea said. "Don't tell us you're planning something rash without us."

"I am Her Grace of Walden. I'll be rash if I deuced well choose to be."

"Then we'll be rash right along beside you," Constance said. "Pity Duncan isn't underfoot. He could do with some excitement."

The Jane who'd turned too many other cheeks did not want any excitement. The Jane who'd married Quinn Wentworth was learning that sometimes excitement, even confrontation, was necessary.

"There you are," Ned said when Jane arrived to the kitchen, the siblings trailing behind her. "Idiot Davies said you wasn't to be disturbed."

The boy glowered at his compatriot, who glowered back.

"Himself said herself wasn't to be disturbed, Idiot Neddy, and now herself is here in the kitchen, where she isn't supposed to be." Davies stood before the wide hearth, the one where the fire was never allowed to die out.

"Why aren't I supposed to be in the kitchen?" Jane asked. "His Grace comes through here every time he uses the tunnel."

"Now you done it," Ned muttered.

Davies blushed, his fair coloring going scarlet. "The duke was planning a surprise."

He stepped to the side and Jane's gaze fell on a small wooden chest.

"Been combing the pawnshops," Davies said, "buying back what he could, making offers for what's been sold on. He's still hunting for one more shawl—has doves on it, I think. He sent a regimental sword and scabbard off to the silversmith for a cleaning and polishing."

A cool ripple passed over Jane's arms and nape. "That is my mother's chest. That is Mama's... that is the chest Mama left to me." She knelt on the kitchen's hard plank floor and opened the lid. The scent of cedar wafted up, along with Mama's signature lemon verbena fragrance.

"Her mirror..." Jane held up the mirror only long enough to assure herself that the tarnish and speckling were as they had been when Mama had owned this same mirror. "Her Sunday shawl, her earbobs, her jewelry box. Quinn did this?"

"Nigh run me ragged," Ned said. "Dragged me to half the pawnshops in London. Man knows how to haggle."

Jane closed her eyes and breathed in the scent of her mother's love. Quinn had done this. For her, without being asked, *without mentioning a word of his plans...*

"That man..." That wonderful, pigheaded, stubborn,

lovely, lovely man. "He's been at this for weeks, and I never suspected." She dabbed her eyes with the edge of her mother's shawl, and fell in love for the third time that day with the husband she never intended to speak to again.

"If you start bawling," Ned said, "himself will sell me to the French Vikings. Are you having a difficult adjustment?"

Jane nodded. "Yes, so please bear with me a moment."

Davies helped her to her feet. Ned, Constance, Stephen, and Althea were all watching her as if she was supposed to know what to do. Quinn had gone to confront the lunatic, idiot countess, and, Quinn-fashion, he'd neglected to bring along reinforcements.

"Ned," Jane said, "perhaps you know where His Grace has got off to?"

Chapter Twenty-five

Quinn had timed his call on Beatrice, Countess of Tipton, for the hour of the day when Lord Tipton was most reliably away from home. The earl was a fixture at his club, and seldom voted his seat. He was solvent—which hadn't been the case when Quinn had worn Tipton livery—and kept a mistress whom he visited most Tuesday afternoons.

Not every Tuesday, according to the flower girls, and thus Quinn was taking a risk.

No matter. The situation with her ladyship required resolution, lest Jane think her husband a socially backward recluse who was ashamed of his wife, and lest her ladyship get up to more tricks of a lethal nature.

"Whom shall I say is calling, sir?"

"Ulysses Lloyd-Chapman."

The butler's brows rose. He was a handsome blond about twenty years younger than any other butler of Quinn's acquaintance.

"I'm playing a jest," Quinn said. "Or would you rather offend one of her ladyship's oldest friends and spoil my little joke?"

"Have you a card?"

Quinn folded his arms, as Jane so often did, and remained silent.

"Very good," the butler said. "If you'll follow me, *Mr. Lloyd-Chapman*."

He showed Quinn to a fussy little parlor that looked out on the garden rather than the street, suggesting Mr. Lloyd-Chapman was one of Bea's familiars, if not a lover. The window had been raised, and the French doors were open, bringing the scent of scythed grass into the room.

Quinn disdained to take a seat but instead rehearsed his speech, for this wasn't a social call. If Jane knew he'd willingly confronted his nemesis, she'd be hurt and angry, for which he could apologize. Jane would forgive him in time—he hoped.

Forgive and forget was her policy, after all.

In typical Beatrice fashion, he was made to wait ten minutes for her ladyship's arrival. She swept into the room in a dress of pale rose with blue fleur-de-lis embroidered on the bodice, cuffs, and hems. Her fichu was cream lace, and her slippers gold.

She was still beautiful, still every inch the lady—to appearances. Quinn waited for some emotion to wash over him. Inconvenient longing, remorse, guilt, anger, *anything*, but annoyance and impatience were all that stirred. With luck, he could return home to Jane before she woke.

These thoughts skittered through his mind in the time it took the countess to come halfway across the carpet.

She stopped, catching her balance on the piano. "Ulysses, darl—*Quinn*?" Her shock turned to a hesitant smile that quickly faded to a chilly dignity. "What sort of ill-mannered deception is this? I was told Mr. Lloyd-Chapman awaited me, and in place of a gentlemanly acquaintance, I find..."

Her hauteur faltered as she took a visual inventory. Quinn had dressed as he always did on a workday: Bond Street morning attire, gold sleeve buttons, watch fob, and cravat pin. The only change was the ducal signet ring winking on his smallest finger.

"Do go on, Bea."

"I am Lady Tipton to you."

He closed the distance between them rather than raise his voice. "Then I am His Grace of Walden to you, which suits me quite well for a change. I refuse to waste even a single extra instant in your company so don't bother ringing for any damned tea. Here's what you need to know: If you ever again attempt to harm me or mine, I will see you jailed and ruined if not hanged."

The fragrance of attar of roses enveloped him, a signature scent that brought back memories of afternoons when perfume had been all the lady had worn. What a rutting, strutting fool he'd been.

She took a step back and bumped into the piano. "I have no idea what you're referring to."

"I was hanged, your ladyship. Felt the platform drop from beneath me, the noose choke the life from my body. I drew my last breath. But for a chance intervention, you would have succeeded in ending my life. Why, Beatrice? I left you in peace, and if you wanted your letters back, you had only to ask for them."

Her gaze fixed on his cravat pin, the lion rampant from the ducal crest. "Quinn—Your Grace—I had nothing to do with your arrest or your trial. I never wanted to see you again, but I wish you no ill fortune."

Even at seventeen, Quinn had grasped that the object of his desire was not a particularly deep individual. Beatrice was easily bored and easily hurt, and now she regarded Quinn not with guilt, but with fear.

Which was puzzling. She'd sent him to his death, a scheme that had taken cunning and confidence in addition to coin.

"If you didn't fabricate charges against me, bribe witnesses, send Robert Pike to France, and all but put that noose around my neck, then who did?"

She looked away. "You should go. If you're intent on taking a place in society, we'll occasionally cross paths. As far as anybody need know, we're strangers. Unless we're introduced by some well-meaning fool, you need not acknowledge me."

That was too easy. "And your letters?"

A soft tread sounded behind Quinn.

"Ask for them back, pet. Demand them back. I know Wentworth plagued you mercilessly and took advantage of your tender female heart, but he really has no need of those letters now."

The Earl of Tipton stood in the doorway, and abruptly the fear in Beatrice's eyes made sense.

"Was your mistress not receiving callers this afternoon, my lord?" Quinn asked.

Beatrice winced. The earl smirked. He made a deceptively harmless figure in a rumpled jacket, but the malice in his eyes was formidable.

"My schedule is none of your business, Wentworth. Give her ladyship those letters and be on your way. You really ought to be ashamed of yourself, preying on a lonely woman, then threatening her with scandal. Not well done of you, but considering your upbringing, one shouldn't be surprised."

Beatrice spared Quinn one desperate glance, which was explanation enough. She'd spun a tale for her husband, painting herself as the wronged party, taken advantage of, threatened even. If Quinn passed the letters over to Tipton, then Beatrice's role in the affair would become obvious, and Quinn's defense against allegations of wrongdoing toward her ladyship would be destroyed.

This was what came of kicking over a hornet's nest. "And if I don't have the letters with me?" He did, tucked into an inner pocket of his coat.

"Then the time has come for you to die."

Tipton withdrew a tidy little double-barreled pistol from his pocket. The distance was such that he stood a good chance of hitting Quinn, particularly with two tries at his target. Doubtless Tipton would have drawn that pistol even if Quinn had produced the letters.

Quinn stepped in front of Beatrice. "Put that damned thing away. The noise will bring a half dozen servants running, and you will be the only suspect in my attempted murder, unless you'd like to see your wife arrested for that crime."

Tipton's smile was downright merry. "Oh, my dear fellow, how little you know of the company you seek to keep. When an earl, a peer of the realm, uses deadly force to defend his wife from the untoward advances of a brute who has already been convicted of taking a life once, then that earl is not a suspect. He's a bloody hero."

"Quinn, he's not bluffing." Beatrice spoke softly, pleadingly.

"He's not a hero either. Go ahead and shoot me, Tipton. I am a brute, but I've survived more misery, cold, pain, and hunger than you can imagine in the worst of your pampered nightmares. I am also a duke, and I will not give quarter to a cowardly blackguard."

Quinn watched Tipton's eyes for the telltale shift that would presage a squeeze of the trigger. Tipton was quietly furious—perhaps with his wife, definitely with Quinn.

"Must you remind me?" the earl snapped. "Had you been content to remain wallowing in your wealth in Yorkshire, or even kept to your counting house in London, I might have allowed you to live. But no, you had to inherit a title, and not just any title. Your land all but marches with mine, and when the College of Arms came around asking pointed questions about the village gravestones, I knew where the answers would lead. It isn't to be borne."

Behind Quinn, Beatrice made a sound that conveyed dread and grief.

"At least you didn't get a child on her," Tipton said, "the smallest of mercies, that. Beatrice, step away from him, or all of London will soon know that your gowns and jewels were purchased with rents owed to the Walden dukedom."

The irony was exquisite: For years, Quinn had carried guilt and regret about his liaison with Beatrice, while Tipton had probably enjoyed having the leverage the affair gave him over his countess. All the while, Tipton had been stealing Quinn's birthright, and that—the earl's theft, not Quinn's lack of restraint with the countess—had put Quinn in danger.

Tipton was prepared to shoot an unarmed man when sending that man to the gallows had failed. What would the earl do to an unarmed woman?

"You are the reason my dukedom is in such disarray?" Quinn asked. "The reason an old and respected title has fallen into ruin? You put Arbuthnot up to pilfering the Walden coffers, you warned him when the College of Arms was asking too many questions."

The pattern made sense now, though the insight wasn't likely to do Quinn much good. The aristocracy was inbred, and the old duke would naturally have turned to a titled neighbor for support when advancing age made managing the ducal properties difficult. Tipton doubtless had encouraged the late duke to bide in Berkshire while the Yorkshire family seat was plundered by Tipton's minions.

"You stole from an old man who had no family to look out for him, and then you tried to have me killed," Quinn said. "My duchess says I should forgive and forget, but that—"

"I'll hear no talk of *your duchess*," Tipton retorted. "That you, of all people, should inherit the Walden title is insupportable. I'm glad I was able to all but bankrupt the estate you inherited, Wentworth. You deserve penury at least for poaching on my preserves. Beatrice, for the last time, get away from him."

"Stay where you are, my lady." Quinn considered distance, angles, hard surfaces, and his own reflexes, but if he managed to dodge two bullets, he'd be leaving Beatrice at risk. Even as he weighed odds and options, he spared a thought for one more regret.

He should have listened to Jane sooner. He should have heeded her sense of caution, should have let her legion of nannies keep him safe, because he was about to do something very, very stupid—even stupider than confronting Beatrice under her husband's roof—and kick over yet another hornet's nest.

"Go ahead and shoot me, Tipton, and my duchess will see those letters published in the *Times*."

* * *

"Told you he were in trouble," Ned whispered.

Jane brushed a rhododendron frond aside. "I will kill him."

"Quinn?" Althea murmured from Jane's left.

"That puling disgrace of an earl. How dare he?"

"You won't have to kill him," Stephen said. "I'm happy to oblige."

"That leaves the countess to me," Constance added.

Ned had led them to this garden, but the next step was up to Jane. Inside the little parlor, Tipton was holding forth again.

"You all but imposed yourself on my wife," Tipton said. "Beatrice confessed all when certain rumors reached me on the Continent. Thank God somebody had the presence of mind to notify me of the goings on in my own household or there's no telling how many of your brats I'd be supporting."

"Himself will do the killing," Ned murmured. "Has a fearsome proper temper, he does."

"You sent an innocent man to the gallows." Quinn spoke from the depths of an arctic fury. "You brought scandal down upon my house, abused the privileges of your station, and broke the law, all for the sake of your stupid, *stubborn* pride. So you can't live as extravagantly as some. You still live better than most. And if your neglected wife grew lonely, what of it? Is that worth having murder on your conscience? Why couldn't you let it go?"

The hairs on Jane's arms raised. "Ned, you stay here, Stephen and I will lead. Quietly, now."

"Have you any idea who so kindly summoned you from the Continent to your family seat all those years ago?" Quinn went on.

"Of course not. Gentlemanly honor demands discretion, not something you'd grasp. Beatrice, *step away from him.*"

"Stay put," Quinn retorted. "Two little bullets from that peashooter won't bring me down. I'm not about to oblige yon titled arsewipe by dying when my duchess expects me home in time for supper."

Jane paused immediately to the left of the French doors. Stephen waited behind her, leaning heavily on a cane. Jane held up three fingers, then two, then one, and marched through the door.

"Your Grace," Jane said, coming up on Quinn's right side. "Introductions are in order."

Tipton swung his gun from Quinn to Jane, then back to Quinn. "Madam, I know not who you are, but you've chosen a very unfortunate time to break into my home."

"Timing is so important," Stephen drawled. "Lovely day for a social call."

Quinn's smile was positively menacing. "I see my sisters refused to be left out of the gathering. What say you now, Tipton?"

"I say I have the only loaded gun."

Quinn shook his head. "Stephen?"

Stephen raised the pistol he'd been holding in his free hand, a stout, ugly firearm capable of bringing down a…a pompous arsewipe.

"Althea?" Quinn added. "Constance?"

Two bright silver blades appeared in the ladies' hands.

"All very barbaric," Tipton said, "and my bullets might not kill a hulking specimen like you, Wentworth, but they will do the lady here grievous injury."

Oh, no they would not. Jane dipped her hand into her right pocket while the countess remained cowering behind Quinn.

"You'd take the life of an unarmed woman?" Jane asked, using her left hand to link her fingers with Quinn's. "An unarmed duchess? Who do you think summoned you home from the Continent, my lord?"

For on this point, because Quinn himself had raised the question, Jane was certain.

"I neither know, nor do I—"

"*My lord*," Quinn recited. "*I regret to suggest that your lady wife has formed an irregular association with a footman in your employ. Your immediate return to the family seat would be well advised.* I sent that letter myself. Labored over the penmanship for days. Debated my obligation to you as my employer. I also fretted over my obligation to her ladyship as a woman who'd been treated cavalierly by the man who'd vowed to honor her. Then I considered that a child could all too easily result from my continued folly, and the way was clear."

Quinn took a step closer to the earl. "Damn you, Tipton, damn you to the dungeons of Newgate, for giving my family cause to worry, for jeopardizing the financial well-being of every customer at my bank."

Quinn's indignation took up the entire room, but his confession—he'd summoned the earl home himself—put confusion in the earl's eyes.

Jane squeezed her husband's hand slowly. Once, twice, three times, then flung the fistful of sand from her pocket into the earl's eyes.

Quinn was on him in the next instant, the gun skittering across the floor. Stephen caught the countess as she sagged against the piano, and two apples went sailing at the earl's head.

"Got him!" Ned crowed as one missile connected with its target.

"Hold your fire, Ned," Jane said. "His Grace has the matter in hand."

The *matter* was on the floor, Quinn towering over him. A butler hovered in the doorway looking helpless and agog.

"Bugger off," Stephen said, gesturing with his cane. "We're busy here."

The countess, who'd draped herself against Stephen, fluttered a hand. "Do as he says, Parker."

Parker cast a glance at the earl, facedown on the floor, Quinn's cravat knotted around his wrists. The butler smiled, bowed, and withdrew.

"Get up, Tipton," Quinn said. "Get up, and if you are very lucky, the ladies will allow you to live."

Chapter Twenty-six

Stephen was perched on the box, Ned with him. Althea and Constance sat opposite Quinn, looking as pleased as Hades in contemplation of a plump robin.

Quinn sat beside his duchess, who was ominously quiet.

He gathered his courage and plunged into battle. "I should have told you what I was about."

Jane's gaze remained straight ahead. "Not now, Quinn."

If he didn't fight for his marriage now, he might never have another opportunity. Jane would be decent to him, accommodating even, but she wouldn't plague him with discussions of names and nurseries, wouldn't be his rutting heifer.

He tried another tack. "I meant well."

His sisters glared daggers at him. "Not now, Quinn," they said in unison.

The coach swayed around a corner, the pace sedate, but the journey home from Tipton's town house was already half over.

"I'm sorry," Quinn said, though he wasn't sorry he'd never lay eyes on Beatrice again.

Constance sent him a wan smile. "Quinn, please. Not. Now."

He permitted himself a tactical retreat until the coach had pulled into the mews and he'd handed Althea and Constance down. By rights, Jane should have been first out of the carriage, but she was making a point.

She looked at Quinn's proffered hand, picked up her skirts, and stepped to the ground without touching him. She'd taken two steps in the direction of the garden gate when Quinn spoke.

"I am in more peril now than when the noose was placed about my neck."

She turned slowly. "Explain yourself."

Had he ever faced a greater danger than the hurt in Jane's eyes? "I keep my family safe."

Jane was mentally counting to three again, and that made him wild.

"Quinn, you keep your family *out*. They think you want to be left alone, so they return the favor. The lot of you rattle around in this gorgeous house, captives to a past that matters less by the year. What am I to do with you?"

A chance comment Stephen had made outside the walls of Newgate came back to Quinn. "What would you like to do with me?"

He was encouraged by her brooding regard. She was thinking, and thinking was better than walking away.

"I would like to be your wife, your friend, your duchess, your lover, but handing my heart to somebody who marches into harm's way without me won't serve."

Without me. "You're not upset that I confronted the countess. You're upset that I went alone."

"And that you purposely loved me witless first, thus assuring I'd be sound asleep while you took on a jealous earl, his half-daft countess, stray butlers...Quinn, a duke is a *leader*. He leads armies, he helps lead the nation. He does not charge off all on his own without a friend or ally to be had. I would like to be the wife of a duke, rather than the domestic convenience of some self-appointed warrior who might never come home to me."

They should not be having this discussion in the benighted alley, where Quinn didn't dare take Jane's hand....

Ask her. "Could we continue this conversation in the stable?"

She shot a glower toward the house. "Excellent suggestion."

Quinn offered her his arm. "Ned!" he shouted. "Wherever you are, get into the house and stay there, or your name will be Ned Can't Sit Down for a Week."

The bushes on the far side of the garden wall rustled as Quinn led his wife to the cool, quiet surrounds of the stable. Horses were dozing in their stalls, an all-black cat rose from a pile of straw and stropped itself against his boots.

"Is that the fellow from Newgate?" Jane asked.

The fellow who'd nose-kissed Jane while Quinn had tried not to envy a cat. "The warden kindly surrendered him when I sent a note requesting the favor. I can offer you a choice of trunks to sit on, or we can repair to the harness room."

Jane preceded him down the barn aisle, the cat at her heels. The harness room was humble, redolent of horse and leather. Jane perched on a trunk, Quinn turned a wooden bucket upside down and planted his arse upon it.

Jane spoke first. "Ned said you gave him the Wentworth family name."

"He hadn't one of his own, and Wentworth is an honorable name, lately."

"You gave me that name as well, Quinn. I gather you will give it to my firstborn too."

"The child may use whatever name you please," Quinn said. "MacGowan was your husband, and a child should be encouraged to honor his father. I would certainly be honored if your baby had the same last name as our other children."

Jane wrinkled her nose. "I want to be furious with you, but I'm far more wroth with that blasted earl. He could not bear for his wife's former paramour to obtain a higher status than he had."

"Her former footman, Jane. When status is all a man has, he guards it jealously. Then too, Tipton has no heir of his body, and to an aristocrat, that's a bitter pill. I can make no excuses for his thieving from the late Duke of Walden, but that wrong was committed against a party now deceased."

She stared at her boots. "You are forgiving and forgetting, and all I want is to see that man in Newgate, counting the hours that remain to him, hanging his food from the rafters so the rodents don't steal it. Not very charitable of me."

Sitting on a dusty trunk, Jane yet exuded all the dignity of a duchess. She'd stood before a loaded gun for Quinn, and the weight of that...he leaned forward to press his forehead to her knees.

"I went there to give Bea her damned letters, to tell her she needn't worry that I'd ever betray her confidences. I have much more enjoyable tasks to occupy me than brooding over the past. You were right, Jane. The time has come to put youthful stupidity behind me."

To put all of the past aside, including Jack Wentworth's insults, York's endless bitter winters, and too many missed meals to count.

Jane stroked a hand over Quinn's right shoulder.

"He could have killed you, Quinn. He could have taken you from me, when I've already gone and fallen in love with you. I could not have borne..." She folded down over him and kissed him—the right cheek, then the left—and wrapped her arms around him. Quinn rested his cheek against Jane's thigh, surrounded by her warmth and the fragrance of lemon verbena. He pushed aside the terror he'd endured when she'd faced Tipton's gun, and instead clung to pride in her courage.

She sat back and Quinn took the place beside her on the trunk. Her relenting came as a profound relief, though the discussion wasn't over. Somehow, he must tell his duchess that he loved her. He'd never said the words, not to anybody, not even to Bea in a moment of maudlin excess.

Thank God.

"You want to be free of your past, Quinn, but I think you will have to assist her ladyship if you're to achieve that result. Tipton has doubtless held her indiscretion over her head for years, while he went lifting skirts all over the Continent. A woman can only bear so much."

"I'm willing to pursue any course you please, Jane, but I'd as soon be spared any further dealings with her ladyship."

By rights, Jane should hate the countess, but something of Beatrice's circumstances had come clear to Quinn. She was a captive to her station, neglected and scorned by a man to whom she was bound to grant intimate favors. Her ladyship was also without true friends and allowed only an occasional season in London to alleviate her boredom.

"You should settle a sum in trust for her," Jane said. "Give her enough to live separate from the horror she's married to. The woman wants rescuing, Quinn, though I expect that butler of hers will accompany her to any household she establishes."

"*Rescue her?*"

"She'll have a good deal less trouble forgiving and forgetting you if she's the toast of the gentry in Cornwall and you're here in London. An estrangement will make life splendidly awkward for the earl."

Quinn kissed Jane's cheek, because even his tolerant duchess had a sense of justice. "A set of prison bars would make life awkward for the earl." A peer could be arrested for criminal wrongdoing, but he'd be tried in the Lords and possibly acquitted. Perhaps that privilege had inspired Tipton's timing where Quinn's downfall had been concerned. The House of Lords would hesitate to convict a duke, while a jury of twelve commoners adjudicating the fate of an upstart nabob had been easy for Tipton to sway.

"Your family's name would come up if you pressed charges," Jane said, "and Tipton would of course tell the world why he'd carried a grudge. Whoever assisted him to empty the Walden coffers has doubtless decamped for foreign parts. We must be creative about this."

We, the most beautiful word in the language. "As long as I can guarantee the safety of my family, I'm willing to be as creative as you please."

Jane cradled his hand in her lap, and for a moment, the only sound was the rumbling of the black cat, who'd curled up on a pile of woolen horse blankets.

"Rescue the countess, then, but as your wife, I have a few things I need to tell you too."

* * *

Jane had castigated Quinn for being too battle-ready, too willing to confront all foes, but his fault was that he was too devoted to those he loved. He'd stuck his neck in a noose rather than put his liberty before his family's well-being, and today he'd faced a bullet from the same man who'd schemed, connived, and bribed to send Quinn...

Jane could not bear to finish that thought.

"Are you in need of ginger biscuits, Your Grace?" Quinn asked, bumping his shoulder gently against hers.

"I'm in need of absolution, Quinn. I lost my temper with Papa."

He kissed her fingers, such a casual, intimate, husbandly gesture. "Did you hurl a knife at him across the breakfast parlor? Not exactly at him, but close enough so as not to matter?"

"Be serious." Jane wanted to tuck her face against his shoulder and breathe him in, but some words needed saying. "I had Papa thrown out of the house. He's not to come back until he's patched things up with his bishop or otherwise found gainful employment."

When she put the situation in plain English, her decision didn't sound so awful. Wastrel sons were cast out into the world frequently, and for the most part, they grew up or at least acquired some humility.

"He must have provoked you."

"I don't want to tell you how."

"Jane, you just stood beside me in front of a loaded gun and all but ordered a titled swine to bugger himself. What could you possibly fear to tell me?"

He wrapped an arm around her shoulders, and Jane's throat ached. "I don't want to admit to you that I was wrong. That sometimes, we must call others to account and demand that they behave honorably. We must fight sometimes, even when we don't want to, because..."

Hot tears slid down her cheeks. Quinn brushed them away with his thumb. "I'm glad you fought for me, Jane. If you hadn't shown up..."

"I almost didn't!" Jane stormed off the trunk, startling the cat, who leapt from its pile of blankets. "I almost left you to face your enemies alone, because you were trying to spare me any cause for worry. Then Papa came by, spouting his daft notions about taking guardianship of the baby, and I could not listen to him. I could not bear to be under the same roof with him."

She faced Quinn and crossed her arms, because the feelings inside her wanted containing, lest they break her heart.

"Sometimes, we have to fight," she said. "Turning the other cheek, letting go of the past, they have a place, but for who and what we love, we can't help but risk everything when called upon to do so, and I love you so very much."

Quinn rose, the small space making his size more imposing, as did the gravity in his gaze. "Your father threatened to petition for guardianship of your child?"

Even here, surrounded by wool, leather, and hay, Jane could discern the fragrance of Quinn's shaving soap.

"The notion is laughable," she said. "I told him as much. Told him a man who couldn't pay his own bills wasn't fit to take on the expenses of a child, and I left much unsaid."

Quinn tucked a lock of her hair behind her ear. "Such as?"

"Such as a child needing a father figure to trust and love, not some pontificating buffoon to make excuses for. I eloped to Scotland rather than deliver Papa the dressing down he deserved. Accompanied him to the prisons, said nothing when he stole my inheritance . . . and I've turned into a watering pot."

Quinn took her in his arms. "My watering pot."

"You found Mama's treasures and brought them back to me."

"You were your mama's greatest treasure, and you're mine to treasure for all time."

He was such a poet, such a good, dear…Jane simply cried in Quinn's arms for a good long while. Cried for her mother, for Gordie, for disappointments and losses too numerous to name, and for the sheer relief of having Quinn to love.

She clutched his handkerchief and clutched him, until the tears were spent, and lightness replaced her sorrow and anger.

"We have four more months of this?" Quinn asked, kissing her forehead.

"More or less."

"I like it. You're very cuddly when you weep."

She smacked his chest, then looped her arms around his waist. "What will you do about the Earl of Tipton?"

"I'd like to forget about him, but instead I'll ask you if we might decide his fate later."

We… "Yes, Your Grace, though not too much later. Somebody has been considerately collecting invitations to discuss with me. That will not be a short conversation."

He scooped her into his arms and sat with her on the trunk. "I meant to do just that, but then I realized I was being followed by Tipton's man and my patience came to an end. The conversation regarding the invitations will be short, Jane. You tell me whom we're to call on, and when we're to call. I dress up in my duke clothes, and we pay calls."

Jane closed her eyes, because the comfort of Quinn's embrace was irresistible. "It's not that simple."

"Yes, love. When a duke loves his duchess, it's exactly that simple, and I do love you so very, very much."

The baby moved, or maybe Jane's heart turned over. "I love you too. I'd like to take a nap now."

Quinn rose with her in his arms. "I'd like to join you."

"I'd like that too."

Quinn had carried her as far as the garden gate when a gig clattered up the ally, Duncan at the reins. A smaller man in laborer's attire sat beside him on the bench.

Quinn settled Jane on the garden wall. "Duncan, welcome home and thank you for a job well done. Mr. Pike, so glad you could join us. The magistrate will be wanting a word with you, so don't think to decamp anytime soon."

"Mr. Pike wouldn't dream of being so cowardly," Duncan said. "Duchess, good day."

Jane hopped off the wall and threw her arms around Quinn. "Well done, Your Grace. Well damned done."

"Somebody has become a Wentworth," Duncan said, offering a rare smile. "You're in good looks today, Duchess."

"My duchess is fatigued," Quinn said. "I'll see her upstairs. Thanks again, Duncan, and we'll chat further at dinner."

As it happened, Jane and Quinn did not come down for dinner, though Mr. Pike did indeed bide long enough in London to offer a sworn statement to the magistrate: Quinn Wentworth had made him a small loan in that dark alley, wished him well, and gone about his business without doing anything more violent than shaking Pike's hand.

Word was all over the newspapers within a week, and by then the invitations and calling cards had reached flood stage.

Epilogue

Nothing helped, not looking forbiddingly ducal as Almack's patronesses approached, not hovering protectively near Jane, not casting threatening glances at Duncan and Stephen.

Althea and Constance were too busy fending off handsome bachelors to do more than smirk in Quinn's direction between dance sets, and Joshua was tucked in some corner with a widowed marchioness doubtless advising her about how to conserve her assets.

Quinn was doomed to bow over the hands of a legion of debutantes and to lead each blushing young lady onto the dance floor like the ducal paragon Jane was determined to fool the world into taking him for.

What a lot of bloody nonsense.

"Might I ask Your Grace a question?" Lady Marianne Honeycutt's blue eyes were lit with the determination of the very young.

"Of course." Quinn turned her ladyship down the room, though the waltz was German, which meant the tempo was funereal. Lady Marianne would probably have his life history before the set ended.

The prettied-up version of his life history Jane had made him rehearse, a taradiddle about humble origins, working hard, finding favor with a kindly elderly banker... That Jane's story was entirely true was mere coincidence, for it was also entirely misleading.

Lady Marianne stared hard at Quinn's shoulder. "I have a bit of coin, a very little. I'd like to invest it. Have you any advice for me?"

What the devil? "Surely you've a father or brother—"

She shook her head, making the violets affixed to her coiffure bob as if in a gale. "I'm not to trouble my pretty head, they say, as if my pretty head can't foresee the day when I'll have to sign marriage settlements or maintain my own household as a spinster or a widow. The gossips say you built a fortune from nothing."

"One cannot always believe gossip; in fact, one rarely should."

"You have enough money to establish a charitable trust for women seeking to join transported spouses—a large trust. Papa grumbled about it, but I know he admires you for it."

"My duchess established that trust in memory of her mother." *Would this waltz never end?*

"But Your Grace"—Lady Marianne leaned closer— "Papa says that the charitable endowment is enormous, and if you have that much money to give away, then you know how to turn a few coins into a modest sum. I don't need a fortune; I simply need..."

She frowned, though Quinn had it on good authority— Constance's—that young ladies were discouraged from adopting any expression that wrinkled the countenance.

"You want some say in your future," Quinn suggested.

"Some security against a rainy day." The same goals that had motivated Quinn as a youth, the same objectives that sent most people to their labors day after day and year after year.

"Exactly. My brother has control of his funds, though he's squandering his allowance quarter after quarter. Mama says he's headed for scandal."

This conversation was scandalous, and yet, Quinn appreciated the young woman's initiative. Fortunately, Jane had admonished Quinn that a duke did not take on every challenge as an army of one. A duke led a loyal force and contributed his cunning and courage without taking any unnecessary bullets himself.

"When we conclude this interminable penance of a dance, meaning no insult to present company, I will introduce you to my brother, Lord Stephen. His grasp of finances is superb, and he's blunt to a fault. He will explain all you need to know and arrange for your funds to be handled through one of our investment accounts, if you so choose."

Nothing in that offer broke the law, though it certainly broke with convention, and required a good deal of trust on the lady's part.

"Lord Stephen is your heir?"

"For now." Which status Stephen exploited with all the delicacy of a large hog untroubled by pretensions to dignity.

"His lordship has a nice smile."

Stephen had a naughty smile, though dragooning him to Almack's along with Duncan and the sisters seemed to please Jane. Quinn's duchess roosted amid the potted palms like a partridge nestled in a sunny hedge, though of course she was *not* as plump as a partridge—yet.

"Someday," Lady Marianne said, "I want the esteem of a man who will look at me as you look at your duchess, Your Grace."

Jane waggled gloved fingers in Quinn's direction and provoked half the room to smiling. Had any other duchess assayed the same informality in these surrounds, unkind talk about standards and decorum might have ensued. With a few smiles, a few soft answers where another woman would have offered criticism, Jane had made informality a virtue and marital affection fashionable.

Quinn's duchess worked miracles, witness a guttersnipe from York was waltzing his evening away with the year's current crop of debutantes.

"Thank you," Lady Marianne said, as Quinn bowed over her hand at the conclusion of the waltz. "You promised to introduce me to Lord Stephen."

As if an old dodderer like Quinn might forget a promise made five minutes ago. "His lordship does not dance, but you will enjoy sitting out with him."

"A man who doesn't dance?" Her ladyship brushed the violets aside. "Surely I will fall in love with him on sight. Lead on, Your Grace."

Before Jane took pity on Quinn and let a plea of fatigue end the outing, Quinn introduced Stephen to three young ladies with pin money to invest, Joshua to a widowed viscountess who did not trust her solicitors, and Duncan to an aging baroness whose articulate contempt for lawyers would have put a Yorkshire drover to the blush.

"You knew this would happen," Quinn said, as he settled beside Jane in the town coach. "You knew I'd be mobbed by sweet young things mad to control their own funds."

"And by sweet old things. What better man to entrust their hopes to than you?"

She had such faith in him. "What makes me so special? The Dorset and Becker has been around for centuries and they also claim a connection to a duke."

One who'd called on Quinn's sisters twice and invited Quinn to an evening of cards that had been positively friendly. The lot of them—two dukes, a marquess, and a smattering of lesser peers—had played for farthing points with more intensity than school boys betting on a tin of fresh biscuits.

"You make you so special," Jane said, taking Quinn's hand. "You know what it is to have nothing, to be without allies, to be at the mercy of an unkind fate. Speaking of which, Lady MacHenry said the Earl of Tipton is in for years of unrelenting misery and an ongoing battle with dysentery."

Quinn laced his fingers with Jane's, for she liked holding hands and he liked any excuse to touch her.

"Should I know Lady MacHenry?"

"Her uncle was governor of the Westward Orejas Islands some years ago. Her aunt claims a more surly local populace, a hotter sun, a denser jungle, or a greater variety of large and menacing insects does not exist this side of the Pit. Tipton's diplomatic assignment will include years of dodging fevers, uprisings, snakes, and spiders."

"Ned will rejoice at that news." Quinn was pleased as well, but the burning need to wreak justice on Tipton had moderated to a more philosophical inclination. Tipton was fundamentally unhappy, could not manage money, lacked the self-respect to earn any coin of his own, and had ruined all hope of joy in his marriage.

The earl deserved the fate he faced—one Quinn had arranged with Elsmore's aid—but his lordship also deserved a crumb or two of pity. The countess had purchased a villa near Lyme Regis, and the Tipton estates in the north had been leased by a wealthy haberdasher intent on becoming a respectable squire.

Tipton was a laughingstock, and his "diplomatic post"

was the merest fig leaf of mercy granted to a disgraced peer.

"The baby is restless," Jane said, nestling against Quinn's shoulder. "Will you take me north after the child arrives?"

I will breathe again after the child arrives. I will cease dunning the Almighty with my prayers for Jane's safety. I will have sex with my wife against the wall again, and possibly on the billiards table as well.

"You want to peek in on your papa," Quinn said.

The light of a passing lamp illuminated Jane's features, and if anything, advancing pregnancy had made her more beautiful. She had the loveliest brown eyes, the sweetest smile....

Quinn kissed her fingers, the easiest part of her to reach.

"I correspond with Papa," she said. "He seems to be rising to the challenge of ministering to a congregation, though the bishop has reminded him that brevity is a virtue. I don't miss him."

"Ah. The guilt of not feeling guilty. I know a certain cure for that."

The reverend had been packed off to a living in the West Riding, and bad roads ensured he'd stay there rather than make a nuisance of himself at the ducal seat.

"I do like your certain cures," Jane said. "I'm getting too big to carry all over the house, though."

Quinn's cures generally required bedrest, after a lusty expression of marital accord. Jane prescribed the same recipe frequently, to the point that Stephen and Duncan had agreed to leave on a grand tour in the autumn.

They—like the rest of creation—were waiting for the baby to arrive in another three months or so.

"You are not big," Quinn said. "You are merely a heifer who's been at summer grass."

Jane smacked his arm, then resumed cuddling. "I'm the Duchess of Walden. I'll thank you to recall the dignity of my office, sir."

Quinn tucked his arm around her shoulders and kissed her ear. "You're my duchess of rutting heifers, and I'm your gutter whelp from the slums of York. Who knew being a duke could be so diverting?"

Jane peered at him in the gloom. "Speaking of diversions, I do believe we need to find a wife for Joshua."

"I thought Duncan might be your next project." *Forgive me, cousin.*

"I'll take them both in hand, and your siblings as well, though Stephen has some wild oats to sow first. Do you mind very much being a duke?"

He loved that Jane would ask him such a blunt, personal question. She was no longer the minister's accommodating daughter who had spoken vows in prison, though she had become exactly the wife Quinn needed.

Did he mind waltzing with earnest young women, playing cards with peers, and driving Jane in the park at the Fashionable Hour? Did he mind the theater, the social calls, the subtle overtures from ambitious members of Parliament?

"I will never be fond of opera." Ned loved all the drama and caterwauling. "The rest of it is no great burden, as long as my greatest treasure remains safe. Take away my coin, my fine clothes, my fancy house, and the title, and I will contrive. If anything should cost me your love—"

Jane offered him a lemony kiss that turned into several kisses. "You say the loveliest things, and you express my own sentiments. Let the title be hanged, as long as the man I love stays by my side."

The coach rocked to a halt, though even Ned had learned not to intrude on Their Graces until the door opened from

within. Quinn handed his duchess down and escorted her
into the house with all the dignity inherent in her station.

In other words, he scooped her into his arms and carried
her up the steps, straight to the ducal apartment, while the
footmen smirked, the chambermaids blushed, and Her Grace
of Walden mooed against the duke's elegant, lacy cravat.

Author's Note

Newgate was an awful place. The name refers to the fact that the prison was built along the old Roman walls that encircled the City of London. In the twelfth century, the gate itself was rebuilt ("new"), and thus the name stuck through the more than 700 years the prison was in use. Newgate was demolished in 1904, though we have enough photographs, journal entries, and sketches to confirm that it was a visual as well as a social blight in its day.

Oddly enough, there is a significant tradition connecting prison reform and banking families. In 1813 Elizabeth Gurney Fry, daughter of a prominent Quaker family connected to both Gurney's Bank and Barclays Bank, visited Newgate. She was so horrified by the conditions there—horrendous overcrowding among the women (and the children locked up with their mothers), nothing to sleep on but filthy loose straw, rampant illness, prisoners incarcerated without any trial or conviction—that she spent the last twenty-eight years of her life as a prison reformer.

She spent nights in prisons; she invited politicians to do

likewise. She visited transport ships by the thousands and instituted the radical notion that prison could offer rehabilitation as well as punishment. She stocked the women's transport ships with scraps of fabric and sewing supplies so the ladies would arrive to their new lives with sewing skills and quilts to sell.

She spent much of her personal fortune on these endeavors, and when her husband's bank failed, she turned to her philanthropist brother to finance her charitable work. The world is a different and better place because of Elizabeth Fry.

I've taken a few liberties with the logistics of prison life in Quinn's day, but the basics are accurate: Money bought privileges, graft was rampant, and prison conditions for both debtors and felons were awful. So when I bethought myself, "Who is the farthest person from a duke? Who has the least in common with the typical graceful, charming, aristocratic hero?" a condemned felon in Newgate came to mind.

I hope you enjoyed reading Quinn and Jane's story, because I had a great time writing it! And yes, our dear, reserved, scholarly Duncan is my next candidate for a happily ever after, though Joshua and Stephen are on the list too!

Don't miss the next novel in the
Rogues to Riches series,

WHEN A DUCHESS SAYS I DO

Coming in Spring 2019

About the Author

Grace Burrowes grew up in central Pennsylvania and is the sixth out of seven children. She discovered romance novels when in junior high (back when there was such a thing), and has been reading them voraciously ever since. Grace has a bachelor's degree in political science, a bachelor of music in music history (both from the Pennsylvania State University); a master's degree in conflict transformation from Eastern Mennonite University; and a juris doctor from the National Law Center at the George Washington University.

Grace writes Georgian, Regency, Scottish Victorian, and contemporary romances in both novella and novel lengths. She's a member of Romance Writers of America, and enjoys giving workshops and speaking at writers' conferences. She also loves to hear from her readers, and can be reached through her website, graceburrowes.com.

**Keep reading for a special bonus novella
from *New York Times* bestselling author Elizabeth Hoyt:**

ONCE UPON A CHRISTMAS EVE

Adam Rutledge, Viscount d'Arque, really rather loathes
Christmas—especially the obligatory trip to the countryside.
His grandmother, however, loves the holiday, so he'll brave
the fiercest snowstorm to please her. But when their carriage
wheel snaps, they're forced to seek shelter at the home of the
most maddening, infuriating, and utterly beguiling woman
he's ever met...

Sarah St. John really rather loathes rakes. But in the
spirit of the season, she'll welcome this admittedly handsome viscount into her home. As the snowstorm rages, the
Yule log crackles, and the tension rises, Sarah and Adam
find themselves wondering whether love is the true meaning
of Christmas, and it's the one gift this mismatched pair can't
wait to unwrap.

ELIZABETH HOYT

ONCE UPON a CHRISTMAS EVE

Chapter One

Now once upon a time there was a prince who was handsome, vain, and really rather full of himself. His name was Brad....

—From *The Frog Princess*

DECEMBER 1741
UPPER HORNSFIELD, ENGLAND

Adam Rutledge, Viscount d'Arque loathed Christmas. The banal cheerfulness. The sly demands for charity. The asinine party games.

Oh, and the obligatory journey to the countryside.

The last was the reason he found himself in his present predicament. Late at night. In a snowstorm. In a wrecked carriage. On some godforsaken road. With his grandmother, Victoire Moore, Baroness Whimple.

His grandmother *loved* Christmas.

And Adam loved his grandmother.

"Hal informs me both the wheel and the axle are broken," Adam said as he tucked the furs more securely around the delicate skin of *Grand-mère*'s chin. She'd been trying to hide a cough from him for the last several days. "The heated bricks should keep you warm. I'm taking one of the horses and striking out to seek refuge. I pray for a fat country squire with buxom daughters—or at least good brandy."

His grandmother snorted. "Attempt not to be so distracted by the buxom daughters that you leave your grandmother to freeze."

"Never, darling." He leaned down to kiss her on her creped cheek, glanced at his grandmother's elderly maid, sleeping beside her, and then turned and swiftly left the carriage.

Outside, the wind drove fine, icy flakes of snow into his face as he trudged to Hal and the two footmen.

Hal, the driver of the wrecked carriage, looked up as he neared. "We've got 'er un'itched, m'lord."

Adam nodded. "Good. You've your pistols?"

Richard, the elder of the footmen, nodded. "Yes, m'lord."

"Stay with my grandmother," Adam ordered. "I doubt there'll be any highwaymen out on a night like this, but be 'ware in any case. I'll return as soon as I can."

Richard gave him a leg up on the mare, and then Adam was off.

They'd passed the light of a house not that far back—two miles, maybe less, according to Hal—but he was riding into the wind, without a saddle, and could see only a few feet in front of the nag's nose.

His main concern was making sure he stayed on the road. The land dropped off a bit on the right, and if the horse wandered in the darkness they'd take a tumble that would be rather a bother—especially if he broke his neck.

He bowed his head against the wind and nudged the mare onto the road.

A half hour later Adam had managed to coax the mare

into a jolting trot and was just beginning to wonder if his fingers were completely frozen when he caught sight of glowing lights.

Thank God.

He wanted Grand-mère out of that carriage and in front of a roaring fire as soon as possible.

Stone pillars marked a drive, which was a good sign—a country residence of some standing, then. He turned the mare's head, and they made their way down a winding approach that might've been scenic. At the moment he could see naught but the blinding snow and the growing glow of those lights.

The drive ended abruptly before a massive mansion. Lovely. Hopefully he hadn't seduced the country squire's wife in London during his rather checkered past—or at least, if he had, he hoped the country squire wasn't aware of it.

Adam dismounted his gallant steed—with less grace than usual owing to the fact that his feet appeared to have turned to ice—and climbed the front steps. He pounded on the door—and continued pounding until it was opened by a coldly unwelcoming face.

The man, though untitled, was from one of the oldest aristocratic families in Britain. He was tall, wore a gray wig, and regarded Adam over a pair of half-moon spectacles. Many people might think the man standing in the doorway benign and boring on first glance.

Many people would be bloody *wrong.*

Damn. This was worse than a cuckolded country squire.

"Yes?" said Godric St. John.

Adam affixed a genial smile to his lips, though he wasn't entirely sure it worked because he couldn't actually *feel* his lips. "St. John. How fortuitous. My carriage has wrecked on the road several miles back and I wonder—"

"Has it?" interrupted St. John rudely.

Adam narrowed his eyes, his smile still in place. Or at least he hoped so—frozen lips and all. "Yes, my *grand*—"

"Who is it, Godric?"

And here came the reason for St. John's boorishness. Dark-brown curls tumbling down from a haphazardly made coiffure, pink cheeks blossoming sweetly, brown eyes alight with curiosity, one small brat on her hip and—*good God*—another swelling her belly to alarming proportions, Lady Margaret St. John sailed into the hall behind her husband. Flirt with a man's wife once—quite innocently!—and he never seemed to forget it.

At least, that is, if the gentleman in question was Godric St. John.

"Oh," Lady Margaret exclaimed at the sight of him turning to solid ice on her husband's doorstep. "Lord d'Arque, do come in out of the cold."

"Thank you, my lady." He did as he was bid and cast his rictus grin on the mistress of the household. "How enchanting to find you, Lady Margaret, blooming even in the frozen midwinter night like a full-blown rose, sweetly scented, gorgeous to behold, and impossible to ignore." He took her hand and bent over it, making sure to linger until he heard a faint growl from St. John behind him.

When he rose the child was staring at him, her finger stuck between stickily pursed lips.

He blinked.

Larvae were not his area of expertise.

"Bees." The new voice was feminine and husky, and held just a hint of scorn.

Adam couldn't help it. His head jerked up at the sound.

St. John's half sister stood behind Lady Margaret.

Sarah St. John was blandly blond, of average height and everyday beauty.

The look she was giving him, however, was anything but everyday: it held pure disdain.

"I beg your pardon?" he drawled with exquisite politeness.

"No need to apologize, my lord," Miss St. John replied. "I believe you were just about to allude to bees and flowers, perhaps with yourself as the bee?"

He winced, inhaling sharply through his teeth. "Dear me, no. Rather banal, don't you think?"

She smiled sweetly. "Oh, is banality something you worry about, my lord? I hadn't noticed."

The little witch.

Adam kept his urbane smile with difficulty, though he had the feeling it might be more a baring of the teeth at the moment.

Sarah St. John should have been utterly forgettable. He'd met the lady only *once*, and that fleetingly.

Yet he remembered her for two reasons.

The first was that Miss St. John had made it plain she hated him on sight—an occurrence unique in Adam's experience.

The second was that on that occasion he'd found himself immediately and overwhelmingly attracted to Miss St. John.

Or, to put it another way:

He *wanted* her.

Sarah St. John loathed rakes.

The self-satisfied smirks. The sly predatory gazes. Oh, and the constantly witty banter rife with double meaning.

She especially hated that bit.

A lady who was the object of this sort of thing was supposed to bat her eyes and look coyly amused at the rake's supposed wit—even if it endangered her own dignity.

Viscount d'Arque was the epitome of the breed.

Tall and elegant, even when in a defrosting greatcoat dripping onto Hedge House's front hall, his high cheek-bones reddened from the winter cold, he exuded aplomb and dash. His mobile mouth with its prominent Cupid's bow quirked in a crooked smile at her, his dark brows arching up over cool gray eyes that sparkled with amusement.

At her expense, no doubt.

Lord d'Arque's smile didn't falter at her admittedly nasty jibe, but she watched as his shimmering gray eyes narrowed just a bit.

He said gently, "And you know me so well after one passing meeting, Miss St. John? Perhaps you've made an overhasty judgment."

Beside her, Megs, her best friend and sister-in-law, seemed to choke on nothing at all, while Godric coughed.

Sarah felt her face heat—and knew she was blushing, most probably unattractively.

Damn the man.

She opened her mouth to make a retort, but Megs beat her to it. "Do stop badgering His Lordship, Sarah, and let the man thaw a bit so he can properly defend himself." Megs turned her wide smile on the viscount. "My lord, would you care for some hot mulled wine in the sitting room? My mother-in-law's cook is known for her spiced wine and guards her recipe as if it were the crown jewels."

"Thank you, my lady," the viscount replied, aiming his overly charming smile at her, "but as I was attempting to tell your husband, I am traveling with my grandmother, who is still in my carriage. I wonder if I might impose upon your goodwill so far as to ask for help in retrieving both her and our servants and inflicting ourselves on your household until the morning?"

Sarah's mouth snapped shut at that. They were suffering through an unusually cold winter and she didn't like to think that anyone, let alone an old lady, was caught outside in this weather.

Fortunately, her brother Godric was already motioning for a footman. "Have the carriage readied and brought round." He turned to Lord d'Arque. "I'll accompany you to bring back Lady Whimple."

"Thank you," the viscount said. "I confess your help is much appreciated."

"Think nothing of it," Godric replied. "We have several rooms to spare. I trust you'll stay as our guests until your carriage is mended and you and your grandmother can travel again."

"Yes, indeed," Sarah said more soberly. "I know Mama will want you and your grandmother to stay. We'll see to readying the rooms while you fetch her."

Lord d'Arque's heavy-lidded gray eyes seemed to glint as he bowed toward her. "Your graciousness humbles me, Miss St. John."

The words were serious enough, but the viscount's drawl always seemed to hold a mocking undertone, giving Sarah the uneasy feeling he was making fun of her.

Her eyes narrowed, but she refrained from snapping at him. Lady Whimple was the main concern at the moment.

Godric was already donning gloves and a hat as well as a fur-lined cloak. "Let's fetch your grandmother," he said to Lord d'Arque, and both gentlemen went back out into the storm.

Sarah eyed the closed door. "Evidently our Christmas party has expanded."

"It has indeed," Megs exclaimed, withdrawing an errant lock of her hair from baby Sophie's mouth.

Sarah nodded, turning to the back of Hedge House—or simply Hedges, as the locals called it. She and Megs had been taking tea when they'd heard the knocking at the door. "We'd best inform Mama and then Mrs. Harris so she can make ready two more bedrooms."

"Mm," Megs murmured beside her. "What do you think? Old Dreary and the blue and white that overlooks the back garden?"

Sarah knit her brows. "Old Dreary for Lady Whimple?"

"Oh no," said Megs, looking a little scandalized. "What if she woke in the night and saw *him*? It might give her a fatal fright. Old Dreary for Lord d'Arque, I think. He doesn't seem the sort to turn a hair at anything he might find after midnight."

"You sound very like the viscount now," Sarah said with deep disapproval, "dropping double entendres here and there." She stopped to lift her niece from Megs's arms before continuing to the buttercup sitting room. "I think he's a bad influence."

"You'd say that anyway," her sister-in-law replied, not unkindly. "We all know your views on rakes."

"Humph," said Sarah, and chose to kiss Sophie with a loud *smack* that made the baby giggle instead of replying.

She knew whatever she said would sound petty and mean.

She *was* biased. It was a simple fact. She had reason to know that rakish gentlemen caused heartache to ladies and she wouldn't—*couldn't*—simply turn aside from their flirtatious ways with a simper or a mere censorious frown.

"But you must admit he's very exciting," Megs mused as they arrived at the door to the sitting room.

"Perhaps," Sarah said, "but I don't especially like exciting gentlemen."

"Don't you?" Megs asked doubtfully.

"No," Sarah replied quite firmly and squashed the small rebellious voice inside her head that whispered, *Liar*.

Chapter Two

꧁꧂

One day while Prince Brad was jaunting around the
forest with his retinue he stopped by a pond. There he
decided to demonstrate his skills in throwing a
dagger and in doing so dropped the dagger into the
pond.
"Bugger," said Prince Brad. "I liked that dagger." ...

—From *The Frog Princess*

An hour later Adam reached into St. John's carriage and
gathered his grandmother into his arms. St. John himself was
dealing with the horses and Adam's servants.

"Such nonsense," Grand-mère said breathlessly as he
lifted her. "I can certainly walk to the door."

"Humor me," he replied lightly as he turned and made his
way through the snow. She hardly weighed anything at all.
Grand-mère was such a forceful personality that sometimes
he forgot how frail she really was. "Every now and again I
enjoy a bit of physical labor just to remind myself that I'm
not quite a fop yet."

Miss St. John held open the door to Hedge House as they
neared.

She bestowed a sweet smile on his grandmother, all but

ignoring Adam. "Welcome to Hedge House, my lady. We've prepared a room for you with a fire, and I've asked for tea to be brought to your room."

"Thank you," Grand-mère said, and then had to stop to cough. "I don't suppose you have any brandy as well?"

Miss St. John didn't even blink. "Of course. I'll send for some." She nodded to a hovering footman and then turned to lead them up the stairs.

"Really, Adam, you can set me down now," Grand-mère growled.

"Nonsense," he replied. "Miss St. John already thinks me a feckless rake. Were she to see me abandon you in the hallway she would lose what little respect she might still have for me."

The lady ahead of them didn't bother turning, but he heard a faint "Humph."

He grinned, watching the sway of her skirts as she climbed the steps.

When he glanced back at his grandmother she was eyeing him thoughtfully. "You and Miss St. John have met before?"

"Only once," the lady called back.

"Yes, but even that once was enough for her to set me down," Adam said cheerfully, and then, in a loud whisper to his grandmother, "I have the feeling she doesn't like me."

Miss St. John made the upper level and shot a scornful glance at him over her shoulder as she turned down a hall.

Grand-mère hummed. "How unusual. Most ladies fall at your feet."

"Indeed they do," Adam replied without a trace of modesty. "I begin to think that Miss St. John simply does not like men."

"Not at all," the lady in question said sweetly. She'd paused in front of a door and she gestured him inside. "I am quite fond of *most* gentlemen."

Adam found himself perilously close to losing his temper with the little virago.

Which was ridiculous. He'd traded far more cutting barbs with other ladies. There was just something about Miss St. John that made him feel savage.

Not that he was about to let her know that.

"Gentlemen in their eighth decade, no doubt," he murmured as he edged past her with Grand-mère in his arms. He shot Miss St. John an easy, guileless smile. "I do understand. A lady such as yourself might find any younger gentleman too fearsome."

He turned before he could see her reaction, but he rather thought his volley had hit by her indrawn breath.

"A lady such as myself?" she asked with terrible calm.

Oh, yes indeed, he'd gone over the walls with that last one. Adam lowered Grand-mère to the bed before glancing up at his feminine adversary. "A lady of..." He paused delicately. "A certain *age*." Adam widened his eyes innocently. "That *is* why you're not wed, yes? Because you're, what? Two and thirty?"

"Seven and *twenty*," she bit out. "And I can't believe you're so concerned about *my* age when you're older than I."

"Ah, but I'm a man," he replied, "And but five and thirty. A mere youth relatively."

A blush had risen in her cheeks—no doubt a sign of ire rather than embarrassment—and he couldn't help but note how ravishing it made her look. Her light-brown eyes were wide and nearly shooting flames at him, her head thrown back, her soft red lips parted in outrage...

Well.

He wondered if this was how she might look in the throes of passion.

The thought went straight to his groin. He might not particularly *like* Miss St. John, but he couldn't deny her allure.

Even if he suspected she was quite unaware of it herself.

He cursed under his breath, glancing away, just as Grandmère spoke.

"I wonder..." She paused to cough and his attention was immediately on her. Grand-mère's hand shook as she raised a handkerchief to her lips, the huge sapphire ring on her left hand winking in the candlelight. "I wonder if I might have that tea now. And perhaps the brandy as well."

Her voice sounded thin and frail.

Adam's brows snapped together. "Of course, darling. Let me help you out of your cloak so that you can rest."

He glanced up to see that Miss St. John was already pouring a dish of tea from the teapot sitting on a nearby table.

He bent over his grandmother, helping her to remove her cloak and shoes. Cannon, her lady's maid, should be up soon. The maid was nearly as old as her mistress and had been with Grand-mère since her marriage. They were fiercely loyal to each other, and Grand-mère would not hear of acquiring a younger lady's maid.

Even if that meant waiting on the elderly maid climbing the stairs.

"Here," Miss St. John murmured.

He looked up to find her at his elbow, holding the dish of tea. Her brows were drawn together, and when she met his gaze, her eyes held concern. "Dr. Christopher Manning is one of our guests for Christmas. He's a friend of Godric's and quite a good physician. Perhaps I might have him attend Lady Whimple?"

"Thank you," he replied, truly grateful.

She turned and quickly left the room.

Adam picked up his grandmother's hand and chafed her cold fingers between his hands, absently noting that her sapphire ring was loose on her finger. She'd lost weight. "I know that you don't like doctors, but perhaps a quick look before you undress for bed."

"If you think it a good idea," she replied in a wan voice so unlike her usual brisk tones that he felt his heart sink in fear.

"I do," he replied, careful to not let any of his apprehension show.

"That gel, Miss St. John..." She paused to cough again. "I rather like her."

He raised his eyebrows. "Because she hates me?"

Grand-mère ignored that. "She challenges you. She isn't won over by your charm."

He winced, remembering Miss St. John's thrown-back head. Her fiery eyes as she set him down. Odd that she should arouse him so. "Yes, and I find her bellicosity the most irritating thing imaginable."

Grand-mère watched him with eyes that had always been much too perceptive. "Do you?"

Sarah hurried to the ivy sitting room, where the house party had assembled after dinner. Lord d'Arque had worn a small wrinkle between his brows when she'd left his grandmother's room. For such an urbane man—one skilled in hiding his true feelings—that wrinkle had been like a horn blaring his worry for Lady Whimple. The viscount was a vain, bold man like all rakes, but she found his devotion to his grandmother rather...sweet. Had it been any other man, she might even go so far as to call it endearing.

She shook her head. This was Lord d'Arque, one of the most notorious roués in London, a man known for his seduction of women. *Endearing* was the very last epithet one would choose for him—and she must remember that.

With that thought Sarah opened the door to the sitting room.

Inside, the party was gathered around her mother, Clara St. John, and Godric, who appeared to be delivering a summary of his journey with Lord d'Arque to the wrecked carriage.

Everyone looked at her when she entered.

"Oh, Sarah," Mama said, "how is Lady Whimple? It's such a cold night for an elderly lady to be out."

"I'm afraid not well," Sarah replied. She looked at Dr. Manning, a handsome man of eight-and-twenty with cheerful blue eyes and a broad, open face. He eschewed the bobbed wig worn by most of his profession and instead pulled his ginger hair into a simple queue. "Will you come, Dr. Manning?"

"Of course." He set aside his teacup and rose at once. "I'll need to go to my room to fetch my bag."

Sarah nodded, turning toward the door with the doctor immediately behind her.

"I believe Mama put you in the blue room?" she asked when they'd made the hall.

"Yes." He grimaced. "An unfortunate business, this, Viscount d'Arque's carriage going off the road."

She glanced at him curiously as they mounted the stairs to the next floor. "You sound as if you know Lord d'Arque?"

"Not as such," Doctor Manning replied. "I...er...have heard of him, naturally."

"Naturally," Sarah murmured.

Dr. Manning cleared his throat, darting a glance at her. "I doubt a lady such as yourself would know of his reputation, but he's rather notorious."

"Ah," Sarah said noncommittally.

It was sweet that Dr. Manning thought that ladies didn't gossip about such things.

She waited outside his room as the doctor retrieved his bag, and then led him around a corner to the east wing.

They came to Lady Whimple's room, and Sarah knocked lightly before opening the door.

Inside, Lord d'Arque was just rising from where he'd been perched beside his grandmother on the bed.

"My lady, my lord," Sarah said, "This is Dr. Christopher Manning, late of Oxford. Dr. Manning, Lady Whimple and her grandson, Viscount d'Arque."

Dr. Manning bowed, looking quite competent and dashing with his professional bag and serious air.

In contrast, Lord d'Arque seemed an indolent aristocrat as he strolled forward to shake the other man's hand. "Thank you for coming, Doctor."

The viscount's saturnine good looks differed sharply from the doctor's boyish fair complexion and hair.

"Not at all," Dr. Manning said. "I'll need a moment alone with Lady Whimple, if you don't mind. Her lady's maid may stay, of course." He nodded to the elderly maid sitting on a chair on the other side of the bed.

"If that meets with your approval, Grand-mère?" Lord d'Arque asked his grandmother.

"Yes, yes," she replied, waving her hand at her grandson in a shooing motion. "Go and have some tea...or more likely brandy."

The viscount smirked as he bowed to the old lady. "As you wish."

He ushered Sarah out of the room and then paused, staring back at the door with a small frown.

He looked so worried.

She cleared her throat a little awkwardly. "We do have tea and brandy in the sitting room, my lord. I find tea can be quite refreshing to the spirits."

Lord d'Arque turned at her words, a cynical smile immediately replacing his frown. "Sympathy for the devil, Miss St. John? How easily you are won over by a bit of melancholy."

Sarah stiffened, reminded once again why she disliked this man.

"If you'll come with me," she replied, turning without waiting for him.

He made a *tsk*ing sound, easily catching up to her with his long legs. "Now, now. Don't be that way. I've a secret fondness for tea myself. Drink gallons of the stuff, I assure you, usually after a vigorous romp with some lovely lady."

"Must you be so vile?" The words burst from her mouth quite without her volition.

There was a short silence as they came to the stairs.

Then he spoke, his voice lower, though still as mocking. "Oh, I think so. Feminine flesh and debauchery are my bread and water—without them I wither and die. If you wish for gentleness and chivalry, apply to your Dr. Manning instead."

Sarah found herself at a near run now, her fury lending speed to her descent. It was no wonder, then, that she caught her heel on one of the treads.

For a moment she felt the sickening swoop of her stomach and the sure knowledge that she was about to fall headlong down the stairs.

Then a strong arm wound around her waist and jerked her close to a hard chest.

She breathed deeply, feeling his heat behind her, his legs against her bottom.

"Careful, sweetheart," he rasped in her ear, his breath brushing her neck, and it was strange because she could've sworn there was real concern in his voice. "You nearly fell at my feet just then."

Chapter Three

❧

A tiny voice piped up from the middle of the pond. "I
can fetch you your dagger, Prince."
Prince Brad looked around. "Who said that?"
"I did," said a grass-green frog sitting on a lotus leaf.
"I will fetch you the dagger if, in return, you bring me
to your castle and let me sleep in the bed you sleep in
and eat from the plate you eat from for a fortnight."
Prince Brad smiled. "Very well." . . .

—From *The Frog Princess*

Adam fought down the instinctive fear he'd felt when
Miss St. John had wobbled on the stairs. She hadn't fallen.
He'd caught her. There'd be no blood at the bottom of the
staircase this time. He watched as Miss St. John's breasts
rose and fell beneath her fichu. The sight awoke the hunting
instinct within him. She was ripe for the picking, so close
and so innocent.

Innocent.

He blinked, pulling back enough to put space between
their bodies.

He didn't, as a rule, chase unmarried ladies. Ladies who
were unused to the sport of passion—the pursuit, the sly

dodging and weaving of the prey, the inevitable mutually satisfactory capture.

Miss St. John, for all her quick wit, her rapid verbal parries, was a virgin.

And he did not touch virgins.

Adam let go of her, his fingers lingering even as he withdrew—perhaps to steady her.

Perhaps to feel her in his grasp for as long as possible.

He inhaled, trying to calm himself. It was uncommonly hard, maybe because while his intellect told him this woman was forbidden, the male animal within him considered her his prize.

But man was nothing without intellect.

He forced his lips into a nearly civil smile and held out his arm. "You mentioned tea."

Miss St. John blinked as if waking from a deep sleep. Gratifying, that. One's pride always liked to see a female ensnared, even if she was to be let go.

Then Miss St. John's eyes narrowed at him and any hint of enthrallment vanished. "Tea. Of course."

She ignored his proffered arm and continued down the stairs, chin tilted at an imperious angle.

He bit back a smile and trailed her, watching the twitch of her skirts and the angle of her shoulders.

They made the lower floor and she turned a corner, continuing at a brisk stride that was no doubt meant to outpace him. In that she failed. She was, after all, a full head shorter than he and thus presumably had correspondingly shorter legs.

Legs.

He shook himself. Best not to think about Miss St. John's legs, hidden so well under those swishing skirts. Were they shapely, with a generous curve from ankle to knee? Or did she have lithe thin calves, muscular from walking? And her thighs...

No, no, *no*.

This was incorrigible even for him. He needed to keep his eyes—and thoughts!—*above* Miss St. John's waist.

She stopped at a door and gave him an amusingly stern look before opening it.

The sitting room was all that was considered wonderful in the Christmas season: a roaring fire, green boughs decorating the mantel, two dogs lounging before the fire, and a roomful of people.

Adam repressed a shudder.

"D'Arque." St. John nodded at their entrance. "I hope all is well with your grandmother?"

"We shall soon see," Adam replied, forcing cheerfulness into his voice.

"May I introduce you to my family and our house guests staying for the Christmas season?" Miss St. John asked.

"Please."

She nodded. "You know my half brother Godric and his wife, Lady Margaret, who are visiting from London."

"Half brother?" Adam looked with interest between Sarah St. John and Godric St. John.

"My mother was our father's first wife," St. John spoke up. "Clara"—here he bowed to Mrs. St. John—"was my late father's second wife. Hedges is the dower house."

Miss St. John cleared her throat. "If you don't mind me continuing?"

"Do." Adam waved a gracious hand just to see her eyes narrow.

Miss St. John nodded. "May I present my mother, Mrs. St. John, and my sisters, Charlotte and Jane?"

Adam bowed first to the younger women and then to Mrs.

St. John, a pleasant-looking woman. "Madam. Thank you for your most gracious hospitality."

The smile Mrs. St. John bestowed on him lit her face from within. "Think nothing of it, Lord d'Arque. I'm only glad that we could be of help."

She had the blond hair of her daughters, though now dulled by gray, and red cheeks and chin. Both of Miss St. John's sisters were pretty girls, though Charlotte St. John, with fine green eyes and a perfect oval face, was obviously the beauty of the family. The sisters sat close together like huddled birds, and Adam felt his lips twitch at the sight. They were obviously fond of each other.

Miss St. John turned to the remaining two members of the party. "My lord, may I introduce you to Sir Hilary Webber, our neighbor from the next county, and Gerald Hill, Baron Kirby, a second cousin twice removed of my sister-in-law, Lady Margaret?"

Both men were not much past thirty. The first was large and rather alarmingly athletic looking, as if he were a latter-day Hercules. The second was tall and thin and wore a neat white wig and spectacles.

Adam bowed to both.

"Good to meet you, my lord. Awful business, your carriage wrecking on the high road," Sir Hilary said in a loud voice that was surprisingly high pitched. "Roads are terrible hereabouts. Happens in the country, I'm afraid."

"It's true," Lord Kirby said. "My carriage nearly wrecked as well, and we were driving in fair weather."

"Lord Kirby traveled from Edinburgh, where he is well known as an expert on exotic flora," Miss St. John explained with a small smile at the fellow.

Adam's own eyes narrowed before he remembered: she wasn't his. She wasn't even potentially his. If Miss St. John had an interest in Lord Kirby and his boring plants, then it was no concern of Adam's.

Still. He rather felt like growling.

"My lord."

The call came from the doorway where Dr. Manning stood.

"Excuse me," Adam murmured to the ladies, and strode to Manning. "How is my grandmother?"

The doctor gestured him into the hall and Adam clenched his jaw against possible bad news. Grand-mère was three and eighty, and though she seemed an indomitable force, she was only human.

Manning turned once they were out of earshot of those in the sitting room. His broad country face looked grave. "Lady Whimple is beset by pleurisy," he said bluntly. "She told me she has pains in her chest and a shortness of breath, not to mention a persistent cough."

It was a moment before Adam had himself under control enough to speak. "Can you do anything for her?"

"I can give her such medicines as I have at my disposal," Manning said slowly, "but the most important treatment is bed rest. It's imperative that Lady Whimple not be moved for at least the next fortnight."

Adam stared. It appeared that he and his grandmother were to be uninvited guests at Hedge House for Christmas.

The next morning dawned with the kind of bright, clear light that occurs only when the sun reflects off snow.

Sarah threw back the coverlet of her bed and rose.

Her maid, Doris, was already busy stoking the fire. "Good morning, miss. I do hope you slept well?"

"Yes, thank you, Doris," Sarah replied, making for the pitcher of fresh hot water on her nightstand. "And you?"

"Oh yes, miss, despite all the bother over the viscount's servants come to stay."

Sarah wet a cloth and began to wash her face. "Were you able to find beds for everyone?"

"We did indeed, miss." Doris gave a final brush to the hearth and stood. "Mind, we was crowded already due to the valets comin' with the gentlemen and o' course Lady Margaret's maid, but there. I've shared a bed often enough as a wee thing it's no worry now."

Sarah glanced at her maid. "That sounds crowded."

Doris shot her a smile. "It might be, but it's Bet the scullery maid who's my bedmate. We bunked together so as to give Lady Whimple's maid her own bed. Bet always has a jest or two, not to mention all the best gossip."

"Well, I'm glad everything's worked out," Sarah said.

"Yes, miss. Will the pale-blue dress do today?"

"Please."

Doris helped Sarah with her toilet and then curtsied and left the room with a handful of linens for mending.

Sarah inspected her hair in the mirror one last time, decided to change her earrings to a pair of blue enamel drops, and then left to make her way to the breakfast room.

The house was quiet this morning, many of the guests perhaps still abed, so when she came to a corner of the hallway she could clearly hear a masculine voice talking.

"There you are, sweetheart. What a lovely thing you are. I wonder what your name is?"

For a moment she froze in outrage. She knew well that voice. How dared he...? Sarah set her chin and walked briskly around the corner to confront the brazen oaf.

But as she rounded the corner she found Lord d'Arque crouched over Harriet, one of their two dogs. The spaniel was shamelessly splayed upon the floor as he rubbed her belly.

His lips were quirked up, his eyes intent upon the happy dog, and his long fingers burrowed through her fur.

Sarah felt a bit warm at the sight. Something about the lazy, sensuous slide of his fingers, the gentleness in his face...

It was as if she had caught him unawares, as if his sharp, cynical walls had lowered for a moment and she saw a different man within. The intimate glimpse of the man caught her by surprise. Made her insides soften and tremble. Was this the real Lord d'Arque? The man who cared tenderly for his grandmother and apparently had an affection for dogs? Had she truly been wrong about the viscount all along?

He glanced up and it was as if she could see those walls rising, shielding whatever—or *who*ever—lay at his core. "Miss St. John. Good morning."

She blinked, still a little dazed. "Harriet."

He raised his brows, looking amused. "I beg your pardon?"

She inhaled, mentally shaking herself. "The dog you're petting and who is making a regrettable display of herself is Harriet."

"Ah." He looked down at the dog, who had become so debauched her tongue lolled out of her jaws. "Harriet. I'm pleased to make your acquaintance." He gave her a last rub and then uncoiled slowly, standing much too close to Sarah.

She inhaled and stepped back, her heart—silly thing!—insisting on beating fast. She wasn't a young girl anymore—a girl who'd once fallen under the spell of a cad. She was too intelligent, too experienced for this.

Lord d'Arque smiled, his eyes alight with something wicked. "I'm afraid I'm rather used to females making themselves shameless for me."

Sarah was very proud of herself for not blushing at his risqué comment—he was so obviously trying to shock her.

"*Are* you?" she asked, infusing her voice with just a *smidgen* of doubt.

She turned and continued toward the breakfast room.

If she'd thought to set Lord d'Arque in his place, she failed. He immediately matched his stride to hers, walking along beside her. Harriet scrambled to her feet and followed along, panting happily.

"Oh yes," he said, as if she'd truly been asking a question. "I don't wish to seem vain, but it's rather embarrassing, truth be told, how often ladies make a play for my attention."

"How awful," Sarah said with mock sympathy. "You must be tripping over them constantly."

"Oh, indeed," he replied, his voice lowered to a rich timber. "That's why you are so utterly refreshing, Miss St. John. You resist my charms so completely, you might as well be a maiden hidden in a tall tower."

For some reason that rather hurt. Was he saying she was without passion, without interest to the male sex?

The thought made her grumpy, which was ridiculous. She didn't *want* the viscount's attention. She was *glad* he thought her unattainable.

Still she might've opened the door to the breakfast room with a little more force than was absolutely necessary before marching in.

"Good morning, Miss St. John," Dr. Manning said as he rose along with Sir Hilary and Lord Kirby. The three gentlemen were at the long breakfast table, various foodstuffs piled before them.

"Good morning," Sarah replied, consciously making her tone cheerful.

She crossed to the table and began to take a seat, but Sir Hilary pulled out the chair beside him. "Will you not sit here, Miss St. John, where the light will not hit your eyes?"

Since the sunlight outside wasn't yet coming in the windows, this seemed a rather silly argument, but Sarah smiled and diverted her course toward Sir Hilary.

She sat in the indicated seat and couldn't help noticing the triumphant look Sir Hilary gave Dr. Manning and Lord Kirby, who were on the other side of the table.

"You're quite right, Webber," Lord d'Arque said from her other side. Sarah turned to find the awful man lowering himself into the chair beside her. "The sun is *much* better here." He picked up a basket and turned to Sarah. "Bread?"

"Thank you," she murmured, taking one of the still-warm buns.

"Tell me, Webber," the viscount continued, buttering a piece of a bun. "Are you a married man?"

"Ah," Sir Hilary said, and unaccountably blushed. "No, no. Not as yet."

The viscount raised his eyebrows. "Indeed? And you, gentlemen?"

"I have not achieved that happy state," Lord Kirby said.

Dr. Manning simply shook his head.

"Three bachelors," Lord d'Arque mused. He snapped his fingers. "Oh, pardon me. *Four* bachelors, for of course I haven't a wife or even a fiancée."

Sarah stiffened, waiting for the viscount's next words and dreading them.

But it was Lord Kirby who spoke up. "Do you know that my father had four bachelor brothers? And my grandfather three? In fact there are quite a number of gentlemen who eschew the fairer sex."

Oddly, this provoked a lively discussion among Lord Kirby, Dr. Manning, and Sir Hilary.

Sarah looked on bemusedly as she sipped her tea.

However, she was glad for their distraction when Lord

d'Arque reached across her rudely to pick up a platter of gammon.

He was too close to her, she could feel his heat, smell the faint scent of sandalwood on him.

It was distracting.

So she was utterly unprepared when he asked, "Tell me, Miss St. John, are you on the hunt for a husband?"

Chapter Four

*So the frog dove down, down into the icy waters of
the pond and brought the dagger up to Prince Brad.
"Thank you," he said. And he took the dagger from
the frog, mounted his horse, and rode away with all
his retinue, leaving the frog behind.
"Bugger," said the frog....*

—From *The Frog Princess*

He leaned a little closer to her, inhaling the scent of roses.
"I'm right, aren't I?" His tone was light. Jovial. As if he
didn't care at all whom she might be considering marrying.
"And three gentlemen courting you—an abundance of
choice."

Miss St. John's cheeks turned a becoming pink, and he
felt something inside him clench.

Ridiculous.

"I doubt this is any of your concern," Miss St. John hissed
under her breath like an outraged cat.

"No." He ate a bite of bread. "But it *could* be."

That got her to turn slightly in his direction. The tip of her
tongue darted out to lick her lush lips, making him stare. "I
hesitate to ask what you mean."

"Well…" Adam brought his gaze back up to hers, trying to control the surge of heat in his groin. "It seems to me that you may need some help in deciding on a husband. Perhaps you need an older, more mature adviser, one who knows the world and has seen many a romance blossom…and then wither."

She looked at him, one delicate eyebrow raised incredulously. "And I suppose you consider yourself such an adviser."

"Oh." He widened his eyes as if caught off guard. "I hadn't thought to nominate myself, but now that you've most graciously suggested it…"

She rolled her eyes at him.

He had to control a grin at the sight of proper Miss St. John so far forgetting herself. He couldn't remember the last time he'd been so amused at a conversation.

Or so aroused.

Which brought him up short. This wasn't a flirtation. He was merely passing the time until Grand-mère recovered and they could leave this home of family and Christmas merriment.

Miss St. John meant nothing to him.

"I will help you to decide which suitor would make the perfect husband for you," he whispered graciously.

"Will you?" she replied, dry as dust. Really she was wasted in this backwater.

"Indeed." He glanced at the other gentlemen, now discussing…Good Lord. It appeared to be something about manure and rapeseed. This might be harder than he'd thought. "I suggest we begin by listing the qualities you'll want in a husband."

"You are *not* helping me find a husband," she said very firmly.

"Physical health, for instance," he continued, ignoring

her. He spoke low so as not to be overheard by the other gentlemen, but he might as well not have bothered. They were too caught up in their farming discussion. "Very important, I should think."

She looked at him, widening her eyes in query.

"For the marriage bed, naturally," he explained kindly. "A husband who can't...er...come to attention is worse than useless."

"We're at the *breakfast table*," she hissed. She appeared to be having trouble meeting his eyes. "This isn't the place to discuss such things."

"Then where? I should think it's as good a place as any to contemplate wedded bliss."

"You're incorrigible."

"Yes, I am." He took a sip of tea to hide his smile. Her outrage was terribly entertaining. "So then *health* right at the top of our list."

She opened her mouth and then slowly closed it, staring at him. Finally she said, "How do you know I wish to be married in the first place?"

"Don't all women?" he asked lightly.

"No," she replied seriously. "Most do, but not all. Just as most men wish to marry, but not all."

He raised his teacup in a salute. "Touché."

"But you're right," she said, turning back to her plate and damnably hiding her eyes. "I want a husband. I want children and a home and a *family*."

He stilled, for he rather thought a note of seriousness had been inserted into their play.

"So sure," he whispered. Of course she would want a family and a husband to give it to her.

A man who was as much his opposite as it was possible to be.

Ladies such as she did not choose rakes to father their children.

"Yes." She looked at him and he saw that she had a defiant light in her eyes. "I am sure of what I want."

He pushed aside his maudlin thoughts and gave her a dangerous smile. "Then permit me to help you obtain that which you want."

Sarah stared at Lord d'Arque. What was he playing at? He didn't like her—that much was obvious. Silly to pretend anything else—the man had made his feelings more than plain, and she was a woman who insisted on being scrupulously factual with herself.

Lord d'Arque was toying with her. And yet she felt drawn to him on an animal level.

She *wanted* him despite her own dislike for him.

How humiliating to be betrayed so by her body! She shouldn't feel sensual attraction to a man she disliked. It was horrifying. Why couldn't she be physically aware of Lord Kirby or Sir Hilary, both respectable gentlemen?

Why couldn't her mind rule her body?

She studied him. His eyes were clear gray beneath heavy lids, cynical and world-weary. She knew she was staring into them too long, noting the darker ring around the iris and the fine laugh lines that fanned out from the corners of his eyes.

He was a rake, she reminded herself.

He wasn't to be trusted.

Why was it so hard to keep that thought at the forefront of her mind?

"Good morning!"

Mama's cheerful greeting came from the doorway to the breakfast room, and Sarah started at her voice.

She saw Lord d'Arque's sinful mouth curl at the corner,

as if he knew how lost she'd become in his gaze, and then he turned away.

He stood with the rest of the gentlemen, bowing to her mother. "Mrs. St. John, you brighten the day like the sun, generous and lovely. I thank you again for your bounteous hospitality."

Mama blushed, and Sarah narrowed her eyes at Lord d'Arque, examining him for any sign that he was mocking her mother.

Except...he seemed quite sincere.

Sir Hilary held out a chair for Mama while Lord Kirby poured her a dish of tea.

"I trust you slept well?" Dr. Manning enquired solicitously.

"Yes indeed," Mama replied, nodding her thanks to Lord Kirby as she accepted her teacup. "I do so enjoy retiring for the night under a heap of coverlets while the snow blows outside. It makes one especially thankful to be warm inside, don't you think?"

Lord d'Arque smiled at her comment while Sir Hilary looked nonplussed and Lord Kirby and Dr. Manning hastened to agree with her.

"And how is Lady Whimple?" Mama continued, looking with concern at Lord d'Arque.

"She slept well," the viscount replied.

Sarah noticed that he didn't actually say that the old lady was better this morning. She frowned, watching him, but he had his social face firmly in place and it was impossible to tell if he was worried for his grandmother.

Jane and Charlotte arrived at that moment, closely followed by Godric and Megs, and for a moment there was a flurry of greetings and the distribution of tea.

When the room had somewhat quieted, Mama looked

around. "I'm so glad everyone is here. I have a task for you all. Well, everyone but Megs and Godric." She glanced fondly at her stepson and his wife. "We plan a Christmas Eve ball, and I'd like to decorate the ballroom with holly branches. There's some holly bushes along the road and at the edge of the copse. Could you young people go and gather holly for me?"

Jane immediately clapped her hands. "Oh, lovely! We can don cloaks and muffs and wooly mittens and have a tramp. Pat and Harriet will like that."

"Let's make it into a game," Charlotte added. Her green eyes were alight with excitement. "We can divide into groups. The first ones to return to Hedges with the holly will be declared the winners."

"Do we have a prize?" Jane asked.

"Oh," Charlotte said. "Maybe a slice of the mince pie Cook is making today?"

"But everyone will be partaking of the pie tonight at dinner," Jane objected. "That hardly makes a fitting prize."

Lord d'Arque cleared his throat, drawing everyone's attention. The smile playing about his mouth was quite wicked. "A suggestion. Perhaps—with the blessing of our kind hostess—the winners can steal a kiss from whomever of the house party they choose."

Sarah inhaled, carefully keeping her gaze from Lord d'Arque. Was there a particular lady whom Lord d'Arque wished to kiss?

From the way Godric was glowering at Lord d'Arque, he had a suspicion it was Megs the viscount was interested in. Even if she and Godric were not included in the holly hunt, Lord d'Arque had carefully worded his suggestion so that both Megs and Godric were included in the kissing prize.

Sarah's heart sank. She remembered now Megs telling

her that Lord d'Arque had flirted with her outrageously at a ball when she and Godric had first married.

Sarah bit her lip. She would *not* become jealous of her sister-in-law.

Meanwhile Jane was clapping with excitement while Charlotte clasped her hands together under her chin.

"Please may we, Mama?" Charlotte begged their mother, being sure to employ her extravagantly lashed eyes. "Oh, *please!*"

"Very well," Mama said. Sarah could tell she was trying to look stern, but mostly she looked happy. "Since it is the Christmas season, I'll allow this game and prize. Mind you," she added, casting a stern eye about the company, "any kissing to be done will be in front of all of us so that no reputations might be sullied."

"Huzzah!" Jane cried in what was a rather childish celebration from a lady who often reminded her sisters that she was *nearly* twenty.

"Hm," a male voice murmured in Sarah's ear. "I wonder whom you will pick to kiss should you win, Miss St. John."

Chapter Five

❧

That night Prince Brad had just begun cutting into his beefsteak when the doors to the royal dining room opened and the frog hopped wearily in.
"Pardon me," said the frog, "but I do believe you forgot your promise to me."
There was a short silence from the royal family before the queen turned a gimlet eye upon her son. "Bradley, is this true?" ...

—From *The Frog Princess*

Adam watched as Miss St. John's eyes widened at his words. They really were rather lovely eyes—a light brown surrounded by thick, dark lashes.

He was playing with fire, he knew. He should've walked away from Miss St. John the moment he'd realized his hunger for her.

Instead he'd traded quips with her, badgered her into responding, and, worst of all, inhaled the scent of roses in her hair like a starry-eyed schoolboy who'd just discovered his cock.

Pathetic.

And now, to cap off his insanity, he was making plans to kiss her.

His mouth twisted in self-mockery as he turned away to sip his tea. Why else make the suggestion of a stolen kiss as prize? Surely he knew well enough his own wants and desires by now. After all, he was five and thirty and had lived a life of debauchery. He'd never given an unmarried lady reason to hope for marriage—or anything else—with him.

But the thing was that he *enjoyed* speaking with Miss St. John. Enjoyed the sting of her barbs and the way she looked so indignantly at him.

Were she already married or widowed...

There was a burst of laughter from the table, and Adam glanced up, realizing he'd missed something as he was musing.

"No, no, the *ladies* must choose their partners," Charlotte St. John said. "I think it only reasonable."

"But there's four gentlemen to three ladies," Lady Margaret pointed out. "Someone will have the advantage of an extra person."

"Actually"—Kirby cleared his throat with a slight grimace—"I wonder if I might be excused due to rather painful chilblains on my feet."

"Naturally, my lord," Mrs. St. John said with a sympathetic smile to Kirby. "Perhaps you can help me in planning the placement of the decorations for the ballroom while the others go on their adventure."

Kirby nodded, looking as if he were having second thoughts about forgoing the holly gathering. If he truly were interested in Miss St. John, he might've realized the holly hunt was a perfect opportunity to woo the lady alone.

Adam hid a smile as he took a bite of gammon.

"Youngest first," Jane St. John proclaimed, either ignoring or not hearing her sisters' dissents. "Let me see..." She took her time in examining Manning, Sir Hilary, and Adam. "I choose Dr. Manning."

That gentleman glanced quickly at Charlotte St. John before smiling and bowing to Jane.

Charlotte St. John looked between Adam and Sir Hilary. Adam winked at her and she blushed a deep—and quite becoming—rose.

"Sir Hilary," Charlotte St. John proclaimed.

"Honored," her choice intoned.

"Oh dear, Miss St. John," Adam murmured, turning to her, "it seems you are left with only me."

She pressed her lips together, looking less than pleased.

Which caused her mother to hastily say, "I'm sure everyone is *quite* happy with their partners."

"Let's leave at once after breakfast," Jane St. John exclaimed.

Which was how, half an hour later, Adam found himself trudging through calf-deep snow, the eldest Miss St. John stumping along mutinously beside him.

All around, the bare branches of trees and the evergreen boughs bore a thick frosting of snow. The sky was a crisp blue, and the new snowfall was pristine and lovely.

A true Christmas scene, Adam thought cynically.

He threw his head back, inhaling freezing air and exhaling it in a great white cloud. "Ah, how wonderful is the country air."

Miss St. John glanced at him, her eyebrows so high in disbelief they disappeared into the fur-trimmed hood she wore. "I would never have taken you for a man who enjoys the country, my lord."

"No? But then you don't entirely know me, Miss St. John. As it happens I grew up in the country."

"You did?" she gazed at him with the same amazement she would have worn had he declared he'd been raised on the moon.

"Indeed." His lips twisted. "My family's country estate is outside Bath. Close enough to London that I could venture there several times a year, had I the desire—which I most certainly do not."

She knit her brows. "But...you must not have been on the way there with your grandmother when your carriage wrecked?"

"Oh no," he replied carelessly. "Our destination was a cousin of my grandmother's. A lady nearly as old as she and quite bad tempered. Grand-mère enjoys inflicting our presence upon her for Christmas and then arguing in a veiled sort of way for a month or so."

"That..." She screwed up her lovely red lips. "That doesn't sound nice at all."

"It isn't." He shot a sideways glance at her, noticing how the lightly falling flakes of snow caught on her eyelashes. Her cheeks were a bright pink and her mouth was wet and red. Dear God, she was beautiful. "I generally hide in the library. The old girl has quite a good library."

"The library?" she asked, as if he'd confessed to a taste for keeping newts. "I hadn't thought you a reader, my lord."

"And yet I am quite literate," he replied. "Histories and plays, philosophy and the odd scientific tome. Even a novel every now and again. Will wonders never cease?"

The color rose in her cheeks, and she averted her eyes from him. "I'm sorry. That was rude of me. I meant no disrespect."

He was about to brush aside her apology when the snow on a branch directly above her head picked that moment to fall.

Miss St. John's head and shoulders were covered with cold melting snow.

For a moment she stood frozen in shock, her eyes wide and outraged.

Adam simply couldn't help it.

He closed his eyes and laughed.

Loud and ringing in the still winter air, he laughed and laughed and laughed—

Wet snow was shoved unceremoniously in his face.

Adam sputtered and opened his eyes to the sight of a sodden harpy with two handfuls of snow lunging at him. He ducked.

She followed.

Her eyes gleamed with righteous rage.

Never one to miss an opportunity, Adam caught her and pulled her against his chest.

Sarah stared up into Lord d'Arque's face, startled by his swift action. He'd wrapped his arms around her, and he held her tight against his broad chest.

As if he embraced her.

She inhaled and smelled mint and tea and something lemony, and her breath hitched.

"Do you concede the battle, Miss St. John?" he asked, his voice deep and slow.

"I…" He was so *close*.

And so big.

The snow fell forgotten from her mittened hands.

His eyes dropped to her mouth and his head bent toward hers.

Her heart started beating so fast she knew he must hear it.

"Over here!" The shout, coming from just ahead of them, drove them apart.

Lord d'Arque stepped back just as Jane walked out of the copse of trees. The doctor was a step behind her, carrying the basket that was meant to hold their holly.

Jane waved to them. "You had better hurry! We're almost to the holly behind the thicket."

She turned and disappeared around the trees, Dr. Manning trailing behind.

Sarah busied herself smoothing her skirts, suddenly shy. "We should continue on our way."

Lord d'Arque gave her a look she couldn't quite read and picked up the basket she'd dropped when she'd gathered the snow to attack him. "Lead on."

She nodded, picking up her skirts and stepping through the snow carefully. "There's more holly up ahead past the copse."

He didn't answer.

She inhaled, desperate for something to say. Her face was hot and she ached low in her belly. *Had* he been about to kiss her? Or was she merely imagining things?

She felt quite cross for a minute. Surely she didn't want Lord d'Arque to kiss her? He was a rake.

And yet...

"Do you always decorate Hedge House for Christmas?"

"Yes?" She peered at him sideways. "It's tradition. Don't you bring in green boughs and holly at your houses—or at your grandmother's cousin's house?"

He had a strange little twist to his mouth. "My grandmother's cousin isn't one to make merry. She provides a feast and plenty of mulled wine, but that's all. I don't celebrate Christmas at my residences."

She stopped. "Not at *all*?"

He shrugged. "I give a purse of money to each servant and direct the cook to serve them plum puddings and goose on Christmas. Besides that, no."

"But why?" Sarah frowned as she attempted to step over a snow-covered log. Really it was much too big and she wasn't sure she could straddle it. "I always loved the Christmas season as a child. We would have guests and games and puddings and—"

She broke off with a squeak as he wrapped his hands around her waist and simply lifted her over the log.

He set her down and arched an amused eyebrow at her.

"Thank you," she said somewhat breathlessly.

"Not at all," he drawled, turning to continue on their trek. "My own childhood Christmases were not so idyllic. There were no guests and no puddings."

"Oh." She studied him. Lord d'Arque seemed quite stoic about his lack of childhood Christmases. Except...he was such an expressive man usually, even if it was often in mockery. His very lack of expression now seemed most suspect. She cleared her throat and asked hesitantly, "Was there a reason your family didn't celebrate Christmas?"

"Not an ideological one, certainly." He gave her a sardonic glance. "I hardly hail from Puritans." He faced forward again as they trudged on. "Quite the opposite, in fact. Both my father and mother had numerous affairs."

Sarah blinked, feeling a little shocked. What did one say to such a confession?

But he didn't wait for her response. "No, I think my parents were simply too caught up in their own battles and petty arguments to bother with Christmas." He shrugged carelessly. "And then they died on Christmas Eve when I was thirteen."

She stopped dead in her tracks.

Lord d'Arque continued for another few steps before realizing. He turned and looked at her.

What...what was she supposed to think of his story? She couldn't feel sympathy for this man. She *couldn't*.

And yet, staring at him standing in crystalline snow, the flakes blowing against reddened cheeks, his eyes unable to hide his sadness, she felt herself fall headlong.

He wasn't just a rake. He was a man. A man with feelings—well hidden, but there all the same.

She licked her lips. "How did they die?"

He glanced away. "They had an argument. Yet another argument. My mother shrieked that she was running away with her lover. My father forbade her, even though he had mistresses of his own. She made to run from the house, but my father caught her at the top of the grand staircase."

Sarah drew in her breath, not wanting to hear what came next, though it had happened long ago.

"They fell," he said, his voice flat. "All the way down the staircase. My mother broke her neck and died instantly. My father broke both arms and also hit his head. He never woke up again, though it took him another week to die."

"I'm so sorry," she said with real regret.

He turned to her. "Why? It happened over two decades ago, and besides you never knew them."

"Yes, but I know *you*," she replied gently, "and I am sorry that such a terrible thing happened to you."

He shook his head and whispered, "You are too soft, Miss St. John. If you're not careful, someone may take advantage and pierce your vulnerable heart."

She lifted her chin. "What makes you think someone hasn't already?"

Chapter Six

*Now the queen had quite strong opinions on keeping
one's word. Prince Brad gritted his teeth, smiled,
apologized to the frog, and lifted her to the table
beside his gold plate.*
*"I'm going to get you for this," he murmured under
his breath to the frog.*
*"Will you?" she replied. "Perhaps so, but in the
meantime, be a good lad and cut me a bite of that
steak, won't you? I'm simply famished."* ...

—From *The Frog Princess*

Adam's brows snapped together. The thought of anyone
hurting Miss St. John caused something inside him to twist
and scrabble to get out.

She shouldn't be hurt.

He was about to ask who had caused her this pain when a
shout came from up ahead.

Charlotte waved from the copse. "We've found the holly!
You'd better hurry—we already have a full basket!"

"Oh dear," Miss St. John said from beside him. "I do believe we're going to lose."

Forty-five minutes later they arrived back at Hedge

House, their pitiful basket holding only a few branches of holly. Everyone else had returned ahead of them.

"I never seem to win these games," Miss St. John sighed, watching her mother exclaim over the baskets of holly.

"A pity," Adam drawled. "I suppose you were looking forward to stealing a kiss."

She blushed—which rather intrigued him—but before he could tease her more, Mrs. St. John spoke.

"Charlotte and Sir Hilary are the winners." Their hostess glanced at her middle daughter. "Charlotte, would you like to claim your prize?"

Adam leaned against the wall, watching the proceedings.

Charlotte St. John glanced first at Sir Hilary, then Dr. Manning, and finally Lord Kirby, who, although he'd not participated in the holly gathering, had come to see the judging.

She hesitated for a moment, and the good doctor looked pointedly away from her.

Charlotte St. John lifted her chin and walked to Lord Kirby.

That man's eyes rounded as she stood on tiptoe and gave him a quite chaste kiss.

That was interesting. Since Charlotte had chosen not to steal her kiss from her holly-hunting partner, that left Sir Hilary to pick a lady to kiss. Adam watched cynically to see if the man would ignore Charlotte St. John's slight and take his kiss from her anyway.

But he was already walking past Charlotte St. John.

Adam straightened as realization hit him.

Sir Hilary stopped before the eldest Miss St. John—standing only feet away from Adam—and bowed. "With your leave, madam?"

She smiled, blushing a little, and nodded.

Sir Hilary bent to set his mouth against hers and Adam felt his hands clench.

It was only a second or two, but during that time he could feel the pulse beating in his temple.

A kiss. A simple kiss. Nothing to become agitated about, especially since Miss St. John wasn't important to him.

Except it was rather hard to continue thinking that, wasn't it? Not when he felt perilously close to hitting a man he hardly knew.

Sir Hilary stepped back and made some sort of light comment. The rest of the party was moving toward the sitting room, presumably to participate in more juvenile games.

"Come with me," Adam said to Miss St. John.

He took her wrist and swiftly pulled her from the room, away from everyone else. The hallway outside was empty, but Adam kept going, turning a corner. He opened the first door he came to—a study or small sitting room of some sort—and led her inside.

"What—?" Miss St. John started, but he silenced her.

By pressing his mouth to hers.

Sarah gasped as Lord d'Arque kissed her. His mouth opened wide over hers, one thumb brushing her cheek. He held her with sure knowledge and embraced her as if he'd won the right.

He pulled her tighter against him, her breasts crushed against his hard chest, one of his legs thrust into her skirts between her thighs. He angled his face over hers and nipped at her bottom lip.

"My lord," she whispered between their mouths.

"Call me Adam," he demanded, and then thrust his tongue into her mouth, preventing her.

She moaned.

She couldn't help it. It had been years since anyone had touched her like this—Sir Hilary's chaste peck hardly counted—and the only other man to do so hadn't had a quarter of Adam's skill.

He made her *feel*. Made her want to cast away her inhibitions and doubts and just let him do as he wanted with her.

The thought brought her up short.

She'd felt this way before…and that man had taken everything she'd offered up and then thrust her away.

Not again.

She tore her mouth from his. "No."

"Sarah," he murmured, and her heart clenched at the sound of her name on his lips.

She couldn't let this happen.

She turned her head to the side.

He pulled back and she could actually feel his gaze on her.

Then he abruptly let her go.

"I beg your pardon," he said, his voice flat and formal.

She looked at him and saw that everything she'd discovered in him was gone. His face was without expression, as closed as a locked gate.

"My apologies if I've given offense." He bowed, pivoted, and left the room.

Adam took the stairs two at a time as he made his way to Grand-mère's room. What a fool he was—becoming jealous over a country squire and Miss St. John. She was a respectable lady, determined to marry some poor man and birth a pack of blond, brown-eyed babies, chubby cheeked and solemn.

He paused on the landing. Damn, Miss St. John's babies would be adorable.

He shook the ridiculous thought from his mind. Perhaps he'd contracted a brain fever from the snow tossed in his face. If so it was a relief: he'd be dead within a week and out of his misery.

He turned his thoughts to Grand-mère as he continued up the stairs. She'd seemed better this morning. Perhaps she would be well enough to travel in a few days. He could leave Hedge House and never see Miss St. John and her respectable ways again.

The thought made him unaccountably irritated.

When he pushed open the door to Grand-mère's room, she was sitting up in bed enjoying a late breakfast.

"How are you feeling, darling?" he asked her, bending to kiss her cheek.

He straightened and examined her critically. Her cheeks seemed to have more color than yesterday.

"I'm feeling much better," she said, but her voice was still weak and she started coughing as soon as the sentence was out of her mouth.

Adam looked on with barely concealed concern as she bent over, gasping for breath.

"Perhaps..." She stopped to inhale and take a sip of her tea. "Perhaps we can continue our journey tomorrow?"

Adam pasted a smile on his face. "The roads are near impassible," he lied. She was clearly in no condition to travel. "I think we shall stay another week—until at least after Christmas."

She took his verdict with better grace than he'd expected.

"Then sit here and tell me what is happening in the house." She indicated the chair next to her bed.

He did as instructed, lowering himself to the chair and giving her a report of the holly hunt... with several key moments omitted.

But perhaps he hadn't been as discreet as he thought.

Grand-mère half closed her eyes and said, "Miss St. John seems an interesting gel. What do you think of her?"

He paused to choose his words carefully. "She's intelligent, quick witted, and bent on marriage."

Grand-mère's eyebrows rose to points above her eyes. "She told you this?"

"No." He shrugged. "But the three gentlemen invited to spend the holiday at Hedge House are unwed and of age. No doubt she's thinking of ensnaring one of them."

"Hmm," his grandmother hummed noncommittally. "Her mother probably made the invitations."

He tilted his head. "You think Miss St. John is uninterested in wedding?"

Grand-mère waved an irritated hand. "Most ladies want to be married. I'm only suggesting that she may not have had *these* three gentlemen in mind."

Adam looked away from her, his mouth twisted. "It hardly matters to me. I have no intention of marrying—and certainly not Miss St. John."

"Not all marriages are as vitriolic as your mother's and father's," Grand-mère said softly. "A wife—a *partner*—can be a great comfort."

Adam stared at his grandmother. If he ran mad and some day decided to marry, he might choose a woman such as Miss St. John.

But that was never going to happen, and besides.

The lady was clearly not interested in him.

Chapter Seven

❧

*That night Prince Brad took the frog to his bed and
laid her on his pillow.
"Oh no," said the frog. "I'm a frog, not a toad. I need
water. You'll have to fetch a basin."
Brad muttered under his breath, but as the queen had
followed him to his bedroom to see to the comfort of
their guest, he was forced to comply.
The frog jumped into the basin of water beside Brad's
pillow and sighed sleepily. "Good night."
"I hate you," Prince Brad replied....*

—From *The Frog Princess*

Three days later Adam lounged in the sitting room. It was
after dinner and the party had all crowded into the room,
where a silly game was in progress.

He took a sip of his brandy and watched Miss St. John—
Sarah—as she tried to find the other members of the party.
She wore a scarf tied about her eyes and she walked halt-
ingly, her hands outstretched, and with a small smile on her
face.

He hadn't spoken to her save to say, "Good morning" or
"Pass the bread" since he'd kissed her.

Which was all for the best. He knew that. She wasn't for

him, and that strange feeling of...intimacy, of recognizing someone alike in mind and soul, all that had been false.

There was a cheer, and Adam looked up to see Miss St. John holding Dr. Manning. The doctor was smiling gently as Miss St. John ran her fingers over his face to try to guess who he was.

Rot.

Adam threw back the last of the brandy in his glass and stood.

"Had enough, d'Arque?"

The soft voice was St. John's, and Adam paused to look at him. The other man was watching him carefully and for once without malice.

Adam inhaled. "As you can see, sir."

"I never took you for a man who retreated from...festivities."

Was St. John...*approving* of Adam's interest in his sister? The world had turned upside-down. "Perhaps then you should revise your opinion of me."

St. John glanced at his sister and then at Adam. "No, I don't think so."

Adam gritted his teeth. "Good night, sir."

The other man inclined his head and drawled, "My lord."

Adam strode from the room, a sort of black mood overcoming him. He'd done the only thing he could, he thought as he sprang up the stairs. He'd let Sarah go when she requested it. Had backed away.

Had conceded the field to other men.

Respectable men.

He paused at the top of the stairs and grimaced. St. John had come close to calling him a coward and perhaps he was.

He turned and strode to Grand-mère's room. He knocked softly on the door before opening it.

Inside, Cannon was perched in her chair by the bed, her head at an awkward-looking angle, asleep. He approached the bed and saw that his grandmother was asleep as well. She lay there, her white hair tucked beneath a cap, her hands holding the coverlet to her chest.

Her gnarled fingers were bent by arthritis, the backs of her hands bruised and liver-spotted. The sapphire ring looked huge on her bony hand.

She looked so frail.

He turned and found a blanket, then gently draped it over Cannon and left the room.

He wasn't yet sleepy, so he made his way to the library. He'd found in the last several days that though the Hedge House library was small, it had several interesting and rare books.

But when he entered the library door he found a light within.

Sarah was at the far end, her back to him as she perused the shelves, her candle held high.

He turned to retreat, but he must've made some noise.

"My lord," she called.

He stopped without facing her. "I thought I told you to call me Adam."

"Adam, then." He heard her venture nearer. "Have I offended you?"

"No." He closed his eyes.

"Then will you look at me?"

Had she no sense of self-preservation?

But it was as if he were controlled by an outside force...or perhaps merely her voice.

He turned to face her.

She wore a blue dress tonight, the color of a robin's egg, her hair bound simply at her nape. Her eyes were wide and uncertain, but her chin was level and proud.

She was irresistible to him.

He prowled toward her, feeling a sort of reckless urge rise within his blood. "What is it you want, Sarah?"

Her rose-red lips parted. "I never gave you permission to use my given name."

"Did you not?" He walked right up to her, close enough he could see the pulse beating at the base of her throat. "I think you're wrong. I think you gave me all the permission I need when you returned my kiss."

She blinked, and he could see her swallow. He smelled the scent of roses and it nearly maddened him.

Or perhaps he was already mad.

"Run now," he whispered.

She stared at him, refusing to move.

"Very well," he snarled, and took her into his arms.

She'd stayed away from him as long as she could, Sarah thought dazedly as she opened her mouth beneath Adam's assault. She'd never come within a couple of paces of him, had sat at the opposite end of the dining table from him every night, had made sure not to be alone with him.

And all for naught.

She fell now as easily as she had three days ago.

More easily if that were possible.

It was as if he were a wine she craved without ceasing.

She clutched at his broad shoulders, struggling to get closer.

To feel all of him.

She moaned, suckling his tongue. Gasped at the heat that flamed at her center.

He picked her up, and she broke their kiss to squeak.

He smirked at her, his lazy gray eyes half-lidded and filled with desire as he walked to a settee. He sat down and arranged her across his lap.

Then he bent and kissed her again.

She wound her arms around his neck, feeling drunk from his mouth, from his lips moving over hers.

She was lost.

He broke their kiss and laid his forehead against hers. "Make me stop."

"I can't," she whispered.

"Then we're doomed," he said, his voice husky and low. "For I'm unable to stop myself. I want you. Day and night and all the time in between. I *want* you."

She pulled his head down to hers, capturing his lips, running her hands over his cheeks, his neck. He wore a white wig as he always did, and when her fingertips brushed it she was impatient. She reached up and pulled it off, then dropped it to the floor.

He had dark, nearly black hair, cut close to his head.

She gloried in this intimate knowledge, running her palms over the crown of his head.

He pulled back, panting, and began to tug up her skirts.

The realization woke her from her delirium of want and into near panic.

She jolted and frantically shoved at his arm—the one under her skirt. "No. *No.*"

Had she thought about it, she would have expected anger.

Instead he carefully pulled his hand from her skirts and smoothed them down.

Then he looked at her and said, "I think it's time you told me about him."

Chapter Eight

The next morning Prince Brad rose from his slightly damp
bed and dressed under the interested gaze of the frog.
"Pervert," he said, scooping up her basin and
walking swiftly down to the breakfast room.
"Your Highness," said a courtier, bowing low on his
entrance. "The ladies have arrived for your inspection."
"Inspection?" murmured the frog.
"I'm to be married," said the prince, "and I need to
choose a bride."
"Oh, good," replied the frog. "I'll help." . . .

—From *The Frog Princess*

Sarah stared at him and for a second looked utterly betrayed.

Then she burst into a flurry of movement, shoving at him, kicking, trying to escape from his arms.

Adam dodged a flying hand and then caught it. She arched her back and he wrapped his other arm around her middle, pulling her up against his chest.

"Sarah," he said.

She stopped all at once, sagging back.

He didn't let go of her. "Sarah."

She turned her head away from him.

He sighed. "If you don't tell me, I'll let you go. But know that I cannot continue with you like this—me advancing, you retreating. I need to know *why*."

Slowly her head turned to him, and he saw that she had tears welling in her eyes.

His heart swelled at the sight. Whoever had done this to her would pay. He'd find the man and destroy him.

"I was sixteen," she said in a small, precise voice. "I'd gone to stay with a friend for a month. Her family was hosting a house party and many people came. Among them was an older gentleman—a man of seven and twenty. He…"

Her voice trailed away, and she closed her eyes as if she couldn't bear to look at him while she told her tale. "He was a well-known man about town in London, but his notoriety only made him more interesting to me. I used to sneak glances at him, watching him as I thought in secret. But he knew, I think. He knew."

Adam let go of her arm and raised his hand to her cheek, stroking over the soft skin there.

He knew when a woman watched him as well. He'd hunted women who fluttered with interest about him.

But they'd never been so young as Sarah had been.

The man who had hurt her was without honor. Without common decency.

"He began looking back," she whispered. "At first I thought I imagined his glances. It was so exciting. So wonderful. I spent every moment thinking about him, wondering with great anxiety if he truly returned my regard. The smallest thing became of great significance. When he held the door for me as I entered the room. If he nodded as I passed him in the morning. At night I couldn't sleep for my excitement. I was a fool. Such a fool," she murmured as if to herself.

He brushed a kiss over her cheek. "You were young. It's not entirely the same thing."

She inhaled shakily. "One day he found me in the garden alone. He said things—grand, flowery things—and they were everything I'd been dreaming of. When he kissed me I was completely his."

Adam closed his eyes, cursing this nameless man who had taken her girlish hope and trembling awareness.

"He…" She swallowed. "He touched me. Raised my skirts and revealed my legs…and more. I think he was opening his breeches when my friend, her mother, and half a dozen more of the house party came upon us." She chuckled, but it sounded broken. "If 'twere possible to die from chagrin I would've done so then. I tried to hide behind him, but he stepped away, exposing my shame to all that were there. My friend's mother was shocked, but she accused him of seducing me. He…he told her—told them all—that I was no innocent. That I'd come to him and made an assignation with him in the garden. That *I'd* enticed *him*."

He opened his eyes, looking at her, this self-possessed, strong woman. "What happened?"

"They believed him," she said simply. "I was sent home in disgrace. My friend's mother wrote a note to my parents informing them of my terrible conduct. Mama burned the letter. She really was quite wonderful."

Her smile was sad.

He inhaled. "I'm glad that your mother is a levelheaded woman."

She nodded. "I missed the next three London seasons. There was too much talk. When I did return I didn't receive any suitors—the few who came calling didn't have honorable intentions."

Eleven years ago he had probably been too busy whoring

to worry about society gossip. Or at least, if he *had* heard rumors about her, he'd long since forgotten them.

He looked down at her small, delicate hand. "What became of the cad?"

"Nothing." She shrugged. "He continued to be a man about town in London. He continued to be invited to country house parties. He continued to be popular with hostesses."

"And does he live in London now?" Adam asked softly.

"I don't know." She looked at him, her light-brown eyes sad. "But that no longer matters. What matters is you and I."

"What about us?" he whispered, stroking a lock of her hair back from her face. It was like silk. Spun golden silk.

"What do you want from me?" she asked simply.

"I want you." He fought to keep his voice level. Civilized. "In every way."

"In marriage?" Her words were soft but held an edge of steel.

He stared at her, feeling wild. "I don't know."

Her sigh was inaudible. "You must understand why I cannot do this." She gestured in the small space between them. "I don't wish to risk my reputation again."

"You don't trust me not to expose you to gossip," he said, and it felt like a slim stiletto slipped between his ribs.

"I…" She looked at him, but to her credit she did not prevaricate. "No. I'm sorry. I can't."

Adam could've argued. Could've said that he wasn't the cad from her youth. That he'd never seduced an innocent before. But he doubted mere words would win her trust.

So he opened his arms and let her go.

Three days later, Sarah sat with Megs in her rooms, watching as her sister-in-law attempted to fit into a dress with the aid of Daniels, her maid.

"I don't think it'll do, my lady," Daniels said, surveying the gap at the back of the dress.

"Pooh," Megs said, wrinkling her nose in the vanity mirror. "I don't understand why my upper body should expand along with my lower. After all, it's the lower that has a baby in it."

She frowned down at her bosom, which was indeed fuller than it had been before her pregnancy.

"Although," she mused, "Godric *is* awfully fond of my body this way."

"I don't think I want to know that," Sarah muttered.

"Don't you?" Megs turned sideways to view her tummy in the mirror. "I really look rather like a boiled pudding, don't I?"

"But an attractive boiled pudding," Sarah said loyally.

"Oh, thank you." Megs began the process of taking off the dress. "Now tell me, what will you be wearing to the Christmas Eve ball?"

Sarah shrugged, glancing down at her hands in her lap. "Perhaps the pink brocade or the blue stripe."

There was a silence until Sarah glanced up curiously.

Both Megs and Daniels were staring at her, though Megs was the only one with a frown. "Really? Those are both years old. What about the new forest green you had made when you came to visit us in London last?"

"I suppose I could wear that," Sarah conceded. Would Adam like her in the forest green? She'd thought the dark, lush color had set off her pale complexion...

Except she didn't want his attention anymore, did she?

"Darling." She glanced up to see Megs looking at her worriedly. "Are you feeling quite the thing? You've seemed down these last few days."

Sarah burst into tears.

She was horrified, absolutely horrified, but try as she might, she could not stop.

Warm arms enclosed her as Megs pulled her down to sit with her on the side of the bed. "Oh, my dear."

Sarah inhaled shakily and looked up, mortified, but Megs must have sent Daniels away. It was just the two of them in the bedroom.

Her sister-in-law got up and brought back a glass of water and a handkerchief and pressed both into her hands.

Sarah gratefully accepted them from her and sipped the water. "I...I don't know what's wrong with me."

"Don't you?" Megs asked very softly. "I noticed that ever since Lord d'Arque arrived you follow him with your eyes. Has he done something?"

Sarah choked back a bitter laugh. "No. It was *I* who did something—I told him that I did not wish to be alone with him anymore."

"Ah."

She looked up at Megs's noncommittal reply.

The other woman was watching her with a small frown. "Did he hurt you?"

"Oh no, quite the opposite," Sarah said, sounding depressed even to her own ears.

"Then...?"

"He's a *rake*." Sarah waved the damp handkerchief. "You know that. Everyone in all of England knows that. And you're aware of how I feel about rakes."

"Ye-es?" Megs said slowly, but she bit her lip. "But—"

Sarah blotted her eyes. "What?"

Megs sighed gustily. "It's just that you've never let a gentleman court you. You don't dance at balls and you're so abrupt with gentlemen that most run away with their tails between their legs rather than try any more discourse with you."

"I *don't*..." Sarah's words trailed away as she thought about what Megs had said. Was that how she truly behaved with men? Sarah felt a twinge of hurt. Megs's description made her sound like a harpy. She met the other woman's eyes. "I'm not that bad, am I?"

"No," Megs hastily assured her. "It's just that most men are rather cowardly. It seems to me that a gentleman who persists despite your sometimes daunting exterior must be very interested in you, don't you think?"

"He's a rake," Sarah whispered, staring down at the sodden handkerchief in her hands. "I can't. He can't even tell me if he wants to marry me or not. How can I let him flirt with me, *kiss* me, when I don't know if I can trust him?"

"My brother Griffin was considered a rake by many," Megs said. "He never considered marriage. Yet once he met Hero she was all he thought about. I truly think he'd rather cut off his right hand than hurt her in any way."

Sarah glanced at her. "You think I ought to encourage him?"

"Why not?" Megs asked gently. "As Lord d'Arque becomes more familiar with you, perhaps he will decide it is marriage he's after. Or he may not, in which case you can turn your back to him then. But if you never make that small step of faith, never let a man try to learn your heart, you'll never find the marriage you want. The marriage you deserve."

Sarah looked down at her hands. "Perhaps I should simply forget Lord d'Arque altogether and settle for an ordinary man."

"Tell me, are you at all interested in the gentlemen your mother invited for the Christmas house party?"

Sarah winced. Mama had the best of intentions, but her

ploy appeared to be obvious to everyone. "They're all nice men, of course—"

"Of course."

"And I *should* find one of them interesting..."

"But?"

"I don't," Sarah confessed with a sigh. "I simply don't."

Megs smiled, looking beautiful and wise. "Then follow your heart."

Chapter Nine

*So, after breaking their fast, Prince Brad and the frog
proceeded to a receiving room crowded with every
sort of royal female imaginable.
Brad took one swift look, turned to the courtier, and
had half the ladies dismissed.
"Why?" inquired the frog.
"Too plain," Brad drawled.
The frog looked at him thoughtfully. "You really are
very shallow."* …

—From *The Frog Princess*

That afternoon Adam sat by his grandmother's bed and
had a terrible suspicion. They were drinking tea together.
Grand-mère sat up in bed wearing a lace-trimmed wrap,
her cheeks pink as she delicately ate a bite of mince pie.

Grand-mère loved mince pie.

He narrowed his eyes. "How are you feeling?"

She set aside her plate, slumping a little, and turned sad
eyes on him. "A little better, I confess."

"Well enough to leave?"

"Oh." She plucked at the coverlet and said in a quavering
old woman's voice, "If you think that wise. Although Christ-

mas is the day after tomorrow and it *does* seem foolish to go now."

He sighed. "Grand-mère."

She raised her brows innocently.

"Miss St. John has made it plain that she does not enjoy my company."

She straightened abruptly. "Whatever did you do to the gel?"

He spread his hands wide. "Nothing."

"Well, perhaps that is the problem." She glared at him. "A woman likes to know she is desired."

"I fear we are past that." Adam felt weary all of a sudden. "Miss St. John will not talk to me."

"You may think talk is your most formidable weapon, dear grandson, but I very much doubt it is," she stated. "*Seduce* the gel. It's not as if you lack experience." She picked up her plate of pie again. "What is it for if you don't use it when needed?"

She eyed him wrathfully over a bite of the mince pie.

"Are you suggesting that I corrupt respectable ladies now?"

"Not *ladies*, merely Miss St. John. Adam..." She placed her empty plate carefully on the table next to the bed before taking his hands in her own. Her fingers felt fragile beneath his, her skin thin and so delicate. "I loved your mother, silly, foolish girl though she was, but you are the sunshine in my days. I am in my ninth decade. When I lie on my deathbed—" He shook his head, denying the mere thought, but she glared at him and squeezed his hands. "When I lie on my deathbed, I want to know that you will not be alone after I am gone."

He closed his eyes. "Grand-mère, you needn't worry about me. I'm hardly alone."

"Are you not?" He opened his eyes to see her glaring fiercely at him. "I am your grandmother. I have the right to worry about you—do not try to deny me this. You are alone, my grandson. You may have so-called friends you drink with, ladies you dally with, acquaintances you greet when you see them on the street, but you have no one save myself that you are truly close to. Find someone. Please. For me."

Adam brought their clasped hands to his mouth and kissed her knuckles. "I will try."

But he rather thought that he was doomed to fail with Sarah.

That night Sarah sat in the sitting room after dinner sipping tea and trying very, very hard not to look at Adam.

It was nearly impossible.

She'd told him herself that she couldn't be with him, and yet...

And yet.

Well, that was the problem, wasn't it? She simply couldn't stop thinking about him. Megs said she should try again with him, but to herself Sarah could confess that she was frightened.

She didn't want to be hurt again.

The question was, which was more powerful—her attraction to Adam or her fear? She found herself lighter when in Adam's company. His humor and his quick wit drew her, but it was the somber intellect he buried underneath his banter that snared her.

She rather thought she could spend a lifetime discovering all his many aspects and never grow weary.

In the center of the sitting room several voices rose, among them Jane's.

"A game! A game! Let us play a game."

Sir Hilary called from his seat in a winged chair, "Shall we play charades?"

Jane pouted. "I'm tired of charades and hide the slipper and blindman's buff. I want something new."

"Hide-and-seek," Charlotte exclaimed.

"That's a child's game." Jane turned to scowl at Charlotte.

Charlotte looked as if she'd very much like to stick out her tongue and was prevented from doing so only by propriety.

"I haven't played hide-and-seek since I was a boy," Sir Hilary mused.

"It might be entertaining," Megs said. "Though how I shall hide I don't know." She looked ruefully down at her tummy.

"Oh, very well, hide-and-seek it is," Jane declared. "Who shall be the first seeker?"

This called for several minutes' bickering and the final decision to draw straws.

Lord Kirby ended up with the honors.

"Now then," Jane said, for she seemed to have taken charge of the evening's entertainment. "These are the rules: You may hide anywhere within the house. Outside is not allowed, as someone might freeze to death. Once the seeker finds a person they become the seeker's helper and will also look for those in hiding. The last person to be found wins." She looked at Lord Kirby. "You must count to one hundred slowly before you start."

His Lordship bowed solemnly. "Yes, ma'am."

And with that everyone scattered to hide.

Had either Charlotte or Jane been the seeker, finding a hiding place would've been much harder. All three of them had spent their childhood in this house and knew well every secret place to hide.

But since it was Lord Kirby, Sarah made a beeline for one of the easier hiding places: the room under the main stairs. One had to look very closely to find the seam of the door to the tiny room. It had been fitted with the same paneling as the wall and thus made the door near invisible. As long as Jane and Charlotte were equally clever with their hiding places, she was safe for quite some time.

Sarah found the little room looking much the same as it had when she was a girl: dusty, with various odds and ends stacked against the walls. Fortunately one of the odds and ends was a small chair. She sat in it, holding her breath for a moment to keep from sneezing from all the dust.

Then she waited.

She was almost nodding off when the door to the room creaked open.

A candle was held high, glaring in its brightness after she'd been sitting in the dark for so long.

The door closed with a click.

Sarah breathed in slowly. "You're supposed to bring me to Lord Kirby. That's how the game is played."

"Is it?" His voice was a low dangerous purr.

She opened her eyes to see Lord d'Arque advancing on her.

Chapter Ten

❧

*Prince Brad held out his arm to an ethereally beautiful
princess. "Would you care to walk in the gardens?"
"Why are you holding a toad?" asked the princess.
"I'm a frog, not a toad," said the frog. "Please note
the webbing between my toes."
"What?" said the princess.
"She's very pretty," whispered the frog in Brad's ear,
"but perhaps you should think of the intelligence of
your future children."
Prince Brad sighed....*

—From *The Frog Princess*

He couldn't help himself.

When everyone had scattered to hide, Adam had trailed
Sarah and seen her hiding place. He entered with the idea
of talking to her, but something broke loose inside him
when he walked into the little room and closed them both
inside.

He didn't care.

Not that she was a virgin.

Not that she was the daughter of his hostess.

Not that she didn't trust him.

He needed her like the air he breathed.

"Tell me to stop now or don't tell me at all," he rasped, setting down the candle.

He reached out a hand, brushing his fingertips across her cheek.

She was silent, her expression shocked, and his heart sank as he started to pull his fingers away.

Then she caught his hand and brought his palm to her lips.

"Don't stop," she whispered against his skin, and it was as loud as a shout.

He pulled her to him.

She was small and light and her body fit against his perfectly. He wanted to strip the binding clothes from her, feel the heaviness of her breasts, squeeze her bare arse in his hands, breathe her scent.

He wanted to wear her scent on his skin, wanted to mark her as his.

He'd never felt like this with any other woman.

This was animal.

Adam opened his mouth against her neck, licking her pulse, feeling her shiver under him.

She moaned.

He picked her up and set her on an old table against the wall.

She wound her arms around his neck as he brought his mouth to hers.

Sweet.

She tasted of the dessert eaten at dinner: honey, apples, and cinnamon.

The taste was addicting.

He could feel his cock throbbing against the placket of his breeches as he pulled her skirts up.

She made no protest this time, instead parting her lips beneath his.

He thrust his tongue into her mouth at the same time that he pushed his hand under her skirts.

She was hot. Her mouth silky wet and sweet. Her legs smooth and long.

He trailed his fingers up her calf and behind her knee and she let her legs fall apart.

He wanted to press his hips between her thighs. To unbutton his falls and shove his cock into her.

To find the center of her heat.

But this was not the place for that.

Instead he drew his fingertips over the tender skin of her inner thigh, encountering curling hair.

She pulled away from their kiss, gasping. Her eyes were wild.

He held her gaze and slowly—so slowly—parted the lips of her vulva.

Her mouth opened without sound when he stroked a finger into her.

Wet.

She was so wet for him.

He couldn't help a twist of his lips at the thought.

He brought his thumb to bear on her clitoris and her eyelashes fluttered.

"Adam," she whispered.

She was his. The power of that moment shook him—his hand at her quim, her legs parted in invitation.

He wanted this woman—wanted her forever.

He tilted his head, taking her mouth again as he rubbed lightly across her clitoris and fucked her with his middle finger.

He felt her shudder, felt the minute movements of her hips.

God, what he'd give to be naked with her and in a bed right now.

As it was, he could only bite at her bottom lip and groan, attacking her mouth savagely.

She arched, her head falling back, but he held her to him, unrelenting. He wanted all of her.

"Come for me," he husked against her mouth. "Come for me."

She clutched his shoulders, her fingers digging into the cloth of his coat.

He could feel her rising. His hand was slippery with her essence. She panted.

"Sarah," he whispered.

She froze and he opened his eyes to watch her.

Because he could. Because he'd done this to her.

Her face was flushed pink, her lips, red and wet, were parted, and her eyes squeezed shut as she shuddered.

She was beautiful.

She inhaled and opened her eyes, her expression dazed, and he pulled her against his chest as he petted her little quim.

When the sound came, at first he thought it was her.

He drew back and looked at her.

Then it came again: a faint cry from without.

The cry of a woman in distress: "No!"

Sarah's eyes widened. "That's Charlotte."

Adam flipped Sarah's skirts down and grabbed the candle, then strode to the door to the little room.

He flung it open and looked up and down the hall.

"This way," Sarah said, darting past him. "She must have gone to hide in the old cupboard."

She pointed to the next door, standing ajar.

Adam strode to the doorway.

And saw Charlotte St. John struggling in Kirby's arms.

Lord Kirby had his hand on the upper slope of Charlotte's bare breast—her fichu had been torn away.

Sarah gasped in rage. "How *dare* you—"

Adam had a much more active way to deal with the matter.

He strode into the room and up to the aristocrat, grasping him by the arm.

"I didn't—" Lord Kirby started, but he was unable to finish whatever he was about to say.

Adam punched him in the face.

The baron stumbled back and fell, knocking over a table with a great clatter in the process.

Sarah couldn't help but smile. Her heart swelled at the sight of Adam defending her sister so decisively.

"Oh, Sarah!" Charlotte exclaimed, and ran to her.

Sarah hugged her sister close. "Are you hurt? Tell me. Did he hurt you?"

"N-no," Charlotte stuttered, trying to wipe the tears from her face. "Not really. He grabbed me roughly and as you saw he was embracing me against my will."

"You little tart," Lord Kirby said rather indistinctly from the floor. Blood was streaming from his nose. "You're lying! *You* kissed *me* after the holly hunt. What was I to think but that you wanted more?"

Charlotte's eyes widened in horror...and doubt. Sarah saw the moment when her sister wondered if the toad on the ground might be right.

She saw red.

"Don't you blame this on the girl." Adam bent and hauled Lord Kirby to his feet, shaking him. "You were to think that Miss St. John did not want your attention when she said so."

Sarah walked up to Lord Kirby and slapped him across the face as hard as she could.

Lord Kirby stumbled, but was held upright by Adam.

"Ow!" He held a hand to his cheek, staring at her with wide eyes.

"You disgusting little worm," Sarah said, low and vicious.

"But—"

She looked at Adam. "Please escort Lord Kirby to the door."

His eyes glinted with amusement, but his voice was grave when he said, "Gladly."

"But it's night," Lord Kirby wailed as Adam took him by the collar and forcibly marched him down the hallway. "And I think you've broken my nose!"

His shouting drew the attention of not only the servants but also the guests, who came out of hiding.

"What's this?" Sir Hilary said when he saw the small procession, for Sarah and Charlotte were following Adam.

"A cad who has revealed his true colors," Adam replied, marching Lord Kirby past the other man.

Sir Hilary glanced at Sarah and Charlotte, who still bore tearstains on her face.

His brows lowered into a frown. "Has he indeed?" he growled.

"Lottie!" Dr. Manning's complexion was gray. "Are you all right?"

He made Charlotte's side and took her arm as she laid her head against his shoulder.

Godric came from one of the upstairs rooms. "What is happening?"

Sarah glanced at him and felt tears well in her eyes.

Godric's gaze went from her to Charlotte and he stilled. "D'Arque?"

"I'm disposing of rubbish," Adam replied, shoving Lord Kirby toward the door.

"Are you indeed?" Godric drawled.

Sarah shivered. She'd never heard her brother's voice sound so dangerous.

"Darling." Megs had entered the hallway, and she hurried to Charlotte. Gently she drew the younger woman away from Dr. Manning. "Won't you come with me?"

Megs glanced meaningfully at Sarah.

Sarah looked to where her brother and Adam were tossing Lord Kirby into the snow and decided that she was no longer needed here. She nodded at Megs and moved to the other side of Charlotte. "Let's find Mama and Jane."

They made their way up the stairs. Sarah cast worried glances at her middle sister, trying not to be too obvious about it. At the top of the stairs they found Jane, who seemed to have overheard the fight.

They all went to Mama's room.

Mama had already retired, not at all interested in a game of hide-and-seek. She was abed with cap and shawl, but she immediately rose when she saw Charlotte between Megs and Sarah in her doorway.

Charlotte sobbed out what had happened when Mama took her into her arms.

Sarah quietly turned and rummaged in the bottom of Mama's cupboard. At the very bottom, under a pile of old chemises, she found what she was looking for: a bottle of brandy.

She took it to where the other women were gathered, poured a tiny bit into the glass that Mama kept on her bedside table, and gave it to Charlotte.

"Thank you," Charlotte gasped when she'd drunk.

"Can I have a sip?" Jane asked, sounding unusually somber.

Sarah wordlessly poured more into the glass and handed it to Jane.

"Do you..." Charlotte inhaled and looked at Mama. "Do you think he was right? Did I entice Lord Kirby to attack me by kissing him at the end of the holly hunt?"

"No," their mother said fiercely. "This is entirely Lord Kirby's fault and frankly I'm shocked at how ungentlemanly he's acted." She pursed her lips. "I shall have to warn my friends about him. No one wants a scoundrel like that around their daughters."

"But what if he tells everyone that I'm...I'm a tart?" Charlotte's bottom lip trembled. "That's what he called me."

Mama hugged her close, looking worried. "Then we shall tell everyone he is a liar. It will be his word against me."

"And me," Megs said quietly, and Mama's expression cleared. "No one of any sense at all will believe that man against me."

Sarah sometimes forgot that Megs was the sister of a marquess and thus a lady of importance in society.

"We'll always stand with you, Charlotte," Sarah said, and hugged her sister. She vowed that Charlotte would never feel the social rejection she had.

Sarah watched as Jane took charge of the bottle of brandy and poured a glass for Mama. Charlotte smiled when Mama coughed after drinking, and then they were off discussing the final plans for tomorrow's Christmas Eve ball.

But as they chattered Sarah thought about Adam—his hands and his mouth and how he'd stared at her as he did intimate things to her body. She wanted to talk to him. To find out if he'd decided what he wanted of her. If tonight had been simply an interlude.

Or if it was the beginning of something more.

Chapter Eleven

*Several hours later Prince Brad was deep in
conversation with the last lady, a princess both
erudite and beautiful, when she asked him how he
best liked frog legs prepared.*
There was an awful silence.
*The frog opened her mouth indignantly, but Prince
Brad beat her to it. "I'm afraid I do not care to dine
upon frog legs as I consider this frog my friend."*
And he swept from the room—with the frog. . . .

—From *The Frog Princess*

Three hours later Adam silently walked down the hall to
Sarah's room. After the commotion of rushing Kirby out of
the house—and then gathering his possessions and tossing
them out with him—the members of the party had decided
to retire for the night.

Adam had spent the last several hours pacing his room,
waiting until it was late enough that everyone would be
asleep.

This was folly. Seeking Sarah out in the dead of night.
She'd said she didn't trust him. A quick romp in a hidden
room hardly changed that.

He wanted to change her opinion of him. He wanted—

A sound came from down the hall.

Adam slid into the deep shadows by a statue.

He heard a door closing.

After five more minutes of silence he continued on his way. Sarah's room was at the end of a corridor.

He reached the door and tried the handle.

Unlocked.

Carefully he eased the door open and slipped into the room. A banked fire burned low on the grate, giving a glowing, flickering light. Sarah slept in a curtained bed. He approached it quietly and stood looking down at her. She lay on her side, her golden hair spread upon her pillow like silk, one hand curled by her chin, and at the sight he realized something.

He didn't want this to end.

Didn't want to walk away and never see Sarah again except as an acquaintance, passing by her at a dance or on Bond Street. Didn't want her to become a memory—a lost, regretful dream.

He wanted forever.

Which meant he shouldn't be here tonight. He needed to show her that it wasn't simply an animal impulse for him.

He turned to go, but it was too late.

He saw her eyes flutter open in the mellow light.

She stretched out her hand to him. "Adam?"

And he was lost.

Sarah woke from a dream of Adam to find him standing by her bed.

She had no idea why he was there, but in her dream-laden state she didn't care.

She wanted him. "Kiss me," she whispered.

He groaned low and then he was leaning over her, pressing his lips to hers almost sweetly.

She opened her mouth, licking across his lips tentatively. Her hands slid over his shoulders and she realized he was fully dressed while she was only in her chemise.

She didn't want that.

"Take this off," she whispered, tugging at his coat sleeves. It felt as if this spell would not break if she only whispered.

He straightened to tear off his coat and waistcoat and throw aside his neckcloth. When he placed a knee on the bed beside her hip, bending to her, she pulled his wig off as well.

She shoved aside her coverlet. "Come to me."

"You're a siren," he whispered as he lay atop her. "You'll drive me mad."

This seemed doubtful. It was she who would be driven mad. He was heavy on her, his hard chest pressing against her soft breasts, his stomach and pelvis aligned with hers, his legs sprawled, one between her thighs. And she could feel his penis, heavy and thick, probing her belly even through the cloth of his breeches.

She wanted.

She slipped her hands inside the collar of his shirt and heard a button pop as she wrapped her fingers over his bare shoulders. He was warm and male and she could smell his heat.

His desire.

He palmed her breast and she lost her breath. His hand was big and certain, his fingers splayed over the mound of her breast, her nipple caught between his thumb and forefinger.

He brought his fingers together, squeezing her nipple between.

She called out softly, the sensation was so new, so wonderful.

He lifted and pushed himself down her so that his face

was level with her breast and took her nipple into his mouth right through the chemise.

It was a crude act. A sensual act. She could feel him drawing on her, could feel the material of the chemise chafe her skin.

He drew back and blew on the wet material and she could feel her nipple harden into a small, pebbled bud.

Then he moved to her other breast.

"You're so lovely," he whispered before he took her into his mouth and sucked.

She ran her fingers across his shorn head, feeling the prickly short hair, the strong neck, the working jaw.

She wanted him. Wanted him so much it was a physical ache. "Make love to me."

He froze for a second, and then he was sliding even farther down her body, bunching her chemise up around her waist.

He parted her legs and threw them over the crooks of his arms.

And then he bent his head—

"What are you—?" she started.

He licked her. With his tongue. Between her legs.

She clutched the sheets, her toes tightening, her insides quaking. She'd never felt anything like it, so soft and yet so relentless, his tongue lapping at her folds, circling her bud, driving inside of her.

It was unbelievable.

It was wonderful.

She felt him spread her with his fingers and she wanted to object to his...*familiarity*. To the way he seemed to feel he had the right to do this to her. But she was flying, so light with the pure pleasure he was giving her that she couldn't speak.

All she could do was feel.

And then she was reaching that point, her legs moving without her will, her hands twisting in the sheets, the heat building and building until she could no longer hold it back.

She fell, bursting from within, beautiful warmth flooding her belly and limbs, radiating from her center, reaching her fingertips and toes.

He licked her a few more times, lazily, and then he was climbing up her like a great cat cornering its prey.

He spread her legs even wider and she felt something big and blunt at her entrance.

His cock.

She opened her eyes, looking up at him.

"All right?" he grunted, looking strained. He was holding himself still, waiting on her answer, and she knew that he would pull away if she told him to right now.

He'd stop himself for her.

A wave of affection washed through her. As it happened, she didn't want him to stop.

She twined her arms around his neck and whispered, "Put yourself in me."

He jolted at that, his hips surging forward just enough to breach her.

She waited for pain but felt none.

She watched as he inhaled. Pulled back. Nudged carefully into her again.

A little more.

Inch by tender inch he pressed into her, widening her. Stretching her for his thick, hard flesh.

She tilted her hips, wanting more, impatient.

And then suddenly he jolted home.

He lay for a moment between her spread thighs, on her, pinning her down with his greater weight and bulk, impaling her with his penis.

Then he looked at her, and when she smiled he began to move.

Tiny waves. Small nudges. His hips hardly shifting at all. It was quite, quite maddening.

She squirmed, trying to make him move, wanting more.

He pulled back then and shoved into her. A solid, hard thrust that made her see stars.

And then he did it again. And again. Watching her with unsmiling eyes, much too intently.

She couldn't look away from his gaze. Couldn't hide her face. Couldn't do anything but lie beneath his hard thrusts and *feel*.

And when he bowed his head over her, his lips pulled away from his teeth, his nostrils flared, his eyes tragic and aware, she felt something inside her open.

He was in the throes of orgasm. Lit. Stricken. Wracked.

But she was the one who lost her heart.

Chapter Twelve

*"Now I have no one left to marry," said Prince Brad.
"This is all your fault, frog."
"My fault?" said the frog, and she would have raised
her eyebrows had she had any. "I really don't see
how any of this is my fault."
"Well, I've had quite enough of you in any case,"
Brad snarled. "I wish I could get rid of you."
"You could always kiss me," retorted the frog.
So he did....*

—From *The Frog Princess*

Sarah stared at herself in her mirror the next evening while her maid arranged her hair for the Christmas Eve ball.

She'd woken that morning all alone in her bed, which made perfect sense.

Adam mustn't be found in her bed. It would ruin her reputation.

He was only thinking of her. Being practical.

Still, it was hard to not feel restless. Confused. Had last night been all Adam wanted from her? He had made no promises, unlike the rake who had destroyed her reputation.

And yet...she hadn't had a chance to talk to him alone

today, caught up as she had been in the preparations for the ball tonight.

She badly wanted to talk to him.

She inhaled, steadying herself. He was leaving tomorrow—she'd heard from Mama—but that still left tonight to find out what he wanted from her.

If they could perhaps have a future together.

"There, miss," said Doris, her maid, stepping back. "You do look a treat."

Her hair had been threaded with pearls and looped at the back of her head. She wore more pearls at her ears and wrists, setting off the deep, lush green of her gown.

"Thank you," Sarah said, meeting the maid's eyes in the mirror. "You can go help Charlotte and Jane now."

"Yes, miss."

Sarah took one last look in the mirror and turned to leave her bedroom, then made her way to the ballroom.

She found Mama there, overseeing the last preparations.

Hedge House's ballroom was a long gallery across the back of the house. Tall windows gave a view of the snowy back garden. Night had fallen, but Mama had arranged for tiny lanterns to be lit and hung on the bare branches of the apple trees in the garden.

"It looks like a fairy garden," Sarah said in awe to her mother as she reached her side.

Mama turned and embraced her, then stepped back. "You're lovely, my dear." Mama met her eyes. "I hope you'll enjoy the dance. I just want you to be happy."

They'd never discussed Mama's obvious reasons to invite three bachelors to the Christmas house party.

Sarah smiled, though her lips trembled. "I know."

"It's just..." Mama's mouth twisted with sorrow. "I think life is easier to journey through with a partner." She squeezed Sarah's hands. "With a husband. I was so happy when I met your father."

Sarah felt a pang. Mama didn't mention Papa often, but she knew the older woman missed him terribly. As they all did. "Mama—"

"You've hidden yourself for so long, Sarah," her mother said gently. "You cannot live properly without risk. If you build so many defenses, trying not to be hurt, you simply wall the world out. Open your walls. Let risk—and *life*—in."

"Yes, Mama." Sarah smiled.

"Ma'am," one of the footmen called. "The guests are arriving."

"Oh my." Mama smoothed down her skirts. "We'd best greet them."

Sarah and her mother stood by the door, welcoming everyone as they came in. Jane and Charlotte joined them and soon the ballroom was crowded with a laughing, chattering throng. Ropes of evergreens and holly hung in loops from the sparkling chandeliers, and the hired musicians were playing a lively tune.

At one side of the room, long tables were being laid for a midnight feast: Cold cooked turkey and goose, pheasant, and joints of ham. There were jellies in jewel colors and puddings decorated with sprigs of holly. Huge bowls of hot mulled wine and cold punch stood with lines of crystal glasses, waiting to be served. Clove, cinnamon, and ginger scented the air.

Sarah inhaled. It was perfect—at least it was *almost* perfect.

"May I have this dance?" Adam's deep voice came from beside her.

She turned and found that he was dressed in a black silk suit worked in gold and red embroidery on the pockets and down the edges of the front. His wig was snowy white and his eyes...

His eyes seemed to promise something.

"Yes," she breathed, and placed her hand in his.

There had been several country dances, but now they readied for a more sedate, sophisticated dance, standing in line with the other dancers, their joined hands raised.

The music began, and she and Adam paced forward.

"Do you still dislike Christmas?" she murmured to him.

They turned to face each other, and she could feel her heart beating hard as she looked up to meet his gaze.

His beautiful lips quirked. "I find that I've come to a new appreciation of the season."

She couldn't seem to help the smile spreading across her face. There was something beating wildly in her bosom. A feeling, an emotion she'd never felt before.

They separated, whirling through the dance steps, and then came together again, pacing around each other without touching.

"Will you leave tomorrow?" she asked huskily.

He seemed to search her face. "Perhaps. Much depends on..."

She tipped her face to his. "Depends on what?"

He cursed softly under his breath and took her hand, leading her from the dance floor.

Behind them there were shocked murmurs.

He stopped, glancing around the room, and then headed to the tall glass doors that led to a balcony, pulling her behind him.

Sarah saw her brother frown and start in their direction.

She shook her head frantically at him.

Megs put her hand on Godric's arm and said something to him.

And then Adam was opening the doors to the balcony and taking her outside.

He shut the doors behind them.

Sarah wrapped her arms about herself. Her ball gown exposed her arms and décolleté, and she was already shivering.

Then Adam dropped to his knees, there on the cold stone of the balcony, and she forgot the temperature.

He looked up at her and said, "Will you do me the honor of marrying me, Sarah St. John?"

She opened her mouth, but no sound came out.

Well, save for the chattering of her teeth.

He frowned. "I know this is too soon, but I want to…" He stopped and inhaled, closing his eyes. "I *need* to marry you, Sarah. I love you and it's the most awful thing I've ever felt."

"A-awful?" Sarah stuttered, a bit insulted.

His gray eyes snapped open, glaring now. "I think of you day and night—every hour, every *minute*. When you walk into a room I look at nothing but you. When you leave, I want to follow. If a man looks at you I want to blind him. If you smile at another man, I want to *end* him. I dream of you. Of your breasts, of your sweet quim—but worse, much worse, I dream of your *eyes* and of your laugh. You haunt me and I'm afraid all of the time that I'll turn and you won't be there. It's *terrible*. I've never been so pathetic in all my life," he muttered as if to himself in disgust. He inhaled and said slowly, his eyes locked with hers, "Please. For *God*'s sake put me out of my misery and marry me."

She couldn't help her lips' curving. "Yes."

He surged to his feet and caught her face between his palms, kissing her passionately.

At that moment she didn't care about the cold. Her heart was swelling near to bursting with happiness.

He pulled back a little, his hot breath washing over her lips as he muttered. "Thank you, my beautiful, wonderful Sarah. I love you. I love you. I love you."

"I love you, too," she whispered, and he bent to her again.

The doors opened behind them and the sound of clapping came to them along with a rush of warm air.

Sarah turned in Adam's arms and saw that her family and all their friends were there at the windows, applauding.

She turned her face into his shirtfront, feeling her cheeks heat.

Standing there in her lover's arms, fairy lights all around them, on the night before Christmas, she'd never been so embarrassed—or happy—in her life.

Adam bent to smile against her temple. "Shall we go in and tell them? Though I think on the whole that they already know."

"Yes," she replied, taking his hand.

And they walked together into the future.

Chapter Thirteen

※

*Prince Brad frowned. "I thought enchanted
princesses were always beautiful."*
*The former frog—now a young woman—rolled her
cornflower-blue eyes above cheerfully freckled
cheeks. "I think we've already established that not all
princesses are beautiful. Besides, whatever makes
you think I'm a princess?"*
*Prince Brad stared in horror. "You're not a
princess?"*
*"No." She curtsied. "Miss Sylvia Smith. How d'you
do?"*
*"I can't marry a commoner," Brad muttered to
himself.*
*"Again. Whatever makes you think I'm going to
marry you?" asked Sylvia.*
*"Because," Prince Brad said, getting a devilish
gleam in his eye as he stalked toward her, "you
chased after me when I left you by the pond, you
managed to frighten away all my other marriage
prospects, and you let me kiss you."*
*Sylvia made an indignant squawking sound. "That
was to break the enchantment!"*
"Details," Brad said, and kissed her again.

He was still kissing her when the queen opened the door. "Bradley!"

"Yes, Mother?"

"Who is this?"

"Why, Princess Sylvia, who I just now saved from the frog curse," Prince Brad replied, smoothly elbowing Sylvia in the side and making her oof when she was about to protest this outrageous lie.

"Oh, lovely!" the queen said with deep approval. "I suppose you'll be marrying her?"

"Naturally."

"Then I'd best be off to plan the celebrations," the queen said, and left.

Sylvia turned to Brad. "I never said I'd marry you. Won't you be embarrassed when everyone arrives and there's no bride?"

"I certainly would be," replied Brad. He got down on one knee. "So I hope with all my vain heart that you'll take pity on me and marry me to save me the humiliation."

Sylvia stared at the kneeling prince. "That's it? No protestations of love?"

He cocked his handsome head. "Well I do feel as if my heart might break apart into tiny little pieces if you leave me and I never see you again, but it seems terribly soon to mention it, don't you think?"

Sylvia smiled at him tearfully. "No, it's not too soon to mention it, you great lump of ridiculousness."

So Prince Brad and the newly de-frogged Miss Smith were married and lived happily ever after, though Princess Sylvia did spend a great deal of her marriage rolling her eyes and kicking her spouse

under the table when he said rude things to guests.
But then no marriage—or person—is entirely perfect.
And besides.
Perfection is rather overrated anyway.

—From *The Frog Princess*

Don't miss Elizabeth Hoyt's newest book,
NOT THE DUKE'S DARLING,
the first novel in her new Greycourt series!

When the Duke of Harlowe—the man who destroyed her
brother and led to the downfall of her family—appears at the
country house party Freya de Moray is attending, she does
what any Wise Woman would do: She starts planning her revenge.

Christopher Renshaw, the Duke of Harlowe, is being
blackmailed. Intent on keeping his secrets safe, he agrees to
attend a house party where he will put an end to this coercion
once and for all. Until he recognizes Freya, masquerading
amongst the party revelers, and realizes his troubles have just
begun. But when it becomes clear Freya is in grave danger,
he'll risk everything to keep her safe. But first, Harlowe will
have to earn Freya's trust—by whatever means necessary.

About the Author

Elizabeth Hoyt is the *New York Times* bestselling author of more than twenty lush historical romances, including the Maiden Lane series. *Publishers Weekly* has called her writing "mesmerizing." She also pens deliciously fun contemporary romances under the name Julia Harper. Elizabeth lives in Minneapolis, Minnesota, with three untrained dogs, a garden in constant need of weeding, and the long-suffering Mr. Hoyt.

The winters in Minnesota have been known to be long and cold, and Elizabeth is always thrilled to receive reader mail. You can write to her at PO Box 19495, Minneapolis, MN 55419, or e-mail her at Elizabeth@ElizabethHoyt.com.

You can learn more at:

ElizabethHoyt.com
Twitter: @elizabethhoyt
Facebook.com/ElizabethHoytBooks

Fall in Love with Forever Romance

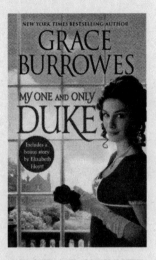

MY ONE AND ONLY DUKE
By Grace Burrowes

A charming Regency romance with a Cinderella twist! When London banker Quinn Wentworth is saved from execution by the news that he's the long-lost heir to a dukedom, there's just one problem: He's promised to marry Jane Winston, the widowed, pregnant daughter of a prison preacher. Also includes the novella *Once Upon a Christmas Eve* by Elizabeth Hoyt, available for the first time in print!

Fall in Love with Forever Romance

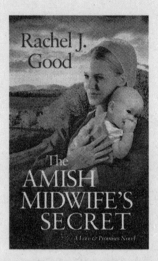

THE AMISH MIDWIFE'S SECRET
By Rachel J. Good

When *Englisher* Kyle Miller is offered a medical practice in his hometown, he knows he must face the painful past he left behind. Except he's not prepared for Leah Stoltzfus, the pretty Amish midwife who refuses to compromise her traditions with his modern medicine...But one surprising revelation and one helpless baby in need of love will show Leah and Kyle that their bond may be greater than their differences.

Fall in Love with Forever Romance

THE STORY OF US
By Tara Sivec

Don't miss this heartbreaking novel about love and second chances from *USA Today* bestselling author Tara Sivec! One thousand eight hundred and forty-three days. That's how long I survived in that hellhole. And I owe it all to the memory of the one woman who loved me more than I ever deserved to be loved. Now, I'll do anything to get back to her...I may not be the man I used to be, but I will do whatever it takes to remind her of the story of us.

Fall in Love with Forever Romance

TIGER'S CLAIM
By Celia Kyle

Two big-cat shifters go undercover as a couple in love to take down an organization that wants to kill all of their kind. But to survive among so many enemies, they absolutely *cannot* fall in love...

THE CAJUN COWBOY
By Sandra Hill

With the moon shining over the bayou, this Cajun cowboy must sweet-talk his way into his wife's arms again...before she unties the knot for good!